THE WITCH
OF
WHISPERVALE

ALSO BY R. A. SALVATORE

THE COMPLETE DEMONWARS SAGA

The Highwayman
The Ancient
The Dame
The Bear

The Demon Awakens
The Demon Spirit
The Demon Apostle
Mortalis
Ascendance
Transcendence
Immortalis

Child of a Mad God
Reckoning of Fallen Gods
Song of the Risen God

Pinquickle's Folly

HE IS ALSO KNOWN FOR
THE LEGEND OF DRIZZT SERIES

THE WITCH
OF
WHISPERVALE

DEMONWARS SAGA:
THE BUCCANEERS
BOOK II

R.A. SALVATORE

SAGA PRESS

LONDON AMSTERDAM/ANTWERP **NEW YORK** SYDNEY TORONTO NEW DELHI

SAGA PRESS

AN IMPRINT OF SIMON & SCHUSTER, LLC

1230 AVENUE OF THE AMERICAS, NEW YORK, NEW YORK 10020

First Saga Press hardcover edition February 2025

SAGA PRESS and colophon are trademarks of Simon & Schuster, LLC

For information about special discounts for bulk purchases, please contact Simon & Schuster Special Sales at 1-866-506-1949 or business@simonandschuster.com.

The Simon & Schuster Speakers Bureau can bring authors to your live event. For more information or to book an event, contact the Simon & Schuster Speakers Bureau at 1-866-248-3049 or visit our website at www.simonspeakers.com.

Manufactured in the United States of America

10 9 8 7 6 5 4 3 2 1

Library of Congress Cataloging-in-Publication Data is available.

ISBN 978-1-9821-7550-4
ISBN 978-1-9821-7552-8 (ebook)

Here's to the adventure
I've been on with Diane and our family and friends.

And to the readers who have been walking this road
of adventure beside me.

What a wonderful journey it's been.

THE WITCH
OF
WHISPERVALE

ONE

MAYORQUA TONOLOYA

GOD'S YEAR 862

(XIMOPOU)

To Father Abbot Braumin Herde and all the masters of St.-Mere-Abelle:

My greetings from Palmaris. I write to you to confirm the whispers that I know have reached your indomitable walls. Lady Tuolonatl and I see no reason yet for deep concern, but the tensions have increased about the city and across the way in Amvoy as well.

But yes, it is true: the pretty faces of our cohabitants hide a darker heart. Necanhu, the Xoconai high priest in Palmaris, has decreed that the year is no longer 862, and that our use of "God's Year" is, in itself, a great insult to the Xoconai. They have declared 862 as Ximopou, as Advent, and the proper recognition of the year as Atlen Xiuitl, which translates simply as "Year Zero"—the advent, you see, of their new name for our world, from the Mirianic to the western sea that borders their homeland: Mayorqua Tonoloya. As our calendar would turn to 863, their reckoning would be Se Xiuitl, or simply, Year 1.

As you know, false religion is oft at the heart of prejudice and calamity. You, Father Abbot, and some of the older masters about you, recall well the victory of Saint Avelyn over the accursed demon dactyl Bestesbulzibar. There are more demons than we know, and as you saw following Saint Avelyn's triumph, these foul creatures are not easily destroyed, if ever destroyed at all.

The teachings of Saint Abelle posit the question of the origin of demons, the central question of our very faith! Are the demon dactyls the source of evil that is in Man, or are the demon dactyls the physical manifestations of the evil within Man? Do they corrupt us, or do we create them?

The latter, I think, for those who have not found the Truth of Saint Abelle.

There are demons all about the world, in our lands, in lands we have only recently found, and, without doubt, in lands we do not know. On the eastern edges of the mountains, the tribes recognized their demon for what it was. They feared the beast they called the Fossa, which is the manifestation of the demon Cizinfozza. They did not worship the Fossa, but they prayed to it that it would leave them alone. You are familiar with Aoleyn of the Usgar and her actions to destroy that demon.

Over those mountains, the Xoconai did worship a demon, the beast Scathmizzane. Yet another manifestation of evil torn down by this extraordinary witch, Aoleyn. She revealed the truth of Scathmizzane to all who would see, but the Xoconai augurs would not, and will not, see. Their fervor for Scathmizzane has not diminished. Quite the opposite! With the rebirth of their great golden city of Otontotomi, they seem more than ever determined to resurrect this demon creature. Thus, my fellow Abellicans, I warn you: the augurs of the Xoconai have not found the Truth of Saint Abelle, and worse, I fear, they have not admitted the truth of their fallen demon, Scathmizzane.

Nor will they ever surrender that misguided faith, Lady Tu-olonatl assures me, but this growing cancer of zealot augurs is no less dangerous—nay, far more dangerous!—than the rise of Marcalo De'Unnero and his heretical followers was to the king-dom of Honce-the-Bear and the welfare of the Abellican Church. For Scathmizzane's teachings tolerate none who are not devout to Scathmizzane.

So yes, Father Abbot, and you, masters of St.-Mere-Abelle, the whispers hold some truth. The tensions rise. Through deception and politics, the augurs battle for control, city to city, town to town, and their control will not suffer the men of Honce to live peacefully and equally beside them.

I am not asking you to come forth, nay, though I beg for support as you may give it, to Palmaris and Amvoy and all the other places where the augurs are trying to gain control.

But, nay, do not come forth! St.-Mere-Abelle is the hope of Honce. Send what lifelines you can, both to the towns of Honce and across the Gulf of Corona to our brethren in Vanguard. Strengthen your walls, triple your guard!

You are the hope of Honce.

Yours in Saint Abelle,
Julian of the Evergreen
Knight of Abelle
Lord of Palmaris
God's Year 862!

CHAPTER 1

KERIDVEN

The woman who called herself Keridven stared at the Xoconai man for a long while, trying to find her breath. From afar, to one who was not Xoconai, he looked much like the others, with his distinct facial markings, but up close, the subtleties of this one's markings looked more like a sunset, or more particularly, like an artist's rendition of one. His nose was the brightest of reds, glowing with vitality, but the transition to the blue skin at the base of his nose was less distinct, a fading glow of soft pink, even a blend thereafter, just a thin line, that hinted of yellow or green depending on the ambient light. His rich brown hair was longer than she remembered, wavy and thick, gathering regally about his shoulders like the furred collar of an Usgar leader or the mane of a grassland lion.

Most of all, though, Keri saw the sadness in his bright eyes, eyes so light an amber that they sometimes appeared almost colorless, and other times picked up the bright colors of his Xoconai facial markings to appear rich and deep and soulful. Sadness

7

was not an expression this one often showed, and now it came as a confirmation of the news he had just delivered: Tuolonatl, the most revered warrior among the Xoconai people, had been recalled to the west, never to return to these lands of Honce on the eastern third of the continent.

Keri had heard the whispers that trouble had come to that region along the Masur Delaval and that their dear friend Tuolonatl was no longer serving as city sovereign of Palmaris, but she had assumed that the woman, so revered among the Xoconai military and civilians, had left by choice.

But no, Tuolonatl had been deposed from her seat and recalled to the west. And there, so said the rumors, the great warrior, still only middle-aged, had retired.

It was surprising news, but really, when Keri thought about it, her shock disappeared. Tuolonatl had been taken away because it was all unraveling.

All their work, all their battles, all their compromises and diplomacy.

All of it, unraveling.

"Why?" she asked, though of course she knew the answer.

The man, Ataquixt, shrugged.

"We had a deal," she pressed. "A treaty."

"*You* made a deal," he reminded. "With Tuolonatl. And the deal was to try. You both knew, as did all who witnessed the covenant that day after the fall of the god Scathmizzane, that your treaty was more aspirational than predictive."

"Tuolonatl wouldn't abide by the commands of the augurs," Keri said.

"Yes, and the augurs here speak directly to Scathmizzane's greatest priests in the west."

"Who forced her recall back to the west to prevent her from interfering in their plans for these eastern lands."

Ataquixt nodded. "So it would seem. Great Tuolonatl stood on principle, but the Xoconai leaders in the west are more interested in profit and power. They see a chance for conquest over the agreed-upon compromises and they take it. They know they will win."

"Because they used the good faith, even the undeserved generosity, of the people here to assemble their armies for their treachery."

"Does it matter?" Ataquixt asked. "Augur Necanhu is now the city sovereign of Palmaris."

"Augur?" she replied, rubbing her face. She didn't know the man, but she felt as if she didn't have to, considering his title. In Xoconai society, the augurs served as the religious leaders, while the position of city sovereign was traditionally elected, and almost always secular. In her limited experience with these fierce but physically beautiful people, that separation had proven all-important, particularly for those non-Xoconai humans who now had to share their land with the mighty people from the west.

In Keri's experience, augurs were to be feared, and not to be trusted, without exception. They were zealots, and their god, Scathmizzane, taught that they, the Xoconai alone, were true humans, with all the other peoples no more than the goblinkin, the *sidhe*.

"Aoleyn," he began.

"Don't call me that."

"No one can hear us," Ataquixt assured her.

"It does not matter. That is a name I must forget, a name that when uttered near me must not bring from me a reaction."

The Xoconai nodded. "Then . . . Kerid . . . Keridven?"

"Keri," she replied. "My friends of the villages call me Keri."

The Xoconai nodded. "Augurs serving as city sovereigns are becoming common in the eastern towns and cities," he lamented.

"Alas for Honce," Keri said.

"Honce? The Xoconai augurs are already whispering the name 'Quixi Tonoloya' in their private gatherings."

"Quixi," Keri breathed. The Xoconai word for "eastern."

"The line between faith and governance has blurred," Ataquixt continued. "The augurs have resumed the magic of the golden mirrors on the pyramids, where the armies and the goods can be quickly transported across thousands of miles, to the great gratitude of the leaders in the west. The military advantage of moving the macana and mundunugu warriors is overwhelming, and so the leaders of Mayorqua Tonoloya have given the augurs much more latitude and control here in the east than they had ever known back home."

"Mayorqua Tonoloya," she muttered, not as a question, certainly, for she understood the Xoconai language well, and knew "Mayorqua" as their word for *empire*, their golden empire from sea to sea.

"And because to have elected leaders here would mean that we, who are considered lesser humans, would vote," Keri remarked sourly, then added even more nastily, "We are not even human to the Xoconai."

"I do not think of you and your people in that way," Ataquixt replied, and he seemed sincerely wounded—of course he was, particularly with the painful truth coming from her!

She nodded and softened her expression, and reminded herself that not all the Xoconai agreed with these prejudices. Certainly not Ataquixt, who was far more worldly than almost any man she had ever met—one reason she had been so attracted to him in the first place.

Still, as Ataquixt had spoken of the logistics, she couldn't help but wince. She understood well the powers of those golden mirrors the Xoconai had planted strategically across the eastern half of the continent. They were teleportation devices, magical transports through which the Xoconai could move armies hundreds of miles in a matter of an hour. The powers of the devices had been greatly diminished in a mighty battle halfway across the continent, and she had thought that a good thing—indeed, the only real hope she had entertained that the agreement, a sharing of the land between the Bearmen of Honce and the Xoconai peoples, might hold. For without their magic to maneuver the macana foot soldiers and the mundunugu cavalry, the Xoconai could never really secure these populated lands known as the kingdom of Honce-the-Bear, home to a proud people not without well-trained foot soldiers and heroes and magic-wielding monks.

"In the eyes of the leaders of the Xoconai," Ataquixt explained, "the augurs will soon tame Quixi Tonoloya."

"Tame? You mean conquer and enslave."

Ataquixt didn't answer other than to sigh, once again reminding her that he was not her enemy here. Far from it. He was Ataquixt, a ranger trained by the Touel'alfar. Ataquixt, who had betrayed that demon named Scathmizzane by throwing the spear that had finished off Scathmizzane's dragon mount. Ataquixt was no friend to the augurs, certainly, and he had been a true friend to Tuolonatl, the great general, the great warrior, whom Keri knew to be decent and honest and trustworthy.

She studied the man then, seeking silent hints. He was thin, but no one would ever think him weak, for his golden-skinned arms were tight with muscles, and the fluidity of his movements showed years of training in the fighting arts. He was unquestionably handsome, beautiful even, with expressive eyes that could chill an enemy or warm a friend. His distinctive Xoconai markings shone with life energy, from his wide nose, which shone the color of fresh blood in the sunlight, to the wings of bright blue and shining white flowing from the base of that red nose to the top-center of his cheeks.

Handsome, even pretty, but Keri reminded herself that it was all superficial, all just skin color. It occurred to her then, and certainly not for the first time, that the distinction in the naming conventions of the two peoples, Bearmen and Xoconai, was a silly thing. These were different cultures, not different beings, save the coloring of the Xoconai face, and the slightly different skin tones—differences that were not more pronounced than those of the typically pale-skinned people of northern Alpinador and the darker-skinned folk of Behren and To-gai to the south.

They were all humans, just humans, sharing hopes and dreams, joys and tragedies. Now, particularly, the woman knew that without doubt.

They were all just human, and like the people of Honce-the-Bear or of Behren or Alpinador or To-gai . . . like the people of the tribes around the Ayamharas Plateau or even of her own Usgar tribe, the Xoconai of the west were not monolithic of thought and morality.

This one, Ataquixt, she reminded herself, was a friend, truly, and more than a friend, who had proven himself more than once.

"I know you don't want that," she told him earnestly.

"I want what we thought could be, not what it has become."

"And what has it become?"

"Quixi Tonoloya in the dreams of the augurs," he answered without hesitation. "This land, your land, is to be conquered and occupied."

"I was not of this land until very recently," Keri reminded him.

"And your homeland is now Tahko Tonoloya, the Centerlands, and as you witnessed, the lake you once viewed from your mountain home is now drained to a wider lake below the plateau, and the ancient and shining city of Otontotomi, golden and glorious, is revealed and restored once more. That which was in the Centerlands and here in Honce hardly resembles the home you once knew."

"You underestimate—"

Ataquixt interrupted with a solemn shake of his head. "Palmaris, one of the three greatest cities of Honce-the-Bear, is now

13

ruled by an augur, as are many lesser cities and villages. This is a harbinger, no doubt. Xoconai armies gather in moments at any place they choose, and sweep through any lesser town that refuses to submit to the will of Scathmizzane."

"The monasteries," she said. "The Abellican monks are powerful."

"They are indeed," Ataquixt replied. "And many have betrayed their own people and come over to join with the augurs."

She tried to suppress her shock but was sure that it was clear upon her face. Her hand went to her abdomen, where new life was stirring.

Ataquixt didn't miss that movement, she realized only after she even recognized that she had made the reflexive shift, and those bright eyes of her lover told her that he understood more than he should.

"The great monastery of St.-Mere-Abelle has held strong," he told her. "The Xoconai will not attempt another attack on that greatest of human fortresses, likely ever. They will simply keep it isolated and irrelevant unless and until the monks become too troublesome. Perhaps you should go there."

Keri considered the advice in the good faith in which she knew it had been given. Yes, she would be safe—as safe as was possible for her in this time—at St.-Mere-Abelle behind those towering walls, within those great halls and catacombs and dark meditation chambers, surrounded by monks skilled in combat and expert in the gemstone magic that could lay low an attacking army in short order.

She would be safe there, but she would be miserable

there. And the monks, though they might accept her, surely didn't want her. Some of the highest members of their order blamed her, and not without reason, for all the tragedy that had befallen their once prosperous and peaceful kingdom of Honce-the-Bear.

And there remained another consideration: in St.-Mere-Abelle, she would be known as Aoleyn. There, she could not escape her past, and if word ever leaked out to be whispered in the ears of the ruling Xoconai augurs, if they ever discovered that Aoleyn was still alive and in this conquered land . . .

"What of Entel?" she asked. The coastal city of Entel in southeastern Honce, nestled at the base of the Belt-and-Buckle Mountains and against the dark waters of the great Mirianic, had been an enigma to anyone and everyone who had ever ruled these lands. It contained two monasteries of Abellican monks, though the two were more rivals than allies, and the city boasted, as well, of two distinct cultures: that of Honce-the-Bear and that of Behren, the desert kingdom just around the mountains' edge. By all accounts, Entel had the flavor of Palmaris and Ursal, but even more, the flavor of Jacintha, the great Behrenese city a mere fifty miles to its south.

Ataquixt shrugged. "There has been no fight there of any real consequence, to my knowledge, but I do not know. The city has ever been divided, and sits now in turmoil, sharing three identities. I do not think the Xoconai will press forcefully there, to be honest, because I do not believe they will need to do so in order to get everything they want from the port city. There seems to be a growing respect among the leaders of my people for the powers looming just south around the mountains, which have an enormous trade and cultural sharing with Entel."

"Why would your people do this?" Keri asked. "We who won on the mountain those three years past could have destroyed so much. With the power of the god-crystal in our hands, we could have laid low the golden city of Otontotomi in a matter of a day, and yet we surrendered that advantage so that the land could know peace and new understanding. Cooperation between our peoples."

"For all our worthy intentions, the land has remained at war since that agreement of hope," he told her. "You know this."

"But the battles were quieting! The absence of power was being filled town to town, most often by the will of the people of the towns!"

"And often disastrously. This, too, you know. There were towns where Xoconai would be killed on sight. There were towns where sidhe were . . ."

"Sidhe?"

Ataquixt sucked in his breath, as if trying to bite back the word.

"We are all humans," Keri said. "Haven't you figured that out yet?"

Ataquixt held up his deceptively delicate hands and bowed gracefully in a seemingly sincere apology.

"You use the goblin pejorative," she answered. "As many of the people who look like me call your people the sidhe, a name both of our peoples gave to the ferocious demonic goblins who roam the great mountains that separate east from west."

"It would seem that both groups think the other less than human, and ugly," he said.

I hardly think your people ugly, she thought, but didn't say aloud. *At least, not physically.* She couldn't deny it if she wanted to, particularly not to this man. These strange people who had swept in from the west, over the mountains and all the way through the Wilderlands and through Honce-the-Bear, all the way to the sea, were meticulously groomed and stood straight-backed and vibrant, strong and exuding health, shining within. And particularly as she had grown accustomed to those distinctive facial colorings, she could not begin to understand how anyone could think the Xoconai ugly.

And Keri knew, quite intimately, that Ataquixt did not think her ugly, though she understood that his claims of opposing prejudice were certainly true.

"There remain places of solid resistance, but they will not last for long, or even if they do, they will become more an annoyance than a true rebellion once the augurs have set their flags," he said quietly and evenly. "Your land will be conquered."

"This is not my land," she reminded him again, simply because she was stubborn and proud of that trait, and he nodded and bowed slightly once more, but his expression remained grim.

"What news of *my* land?" she demanded. "Tell me of the plateau."

"Otontotomi thrives as the greatest city of all east of the Teotl Tenamitl range. Three hundred thousand people live on and about the plateau you once knew as home."

"People? Xoconai?"

"Xoconai and those of the tribes who once lived there. People."

"Not sidhe."

"Not sidhe," Ataquixt agreed with a smile. "Certainly not sidhe."

"God's Parapet," the woman translated under her breath, for Teotl Tenamitl was what the Xoconai people called the mountains dividing the west from the wild center and the populated east of this vast continent—the mountain range they had crossed when she had destroyed the demon Fossa. For to the Xoconai, the fall of that demonic beast was the signal for the rise of Scathmizzane, their own demon god. Not the towering mountains but the Fossa had been the one true barrier that had kept them in the far west. She pictured Otontotomi, and remembered the region before it had been uncovered, when the city was hidden beneath the deep waters of the mountain lake that shone beyond the shadow of Fireach Speuer, the mountain she had known as her home for all but the last three years of her young life.

"And . . ." she prompted.

"Who can know? There is peace there for now. The remnants of your tribe and many from the lake tribes hold a superior position high on the mountain, a place filled with powerful magic. The cost of attacking them would be high, so very high, if it could even be successful."

"As with St.-Mere-Abelle."

"Very much," Ataquixt said with a nod. "Perhaps you could—"

"No," she said definitively. "I'll not ever return to Fireach Speuer."

Keri was surely comfortable with her response. That land was her past, Aoleyn's past, and not, and never, her future. Still, she desperately wanted her homeland to remain peaceful and stable.

A small victory, at least.

"If not there, then you should go to St.-Mere-Abelle," Ataquixt told her. "You will be safe there."

"There is more to life than safety." Keri didn't look at him as she spoke. She couldn't. She did briefly lift her gaze enough to see him bow again.

"I hope you remain well, my friend," he said. "And you are my friend. That will not change. You have earned my respect many times over, and both Tuolonatl and I know your heart and love you for it. You are the light, but darkness has come. You might punch little holes in that cloud with your formidable powers, but you'll not lift the veil. I tell you this because you are my friend.

"Look closer to your hearth and home, great warrior, great witch," he went on, and she didn't have to look up to know that Ataquixt was regarding her belly then, and the life it contained. "It is a wide world, after all, and the tide will flood and it will ebb beyond the demands of any one person. You will find happiness here in this quiet and unremarkable place, I believe, but it will not be as you and Tuolonatl and I had hoped. Not on the level of the nation, at least, but make of your home a happy place."

Keri nodded but didn't look up.

Her home. Keridven's home. That place wouldn't be

St.-Mere-Abelle, she knew. She hadn't been treated well there and found the ancient monastery dusty and steeped with the ghosts of ages past, the superstitions and legends beyond reality of men—almost always men, to the near exclusion of women—who had died long ago.

Realizing that Ataquixt had walked away, she glanced up. He was on the other side of the small field already, in the shadows of the tree line of a thick forest nestled against the mountains of south-central Honce. She watched this fierce mundunugu warrior climb atop his mount, but it wasn't a cuetzpali lizard, as was typical.

No, it was a horse, a blue-eyed pinto.

"Pocheoya," the woman mumbled, and she knew in that moment beyond all doubt that Ataquixt wasn't misinformed or lying to her, and that their common friend and the only champion who might reverse these terrible events would not return.

For he rode Pocheoya, the beloved horse of Tuolonatl.

Keridven watched the sunset on a low hillock, looking across the wide fields of southern Honce to the brilliant lines of orange and red splayed across the western horizon. Turning left a bit, she could see the reflections lighting fires on the snow-capped mountains. It was the last day of Toumanay, the fourth month in the calendar of Honce-the-Bear, and spring had come early after a mild winter, with the leaves already in full bud.

She replayed her unexpected meeting from earlier. She wasn't surprised that Ataquixt had been able to find her—that one seemed to know a lot about everything—but she was stunned that he had bothered. They had parted ways in Ursal three months earlier, had said goodbyes that had seemed lasting in that moment. She looked back the other way, just east of her position, to the houses of Whispervale, her new home, the small community nestled between two spurs stretching north into Honce from the Belt-and-Buckle. No one had known that she was coming here—even she hadn't known it!—when she had left St.-Mere-Abelle more than a year before, chased out by the ghosts of her past and the accusations of Abellican scholars. She had gone from the great monastery west, to the city of Amvoy, intending to continue on across the river to Palmaris, to check in on an old and dear friend of hers.

But her friend was long missing, she had been told by a trusted source, and almost certainly dead and buried in an un-marked grave like so many others who had resisted the changes in that city, charged with high crimes by the augurs of Palmaris.

She shuddered as she thought of Xoconai execution, where the convicted were put in a box of four gold mirrors, which would then emit heat into the middle to curl the skin of their victims.

That would have been her fate in Palmaris, she knew with certainty, if her true identity had been discovered by the augurs. Whatever crime anyone else might commit, the witch Aoleyn of the Usgar would ever be the most hunted of all by the augurs. She had slain their precious Scathmizzane and had interrupted their plans for a swift conquest of the east.

With nowhere else to go, Aoleyn had turned south and

fled the region. She didn't know why, but south had seemed as good a direction as any at that desperate moment. She didn't really fear the Xoconai, even the augurs, outside of Palmaris, not then as she did now, but to linger in the area . . . perhaps she had been afraid of what she would find out about her dear old friend's absence.

Finding that man, her lifelong friend, her first lover, in a grave would be too much for her.

She had gone on to Ursal, taking her time, learning the countryside, or the riverside, at least, as she made her way from town to town along the wide and meandering Masur Delaval. At the end lay the greatest city of Honce, high and walled. She had been through there during the conflict and knew the people to be strong and stubborn.

But Ursal had disappointed her and had frightened her, for deep inside, she had known even then that her dream of peace might not hold. She had met up with Ataquixt quite by accident, and the two had shared their troubled thoughts and much, much more. But events in Ursal had become dangerous for her and the whispers of her true identity had been overheard, and so she had once more departed, without real direction.

Entel, perhaps, she had thought even then, and so she had meandered south to the mountains, then turned east. With a hundred miles behind her and a hundred more to go, if the maps were to be believed, she had come upon this place, Whispervale, and here had found true respite, and blissful anonymity. None here even seemed to know much, nor care much, of the Xoconai invasion. Whispervale sometimes saluted whatever king was in place in Honce, but the toasts were more an excuse to drink than any real passion for whomever it might be (with one notable exception, a previous queen and not a king). For these farmers and foragers and hunters and fisherfolk were independent of the lords and kings and landowners who had proven such a plague throughout these lands for centuries untold. The people here were fully self-sufficient. They lived far from the main roads and far from the intrigue of the games of the powerful, and they wanted to keep it that way.

The folk of Whispervale and the five surrounding villages had all that they needed, with fertile gardens, mountain streams teeming with huge trout, and game and wild berries aplenty.

Sitting on that hillock this night, looking back at the sleepy town that had so welcomed her, and had even helped her build a cabin of her own, Keri was struck by how similar this seemed to the life she had known before she had learned the truth of her tribe on the mountain, before she had battled the demon Fossa, before the Xoconai had come and the world had widened terrifyingly. How ironic that she had always dreamed of what lay beyond the Ayamharas Plateau, and now that she had found out, she wanted nothing more than to be back there and back to that simpler time.

Here, she had become Keridven.

Still, despite the warm feelings of this community, she had never meant to stay in Whispervale. Now, though, with a child growing in her womb, she thought that she might never leave.

That wouldn't be a bad thing.

She blew a deep sigh and considered the news from Ataquixt, the dire implications all too clear. Tuolonatl hadn't simply been recalled to the west. She had been hustled there, else she would not have left her beloved Pocheoya behind, even with someone as trusted by her as Ataquixt.

That portended a grave turn for the region, Keri feared, and she hoped that she was wrong, and hoped that, if not, places like Whispervale would not be found out.

The people here were no threat to the Xoconai, nor did they have any wealth the Xoconai could covet. Perhaps the conquerors wouldn't look this way.

She tried to tell herself that, but . . .

She knew better. She was the center of the darkness that had come to the land, and that darkness would find her, certainly.

She had destroyed the demon Fossa that roamed the great mountainous divide for centuries untold. Her intentions had been good, but the act had precipitated the eastward charge of the Xoconai.

If she hadn't killed the Fossa . . .

If she hadn't been little more than a child, meddling in affairs beyond her understanding, and with magical powers too great for one so inexperienced . . .

She hadn't known the consequences, but did it matter? For now, tens of thousands were dead, hundreds of thousands teetering on the edge of subjugation, and the world for all who were not Xoconai was hurtling toward the sunset precitpitating a long night.

The sky was lit by a half-moon and a million stars by the time

24

she wandered back onto the main street of little Whispervale, crestfallen and chased by demons of guilt.

"Been dancin', Keridven?" asked old Biddlebrew, who ran the goods exchange, and who made the finest mead for the common room at the Mountain Shadow tavern. "But ye went without Jilly, did ye? Or th' other Jilly, who's been asking to join ye?"

"Not dancing," she answered with an amused giggle. Biddlebrew could have named a third Jilly and even a fourth, in this town of only a few hundred residents, although that fourth one was a young man, and for him it was Gilly, not Jilly.

Yes, that was a common name in these parts, in all the lands, so it seemed, for people, mostly women, near her own age in their twenties.

She smiled at the thought. She had never met this Queen Jilly, or, more accurately, Queen Jilseponie, but she had met Jilseponie's son, had battled beside him, had been with him when he had died in the mouth of a great dragon, the mount of the Xoconai god.

Her smile became the blow of a sigh. They had all fought so well, so brilliantly, and more than that, they had done the right thing.

So they had thought.

Keri let the ever-present darkness go. She had only been here in Whispervale for a couple of months, having arrived in the middle of the second month, Progos, but the warmth the townsfolk now showed her made her feel as if she had lived here all her life. She had made many friends, particularly the Jillys, and had introduced a small group of women to the dancing tradition of the Coven of the Usgar. Thus she had created the witches of the Coven of Whispervale.

Not with the magical elements she had known among the Usgar, though. Not yet and perhaps never. She had to be careful with that, and she feared it profoundly, given the disasters she had wrought wielding that godly power. The dance itself was magical and spiritual, after all, and quite satisfying—and growing more so as the handful of participants had found a proper setting, a proper grove for it, and had begun perfecting the experience bit by bit, with lanterns and ghostly flowing clothing. Even more than that, the dancers were losing their inhibitions more with each dance, no longer looking around to see if another had noticed a misstep, and instead realizing that there were no missteps, and that the place to look in each witch's dance was into one's own heart and soul.

CHAPTER 2

THE MAGICAL WORD

Ataquixt moved to the prow of the small sloop, keeping his hand firmly grasping the stay rope. He wasn't often on the water and had never gotten comfortable on a boat. Add to that the swirling waters of the Masur Delaval this far north as the tides began to turn, and the man was fairly certain that he would soon remember well his breakfast. He was thankful indeed that this journey up the river to the city of Amvoy wasn't a long one, and wasn't up and down on the wild waves in the Gulf of Corona beyond the city.

"You are passing the dock!" he called back to the round-faced boat captain, who laughed boisterously in reply, his buoyant mood sending his shoulders—which were distractingly wide—rolling up as if to cover his ears. A moment later, the skilled Captain Overbey of Palmaris cut the wheel hard, turning the boat to starboard, then shifted and tinkered the masts enough to catch the wind and pull them in, while the reversing current of the tides, now moving south, pushed the small sloop perfectly in line with the dock.

"You jump near the front cleat and tie us off before the current pushes us all the way back to Ursal!" the captain yelled. "And make sure you put the aft line on it, you lizard-riding goldfish!"

And he laughed again, and Ataquixt smiled and nodded, although the thought wasn't pleasing to him. Ataquixt could trot a horse along a narrow mountain trail with a thousand-foot drop to one side without a care, but the notion of leaping from a boat to a dock had his belly flipping with nerves. He looked past the bridge to two of the other three Xoconai who had accompanied him on this trip north, silently pleading.

That just made them grin and shake their heads. They were quite obviously enjoying Ataquixt's nerves here, a good-natured ribbing they could give to their unit leader.

The sloop came in very near the forward left corner of the dock, close enough that Ataquixt's great and terrifying leap was really no more than a step, coming to the planks of the dock right behind its forward cleat. He looped the aft rope once and again and rushed forward with the prow tie in hand, pulling hard as the sloop began to drift away.

He caught it, though, looping the rope about the cleat and tugging the sloop against the dock, then rushing back to secure the aft rope more fully. The tide was stubborn, though, and Ataquixt had to bring it up tight inch by inch.

"Well done," Captain Overbey congratulated him. "Perhaps ye should be tradin' yer lizard . . ." The man paused and glanced back at Ataquixt's mount, which was surely not one of the collared lizards that served as the mounts of the mundunugu warriors back in the Tonoloya Basin. "Yer nag, I mean, and how can ye ride so high on that thing?"

"It is a pony, not a horse, and not so high."

"But can it climb a cliff?" Overbey teased.

"No, but Pocheoya can outrun any cuetzpali, do not doubt," Ataquixt answered.

That brought a laugh from his Xoconai companions, fellow mundunugu who still rode the collared lizards of the western deserts—their mounts were belowdecks with the fourth of the group.

"Wouldn't ride neither," Overbey told him. "Bah, but the waves are kind to me old legs."

"Legs bowed enough so that it looks like someone stole your fat horse," the lone woman of the mundunugu group, a young and bright-faced lass named Etlquay, put in, and Overbey's shoulders bobbed with laughter once more, and he did a little bowlegged jig that had Etlquay and the other onlookers quite amused.

Ataquixt loved this play between a Honce Bearman and the Xoconai, but it also saddened him as he considered what might have been.

Following Captain Overbey's instructions, the Xoconai lowered and secured the sails. "I'll make sea dogs of ye all!" he boasted, moving to help Etlquay guide Pocheoya to the rail and over to the waiting grasp of Ataquixt.

"Ye're to ride that thing all the way back to Ursal?" Overbey asked, hopping over the side to the dock. "With the rest o' ye bouncing along on lizards? Ha!"

"You have fulfilled your commitment, Captain Overbey," Ataquixt said, formally releasing him. "We will make our way, however the situation demands."

"Well, I'll be here in Amvoy, or across the river to Palmaris, until the first crops flow south. If ye be needin' me . . ."

"I am sure you are easy to find," Ataquixt said.

He took Pocheoya fully from them then, as Etlquay hopped off the pony to help the other two Xoconai with the three cuetz-pali lizards and their packs.

Ataquixt moved to the end of the docks and stood staring west and just a bit to the south across the Masur Delaval, where he knew Palmaris to be. He would see the lights of the city when the sun set, perhaps, but only if the night cooled considerably and no fog came up on the river.

"What is the latest I can coax a ferryman to take me to Palmaris?" he asked Overbey when the captain walked up beside him.

"I could've just dropped ye there."

"No, not to worry. I am not even certain that I will be going there this trip," Ataquixt lied.

"With the incoming tide turning the current to the south, they'll run through most o' the night, not to doubt, if the price is right," Overbey replied. "At the north ferry, I mean, a few miles out of Amvoy. They'll use the current and get ye there within three hours. Might even be within two if they find a favorable wind coming down from the gulf."

"Every night?" Ataquixt asked. "That's the schedule every night?"

"Watch the tides," Overbey explained. "If the Masur Delaval is chasing the tide into the gulf, running north, the south ferries'll run. If the gulf's spittin' it back, go north to find a ride."

Ataquixt nodded.

"Got to rid meself of my sea legs with a pint," Overbey said. "I can show yerself and yer friends some proper drinkin' holes."

"If our schedule permitted, I would surely follow you, good Captain Overbey," Ataquixt said. "But we have early engagements in the morn."

"Always busy, ye goldfish—ah, but I can't rightly call ye that, can I? Ye're not the sea-dog, aye?"

"I brought my pony along so that I wouldn't have to get back on a boat to return to Ursal."

Overbey howled again, slapped Ataquixt on the shoulder good-naturedly, and rambled down the docks, tipping the front of the dirty bandana he had wrapped about his head to each of the other two Xoconai men as he passed, and dipped in a full bow to Etlquay.

Ah, what could have been, Ataquixt lamented.

The four mundunugu secured two rooms at an inn along the north coastal reaches of Amvoy, then went to the common room for a meal where they would be seen and surely noticed, particularly Ataquixt and Etlquay, whose amorous displays had several of the patrons, Xoconai and Bearman alike, shaking their heads and making all sorts of chortles and harrumphs. Even the tavern keeper and his waiters threw dirty looks the way of the couple, though none of them, Bearmen all, had the courage to say anything, of course.

They ordered drinks by the round, poured bits on the table and floor, or let them spill out of their mouths. Ataquixt and one of the other men discreetly swapped their nearly full drinks with ones almost drained by the other two mundunugu at the table.

Two of them, Etlquay and another young mundunugu named Papap, became truly drunk, while Ataquixt and Alleketza, a veteran of many adventures, just acted that way.

"We all know our roles this night, yes?" Ataquixt whispered, huddling them together, then turned it into a toast to cover the intrigue.

All three nodded. Ataquixt took Etlquay's hand, yelled at one of the other men to pay the tab, and pulled her out of the room, the woman giggling and stumbling along at the end of his arm. Up the stairs they went and to their room, falling into an embrace and a kiss as they fumbled through the door.

"Our lovemaking should be very loud this night," Ataquixt ordered quietly when they were inside, with the door closed behind them.

In response, Etlquay moaned loudly, then burst into laughter.

"You are wonderful," Ataquixt told her, and kissed her on the cheek. "Seriously now."

She tried to stop herself from laughing, but couldn't, a huge burst of giggles flowing forth.

"Commander Avitl needs us!" Ataquixt reminded her, trying to sound serious and hold his own giggles back. "She will come up for the position of city sovereign of Ursal soon, and we all agree that would be a good thing, yes?"

Etlquay nodded eagerly, biting back a laugh.

"Make it loud," Ataquixt said with a wink.

"Is this about Avitl's needs or Ataquixt's reputation?" she asked, and burst out laughing again, and this time, Ataquixt simply could not help himself and joined her.

He ushered her to the bed, then moved to the window, opening it and peering out to make sure the way was clear. He looked back and winked, and off he went, through the window and down the side of the building, then off into the night to the north and the ferry.

Papap and Alleketza would make inquiries about the city of Amvoy, while Etlquay would cover Ataquixt's departure by making it sound like eager young lovers were fully engaged in the room.

His own night had barely begun. He flipped a bulky robe over his shoulders and put a mask over half his face.

He stepped off the ferry onto the Palmaris dock sometime after midnight. "You are certain of the third dock?" he asked the ferryman.

"You were on her when she put in, eh?" the old man replied. "So you said."

"I was drunk."

"Seems a common thing."

"I paid you well to get me back here before my dawn watch," Ataquixt said. "Are you to make me miss that watch anyway and find myself swabbing decks?"

The man smiled and held out his hand.

Ataquixt sighed heavily as if in disgust and flipped him another silver coin.

"One less silver for you to drink yourself into trouble with," he said. "Third dock, and good luck getting aboard her without being seen. I'm not for knowing what your tub was carrying, but your captain put many on watch when last I seen her."

"Punishment," Ataquixt told the ferryman. "We were sloppy along the Mantis Arm and nearly beached her. Captain promised to make us pay for that."

"Drinking?" the old man said with a laugh.

"Lonely out there. Not much to do."

"That's why I stay on the river. Keeps you alert, or you die."

"Aye, and if I don't get myself prepared for my watch, I'm sure I will die."

Ataquixt moved off into the shadows, mulling the new information he had luckily collected. "Many on watch," he echoed under his breath, which might well be a bit of confirmation of the rumors that Commander Avitl had heard and sent him to investigate. Of course, he hadn't been on the ship in question when she had docked a couple of days or so before. Avitl hadn't even known her name.

It was just a rumor, after all, but one with potentially huge implications.

He moved down the dock to the boardwalk, then across the planks to the side of a warehouse. With a quick look around, he went up the side to the roof, then crept along to the south, nearer to the lower-numbered docks.

The night was quiet and dark about him, the stillness on the docks as thick as the inevitable fog, whose first wisps were already wafting about the wharf posts still long before the dawn.

Ataquixt was no veteran of the water or of boats, of course, but he was a trained ranger and knew how to angle his gaze to catch silhouettes and movement.

"I hope you're right, ferryman," he said, moving farther, then squatting along the edge of the roof across the boardwalk from what he figured to be the third dock. The ship tied there seemed to fit the expectations he and Commander Avitl had discussed. Certainly, she was of the Tonoloya Armada—Ataquixt could see the decorative flaring at either end of the taffrail so common with Xoconai vessels. Its wide hull showed it to be a cargo ship, and though there were no lights on the deck, Ataquixt had noted no less than five watchers. There he sat and waited and watched as the night deepened.

He heard some talking from the deck, then saw a sailor moving along the stern rail to starboard, pausing there to light a pipe. Ataquixt noted the facial markings in that brief flicker of light.

Xoconai. A woman.

She looked back over her shoulder and called into the shadows to "Stay awake," before turning and walking forward.

The watch commander, Ataquixt figured.

Down the side of the building he went, creeping from shadow to shadow nearer to the ship, until he settled behind a barrel that smelled of fish on the river edge of the boardwalk. There, he waited some more, and finally nodded when the tide began to shift and the waves began slapping more noisily against the docks. He breathed a sigh of relief, for he was running short on time to accomplish all that he hoped before the eastern sky would begin to brighten.

Using the fog where he could, barrels and dock posts when he could find them, the stealthy ranger made his way to the port corner of the stern.

He waited a bit longer, eyes staring up at the rail of the high afterdeck for some sign of the sentry. When no one appeared, he leaped to the securing rope, hands grasping, feet hooking. Up he climbed, twisting to secure himself on the ridge just below the taffrail.

He pulled a thick cloth from one pocket in his coat, then a flask from an inside sheath. He wasn't sure where the sentry might be, exactly, but he knew that he had to take a chance. He soaked the rag with the liquid, a combination of viper venom and lavender and other herbs, and went over the rail, quiet as the fog.

Luck was with him, for the sentry was not far away and hardly alert, leaning against a rope and facing out at the dock to port and the smaller ship next in line.

Clearly groggy, maybe even dozing, the man hardly reacted when Ataquixt's arm wrapped around him, pinning the sentry's left arm and reaching all the way across to grasp the man's right, as well. Ataquixt's right hand flashed around and up on the other side, pressing the scented cloth against the sentry's face.

He had the man locked up for a few seconds, enough so that when the fellow finally wriggled his right arm from Ataquixt's grasp, the sedative was already settling in, weakening him. Even as the caught sentry grabbed Ataquixt's right wrist, the man fell limp in his arms, to be guided down softly to the deck.

Ataquixt took the few moments to position the sentry to

make it look like he had curled up comfortably on his own, even rolling him to his side and tucking the thick cloth under his cheek like a pillow. The potion would fast evaporate, he knew, and by the time anyone came upon this sleeping man, there would be no evidence of an attack.

Just a sleeping man who would be rudely awakened and would then fumble about for an excuse.

Ataquixt crept to the forward rail of the high afterdeck, looking down at the main deck. At least three more sentries were down there, but none of them seemed very engaged at this point.

All the ranger's training came into play then, as he ignored the two staircases descending to the main deck and went over the rail between them instead, dropping lightly, falling immediately to his chest and slithering like a snake to the bulkhead.

The first hold was full of sleeping Xoconai, as expected.

The bulkhead to the lower hold was locked, as expected.

Ataquixt produced a thin metal lockpick and opened it in short order. He lifted it just enough for him to crawl through, then gently closed it behind.

He couldn't stand straight in the bottom hold, which was less than five feet, floor to ceiling. He quickly lit a candle and surveyed the jumble about him in the packed hold, which was filled with unremarkable crates and barrels, most of which had shifted and crowded together in the tossing and turning of the tides. Ataquixt feared he would have a long task ahead in finding one to confirm the whispers.

He drew his heavy dagger and moved about, prying and peeking, prying and peeking, one crate to another, and, on a hunch, one barrel to another.

The hunch paid off.

He extracted himself from the cargo ship as he had brought himself in, with patience and stealth, and was back on the dock before the eastern sky had brightened enough to make his departure from the boardwalk clear to see.

He went south now, not north, near to Palmaris's southern gate, where he turned into an alleyway and pulled out a bedroll, trying to get a bit of sleep, at least.

He was out of the city before dawn, over the low western wall and across the fields beyond. The sun was up when he came to the grave—a fake grave claiming to be the last resting place of a man from the Centerlands, from the Ayamharas Plateau, who had become a hero in the city during the war.

A man who had been Aoleyn's dear friend and first lover.

He moved to a large oak not far to the side, climbed to the second line of branches, and there found a specific knothole. He reached in slowly, fearful that some small animal might have taken it as a home, and was quite relieved to find that was not the case—not recently, at least—and even more relieved to find that the metal block that had been lodged in the bottom of the hole was still there. Getting it out was no easy task, for it had been put in with the magic of the Touel'alfar, the elves, but he managed it. It fit in the palm of his hand, had neither markings nor any indication that it might be opened.

Ataquixt knew that there was an emerald, an enchanted gemstone, within it.

He brought the block to the grave and laid it atop the marker, then sat back and hoped that the magical call would go forth and be received as designed.

Then he went back to the oak and sat down with his back to it, facing the grave, thinking a bit more sleep would do him well.

He didn't get the chance, for within a matter of heartbeats, a green light appeared above the headstone, forming a glowing line from the stone to a height of about six feet. It began to spin and widen in its center area, appearing then as an oblong green top, spinning on its end.

It slowed and then dissipated to nothingness, leaving in its place a diminutive humanoid, four feet tall, thin enough to hide behind a small tree, and with small translucent wings.

"Lord Belli'mar," Ataquixt said reverently, jumping up and dropping immediately into a bow.

"Ag'ardu An'grian," the elf replied, speaking the elven words for the collared lizards commonly ridden by the Xoconai, the name the Touel'alfar had given to Ataquixt when he completed his ranger training. "Why have you called to me?"

"The world spins, perhaps darkens," Ataquixt replied. "I thought you should know, especially since this might well involve the Lady Brynn Dharielle of Behren."

Belli'mar Juravel nodded. "Lady Brynn is beyond us now," he replied. "We choose not to interfere."

"But my duty is to inform."

Again, the elf nodded. "I suspect that I know already, but will hear your words, of course. And if it is what I believe, then yes, my friend, the world will darken. It is the love of your people. It is the weakness of your people. It will lead them to commit acts unbecoming your people, no doubt."

Ataquixt sighed heavily, unable to argue the point.

"How fares Bahdlahn of the plateau?"

"You know that I cannot speak of that. It will be years before that is truly answered, before he completes his tenure with us and is sent back to the world he once knew."

"I hope he fares well," Ataquixt said, and sincerely, for even though Bahdlahn, the man named in the false grave, had been Aoleyn's first love, Ataquixt felt no jealousy toward him. Bahdlahn was a good man, a just man, and a worthy ranger-in-training—indeed, one Ataquixt himself had referred to the Touel'alfar. "I believe that he will pass your tests."

Belli'mar Juraviel nodded, but it was a movement of acknowledgment, not necessarily agreement, Ataquixt knew. As much as he had come to love them, to appreciate their gifts to him in training him as a ranger, and to understand their view of the world, these Touel'alfar could be truly infuriating creatures in their selective, and sometimes seemingly arbitrary, dispassion.

"Before we speak of the state of the world, I have other news as well," Ataquixt said. "I am to be a father."

"A fortunate child, then."

Ataquixt smiled. "Thank you, and more than you understand. The mother is the witch Aoleyn, who destroyed the demons Cizinfozza and Scathmizzane."

"Well, my protégé, you are full of surprises here," the elf lord said. "I suspect that your child will live an eventful life, and hopefully a long one."

"I wish the child's world would be one nearing sunrise, but I fear it may be closer to sunset," Ataquixt said.

The Xoconai ranger winced a bit when Belli'mar Juraviel didn't disagree.

"But come, let us speak," Ataquixt quickly added. "My time is pressing and I wish to relay all that I have learned of the happenings in this land of Honce."

"And I wish to hear it. But remember, the Touel'alfar will not interfere with the doings of men, Bearman and Xoconai alike. Nor Behrenese, even if Queen Brynn decides that this is her fight after all."

"Room for a mundunugu quartet and our mounts?" Etlquay called up to the deck of the wide carrack.

"We've been on the road for many days and are looking for a trip back to Ursal," Alleketza explained. "Might you be bound for the city?"

"I don't know that we have the room, and—" the sentry called down before he was rudely interrupted by the watch commander, who pushed past him, stared down, and called, "No!" in no uncertain terms.

Etlquay tried to call up to the woman, but she just turned about and walked away, pulling the sentry with her.

Papap tapped Etlquay on the shoulder and redirected her gaze to the long wharf and a familiar figure approaching. Leading the four mounts, the three mundunugu headed down to intercept Ataquixt.

"So, how was our magical night?" Ataquixt asked Etlquay when she handed over Pocheoya's reins to him.

"Loud," Alleketza said with a laugh.

"Your reputation is secure," Papap added.

"We believe we found the right ship, yes?" Etlquay asked, glancing back at the carrack they had just left.

Ataquixt nodded.

"They've got something of worth," Etlquay said.

"They came in from the Mirianic Ocean, from south of Entel, though how far, I know not," said Alleketza. "Word is that they put into Entel, but only briefly, before they ran the length of the Mantis Arm and through the gulf at full sail."

"Something of worth," Etlquay repeated. "Information or . . ."

Ataquixt produced from his pocket a yellow nugget, the indents from where he or someone else had bitten it clear to see.

"They've at least one keg full of this in their hold, and many more, I suspect."

There it was, the clear answer to the riddle, the confirmation of Avitl's suspicions and fears.

Gold.

The magical word of the Xoconai, the basis of their

economy, their identity, and quite literally, the conduit of their magic.

"They found gold somewhere in the south," Alleketza reasoned.

"Everything just changed," Ataquixt agreed.

CHAPTER 3

CHILD OF THE WITCH

The tenth month of Hallow neared its end, the edge of winter slipping down from the Belt-and-Buckle Mountains to shiver Whispervale.

In the lands of Honce, this was the month of the final frolic, the harvest, the celebration of good weather, in the knowledge that the darker and colder days were just ahead. It was a holy month in Honce, and one of superstition and whispers of danger.

The harvest month had been no such thing in the land of Keri's birth, with its different cycles of life and death, of wakefulness and slumber, but she thought it a curious and fitting coincidence that this night, the last night of Hallow, Allhallows, was the moment her child, the child of a witch, had chosen to be born.

She knelt on her bed, Jilly and Jilly rushing in and out with towels soaked in cold water for her head, and more towels soaked in hot water to bring warmth to her lower body. They fretted for her—one had known the trial of childbirth—and Keri let them.

But she was not worried.

Here, in this time and place and moment, she had no trouble hearing the magical song of the gem-studded jewelry she wore, particularly that of the wedstone, which the Abellicans called the soul stone, that served as the cylindrical hub of her belly ring.

Through that magic, she felt the health of her child. With that magic, she calmed the pain in her body, and would heal quickly any ruptures that might occur. She was quite safe, as was her child.

She couldn't hide from the doubts, however. She was a witch of the Coven of Usgar, and so this experience had been, and now was, entirely her choice. She had felt, the very next morning after she and Ataquixt had found comfort in each other's arms as they had said goodbye to their previous lives and accepted the reality of the present and future, that their lovemaking had left her pregnant.

Why hadn't she protected herself that night? Her magic could easily have done so, but no, she had not.

And when she sensed the result, she was not afraid and she was not sad.

She was going away, leaving her previous identity and life behind. She was going forward now in a new name and with a more personal purpose.

She had to.

Was there more, she wondered now, in this moment when it was about to become all too real? Had she subconsciously clung to a residual stubbornness, a refusal to surrender the future she had envisioned, the future she knew to be the best course?

If anything was to symbolize that which she had fervently

hoped, after all, it would be a child of a Xoconai and a person not of that culture, a person without the distinctive face markings.

She felt the pressure of the impending birth. She called upon her magic for strength, for healing warmth.

None of the thoughts before mattered in that moment. This was her reality, and she embraced the overpowering sense of the moment, the present. It wasn't about the future right now, and not about any symbolism, and not about the wide world around her.

It was her.

It was her child.

That was all.

His ear pressed against a slight gap in the windowpane, Ataquixt expected to hear the cries of pain of childbirth, but instead heard . . . singing.

The witch singing, softly, calmly, and then came the cry of a child.

The Xoconai rolled back against the wall and exhaled, taking in the moment, trying to sort through so many conflicted feelings. He had been coming back to Whispervale repeatedly since his last meeting with Keridven some six months earlier—when he had come to realize that she was with child.

That truth was only confirmed as the weeks passed, of course.

Was it possible?

They had made love only that one time, a night of despair

turned to distraction, turned to an honest appreciation of each other and what they had all gone through. He had no idea if Keri had taken other lovers before or after that event.

In any case, his child or someone else's, he would not have abandoned her. She was important to him.

He went back to the window and peeked in. A younger woman was with Keridven then, bringing her fresh linens, helping her to get settled with the baby. For a moment, Ataquixt couldn't take his eyes off the new mother. She was glowing, happy, and healthy—more than he had feared would ever be possible after all that had happened. He knew the wings of guilt pressed upon this woman, knew that she, Aoleyn, blamed herself for so much, and that no amount of reasoning or support would push her past that feeling.

Aoleyn of the Usgar was a broken woman.

But maybe, he thought, just maybe, Keridven of Whispervale would not be.

He thought he should leave then, and stay away. He was a danger to her. If his Xoconai commanders ever learned of this secret, that Aoleyn was alive and well and only a few days' easy ride from Ursal, they would come for her, mercilessly.

Any thought of leaving vanished when he got a good view of the baby, as Keri shifted it to her breast to suckle.

No, he could not go. Not then. Not without knowing.

He waited for the young woman to give Keri her privacy, then he gently eased the window open, slipping through so gracefully and silently that he was near to the bed before the new mother even noticed him.

She started when she did, and jerked away, protecting the child, and Ataquixt put his empty hands up unthreateningly, half expecting this powerful witch to magically hurl him back through the wall.

"Ataquixt," she gasped when the moment of surprise had passed.

"Aoleyn," he quietly replied.

"No!" There was no debate to be found in her tone.

"Keridven," he apologized.

"What are you doing here?"

"Would you deny . . . is there something you have not told me?"

The edge came off her harsh expression almost immediately. She looked down at the baby boy and gave a helpless little laugh. "This is your son," she readily admitted. "There is no doubt. Though, look, he has my skin coloring and not yours, not the golden hue of Xoconai skin, not the facial markings of your people."

"You cannot know about the facial markings," Ataquixt started to reply, but he could see that she wasn't listening.

"Good fortune, while he is a young one, at least. He will pass in Whispervale as a child of Honce."

"That is good fortune," Ataquixt agreed. Or was it? He couldn't be sure, particularly given the discovery of golden riches made by the Xoconai sailors.

"Although, if the caste system of the Xoconai holds, perhaps it would be better for him if he looked like his father when he is older," Keri said.

"Would you like that?"

Keri paused then, and shrugged. "I want him with me. And look, he appears as a child of Honce, though neither of us is a child of Honce. And I will give him a name common among the people of Honce to further solidify that identity. Also, the name of an old friend." She looked down at the babe, who had turned from her breast, though whether he was hearing her or seeing her, Ataquixt couldn't know.

"You are Kenzie," she said. "And may you walk the world with his confidence and grace."

"A fine name," Ataquixt said, and his voice cracked a bit as he spoke it.

"Ataquixt?" Keri asked.

"It is nothing. I am a fool, is all."

"You are not a fool."

"Were you going to tell me?"

"No."

"You think that fair?"

She paused and looked away, then back at him. "No, I do'no."

"But necessary," Ataquixt said, and Keri nodded.

"I would like nothing more than to have you here with me, with us," she told him. "But how can we, with the world the way it is?"

"I should not even be here now," he admitted. "But I could not stay away. Will you forgive me?"

"Forgive you? It is I who needs ask that question. I did'no tell you because I feared you would come here, and be here, and so the whispers would spread and the Xoconai—"

"You did the right thing," Ataquixt interrupted. "For Kenzie."

"Keri, are you all right?" came a voice from beyond the door.

"I am well, Jilly. I will call when I need you, I promise." She lifted her finger over her pursed lips and Ataquixt nodded. She raised her arm, inviting him in for a big hug, and he readily complied, hugging them both.

"St.-Mere-Abelle remains secure," Ataquixt said softly.

"And remains no home of mine. Will you speak of the plateau next?"

"No," he answered with a sigh, and not just because he knew that she wouldn't entertain the idea of moving back to the plateau. Given the discovery in the south and the importance of Otontotomi and the plateau, there would be even more scrutiny there than here in the farmlands of Honce.

"Then you're finally hearing me."

Ataquixt shook his head, his grim expression stealing the smile from Keri's face. "Take great care in the coming years, wherever you go," he said.

"What do you know?" Keri demanded.

"The Xoconai interest in this land will not likely abate. It will intensify." He said no more, for she had enough on her mind to begin worrying about gold and trade routes and all the rest that would almost certainly follow the cargo coming in from the south.

"I know too that Kenzie will be safe and raised with the hopes and dreams we share," he whispered into Keri's ear. He kissed her on the cheek, then pulled back to stare at the child, his son.

Keri offered the babe to him, and he cradled little Kenzie in his arms, whispering to the babe for a long while. When he finally looked up at Keri, he told her, "We cannot know of his markings. The children of the Xoconai sometimes do not get the facial coloring until the springtide of life. You will see hints, perhaps, but you cannot be sure until his voice is that of a man, not a boy."

"If the world becomes a better place, I hope he will look like you," she said.

The kind words hit Ataquixt hard, so hard that he didn't reply for fear that he would choke up. This was his son, but it could not be.

For the sake of the child, for the sake of the mother, it could not be. He couldn't even let the townsfolk of Whispervale see him, whatever their kindness, for his mere presence here might lead to larger gossip and deeper consideration of this strange young woman who needed to be Keridven of Whispervale.

Keridven of Whispervale and not the witch named Aoleyn, who had killed Scathmizzane.

He moved in and shared the baby with her, hugging them both and kissing her on the cheek—but she turned to make the kiss on the lips, deep and heartfelt, a physical communion of their joys and their fears for what they both believed would be the very last time.

Ataquixt went to the window.

"I will likely be gone for a long while, but thereafter, may I return, at times, and watch from afar?" he asked.

Keri started to shake her head, but instead she just shrugged, then nodded.

Out went the warrior, through the window, into the cold night breeze, colder still because, although he had just witnessed the birth of his child, and to a woman whom he deeply admired and loved, he had never felt so alone.

CHAPTER 4

FIREACH SPEUER

GOD'S YEAR 865
(NAUI XIUITL)

Though the sun was bright, the day very warm, Ataquixt carried a foul mood. This was the first time since the declaration of Mayorqua Tonoloya that he had been out of the lands formerly called Honce.

He wasn't thrilled with his location, nor with his mount, which surprised him. Pocheoya would not have been a good fit for this mission, and thus, the ranger was back to riding a cuetzpali. This collared lizard was a good one, he understood, but he had grown accustomed to being up much higher while riding the pony, with a better view of his surroundings. Once he had gotten used to not seeing the ground immediately about his feet and once he had learned the rhythm of the pony, moving his legs in perfect complement, the ride proved much smoother than anything a cuetzpali could provide. He couldn't ride up walls as with a sticky-footed lizard, of course, but Pocheoya was much faster on level ground, and could run for far longer sprints.

Not here, though, Ataquixt understood, plodding with his mount up the long stairs from Otontotomi, settled on the bed of what had once been a very deep lake, up to the previous shore of said lake, and with only steep mountain trails beyond.

"What do you fear, Avitl?" he whispered under his breath, too low for any of the other soldiers in the caravan to hear. She was the city sovereign of Ursal now, and overseeing the increasing flow of gold coming from the east and being sent to the west, but this was the first time she had insisted that Ataquixt, one of her most trusted guards, and more importantly, her finest scout, accompany the shipment.

Something was in the air.

He glanced back through the giant rift in the plateau wall to the wide and shallow shining lake beyond the golden city.

There were a lot of ships out there, transports full of macana warriors.

Otontotomi already had a large complement of macana, and more mundunugu cavalry than any Xoconai city east or west.

At the sound of a gong and the blowing of a great mountain horn, Ataquixt's gaze traveled back to the city, to the shining golden dome of the reconstructed and even more glorious temple of Scathmizzane. He could see the crowd assembling before the augur platform for prayers, and though he couldn't make out any individuals down there, he was fairly certain that one of the priests up on that platform was Apichtli, a powerful man who had been quite outspoken about the dream of truly enacting Mayorqua Tonoloya.

Avitl had believed that Apichtli, above all, had been the

one to shift the policies in the east, to declare Honce as Quixi Tonoloya and convince the powers in the west to reset the calendar to Se Xiuitl, and rename the Bearmen as subhuman, as sidhe.

But the east was already mostly tamed. Why were so many of the western military forces sailing into a city already so well defended? Were they going after St.-Mere-Abelle again?

Ataquixt doubted that. The losses would be too great, the gain too little.

Did they have their eyes on Vanguard, across the Gulf of Corona from Palmaris?

Again, the ranger doubted it. There was little in Vanguard worth the effort, and too much unknown to take the risk. Anything they could get from Vanguard could come in from the west, from the great forests north of the Tonoloya Basin.

To the south, then, and the deserts of Behren?

Queen Brynn had a dragon. As a trained ranger (as was Queen Brynn), Ataquixt knew a lot more about that type of monster. A true dragon alone could shut down all shipping off the coast of Behren, and since the gold was coming from south of Freeport, such a move would be against the Xoconai interests.

Ataquixt's mind finally came around to what he knew to be obvious. He looked up at the mountain rising so high before him, ten thousand feet and more.

There was a large settlement up there now, almost exclusively non-Xoconai—the people who had lived there before the invasion and those from the settlements around the lake that was no more.

There were still witches up there, Aoleyn's former coven sisters.

There were caves full of magical crystals up there, culminating in the great God Crystal that protruded from the ground like some great phallus of the Usgar god.

That had been the primary point of the treaty those few years ago. The people of the Ayamharas Plateau had kept control of the mountaintop.

Now the gold was flowing, and so it followed, Ataquixt knew, that Apichtli and others considered the mountain to be a threat to Otontotomi, the shining city that served as the lynchpin to the empire of Mayorqua Tonoloya. With trade from the east becoming so important, would the Xoconai leaders be comfortable with the current situation here, even though by all accounts it had held stable and safe for several years now?

He looked back to the huge lake beyond the chasm in the sheer mountain wall, a chasm burned by a magical beam of pure power from the very God Crystal that topped this mountain. He noted the biremes, troop carriers, crowding into that breach to the Otontotomi docks.

It all fell into place.

It all made sense—horrible, terrible sense.

"You will do as you are commanded," the older woman said to her younger counterpart. "We have made an agreement, and holding true to it is all that keeps us on our ancestral land."

The other woman, Connebragh, chewed her lip, reminding herself that Mairen was the Crystal Maven, the Usgar-righinn. Mairen had not aged well, these last few years in the battered and battle-torn Ayamharas. Her once black hair was gray now, her face weathered from worry and from the mountain winds, her teeth chipped and yellow.

Part of that was because of this agreement, where Mairen and the other witches of the Usgar coven could not fully call upon the magic thrumming in the caves below the God Crystal. The treaty with the Xoconai had put vast limitations on the use of that magic—they could heal wounds and sickness and could chase off the winter snows with the warmth emanating from the God Crystal, and every now and again, Mairen would use her scepter to enhance their ritual dances, to lift them off the ground or to bring up winds, chill and warm.

The Xoconai augurs down in Otontotomi had scouts and ambassadors all about the human settlements up on the mountain, particularly in the main area near the God Crystal, and more determined to watch the witches very carefully. Anything more than those minor spells would bring fast reprisal from the great Xoconai city in the bowl at the base of Fireach Speuer, the mountain the Usgar—and now most of the surviving folk of the other tribes—called home.

"You cannot ignore the signs," Connebragh replied. "The hills crawl with Xoconai lizard riders."

"The mundunugu are hunting," Mairen countered. "They tire of fish, no doubt, and the winter will come soon enough."

"I have never seen this many," Connebragh insisted. "Nor this many refugees streaming up the mountainside."

"Seeking a new home with us, and why would they not?"

"The outer settlements we now have are thick with winter snows."

"Just a short distance from the eternal summer of the God Crystal," Mairen said.

Connebragh was about to mention the vessels in the lake. The entire Otontotomi fleet was out all the time, ferrying back and forth from the city docks to the landings along the northeastern shore, near to the fort where the golden mirrors had been set for the magical transportation. Mairen would just make some remark about the flurry of trade, Connebragh realized.

But no, she was quite convinced that those boats were ferrying soldiers.

She wouldn't convince Mairen, though, and even if she did, or even if she really didn't have to, the Usgar-righinn would brush it off.

Mairen was terribly afraid, Connebragh knew when she looked into the older witch's eyes. They were here atop Fireach Speuer, their ancestral home, resting on the crystal bed of their magical powers. A few Xoconai lived up here with them, mostly scholars who wanted to learn of the people of the plateau and region. Even without counting them, there were perhaps five thousand people up here now, refugees from the plateau and all the surrounding lands.

The Xoconai in Otontotomi numbered twenty times that. The Xoconai warriors alone, macana and mundunugu, in the golden city numbered perhaps twenty thousand—and that was before all the recent activity.

Something big was coming, something bad.

Connebragh saw it clearly, and she suspected that Mairen did, too.

Would their obeisance be enough to save them?

Mairen was apparently willing to make that bet.

Ataquixt rode his cuetzpali to a high bluff overlooking the northernmost settlement outside the central home of the Usgar, the one nearest the trails leading to Otontotomi, thus the most likely first target in any move up the mountain.

He took heart as the hours passed in quiet, save the steady groan of the mountain wind. He went from watching the trails leading up from above to the small encampment, to studying the movements within the place, the everyday goings-on of these people, these *sidhe* to his fellows, who had lived around the great lake covering the Xoconai golden city only a few years previous.

How normal it all looked to him, even though many of these particular people looked very different from the Xoconai. In addition to the lack of face colorings, the lake tribesmen had misshapen heads, the result of the tradition of wrapping the skulls of their children. The practice was to make sure they did not look like the Usgar of the mountain, who had been their sworn enemies back in those days.

Still, Ataquixt understood that if he'd been on a bluff in

the low mountains surrounding the Tonoloya Basin far in the west, the movements he would witness were no different from those below him now.

Children played in the clearings between the large round tents and wooden structures.

The adults went about their chores, maintaining the fires, preparing the meals, shoring up the various structures.

Even the sounds—the laughing, the occasional yell of an adult reining in the behavior of an unruly child—reminded him so much of home.

The scout scolded himself for the distraction when he glanced back the other way to the eastern slopes of the great mountain, for there he saw the lines of mundunugu. They rode their lizards along the steep and broken canyons and trails where a walking man could not go, climbing higher, climbing around this lower encampment.

So many mundunugu!

Ataquixt closed his eyes and sighed, realizing his mistake and understanding the strategy very clearly then.

He went down low, for he didn't want to be seen up on this bluff, certainly, and tried to sort out his best moves.

He had none. There was nothing he could do, no one he could warn who could offer anything about the coming storm.

He climbed up on his cuetzpali and set off at a fast trot, moving west, just north of the village. More than one of the villagers likely saw him, but no matter—Xoconai were often on the mountain singularly or in small groups.

He wanted to turn and ride into the settlement and warn them, but to what end?

He continued to the west, to the trails on the other side of the God Crystal, still far above him. He called for everything his mount could give him, thinking that maybe he could get to the witches and warn them. They perhaps could offer resistance.

Far across, looking down the stony cliffs on the mountain's western decline, that thought, too, was flown.

More mundunugu were there, swarming about the region of the entrance to the crystal caves, the base of Usgar magic.

A cry of surprise and fear from above told him that it had begun.

"Begone!" Mairen cried at the lizard riders as they swarmed into the main encampment of the mountain tribes. People ran all about for their lives, the mundunugu chasing them down and cracking their skulls with the toothed macana paddles, or launching javelins from their deadly accurate atlatls.

"We have done nothing to betray you! Nothing to threaten!" Mairen screamed, scrambling out of the lea that held the God Crystal, through the circling pine trees, waving her arms and the crystalline scepter of her station.

Rushing to the edge of the small field, Connebragh watched the Crystal Maven's run. "No, no," she heard herself whispering, both at the attacks beyond the trees and at the foursome of

Xoconai walking their mounts at Mairen, fanning out to form a semicircle about her.

"Stop this!" Mairen yelled at them. "We are not your enemies!"

Four javelins flew into her body in reply.

Connebragh lost her breath and stumbled backward onto the field.

"Kill them, kill them!" she called, her voice raspy and pained.

The witches began their dance, their song. Connebragh rushed to the God Crystal, joining another witch there. She hugged the crystal, sending her thoughts into it, hearing its song. Connebragh wasn't strong in Usgar magic, but she didn't have to be at this time. The magical energy flowed up from below, from the crystalline formations in the caves beneath this sacred place, speeding to the call of the witch song.

The God Crystal thrummed with power.

All Connebragh had to do was aim it.

She saw the four riders who had murdered Mairen coming through the trees, javelin-filled atlatls lifted high.

Lightning shot forth from the God Crystal, blasting through the trees, throwing the lizards and their riders back the way they had come.

Connebragh closed her eyes and conjured an image of the camp beyond the lea, and the magic of the crystal showed her a vision of the place in real time, the Usgar scrambling, fleeing, screaming, and dying. The merciless Xoconai cutting them down.

Arcing bolts of lightning flashed and flared from the crystal, stabbing through the trees, incinerating Xoconai and lizards, and even the poor tribesmen who happened to be in the path of destruction.

Connebragh felt the tears streaming down her cheeks when she watched a trio of young Usgar thrown like leaves in a mountain gale by the power of the lightning.

But what choice did she have?

The cries around her didn't register to her at first as she continued to call forth the magic, now adding lines of fire to the lightning. The trees before her went up in flames, the sappy pines exploding in the heat of the brutal conflagration.

She noticed the magic fast diminishing, though, and only then realized that the song of the witches, too, was fading.

She opened her eyes and looked around to find a raging battle on the sacred field. Usgar warriors and Xoconai poured onto the lea from the sides and behind the God Crystal, throwing their spears, launching their javelins, leaping at each other with feral fury.

The other witches leveled their small crystals and threw magic into the fray. Waves of healing fell over the Usgar defenders, lightning stabbed at the Xoconai attackers, great winds came forth to defeat the hurled javelins.

The Xoconai angled around and tried to burst through the Usgar warriors to target the witches, who numbered only a dozen, but the skilled heroes of Usgar understood the tactics, clearly, and threw themselves in the way, fighting to the bitter end.

Connebragh hugged the God Crystal once more, imploring it to bring forth more magic.

She heard its song, but distantly.

She opened her eyes and saw more Xoconai riding through the smoke and scattered fires among the pines before her.

One of her sisters crashed against her, then, and Connebragh grabbed the witch's hand. "Help me bring forth the power," she begged. And then she gasped as the woman turned about, revealing a dagger stabbed to the hilt into her chest, her mouth open in a silent cry of futile denial that her life had come to its end.

Connebragh didn't know what to do. She saw another witch fly to the ground under a leaping Xoconai lizard, the fierce beast chewing her face and throat.

More mundunugu poured onto the field. The Usgar warriors were killing the attackers two-to-one, it seemed to Connebragh, but they'd have to score ten times that number to have any chance at all.

Over to the side, another witch dropped her crystals and fell to her knees, hands raised in surrender.

Two riders charged into her, lizards clawing, macana paddles battering her mercilessly.

Connebragh, crying openly, knew she was about to die, knew that they all were about to die. She hugged the crystal and prayed to her god, calling for something, anything—healing, protection, some burst of power to make it all stop.

She was glowing a milky white, as if a magical shroud had come about her, but she didn't know it. All she felt was a bubble of power, like the last cry of defiance, rising from the crystal itself in a general manner, as if of the magic's own accord. It wasn't an aimed blast like the lightning or fire bolts, but just a belch of the entire crystal, of the Usgar god, a sudden, violent explosion of flame, a fireball that filled the lea and beyond.

Connebragh was falling then, or flying. She hit the ground hard and bounced and rolled, ending up face-down on the grass.

She knew she had to get up. She knew she had to run away.

But how, and where?

With the sound of the blast still ringing in her ears, it took her a while to realize that it was just the echo, and that was the only sound, so suddenly.

She looked up.

The trees were burning all about the circular meadow. The grass, even that under her, was scorched and blackened and wafting smoke.

And all about her, Xoconai and Usgar, witches and warriors, lizards—all of them—lay about the lea, blackened and burning.

Horrified, Connebragh pulled herself up, patting at her arms as if expecting them to be on fire. For a few heartbeats, she thought she must be dead, for she felt no pain.

And she was glowing.

She tried to sort it out. What had she done?

What had the crystal done?

Where had her call ended and the roar of her god begun?

She didn't know, but she quickly realized that nothing would protect her now. More mundunugu were coming, she could hear, from the village beyond the trees.

Connebragh scrambled out the back side of the lea, stumbling through the burning pines, pushing fiery branches out of her way, but feeling no bite from the flames.

Not at first, at least, but the serpentine shield she had somehow pulled from the God Crystal was diminishing now. Her eyes and throat began to sting from the hot smoke and embers. She clutched at the one small crystal she carried, a rod shot through with a line of gray hematite, the wedstone of healing.

She stumbled out from the trees and along a steeply descending path, where she was soon falling more than running.

A javelin grazed her back, tossing her fully from her feet to crash hard against some stones.

Desperate, she pulled herself up enough to look back, to see the lizard rider on a bluff far away, loading another javelin. She threw herself forward, over another ridge, and went tumbling down, bouncing and rolling a long, long way, coming to a sudden and violent stop against a stone.

She didn't feel the impact.

She didn't feel anything.

There was just darkness and utter quiet.

He paced his mount along the trails, nodding to his fellow mundunugu and to the macana foot soldiers who had spearheaded the second assault, charging straight up the mountain trails and driving the folk from the lower settlements, like the one he had been watching initially, up into the waiting maw of the lizard riders.

Ataquixt did well to keep his expression calm and one of

satisfaction, giving the outward appearance that he approved of the glorious victory the Xoconai had won this day on Tzatzini, their name for this towering mountain.

Behind that expression, the ranger wanted to throw up, to scream in rage and curse all who had planned this great treachery!

But no, he could not.

He would be of no use to the world if he was dead.

He continued on his way, finally coming to the central village and the smoldering ruins of the pines and meadow that surrounded the famed God Crystal. Just outside a circle of smoking devastation, he found the body of a familiar woman. He rolled from his mount, knelt beside her.

"Mairen," he said, and took the crystalline scepter from her dead hands, holding it up and admiring the beauty of it, the line of red that glowed within, and the casing, which looked as if it had been crafted of starlight.

He blew a great sigh at the waste of it all, then slid the item into a deep pocket within his backpack.

He kissed two fingers and pressed them against dead Mairen's cheek. "Rest well. Know eternally that you tried, that you chose the moral course," he prayed over her. He settled himself and stood straight, took up the reins of his mount, and walked through the carnage.

Dozens of bodies, mostly of mundunugu and their lizards, littered the small field, or were clumped against the trunks of the scarred pines. The leaders of Otontotomi would count this particular battle for the God Crystal as a victory, of course, but between this field and the ruined village beyond the trees, more than a thousand Xoconai families would find grief.

And for what?

He had helped to create the peace, to form the treaty that Tuolonatl and Aoleyn and the others had forged here, and within that arrangement, his people could have found all the prosperity they would now know, and would have made of the people of these sparsely populated regions—and more importantly, those of the great cities to the east in Honce—powerful allies.

Even Queen Brynn of the desert kingdom south of the mountains would have accepted the Xoconai as neighbors—there were no stirrings of war with Behren in the first years of the treaty.

But that was not enough for the insatiable leaders of the Xoconai, particularly the augurs. No amount of gold would fill the holes in their hearts, it seemed, or sate their appetite for complete power.

He moved through the field and beyond, to the rockier chasms and valleys on the far side of the settlement, the western slopes of Tzatzini spreading before him. Perhaps he should go to the crystal caves, he considered, but then dismissed it quickly.

Xoconai were in there, and surviving witches, if there were any, who had sought refuge in their crystal-laced tunnels would surely have been summarily murdered.

He moved to the edge of one sheer drop, wanting to feel the wind on his face to dry his tears, wanting to see the wide, wide world spreading before him. He thought of the Touel'alfar and their hidden, magical lands, not for any hopes of practical assistance—Lord Belli'mar of the elves had made it perfectly clear that this conflict was not their concern—but merely to remind himself that the world was bigger than Tonoloya, even Mayorqua Tonoloya, and that there were many more people out there going about their lives.

Perhaps in peace, perhaps in battle.

He hoped for peace and found a moment of comfort in thinking that he was, after all, a very small person in a very large world and a very tiny speck of time.

The moment proved fleeting. He heard a groan below, one of a human voice and not the wind.

Connebragh tried to react when she saw the toothy maw of the reptile rising over the lip of the ledge where she lay. But she could do nothing. Lying on her belly, broken and battered, she had no strength to fight the creature. She only hoped that it would kill her quickly—even in her dazed and weakened state, the notion of being alive while eaten was too much.

The lizard moved up higher and Connebragh stared curiously at its rider.

A Xoconai mundunugu.

She was surely dead or would be taken prisoner by the fiends.

"You are alive," the Xoconai said, and not in the language of his people, but in the tongue common to the tribes of the Ayamharas Plateau.

Connebragh groaned and tried to turn away, but the warrior put his hand on her and said, "I know you."

She focused on him and tried to sort through her jumbled thoughts.

"You are Connebragh of the Coven, friend to Mairen and friend to Aoleyn."

"Aoleyn?" she echoed. It was a name she had not heard in several years. That surprise gave her more focus as she stared at the warrior.

"The battle," she whispered.

"Many are dead," the warrior started to reply, but Connebragh cut him short, for she wasn't referring to this current fight.

"With the god," she clarified. "You were there, beside the cochcal. Tuo . . . Tuolonatl?"

"Yes. Yes, you remember."

"Your spear . . ."

"In the dragon's eye. I am Ataquixt."

"And now you turn on us. You lied. You all lied!" Connebragh struggled and began to claw at the stone, trying to pull herself away from the man, and thinking then that if she could manage it, she'd hurl herself from the ledge and be done with it.

"No, I did not," Ataquixt answered quietly. "Not then and not now. You are not my enemy and I am not yours."

Connebragh fixed him with a perfectly incredulous stare.

"Come, I must hide you from the raiders. We must let you heal and must be on our way."

"Where? How?"

"Far from here. There is no place for you on the plateau any longer."

"Where?" she insisted.

Ataquixt shook his head, unsure—but he was already getting some ideas.

TWO

—

WHISPERVALE

GOD'S YEAR 872

(MAHTLATLI XIUITL)

Forgive my silence, Father Abbot. These last years have tested me to my limits and beyond. As you requested, I traveled to the west, to the Ayamharas Plateau and the great mountain known as Fireach Speuer, where Scathmizzane was killed. The journey there was facilitated by the golden mirrors our nemeses use to far-step across the leagues . . . a well-placed bribe to a corrupt Xoconai commander got me to the gates of Otontotomi, the great Xoconai city nestled in the canyon that used to be the lake below the mountain. Once there, however, my journey grew far more challenging. Abellican monks are welcomed not at all anywhere near to Otontotomi.

I have killed, Father Abbot, and though only in self-defense, my actions horrify me and will require a great penance, one that I hope you will bestow fairly and firmly when we meet again.

I did get up the mountain, and it is everything we feared. The Usgar tribe and those other people of Ayamharas who moved high on the slopes near the protective magic of the crystal caves are no more. The caves, the great crystal, and all the mountain are now in Xoconai hands alone. People of the Ayamharas or folk of Honce, or of any other region who are not Xoconai, are simply not allowed on the slopes of Fireach Speuer. I do not know how proficient the Xoconai have become with the crystals and their magical properties. How much they have learned or how powerfully they can utilize the sacred stones within those crystals, I cannot say.

They are not a stupid people, and not unaccustomed to magic, as you know.

For my journey back to Honce, I had no way to access the teleportation powers of the golden mirrors. It took me nearly a year, and without my sacred stones, I would never have survived. It is not an easy journey, full of monsters, fierce animals, and long stretches short of water and food. The promising news, though, is that there are few Xoconai soldiers across the nearly two thousand miles from Otontotomi to Ursal. They are thick in Honce, no doubt, but their reserves are far afield.

If ever we could defeat their mirrors, those here would wither.

But they are here, as we know, and they grow bolder and more dangerous with every passing week. And more hostile to those of us wearing Abellican robes. At one point, near the end of last year, I was taken prisoner by a Xoconai patrol, and survived only by appealing to an old associate, one I knew in those few months when I was following the teaching of Marcalo De'Unnero. He convinced the Xoconai to let me go, that I was no devotee of Saint Avelyn and the Reformed Abellican Church.

Believing me a disciple of Marcalo De'Unnero, the Xoconai released me.

How it pained me to pretend that I still believed the heretic's teachings to be correct and just!

My choice was to lie or be revealed as an Abellican spy sifting about the villages of Honce. My Xoconai captors would have put me to death, no doubt. They have become merciless and utterly uncaring for we men of Honce-the-Bear.

I do not ask for your forgiveness, for I know in my heart that it was not weakness or fear of death that drove me to lie. The situation out here in the land of Honce beyond the walls of St.-Mere-Abelle deteriorates daily. Towns and cities are falling to darkness. The augurs celebrate Scathmizzane, their Glorious Gold, once more, and the throngs of Xoconai who attend their liturgies are loud with their praise of the demon god, and louder still with their cheers that they are the chosen people, the true humans.

There is no truce.

There is no peace to be found.

And thus, my calculation that you need me out here collecting information as I can was the factor that made me seek out those old De'Unneran accomplices—brothers and sisters who are now wholly traitors to the folk of Honce, I fear. While I do not believe that these heretics of our faith truly embrace Scathmizzane's teaching or even the Xoconai as their brothers, their cooperation with the Xoconai is a calculated ploy to give them supremacy within the Abellican Church and with the folk of Honce.

I fear it might be working. We are hiding away, and with good reason, of course, yet I suspect that the common folk of Honce do not fully appreciate that reason. Thus, they think that we have abandoned them, leaving a void the De'Unnerans are all too willing to fill.

In my heart, I wish that this was delivering better news to you, my beloved Father Abbot, although I suspect that I am only confirming many whispers that you have heard from those few fortunate folk who make their way to the doors of the great sanctuary that is St.-Mere-Abelle.

Perhaps I will be one of those fortunate souls soon, for I am making my way north across central Honce now in the hopes that I might return to my home, to St.-Mere-Abelle, soon to deliver a fuller report. But I must take care, and I urge secrecy on your and the other masters' parts. It is better for us all if it is not revealed that Brother Thaddius has returned to welcome arms at St.-Mere-Abelle.

I serve our Blessed Order and the folk of Honce-the-Bear better if the De'Unnerans believe that I remain with them and if the cursed Xoconai think me no threat to them.

By the pen of Brother Thaddius Roncourt,
Your servant in Abelle, from the town of Youseff
This 15th day of Toumanay,
Fourth month of God's Year 872

CHAPTER 5

THE COVEN

"The moon isn't to be full this night," Connebragh remarked, coming out of the bedroom of the house she shared with Keridven, noting the woman gathering the lanterns and placing them beside her folded white gown, which was really just a simple shift of sheer and flowing material.

"It's not needing to be, is it, Connie?" Keri answered, and she glanced back to show her partner her crooked little smile.

It took Connie a while to respond, for the morning sunlight streaming in through the small house's window had cast such a favorable glow over Keri that the image had thrown Connie back to their younger days. And truly, Keri didn't appear to have aged much in the decade and more since she had left their homeland, even given the many trials she had endured. Keri had never been considered beautiful, or even pretty, among their tribe, for she didn't much resemble the typical Usgar woman. She was barely more than five feet tall, whereas Connie, like most, was closer to six, and Keri had black hair and black eyes, colors that were quite uncommon among the tribe. Even her skin was different, a bit darker and with olive undertones. The whispers hinted that she was not fully Usgar at all, and that her mother had been impregnated by one of the few travelers who had made their way among the tribes of Loch Beag and Fireach Speuer. It was just gossip, of course, for how might such a tryst have even happened? But somewhere in her past, perhaps, some ancestor . . .

Looking at her now, though, Connie understood how much her tribe's traditions had influenced them all, herself included, in the disdain for the different-looking Keri. For the woman, now in her mid-thirties, was surely beautiful, and that crooked smile so mischievous and imp-like. She didn't need the morning sunshine to make her eyes sparkle with life, and she gave a warm glow in any lighting or no lighting at all.

"I'm only thinking you were meaning to wait for the moon's full light this month," Connie explained.

"My mind's filled with possibility and worry," Keri said.

"Because the Xoconai were seen in the hills."

"Aye, and there're whispers of changes all about the land. I'm not sure what that might be meaning for Whispervale, but nothing good if it's to change at all."

Connie smiled and nodded at that. She had been led to Whispervale after the fall of Fireach Speuer more than a half-dozen years before, and by a most unexpected rescuer, the Xoconai named Ataquixt. He had nursed her back to health in a cave near the mountain, then had escorted her across the thousands of miles, even arranging a transport through two different teleportation mirrors of the Xoconai to move vast distances with a single step. Still, the journey had been arduous, with months of travel and always on the edge of disaster.

She had been welcomed into the house of Keri and her then three-year-old son, Kenzie. They had raised him and then added two other boys who had been orphaned in a terrible hunting tragedy a couple of years later. Their home had been, and still was, a most happy place, full of love and trust, and shared laughter before the hearth when the cold mountain winds blew.

As it was with all of Whispervale around them, a close-knit and caring community that worked together through tough winters, bad harvests, and any other trials that might arise.

"So, are you thinking to dance?"

"Dancing's where I'm feeling most free," Keri answered. "Dancing's where I hear the call of the music and the magic of life itself. 'Twas yourself that brought the dancing back to Whispervale, if I'm remembering right."

"You started the dancing here before e'er I arrived," Connie countered with a wide smile.

"Not like this," Keri protested. "Not with the magic. It was just a dance before that, spiritual and holy, aye, but without any use of the stones. I was afraid of showing the true magic of it to the local folk, but it was Connie who changed my mind."

"You weren't afraid of showing them, you were afraid of using the crystals," Connie bluntly replied.

Keri sucked in her breath, but could only nod. She still was afraid of the stones and the power they wrought—so much tragedy had followed Keri in her previous life when she had put the magic to powerful and often terrible use! But because of Connie, she had begun at least using them once more for the small things and the good things, like healing wounds and sickness, and, of course, for the dance. She had done so secretly, pretending that herbs and salves were healing the injured and sick, not the wedstone magic. And with the dance, the women were just attributing it, with Keri's guidance, to a communal lifting of the spirits and the imagination. "'Tis our gift, my old companion, my dearest beloved," Connie said more seriously, and she walked over and dropped one hand on Keri's shoulder, the other going under Keri's loose shirt and to the dangling, magical gemstones hanging on short chains from her belly-button ring—and even the rings and chains were magical, all fashioned of wedstone. "'Tis who we are, particularly who you are, for who has ever been more attuned to the song of the crystals than Aole . . . than yerself?"

"I do'no wish to be that woman anymore," Keri flatly stated. "She's left behind, on a mountain."

"I know," Connie said, and she hugged her partner tight and kissed her gently on the cheek. "You fear what you were."

Keri gently pushed her back to arm's length. "No," she said, her expression and the slight shake of her head telling Connie that she was sorting it out more than insisting it wasn't true. "Just tired of the fighting."

"Of the killing, you mean."

Keri replied by holding up her hands and turning them so Connie could see her palms, decorated with tattoos to resemble the paw prints of the cloud leopards that had floated gracefully across the cliff facings of their old mountain home.

Connie nodded sympathetically. Keri could not escape her past with or without the magical gemstones she wore in the piercings and jewelry that she rarely removed. Connie came forward and kissed Keri once more, softly and on the lips this time.

"Should I whisper of a dance this night?" she said quietly when she pulled back.

Keri nodded.

"Are you going to teach them the song?"

Keri's eyes blinked open wide and her expression became one of shock. "The song of the crystals? No. No, never. That would damn them if all that I'm fearing is coming true. No, this is our secret, Connie, and ours alone. I've not even revealed the depth of it to our children, nor will I. Nor will you."

"I agree," Connie said after a moment of reflection. "But aye, let us dance and sing together this night, in all its exhilaration and beauty." She moved for the door, but turned back and winked at Keri, saying, "Even though 'tis no' a full moon."

"I need no excuse to bask in the dance," Keri replied.

Connie laughed at that but noted that Keri's smile was strained. Her partner was truly concerned here.

Connie was barely out of the house before Keri began her preparations. She smoothed her white shift flat on the table before her, then slipped off the ring on her left index finger, feeling the pinch and drag as the needlelike wedstone connective jut scraped at the underside of her finger. She winced, considering the power of this ring, which was set with two gems: ruby and serpentine, one for bursts of magical fire, the latter to create a shield to protect her from the devastation of the former.

Keri didn't want to think about it. She shook her head as she removed her right-hand ring, and for a different reason, as she felt physically weaker as soon as she slipped it off. The bloodstone set in it continually granted her strength. Keri smiled, recognizing that she did indeed feel physically weaker without the bloodstone connection. She wasn't even consciously using the magic of the stone, but simply removing it was proof enough that the strength offered by it was always with her, at least a bit.

In that ring, too, was a citrine, another stone of magic. What a fine combination these two had provided, granting an ability to shape solid rock and the strength to move heavy stones about.

She removed her left shoe and reached down to her anklet, its wedstone chain set with deep blue sapphires and a lighter blue zircon, and with small graphite bars that snugged tightly to the sides of her ankle. She took great care in unclasping the anklet, then slowly pulled it from around her leg. She sent her magical energy into that wedstone chain as she did, healing the little punctures as the connecting hooks pulled out of her flesh. She brought it up before her eyes to inspect the piece carefully, and thought herself clever once more with her innovation to actually anchor the jewelry to her skin with the worked wedstone wires. Her connection to the gems was so much stronger, its magical music resonating so clearly to her!

Perhaps it was a connection to a god, as the Abellicans

believed, though Keri's so-bitter experiences could only lead her to think of the gods as demons.

Next came her right earring, with its deep red garnet stone, and then the left, holding a turquoise ear cuff set with a cat's-eye gem that allowed her to see quite well in the night. When she was satisfied that the socket was firm, the ear cuff joined the other pieces on the folded white shift.

Keri looked out the window to make sure no one was nearby or approaching the house, then untied the laces of her blouse, removed the shirt altogether, and dropped it to the side.

She stepped back from the table and turned to garner more light from the window, then bent over and carefully worked the wedstone fasteners on her belly-button piercing, her most prized piece of jewelry. For this piece held the strongest and largest wedstone, through which Keri could heal grievous wounds. It also held a separate magical stone at the end of each of its four finger-length chains: a flat green malachite that allowed her to become weightless, or even to magically float objects about her from the ground; a white-and-gray dolomite, which made her hardier—had she even sniffled with a cold through the years since donning it?—and with which she had cured many of Whispervale's farmers from some very nasty diseases; a glittering diamond that allowed her to make brilliant light, or to reverse its magic and suck up all the light around her and create a globe of utter, impenetrable blackness. And finally, perhaps her favorite of all, a milky white moonstone that gave her the power to create breezes, even great gusts of wind, and with which Keri could even fly for short distances. Oh, but how she had loved flying, gliding along the mountainsides of the towering peaks back home! She wouldn't dare use this stone for such a visible purpose now in these uncertain times, of course, but the temptation was ever there.

For the freedom she felt when released from the bonds of the world was truly a miraculous sensation, and one that reinforced her belief in the magic and the purpose of its use, and her faith in the beauty of this life, and the hopes of something beyond the mortal experience. Yes, this was her favorite stone, her favorite, freeing magic. The wedstone and the dolomite allowed her to heal herself and others, and indeed, had saved several lives, at least, but this one, this moonstone, truly held her heart.

She gently placed the belly ring on the folded shift, then retrieved a swatch of soft, unbleached cotton and a weak soapy solution. Very carefully, she polished the various stones, inspecting all the settings. When she was done, she began slowly putting her jewelry back on, savoring each piece as its wedstone connector pricked and slipped back into her skin, feeling the magic, hearing the songs of each individual gem.

Reminding herself of the power here and the beauty, of who she had been, of the things, good and bad, that she had done.

Yes, they were going to dance this night, and Keri was determined that this one would be special, that she would bring forth the song of every gemstone so powerfully that every woman of the Whispervale coven would share fully in that magic and beauty, that they would know through the dark days ahead that there was something to hold on to, some hope that they would know this joy one day in the future.

Keri closed her eyes and bent her head back and let the malachite lift her from the floor, then felt the breeze tickling her bare skin as the song of the moonstone harmoniously joined in.

Freedom.

No one, she decided then and there, could take this from her. She never wanted to use this power in a violent way against another again.

But no one could take this from her.

Seven women walked together, some hand in hand, up the low hill northwest of Whispervale, enjoying the warm early-summer breeze and almost giddy with anticipation for this unexpected dance. The youngest, Shivahn, was still in her teens, and the twin sisters walking before her barely out of them. They came through the trees to the open lea, and there removed their cloaks and shoes and gowns. Wearing only the white shifts of flowing light fabric, they lit their small lanterns, two each, and walked to the starting points of their performance, forming a wide circle. There, they all paused in silence and considered the night around them, the sounds of night birds and frogs and various insects. The distant howl of a wolf or hoot of an owl. The light of the stars above, and a fingernail waning moon hanging low in the east.

They remained at quiet peace for a long while; then, on Keri's call, they began to slowly move, stepping rightward in unison, swaying and turning about with easy individual motions, an expression of self, an inner inspiration, within each coordinated step.

Like a great natural heartbeat, there came a slight, barely audible drumbeat—Keri using her skill with the dance, they all knew when they thought about it, though none of them would think about it in that moment, as they were lost already in their movements and the harmony of the night.

The rhythm increased gradually, the unified steps coming a bit faster. The women began to sing, to hum, to chant—whatever expressions of joy the night pulled from them.

Some began to turn their own circles within the larger circle; all held their arms out to either side, the lanterns sweeping wide at the end of each.

The music grew, more than just a drumbeat now, as if the sounds of horns and strings had been created of nothingness. Inspiring them to dance, continuing and hastening their circle, dipping and rising between steps or during, turning slowly or spinning fast, crouching low or leaping through the procession. They began to sing, all of them, and found harmony even though the women who had been raised in Whispervale didn't understand all the words of the song they shared. But their voices were smooth and synchronous, and the forest about the small lea on that high bluff seemed as if it was supplying the melody—which it was, to some extent, because of the magic of one of the dancers, but that, too, was something quite removed from the women who had spent all their lives in the small town nestled in the foothills of the Belt-and-Buckle a mile or so to the southeast of this hillock.

They could all feel the magic, its energy unmistakable. It carried them in their spins, made them lighter on their feet, even guided the fog that had risen this night under the full moon to make them feel as if they were dancing on a cloud.

They sang and they were solemn. They sang and they were happy. The intonations brought forth from them the entire range of human emotion, heightened and spiritual.

Their shifts flowed and swept to exaggerate every movement, making them all seem ghostly, more spirit than flesh.

So fittingly.

A breeze came up, tickling them, hair flowing, shifts flowing to their limits. And the wind was warm, then it was cool, then cold even, before warming once more.

That almost broke Connie from her growing trance, for she knew it to be Keri manipulating the temperature of the wind with her ruby and her zircon, something the powerful witch had not done on their previous dances with this coven. She opened her eyes just long enough to see that Keri had moved from the turning outer circle to the very middle, a sight that reminded her of the dances on a distant mountain, when the leader of a different coven had so typically centered it.

The distraction didn't hold, for the music grew, now accompanied perfectly by the whistling of the magical wind. Connie felt herself growing lighter, her strides becoming long, her leaps higher. The breeze was comfortably cool now and blowing stronger, and swirling, almost as if to catch her and enhance her every movement.

She fell under the spell of the dance, of the night, once

more. She lifted from the ground and slowly spun about, but as she descended, she felt as if her spirit kept lifting, as if she was breaking free of her physical body. And she saw the dance then as if she were a night bird, looking straight down from on high! And she heard within the song several gasps and understood that she was not alone up there, seeing through the eyes of some flying creature!

She was seeing the dance in total, from above, her fellow witches turning and leaping, and now weaving in and about each other, their lantern lights, spots of flame, moving in harmony to the music that was all around and all-encompassing.

And in the middle, there stood Keri—or rather, there floated Keri, off the ground, her arms extended, her head lolling in her trance. She dropped back down suddenly, and a burst of sparkling blue energy rushed out from beneath her feet, spreading wide, rolling out underneath the six dancers.

Connie felt the shock, the joyous tingle of energy rushing up through her feet to her legs and throughout her entire body.

The tempo increased, the circle tightened. As if on command, though there was no call, no practiced routine, three of the witches reversed direction, and all six began to weave about the again-floating Keri.

On and on it went. Keri dropped again and again, infusing the coven with energy. The wind grew hotter and hotter, then suddenly cold once more, the shifting sensations only bringing the women more deeply into the reality of the deep night.

Then a light began to grow in the center, in Keri's uplifted hand. A single sparkle of light brightening well beyond the glow of the lanterns. Brilliant and powerful, like looking into the sun, and they could not hold their gazes upon it.

And it stopped—no, more than stopped. It reversed, winked out, and took all the other lights with it: the lanterns, the stars, the fingernail moon. All of it, gone. The music became once more the simple beat of nature's night drum, the wind calming to nothing in the blink of an eye.

And the dancing stopped, leaving the seven in utter blackness and stillness and silence, as if all sensation had suddenly been stolen away.

None moved. None spoke. None did more than stand there in the nothingness, caught only in their own thoughts and feelings, physical and emotional.

The world began to slowly grow around them once more, the lights returning, a bird calling out from high above.

All six of the circling witches stood there overwhelmed, staring at the woman in the center, who seemed just as disheveled and surprised as they.

"We must never tell anyone about this night," Keri said to them.

"They would not understand," Connie agreed. "How could we begin to explain?"

The dancers, the witches, all looked to each other, and the youngest began to giggle, and it became infectious, all seven soon laughing and giggling as if they knew not how to feel after an experience that had so transcended anything any of them had known before, a feeling so intense and a release so full of power that there was only one experience any of them, and not the youngest, who had not yet known it, could equate to it.

Any of them except for Keri, of course. The precipitator, the sharer. She had fallen into her magic more fully in the many minutes of that single dance than she had since a fateful and brutal battle on a mountainside far, far away.

Perhaps she had finally fought past her fears and her hesitancy.

Perhaps not.

And that led her to fear that this would be the last time she would ever achieve this level of harmony with the world around her and with the magic within her and the conduit gemstones that decorated her body.

CHAPTER 6

SHIFTING TIDES

"It feels much the better," the little girl said, looking up at the robed monk with smiling eyes and a gap-toothed grin.

"Of course, my little love," Abbot Melchor of St. Honce of Ursal answered. "I told you that I would never let them hurt you."

The girl threw her arms around the man's neck and gave him a big kiss on the cheek.

Watching from the other side of the room, the young mother, Melody, felt the tears welling and reached up to press them back with her thumb and index finger when her younger daughter said, "I love you, abbot."

"I love you, too."

"Go and play with your sister, and try not to get hurt again," Melody told her daughter, who skipped away. She didn't watch her daughter's departure, but instead studied Melchor as the girl left the room, noting the wistful look on his face. If only it could have been different.

"She should call you da, not abbot," Melody said.

"We both wish it could be so," Melchor replied. "But we

each have our place, and we must serve Ursal well in these troubled times."

"You must serve Ursal well, you mean. I serve only my girls, and no hard task that, since you provide so much that we need. I'm grateful to you, don't you doubt, but . . ."

"But you wish it could be more," Melchor said, coming up to her and wrapping her in a hug. "I know. I feel it, too. I would move you into St. Honce if I could. It is simply too dangerous."

"I know."

He shifted back just a bit and stared into Melody's eyes.

The moment was stolen by a loud, sharp knocking. Melody started for the door, but Melchor held her back and went himself.

Nervously, she watched. Melchor hunched his shoulders—she thought she heard him gasp. He stepped back fully into the small apartment and closed the door a bit, but before he turned around, he dropped his face into his hands.

"What has happened?" Melody asked.

Abbot Melchor turned to her, his face a mask of apprehension. He seemed to be shaking.

"Something terrible," was all that he would say. "Recall the girls and keep them inside. Something terrible."

And he was gone, rushing out onto the cobblestoned street in the great city set at the end of the Masur Delaval. Snow was falling, this fittingly gloomy first day of 872's last month, Decambria.

Even thinking of the year, of *God's Year*, reminded Melody of the danger. No, this was Year Ten now, not 872. Or Mahtlatli Xiuitl, as the Xoconai said. It was as if their words alone could simply erase more than eight centuries of the Abellican religion and the history of the kingdom of Honce-the-Bear.

Perhaps they could.

Melody moved to the door and watched the abbot rushing away, escorted by a trio of monks from the monastery of St. Honce, and soon met by lizard-riding guards bearing the pennant of Avitl, the Xoconai woman who ruled as city sovereign of Ursal.

She knew the news was bad, very bad.

When, of late, was it ever good?

"The wound is grievous," Abbot Melchor explained soon after to City Sovereign Avitl in the hallway outside the private quarters of the very important visitor to Ursal. They were in the new temple the Xoconai had constructed in the great city, a brilliant shrine to their god, Scathmizzane.

Scathmizzane, who had fallen into great disregard among the Xoconai after the fight on the distant mountain, but who was resurging now, led by the zealot augurs, mostly by the man who lay wounded behind this very door: Apichtli, the appointed Grand Augur of Quixi Tonoloya.

Avitl held up her hand to silence the abbot. She turned to the guard at Apichtli's door, who nodded in recognition of her concern. Realizing the guard to be Ataquixt, the city sovereign returned the nod.

"Apichtli is the Grand Augur of all the eastern reaches of

Mayorqua Tonoloya," Avitl reminded Melchor harshly. "He may well succumb to his wounds. Do you understand the implications for you and the rest of your sidhe brethren if this assassination attempt ultimately proves successful?"

"Mayorqua Tonoloya," Melchor echoed quietly, shaking his head. It had happened so gradually, bit by bit through those first years, with back-and-forth skirmishes both martial and political as the Xoconai built up their dominance. And then, after nearly a decade of this struggling experiment of coexistence, Apichtli had been named Grand Augur and the Xoconai had simply announced their dominance, had simply declared, against all agreements, that Honce was conquered and that the treaty forged on the mountain halfway across the continent after the destruction of the demon god of the Xoconai and his dragon mount was no more. For three years, the prospect of the two peoples, Bearman and Xoconai, living side by side had been an uneven one, which had proven to be as much a cause for concern, as was shown from the start in this principal city of Ursal, as it was for optimism, as had been the case in the truly enlightened power sharing that had been known in the city of Palmaris, north of Ursal along the Masur Delaval.

Even when the Palmaris experiment had failed, Lord Julian of the Evergreen gone missing and the wife, the city sovereign, the great Xoconai general Tuolonatl, recalled to the west, hopes had remained that the troubles would quiet and the treaty would hold.

Almost before Melchor and the rest of the leaders of Honce-the-Bear had realized it, what had become a sharing of land

and resources, a joining of two peoples for a common good, had become an open occupation. Quietly had the Xoconai used their greatest magic, the mirrors that allowed people, armies even, to walk great distances in a single step, to establish footholds in many remote corners of Honce. They had coerced with threat and with treasure, and now what had been known as Honce-the-Bear was no more. Abbot Melchor could not deny it: the great Xoconai nation of Mayorqua Tonoloya now stretched more than three thousand miles, from the shores of the western ocean to the banks of the great Mirianic.

Abbot Melchor was only three years into the job as the leader of St. Honce of Ursal, but he had known from the beginning that his position and likely his very life hinged on the approval of City Sovereign Avitl, and particularly, of late, on appeasing the temperamental and highly prejudiced Grand Augur Apichtli. Avitl was a reasonable woman, Melchor knew. He actually quite liked her. But even she would never consider him, or any Bearman, or any human who was not Xoconai, to be her equal.

Grand Augur Apichtli had taken that prejudice to extreme levels, and now, of course, Melchor's fate was sealed completely under the suffrance of the man. There was no longer any chance of Melchor denying it, even to himself. Apichtli had come to prominence by waging and decisively winning a second great battle on that same distant mountain where Scathmizzane had fallen more than a decade earlier. In simple truth, the same place where the truce and alliance had been conceived and decided was where it had fallen apart.

Riding the winds of that victory, Augur Apichtli had then

come east, where he and his minions had seized control of Palmaris, forcing the recall of Tuolonatl. More insidiously, Apichtli had brought an important distinction between Xoconai and Bearman: the notion that no, these two different cultures were not commonly "human." No! In Apichtli's jaundiced eyes, the Xoconai alone were the "true people," and the rest, something lesser.

Much lesser. The conquered people were sidhe, goblinkin, subhuman. There could be no more argument. In the early days, there had been marriages, children even, between the bright-faced humans of the west and the ruddy-skinned people of the central and eastern lands.

No more. Such unions, and particularly such offspring, were expressly forbidden under penalty of death—for both parents and the child!

For the children who had already been born to Xoconai and sidhe, from everything Melchor had been able to discern, the results were wildly disparate. Many had been killed, so said the rumors, while others had been placed in a sort of limbo, their fates greatly dependent upon their ascent to adulthood, when it would become clear if they favored their sidhe or Xoconai parent in appearance.

It was all so very wretched and cruel.

And effective. The old deals were gone, the Xoconai had gained complete control over the entire land of Honce-the-Bear south of the Gulf of Corona now, with but two exceptions: St-Mere-Abelle and, to a much lesser extent, the city of Entel in the southeastern corner of the land.

In the midst of this shift from cohabitation to conquest, from collaboration to subjugation, the one undeniable reality was that Grand Augur Apichtli had gotten results in the eyes of those in the far west, the home, the true seat of power, of the Xoconai.

And he continued to do so.

Now Apichtli lay on a deathbed, likely, and though the source of the attack, either the assailant or the weapon, had not been determined, Melchor had a very good idea of both—and if he did, then so did Avitl.

"Do you understand?" Avitl asked again.

"Of course."

"I think you do not, Abbot Melchor. Perhaps somewhere in your mind you think it a good thing to be rid of Grand Augur Apichtli. I'll not deny that the man is . . . severe. Whether or not he survives this cowardly attack, no good will come to your people from this assassination attempt. But those troubles will multiply many times over if he dies, I promise you. Grand Augur Apichtli is revered by my masters in the west, both secular and religious. He has brought great wealth to the city sovereigns, renewed hope to the augurs, and renewed faith to the Xoconai masses."

Melchor chewed his lip to prevent himself from uttering aloud what he was thinking: if this attack had only happened a few years earlier and had indeed proved fatal, it might have made a difference. But now Apichtli's disciples were far too entrenched throughout the lands for his removal to bring any substantive changes or any revival of the notion of cohabitation and collaboration between Xoconai and Bearma—

Melchor's thoughts skipped a beat at the mere internal rec-
itation of the word for the people of Honce. He couldn't even
think of his own people alongside that lost identity. No, they
were sidhe now.

Subhuman.

He wanted to deny Avitl's claims, but he knew he could not.
The gold and sugarcane flowed up from the southern lands to
the eastern port of Entel, and then across the lands through the
magical mirrors to the cities farthest west. In but a few short
years, what had been the mighty and proud kingdom of Honce-
the-Bear had become a mere farm for food, slaves, gold, and
other treasures, feeding the voracious western beast. And the
powers of the west had responded by providing more skilled
augurs and soldiers to the city sovereigns like Avitl, along with
a consolidation of political power that had secured the rule of
the most fortunate Xoconai.

Merely ten years ago, well more than half the cities and
villages of Honce had been governed by a man or woman of
Honce, and previously, another number of them, like Palmaris,
the third-largest city of the land, had formed power-sharing
agreements determined to benefit all the people of the city.

Now, no sidhe could run for elected office, and woe to any
who was not Xoconai who claimed any authority. There were
no elections unless the Xoconai religious leaders decided to hold
one, and sidhe were prohibited from voting, let alone running.
The city governments were wholly Xoconai and would remain
so. Avitl would remain the city sovereign of mighty Ursal for
as long as she desired, or as long as she kept the augurs happy.

Grand Augur Apichtli lay with a potentially mortal wound. He had been struck down in Ursal.

Avitl wasn't keeping the augurs very happy right now.

The door opened and an old monk walked out, his scraggly beard, downcast and defeated eyes, and perpetually dour expression on his thin and hawkish face offering no immediate hints to the two, who held their collective breath. Behind him came a grim-faced Xoconai macana warrior, holding unsheathed the weapon that gave him his moniker.

"The grand augur rests more comfortably," Master Marlboro Viscenti said.

"You have cleansed the wound?" Avitl demanded.

Viscenti nodded, and when he didn't immediately continue, the warrior nudged him with the tooth-edged macana none too gently. Viscenti cast a scowl at the young woman, then reluctantly held up his bloody hand, a small metal ball pinched between his fingers.

Avitl sucked in her breath and shifted her judging gaze over to Abbot Melchor, whose worst fears had just been confirmed.

Viscenti was holding a lodestone, a magical gem, which those trained and skilled in the use of the sacred Ring Stones could release like a bullet from their fingers. Such a gemstone had been used very notably once before in the history of the land, in an attempted assassination, when future Queen Jilseponie had struck down demon-possessed Father Abbot Markwart decades before anyone in Honce-the-Bear had ever heard of the Xoconai.

There were few magical Ring Stones circulating in Quixi Tonoloya outside of St.-Mere-Abelle, the one remaining stronghold of the Abellican Church, the one place in all of Honce south of the Gulf of Corona that had fully resisted conquest. Fewer still were the number of people who could put such stones to use, particularly to powerful effect, as was clearly exhibited by whoever had taken the shot so effectively at Grand Augur Apichtli.

"Will you find the assassin or will I find and eliminate the suspects?" Avitl asked.

Melchor winced and conjured the image of every monk in Ursal hanging by their necks in a long, long line.

"I will go and use my soul stone with all my strength to bring more complete healing and comfort to the Grand Augur," he replied.

"That is not what I asked."

"It is likely an assassin from a distant land," Master Viscenti dared to interject.

"From St.-Mere-Abelle, you mean?"

"Or Entel?" Viscenti asked as much as suggested. "Or even from Behren. There have been skirmishes off the desert coast between boats flying the flag of Tonoloya and those sailing under the pennants of Chezru Chieftain Brynn Dharielle, so say the rumors."

Avitl's hand snapped up and plucked the lodestone from Viscenti's fingers, her precise and lightning-fast movement a reminder that she had been a renowned macana foot soldier in the invading Xoconai army those thirteen years earlier.

"You ask me to look afar when the assassin is likely much closer at hand," she warned Viscenti. "Noted."

"You cannot know . . ." Viscenti began to argue, but Avitl ignored him, turning back to Melchor.

"Who in your monastery is capable of this?" she demanded.

"Milady," he answered, blanching. "None. None. We are humble brothers sworn to uphold peace and to—"

"I do not mean emotionally, you foolish sidhe. Do not pretend to know the heart of any other. No. Who *could* do it? Who is possessed of enough of your strange magic to so powerfully throw this stone?"

"I . . . we do not take measure of such things," the abbot stammered.

"But you all train in the use of your sacred stones? Any of your brethren could launch one of these?"

"Most, yes, but not all. Many people, even many brothers, have no affinity for the divine blessing."

"You are treading very close to heresy," Avitl threatened.

"The blessing of *our* god, I mean."

"The magic properties of the stones, that alone," Avitl corrected. "Secular powers and surely not divine. Need I remind you that there are other people in this world known to use such gemstones?" She turned to the Xoconai guard at Apichtli's door. "Isn't that right, Ataquixt?" she asked. "You were there, on the mountain above Otontotomi, were you not? You witnessed the power of these curious stones without any Abellicans involved in their usage."

"Crystals, my sovereign," the man replied. "They used gem-filled crystals much the same as these Abellican Ring Stones, with identical properties depending upon the gem or mineral involved. There were some monks there later on, but those indigenous to the plateau had no concept of, let alone any connection to, Abbot Melchor's church, certainly, though some possessed great affinity with the magic."

"Then perhaps you turn your eyes in the wrong direction when you look to the monastery of St. Honce," Master Viscenti put in. "There are others in this city, in all the cities of Honce-the-Bear, who possess some stones and can utilize them."

"There is no Honce-the-Bear," Avitl said, biting off each syllable.

"Your pardon," Viscenti said unconvincingly, and with a rather superficial bow.

"To your other point, those rogue magical stones, too, are the responsibility of the sidhe church, are they not?"

Viscenti stammered, but didn't really say anything.

"If the Grand Augur dies, your monastery will be dismantled, brick by brick," Avitl warned the two monks. "You can only imagine how you and your brethren will share a similar fate. I expect a procession of your most powerful magicians carrying your most powerful soul stones. On your lives, he will be healed, fully so, in short order."

"Yes, my sovereign," Abbot Melchor replied with a bow.

"Go!" she shouted, and the two monks hustled away.

Avitl slipped over next to Ataquixt as they departed. "Watch them, note them," she instructed. "They will send their most powerful to tend the Grand Augur under such a threat. I would have every name."

"Yes, my sovereign," the renowned mundunugu scout answered, and he straightened and presented his macana in formal posture before the door.

He breathed a sigh of relief when Avitl, too, took her leave, for he wasn't sure how well he was hiding his dismay. She would have every name. Thus, a healed Grand Augur Apichtli would have every name.

Ataquixt realized that the list he had just been tasked to provide would not be a good place for any name to be.

Only two days later, standing his post in the city throne room, guarding City Sovereign Avitl and a fully healed and frothingly angry Grand Augur Apichtli, Ataquixt found his worst fears realized.

"Every day that passes, these sidhe grow bolder," Apichtli growled.

"They are mostly subdued," Avitl replied calmly. "But yes, there are outliers. We knew there would be."

"They are animals. They understand only one thing."

"When we find the assassin and any associates, they will be dealt with severely and publicly," Avitl assured him.

He snorted with clear derision. "When you find them? Pray tell me how you intend to find them. There is no signature on the lodestone, even if the assassin was one of the few of these sidhe who know how to write. We do not even know where this particular stone came from. There were a score of witnesses in the square when I was stricken—why have they not told us anything of value?"

"Not one of them saw anything more than you falling."

"So the animal sidhe would claim."

"There were people in that square as well," Avitl reminded. "Your own guard among them."

Ataquixt grimaced just a bit at the continuing reference to the folk of Honce as sidhe, and more so at Avitl labeling only the Xoconai as "people." It was certainly not an opinion the worldly ranger shared.

He had a son with a woman who was not Xoconai, a wonderful and beautiful woman he did not think of as lesser than he—quite the opposite! They remained friends from afar, though no longer lovers, and hardly saw each other, of course, but only because they knew how dangerous it would be for any to find out. But he knew that the boy—a budding young man now—was well cared for and much loved. Every so often, Ataquixt would sneak to Whispervale and watch from afar.

"Abbot Melchor knows that it is in his interest to discover the assassin," Avitl assured the Grand Augur. "We have eyes all about. We will have our answers."

"Oh yes, but we will," Apichtli said, and nodded to his own soldiers, who stood by one of the grand room's side doors.

One of them turned and pulled open the door, and into the chamber strode a tall, lean, broad-shouldered Xoconai man dressed in a loose-fitting, brilliantly white shirt and tight trousers of the richest blue, tucked into extraordinary shiny black boots that reached to his knees. The sleeves and leggings were trimmed down the sides in gold, as was the crimson sash he wore from left shoulder to right hip. Gold-handled baskets of marvelous weapons—swords and not macanas!—stuck up diagonally above either shoulder. A second sash crossed his face, similarly left to right, and covering his right eye.

He carried his stovepipe hat, which was tight-brimmed and black like his boots, under his arm until he stopped before the seated city leaders, where he presented himself with a deep bow. Then he tossed the hat atop his shaven head with a clever flip of his wrist.

"I believe you know Cochcal Yaqui, or of him, at least," Apichtli told Avitl, whose nervous shift in her seat confirmed that she had indeed heard of this one. "More likely, you have heard of him as the Coyotl."

Her scrunched face revealed that she had indeed, and so had Ataquixt, and it took all his training to remain perfectly steady at that moment. The Coyotl, or "Coyote" in the language of Honce and the Wilderlands, was known to any Xoconai who ranged the forests and fields east of the mountain divide and was known to many people west of the mountains as well, for this hunter had been plying his trade since before Ataquixt was born, and had been among the first Xoconai to come into Honce after the treaty.

Coyote was prized by men like Apichtli, Ataquixt understood well, but not for his hunting skills, though they were solid enough. By all accounts, he was a great warrior, and thought to be a skilled tactician, which had led him to such a high rank among the macana foot soldiers. His shirt was blousy and loose-fitting about his arms, but when he moved and the fabric tightened, it revealed tight and large muscles beneath. Even more imposing than his battle acumen and obvious personal power, however, Coyote was utterly ruthless, which meant that he brought the fast and overpowering results that leaders like Grand Augur Apichtli craved.

Ataquixt didn't agree with the common perception, and didn't think Coyote a fine tactician. More like a bludgeon, who traded finesse for sheer ferocity. There were no lines of decency in Coyote's cynical world, no.

Boundaries were for the weak.

To Ataquixt, Coyote was to justice as torture was to interrogation. As the latter would elicit the words you demanded, even if they were not the true answers, Coyote would elicit the results you desired, even if the victims of his "justice" were not the true perpetrators.

"The investigation is mine now, City Sovereign Avitl," Apichtli informed her.

"Ursal is my domain." Her argument didn't show much conviction, Ataquixt realized.

"I was the one assaulted . . . and are you so sure of that claim?"

The two stared intently at each other for what seemed like a long, long while.

"Summon the abbot and that miserable old master," Apichtli insisted. "Send them to me so my investigator here can learn all that they have discovered, and likely much more from them than they care to admit."

"There are near to twenty thousand sidhe in or about this city," Avitl warned. "The monastery is the façade of relevance to them. They recall its previous power and so still feel as if Ursal is theirs as well as ours. Take care your every move."

"Relevance?" Apichtli snorted in reply. "They are sidhe. Feed them and only beat them when you must and they will be content."

"Who can say when that is necessary, Grand Augur Apichtli?" Coyote asked with a shrug, and the augur laughed jovially.

"You served under Abbot Ohwan, did you not?" Coyote asked Abbot Melchor later that very same day.

Strapped into a hard wooden chair by his ankles, wrists, and neck, the abbot replied through gritted teeth, "I was just a boy."

"Yes, an orphaned child working at the abbey, and a disciple of Abbot Ohwan, who was no friend to St.-Mere-Abelle."

"I protest this!"

"Of course you do," said Grand Augur Apichtli, the third and last man in the room. "But it is of no consequence in any case. What is past is past, and what is past for the sidhe of this land really holds little interest from me. Coyotl's point here remains. You, abbot, understand the complexity of power, of power structures, and of politics and the need, sometimes, to corral the tendencies of man and sidhe to serve the greater good. Am I wrong in this?"

"No, Grand Augur."

"Good," Apichtli answered. He turned and nodded to Coyote, who produced a large golden ring and approached the bound man.

"We have magic of our own, of course," Apichtli explained as Coyote stepped up beside Melchor and put the ring over the top of his head, settling it just above his ears. Coyote began to chant quietly and Melchor felt the band tighten, and for a moment, he feared that it might keep tightening until it simply crushed his skull.

But no. The shrinking ring stopped, though it remained uncomfortably tight about Melchor's skull.

"This is a ring of truth," Apichtli explained. "I had hoped to forego using it, but I have had quite too much of this evasiveness. You have answers that I wish to hear, and so I shall ask politely. And do understand, Abbot Melchor, that any lie coming from you will cause this divinely magical ring to tighten a bit more. Your skull will not survive many lies."

"I am loyal, Grand Augur," the frightened young abbot replied, and the ring tightened just a bit. "I have served City Sovereign Avitl well in all that she has desired . . ."

"I know," Apichtli interrupted. "Or at least, so I have been informed. So you see, abbot, you have nothing to fear here. Do not deny that you have been hesitant in divulging the fruits of your investigation."

"I wish to be careful, Grand Augur. I do not wish to see innocent people put to death."

"Of course you do not."

"I am a loyal servant of Mayorqua . . ." The band began to tighten, turning the end of that sentence into a growl of pain.

"You see, this is where our understanding of the best courses of action diverges," Apichtli explained. "There are times, abbot, when brutality is mercy. This is one such time that we both face now, and there will be many more before the world is properly settled. Now, we are going to have this very frank discussion, and you will answer my every question, and you will learn your place and accept that place. Or your skull will crack and warp and eventually your head will simply implode, and oh, the agony will be exquisite."

He motioned to Coyote and said, "Do proceed, my hunter."

CHAPTER 7

KENZIE

K eri slept late the next day, then wandered about her house and garden as if in a dream. Truly, she was exhausted, more so than in many years, perhaps even back to the day she had given birth to her son. Fortunately, she had no duties about the town that day, and no one came to her with any emergency requiring her healing powers.

She puttered about her garden through the cool autumn afternoon and was glad when she looked up from her weeding and saw her three boys returning for dinner.

"Boys," Keri muttered aloud when she saw them coming up the path, for that description was fast failing, particularly for Carwyn, who was now a teenager, three years older than his two companions: his brother by blood, Dafydd, and his stepbrother, Kenzie, who would turn eleven in less than a month. How slight and delicate Kenzie looked next to the other two, Keri thought. Carwyn and Dafydd were the children of a Whispervale couple, both deceased. Keri and Connie had adopted them nearly a decade earlier. Hearty lads both; their father had been the town's blacksmith, a giant of a man, and his wife had stood a foot taller than Keri, with broad shoulders, thick limbs, and strong facial features, all of which were evident in the orphaned boys.

The pointed discrepancy in size didn't surprise the woman. Keri was not tall, and Kenzie's father was lithe and lean, like most of the Xoconai people.

"So, are you thinking you might be helping me in setting out the supper for our hardworking boys?" Connie called from the house's open doorway.

Keri nodded to her and pulled herself up from the ground— poorly, she realized when Connie laughed at her.

"I will set out the meal," Connie offered. "You go and wash your face and hands."

Keri appreciated the offer, though the well seemed far, far away to her in that moment. She stood straight and settled herself with a calming breath, closing her eyes and recalling the previous night in all its beauty.

Even with that appreciation, her exhaustion this day could not be denied. A meal and a large amount of water would do her good.

When it came to it, Keri didn't eat much, though, and didn't even hear, let alone join in with, most of the conversation around the table, the three boys relating at length their work that day at the smithy. She did perk up when Carwyn noted that his apprenticeship was nearing its end, however.

"I might have to go to Three Peaks or Masur Celthwin to find proper work," he said.

At least those two towns were near, Keri thought.

"Fester Magni only agreed to hold your father's smithy until you were old enough to take it," an obviously alarmed Connie replied to that. "That's just a few years from now. Fester's hoping to get back to the hunt instead of the smoke of the smithy, aye?"

"He's still got two other apprentices, though," Carwyn explained. "The whispers say that Three Peaks is short a smith, and that the man working the forge in Masur Celthwin is looking for an apprentice far along in learning. He's hoping to move his family to the north, somewhere about Ursal, before the winter sets in."

"Claim the smithy here in Whispervale. 'Tis your birthright. Let Fester Magni go back to his hunting, and you'll have two worthy apprentices sitting right here at the table," Connie said.

"I do'no think I'm quite ready for that, Mum."

"It's been my own experience that a person is never ready and always ready," Keri did then put in. "It's the need of the action that moves the mind and heart."

"Listen to your mother, aye?" Connie said with a wink to Keri.

"Which mother, then?" Carwyn replied.

"Yes!" Connie scolded, and all five had a good laugh.

"I think one apprentice, not two," Kenzie unexpectedly put in, and the laughter stopped and all eyes turned to the boy.

"I'd rather ride them than shoe them," Kenzie added. "I see my place working the stables, or maybe riding scout for Whispervale, or even serving as the courier to the other towns."

Mundunugu, Keri thought, but held silent. She could picture the smile the boy's father would be wearing right now if he had heard that proclamation.

"Dangerous work, courier," said Connie, but Kenzie just shrugged it off.

"No worries for this day," said Keri. "The world ever changes and so do the minds of teenagers."

"Aye," Connie agreed. "Likely that one or th'other will fall to the batting lashes of a pretty lass, and then what they're wanting won't much matter!"

Another laugh followed, and Keri checked out of the conversation, closing her eyes and letting her mind wander back along the path that had taken her to this pleasant and uneventful life—and how she hoped it would remain that way! She stayed deep in her memories with the clatter of plates all about, the arguments about whose turn it was to wash them, followed by the ringing and scraping of the utensils. Even when all was sorted, the house didn't quiet down; it took on the general bustle of three boys—nay, young men—who wished to find some playtime with their friends before the night set in.

It was all so perfectly normal, and a younger Keri might have been bored by it.

But now, after so many trials and battles, so much blood and so many losses, she just appreciated it.

Keri wandered out of the house soon after dinner, leaving the din behind as she reclined on a couch set out on the long front porch. She let the sounds of the night take her away, her thoughts riding along on a cool breeze.

"You can'no be comfortable," she heard sometime later, and only then did Keri realize how far the moon had climbed in the sky above her, and thus, how long she had been lying out here basking in the night sounds.

She felt a blanket falling over her and looked up to smile appreciatively at Connie. She crushed in against the back pillows of the divan, shifting her hips and making room for Connie to lie down beside her and share the blanket.

"A cold one," Connie remarked, giving a bit of a shiver.

"Aye, but the wind's keeping the biting bugs away."

"You could probably warm the wind if you wanted, aye?"

Keri turned her head, her face very close to her partner's. "Do'no speak of such things," she whispered. "Please, I beg."

"I know," Connie admitted. "It's just that last night's so thick in my thoughts. 'Twas a night I'll not ever forget, and unlike those other memories burned into my dreams, bad memories, this was one of beauty. I've never seen such a display from you, or from any of the witches of Usgar."

"You've seen more magic than that."

"In a fight, aye, but in the dance?"

Keri shrugged. She couldn't really deny the level of the previous night's magical intensity.

"I thank you for that, with all my heart."

"I'm not sure you should be thanking me," Keri admitted. "I was hardly aware it was happening, almost as if it was more happening to me than because of me."

"The dance is a trance. Isn't that what Mairen so oft told us?"

Keri looked back up at the stars and nodded. A trance, indeed, and this one more profound and powerful by far . . .

Why?

"The dance takes us," Connie said, and Keri nodded again, for surely it had taken her the night before.

"We had talked of widening our home circle," Connie continued. "Have you given it more thought?"

Keri knew that she was referring to their children, and understood why she was broaching the subject, given the dinner conversation. She was afraid of Carwyn leaving and thought that an introduction to the beauty of the music of magic would make him, would make all three, far less eager to go out into the wider, brutal world.

But now wasn't the time, Keri understood. Xoconai scouts had been in the region and had almost certainly seen the night lights of Whispervale and the other towns. This had happened before, of course, but something just nagged at Keri that this time might be different. Maybe it was because the boys were growing up, were young men now in many ways. Maybe it was simply because the idea of more conflict sat ill in her gut—she slipped her hand under the blanket and under her shirt to her belly ring at that thought.

"Are you wishing that we had a girl or three, then?" she asked.

Connie's laugh warmed her. "No," she replied earnestly. "Weren't it the first thing ye told to me those years ago when Ataquixt led me back to you, when first I learned that you were dancing again? Should it really only be women? That was your question, not my own." She did an impression of Keri, even reverting to the thicker accent that both of them once carried, as she finished, "Can't we give this gift to them? A dance of their own?"

"To him," Keri corrected. "At that time, it was just Kenzie in our home."

"The point holds."

"Aye, and so's the thought. But I'm afraid to," Keri admitted.

"Afraid for all three, or for your Kenzie alone?"

"Kenzie, mostly, but not because he's my own son—or maybe part because he's my blood, aye."

"He'll likely hear the song o' the crystals, aye? That's your fear?"

"Part, aye, and it might be a burden to him in the times coming." Keri took a deep breath. "But more, don't you see?"

"He favors his mother."

"Because he's still a boy, but not for much longer. The Xoco-nai get their face coloring when they pass through the awkward stage and leave their juvenility behind."

"It might be nothing."

"Not nothing, no," Keri said. "Look closely at him when the sun's high and splashing its beams on his face. The coloring is already beginning to show. Aye, it'll likely be muted, as I'm his mum, but his da's a powerful one and his contribution to the boy'll have its say, I do'no doubt."

"The folk of Whispervale are goodly, and they've known Kenzie since the day you birthed him. They'll not—"

"It's not the folk of Whispervale that worry me," Keri interrupted. She paused and took a deep breath, and then gave a helpless little laugh about another out-of-place boy she had first met when she was but a little girl. He had been born in a cave near her tribe's encampment, his pregnant mother kidnapped by the Usgar on a raid to a village on the lakeshore below their mountain perch. Away from the tribes that had settled along that lake, this child hadn't been subjected to their skull-wrapping rituals and had grown up looking far different from his blood relatives, more like an Usgar man. That fact didn't save him from his life as an enslaved person, however.

Her mind went back to that night when she had found comfort in the arms of Ataquixt, and he in hers. She had known of the creation of a child so soon after but had made the decision to have the baby. In the height of hope, Keri had believed that the child of this particular man, who ranged the region, worldly and kind and formidable when he had to be, would somehow rise above the troubles of the times.

Now, though, she greatly doubted any such thing. Even way back then, with trouble brewing, this land had been a far brighter place.

She could never regret Kenzie, of course. He was the joy of her life, the sustenance that had kept her going and made her try this more mundane, but quite acceptable and pleasant, existence.

There were other children like him, so the boy's father had told her, and of course there were, with the two cultures living together in this land—in relative harmony back then. But not so many.

The other thing that Ataquixt had told her was that there were children—few, but not unknown—of mixed blood back in the far west, beyond the mountains in the Tonoloya Basin, the very heart of the Xoconai homeland. He had told her that, warned her of that, before their unexpected tryst, even, for back in Tonoloya, those children had not been treated well. They were menial laborers, nothing more, and could aspire to nothing of true worth in Xoconai society. Would it be the same here?

Almost certainly worse, given the recent changes, she now believed.

A dozen years ago, Keri thought for certain that it would not. But that was when the land was shared, not when the Xoconai were once more taking the role of conquerors.

"If he properly shared your features and his da's colors, Kenzie will be a beautiful man indeed," Connie offered.

Keri just smiled beneath the nighttime canopy. Kenzie already was beautiful. He could be nothing but beautiful to her. And yes, Keri had thought Kenzie's da quite handsome, and quite wonderful and decent.

But that was all a decade and more ago.

Now Kenzie was real.

The world around them was real.

And increasingly harsh.

CHAPTER 8

REMINDERS

The midsummer day was hot and gray with heavy clouds, and a dreary mist hung in the air.

Perfectly fitting.

In the main market square within the huge walled city of Ursal, the people gathered nervously, Bearman and Xoconai alike, for the recovering Grand Augur Apichtli and his inquisitors had kept very secret the outcome of their hasty investigation.

Whispers rolling through the gathering spoke of an incursion into St. Honce monastery two nights previous, though, and Abbot Melchor had not been seen since. Also, several longtime prominent Ursal citizens, nobles held in the highest regard, had not been seen in several days, their mansions eerily quiet.

Everyone coming onto the square counted the ten nooses hanging from the gallows that had been hastily constructed.

Xoconai soldiers lined the parapets all about the area, their atlatl throwing sticks readied upon their shoulders, deadly javelins loaded.

Inside a high chamber overlooking the square in the main

keep, the city's seat of power, City Sovereign Avitl ground her teeth nervously as she watched the growing mob. Behind her, Grand Augur Apichtli and his hunter, Coyote, riffled through papers.

"We have them all?" Apichtli asked at one point.

"More than all," Coyote said lightly, and Avitl grimaced. This wasn't about justice, but about a show of strength.

"The assassin is one of these ten?" the augur asked.

Coyote made a dismissive sound, and Avitl didn't have to turn about to realize that he had shrugged noncommittally, as if mocking any idea that such a fact would matter.

"Likely," Coyote admitted. "But who can know, really, when we are speaking of these ugly sidhe creatures? Most treacherous and mendacious, and ridiculously proud, given their inferior intellect and, sadly, their sheer ugliness."

"So true," the Grand Augur Apichtli agreed.

"Even if the killer is not among them, let him spend his days in misery, knowing that he failed and that he doomed his fellows to such a fate," Coyote added.

A sharp knock on the door turned Avitl about.

"Abbot Melchor," Apichtli said, even before the man outside in the hallway yelled out, demanding they open the door.

"As expected," Coyote agreed.

Avitl nodded to her guards, who pulled open the door, whereupon Abbot Melchor and Master Viscenti verily spilled into the room as if they had been leaning on the wood.

"You cannot do this!" Melchor yelled, rushing forward. "You invite—"

"Perhaps your assassin should have considered that before launching his missile at the Grand Augur of Quixi Tonoloya," Coyote returned.

"My assassin?" Melchor gasped, poking his finger against his chest, his expression full of outrage and shock. He snorted in disgust at the two men and moved past them, fixing his gaze on Avitl. "This is madness and will create great unrest, not just here in Ursal, but throughout the lands. They have taken seven of my brothers and sisters, a quarter of my clergy, and all of my masters other than Viscenti!"

"Seven who have had dealings with the three convicted conspirators," Coyote said.

"Convicted?" Master Viscenti put in with a chortle. "You dragged them from their homes and beat them until they told you what you wanted to hear."

"Beat them?" Coyote echoed with feigned shock. "Dear master, I am much more subtle than that in my techniques, I assure you. Not one will show any scars of beatings at all—well, perhaps the bald one, whose head is now a bit misshapen."

"Abbot Melchor, do you deny that these two women and this man, high citizens of this city, were in possession of magical items fashioned of the gemstones that are supposed to be the sole province of the Abellican Church?" Grand Augur Apichtli asked.

"The sacred stones were never the sole province of the church, Grand Augur. Mostly so, yes, but never exclusively."

"Because the wealthy lords of Honce-the-Bear were able to purchase them, to gain even more power over the peasants who groveled about their lands, working their fields for pittances,"

Apichtli said. "Quite fine servants of the common man, your clergy."

Melchor sputtered while trying to respond, then backed off completely. He looked to Viscenti, who was obviously flustered, for the old monk couldn't deny the corruption involved. The side dealings of the Abellican Church, trading some of the extra magical stones in exchange for wealth and power, had been a quiet business that had gone on for centuries in every city of Honce, with much of it even emanating from the great monastery of St.-Mere-Abelle. Such corruption had been a point of contention and even open battle within the order several times in history, most recently in the rise of Avelyn, and subsequently, in the heresy of Marcalo De'Unnero, who used such corruption as a cornerstone cause for his insurrection against the church. Even now, more than three decades after his death, the memory of De'Unnero held his followers in his thrall, and every monastery had whispers of some in their ranks who quietly nodded in approval whenever that cursed name was spoken.

"Practical considerations for the greater good," Viscenti said now when it became apparent that tongue-tied Melchor wouldn't respond.

Coyote laughed at him. "I have spent many hours studying the recent history of your church, I assure you."

"If you wish to join . . ." Viscenti started.

"I like to know my enemies," Coyote cut him short, and the two men glared at each other.

"Enough of this banter," Avitl demanded, and turned to Apichtli. "What do you intend to do?"

The monk and the hunter continued to stare a moment longer, until Coyote bluntly noted while glaring at the old monk, "I asked for eleven nooses."

Master Marlboro Viscenti, a close associate of the great Avelyn Desbris, who had fought in the Demon War, who had survived the rosy plague, who had served as the closest advisor of Father Abbot Braumin Herde, who had battled King Aydrian and De'Unnero, did not flinch at that announcement, did not blink, and did not back down.

"Grand Augur?" Avitl demanded, deflecting the conversation to the matter at hand.

"I don't know how these pathetic sidhe manage such magic with their stones," Apichtli replied. "But then, we witnessed similar problems with the sidhe on the mountain overlooking Otontotomi, of course. The last battle there was quite bloody. Even the dim-witted find their weapons, I suppose."

Avitl eyed the newcomers during that diatribe. Abbot Melchor chewed his lip through every word and seemed unable to lift his gaze from the floor, but Viscenti just stared hard, unblinking. Avitl knew in that moment, though truly she had seen it coming for quite some time, that any hopes of true alliance between the people of this land and the Xoconai were quite dead. The sovereigns in the west didn't want it, and they had systematically turned a coexistence into an ever-more-brutal occupation.

The realization devastated her. She had served under Coch-cal Tuolonatl, and had believed that the treaty on the mountain above Otontotomi would be beneficial to Xoconai and Bearman alike—indeed, to the whole world. What magic and wonders might the two cultures learn from each other! What power in their combined strength to pull the whole world in a better direction!

Even beyond the scholarly and practical means, Avitl didn't like killing, and surely didn't much appreciate the mere notion of slavery, a practice that was becoming common in Quixi Tonoloya in all but name. To her, these people of the east, and of the central lands, and likely of all lands, were not sidhe. Yes, Cochcal Tuolonatl's designs for Quixi Tonoloya had been quite different in those early years. The visionary warrior had believed that the Xoconai and the people of Honce, and of all the Wilderlands in between, could become one great nation, sea to sea. She hoped for an alliance with Chezru Chieftain Brynn Dharielle, the famed Dragon Rider, who ruled the desert kingdom south of the mountain chain known as the Belt-and-Buckle. Tuolonatl had even reached out to Brynn once long ago, begging parlay, and her request was accepted. Tuolonatl knew that she could draw fast bonds with Brynn, for the two shared a love of horses, particularly pintos.

Avitl had hoped to travel with Tuolonatl on her planned journey to Jacintha, seat of Behrenese power, at Chezru Chieftain Brynn's invitation. Then City Sovereign of Palmaris, Tuolonatl had outfitted a ship to take them out of the Masur Delaval, through the Gulf of Corona, and down the eastern seaboard to the port of Jacintha. But alas, only a week before the day of departure, Tuolonatl had been hastily recalled to the west, her city of Palmaris given to an augur who so clearly did not share her vision.

That had been before the official advent of Mayorqua Tonoloya more than a dozen years before, but still, as the years passed, Avitl had held out hope that Tuolonatl's way would prevail. She, who did not hate these people, had been named as city sovereign of Ursal, after all, the most powerful and important settlement in all of Quixi Tonoloya.

But now, in this moment, in watching the exchange between Master Marlboro Viscenti, perhaps the most renowned and revered Abellican monk outside the unconquered St.-Mere-Abelle, and Grand Augur Apichtli's murderous huntsman, she knew that her private hope, Tuolonatl's dream, was fully dead.

As dead as the ten who were soon to be hanged.

She listened as if from afar as the argument stewed between the monk and the augur.

"Do you not understand the consequences?" Abbot Melchor shouted at one point, his voice so full of frustration and finality that it stirred Avitl to observe more closely.

"Of course he does," Master Viscenti said with a sarcastic grin and a shake of his head. "He seeks them."

"You have not come to understand your betters," Apichtli told them. "Or accept that you are a conquered people."

"That was not the truce," Viscenti said.

"There is no truce!" Apichtli uncharacteristically shouted. "And there is no negotiation. You are beaten. You remain in Quixi Tonoloya, indeed, anywhere within Mayorqua Tonoloya, at our suffrance and whim, and only by the generosity of Xoconai spirit. The sooner leaders of the sidhe such as yourselves realize that truth, the sooner the sidhe who once called this land Honce-the-Bear will come to understand and accept their new lot in life."

"You are a fool," spat the old monk.

"A fool who can move armies all about the land in the time it would take you to crawl back to St. Honce," Apichtli reminded him. "You and yours think to strike from the shadows, to inflict pain on the Xoconai, to kill our leaders? Well, today you will see the consequences of that unacceptable attitude. Now, go and find your place beside the other sidhe witnessed among the assembled crowd, and after the pronouncement of the verdict, when I call your name, speak words that will calm the bile, blood, and phlegm of your fellow sidhe, or what will be a proper and just execution will become instead a proper and just massacre."

He turned to Coyote. "Your warriors are in place?"

"Hundreds," the harsh man replied contentedly. "They filter throughout the gathering, macana and knives ready on my word."

The Grand Augur slowly turned back to the abbot. "You have your orders, Abbot Melchor. Now go and do well by your people, for their sake."

Abbot Melchor bowed obediently.

"You are a monster," Viscenti said.

"I am a Xoconai and you are a sidhe," Apichtli stated evenly.

"One who does not understand the inevitable disaster he has invited."

Apichtli laughed at him. "You are conquered. That is all you need to know."

"I know that you will never set your foot inside St.-Mere-Abelle," Viscenti answered calmly, and Avitl noted Apichtli's unintended wince, the first sign of weakness she had ever seen from the cruel man.

"And that is enough?" Apichtli said, trying to diminish the remark.

But Viscenti wouldn't blink, and replied with a grave, "For now."

The mood of the crowd wasn't uniform, but it was clear that those who were not Xoconai, the people whose families had resided in the Ursal region for generations, weren't pleased to see the seven monks of St. Honce, gagged and with their hands tied behind their backs, marched past and up the steps to the gallows. The crowd became even less pleased when the three condemned nobles followed close behind. These were three of the most powerful and influential people in the Ursal region, and one in particular, an old woman named Lady Kyrsteen Ursal, was renowned for her generosity and kindliness and a distant relative by marriage to beloved King Danube Brock Ursal, who had ruled Honce fairly and generously many years before.

The gasps became hisses as this old woman, in her eighties, was roughly pushed and pulled up the stairs to the gallows platform.

She kept her chin high, though, and didn't flinch when Coyote dropped the heavy rope over her head and roughly tightened it about her skinny neck.

Across the square, above the crowd and facing the platform, City Sovereign Avitl and Grand Augur Apichtli stood on a balcony.

"They are growing restless," Avitl warned. "This may prove disastrous."

"Hardly," the augur replied. He raised his arm, signaling, and horns began to blow all about the square, drowning out the complaints and continuing until the gathering settled.

"Ye folk of Ursal," Apichtli called. "Witness before you ten criminals who have betrayed you!"

The proclamation was met with boos and hisses and a smattering of cheers—the latter almost exclusively from the many Xoconai in attendance. But even some of them weren't cheering and seemed less than enthusiastic, Avitl noticed.

"We seek to be beneficent sovereigns to you all," Apichtli continued. "To let you live your lives in proper service, but without such consequences as that which you see before you. But these criminals deny that. From the shadows, they struck, and at me, who comes to you as a spiritual guide. Do not suffer them among you, I warn, for we Xoconai are beneficent when we can be, but do not doubt our resolve to see justice properly realized."

He turned and nodded into the room behind him, and Abbot Melchor was brought forth to stand beside the augur.

"Do affirm the sentence of the criminals," he whispered to Melchor.

The abbot stiffened his back and tightened his jaw.

"Guards!" Apichtli yelled down. "Guards, bring forth ten sidhe witnesses to stand before the stage to bear witness."

As he spoke those last two words, Apichtli turned a side-long stare at Melchor, letting the abbot know beyond any doubt that these ten would be much more than witnesses if he didn't promptly and correctly comply.

That shook Melchor, of course, but not as much as when the "witnesses" were pushed forward.

Children, some likely not even ten years of age.

"Please, Grand Augur," Melchor muttered. "You cannot."

"But I would, as easily as you eat veal," the augur promised quietly.

Abbot Melchor glanced behind him into the room, to see Viscenti snarling and clenching his fists so tightly that Melchor feared the old monk would pop his knuckles out of joint.

Melchor cleared his throat.

"The evidence was clear," he said loudly, but shakily. "And confessions were given. These ten conspired to murder the Grand Augur of Quixi Tonoloya. My people, this we cannot have! Since the time of King Danube the Elder, we have been a kingdom of laws and justice, and most here are old enough to remember when such order was lost to us, when a tyrant took the throne in Ursal. We did not wish the reign of King Aydrian to continue, but neither did we allow for murder from the shadows."

"Jilly!" one man below yelled.

"Aye, Jilly!" yelled another, a woman, and the crowd began chanting for their deceased beloved hero, Jilseponie Ault Wyndon, wife of the famed Nightbird. "Jilly!"

"She hated that nickname," Melchor heard Master Viscenti say from behind. "Pony, ah, Pony."

"Calm them, or the nooses will be used more than once," Apichtli warned Melchor. "There is a needed example to be made this day. It can be made with ten, or with a hundred. Or with a thousand. I do not care."

There wasn't a doubt in Melchor's mind that the augur meant every word.

"Silence!" Abbot Melchor shouted repeatedly, until the crowd at last quieted. "My friends, without laws, without consequences, we are nothing. You know this and I know this. It saddens me to think that we, that I, was betrayed by those standing on the stage before you. My seven brothers and sisters, whom I thought good Abellicans, should have known better. We do not murder!

"Perhaps I am partly to blame for not instructing them better . . ."

"Jilly!" the same woman called again.

Melchor saw Apichtli nod to someone below.

"A different time and circumstance!" Melchor yelled before the chorus could begin anew, and he averted his eyes when he saw a Xoconai warrior move up behind the protesting woman and silence her by slapping a hand over her mouth. She started to struggle, but jerked suddenly, and even from this distance, Melchor knew that a dagger had been shoved into her back, quite expertly.

Other soldiers came up about her, surrounding her, shielding her from onlookers. They hustled her away, off the square and out of sight, through a door.

"So, no!" Abbot Melchor yelled. "Bear witness, as is your duty to Ursal, to me, to City Sovereign Avitl. To civilization itself."

"You see, Melchor," Apichtli noted. "You are quite good at this when properly inspired." Clearly trying not to laugh aloud, the callous man turned to his huntsman and nodded.

At that same moment, Lady Kyrsteen finally was able to work the gag out of her mouth, and even as Coyote lifted his arm to signal the executioner to pull the lever, she spat in his face.

"Cowards and killers, all!" she cackled. "And ne'er will ye break the will o' Honce!"

The lever was pulled, the plank fell out, and the ten prisoners dropped, but only nine to the end of their ropes, their necks snapping. Some jerked only once before expiring, while others kicked and spasmed through a few last heartbeats.

But Coyote caught the tenth before her neck was stretched, and he held her there, laughing at her. Lady Kyrsteen thrashed and struggled, even bit at him, but the incredibly strong Xoconai just smiled and eased her down.

She hung there, choking slowly, her eyes bulging, her lips beginning to foam.

"Pull her legs!" some cried after a long while.

Coyote hugged her again, as if to comply.

But he lifted her up, not down, and loosened the rope just enough for her to draw a breath.

Lady Kyrsteen glared at him, and he laughed at her and commanded, "Beg."

The woman was shaking. She turned her head just a bit and seemed as if she was about to spit again, but then faced forward and steeled her visage.

Coyote began lowering her again, slowly.

And it began again, the woman struggling. Clearly, she was trying to maintain her dignity, trying to still her movements and not show her fear.

But she couldn't draw breath, and whatever her mind wanted her to do, her body couldn't comply. She jerked and kicked and frothed, her eyes bulging again, and she seemed about to lose consciousness.

So Coyote lifted her up again.

The crowd hissed and called for mercy. "Pull her legs!" they yelled. "Oh, but get it done with!"

"What is that fool doing?" Avitl demanded of Apichtli. Beside her, Abbot Melchor was spitting with rage and horror.

"He is teaching the sidhe their place," the Grand Augur replied smugly.

"Mercy!" the crowd began to chant.

"You wish mercy?" Coyote shouted.

"Mercy!"

"You, filthy boy," Coyote called to a young teenager among the ten who had been brought up to stand immediately before the stage. "Come here."

The boy's eyes widened in horror and he shrank back—or started to, until a Xoconai soldier behind him grabbed him by the arms and hoisted him to the front lip of the stage, where one of the soldiers on the platform ran over and pulled him all the way up, then delivered him to stand before Coyote.

"Should I grant her mercy, filthy sidhe boy?" Coyote called.

The boy looked around, clearly terrified. He bit his lip and began to shake violently.

"Grow some courage, you silly child," Coyote yelled at him. "I am not asking you to take her place. Should I grant mercy to this old woman?"

"Mercy!" shouted many in the crowd.

"Boy?" Coyote screamed at him.

"Yes, please, sir," he blurted back.

"Come here," a grinning Coyote ordered. "Hold her."

When the boy hesitated, Coyote grabbed Lady Kyrsteen by the scruff of the neck and held her there with one hand, then snatched the boy with the other, pulling him forward to slam into the woman.

"Hold her!" he ordered, and moved away, and the poor boy grabbed tight and tried to keep the woman from stretching to the end of the rope. She was old and withered and weighed little, to be sure, but he was still a boy, his arms skinny. Stubbornly, desperately, he set himself and held Lady Kyrsteen aloft.

"If you hold her long enough, I will let her go free," Coyote told them all. "But if not, well . . ."

And he laughed and the crowd gasped, and they all went quiet, watching, watching, as the moments slipped by.

Some in the crowd began to shout encouragement to the boy. Others shouted curses at Coyote. Soon, the boy was sweating, and shaking again, this time out of exhausted muscles and not simple terror.

Coyote moved over and taunted him. "Her neck will stretch so beautifully, do you not think, filthy boy? You will fail her and she will die in your arms, and you will know that guilt for the rest of your pathetic days. Oh, if only you had been stronger."

The poor boy whimpered. Shouts of encouragement stilled, became a hush of horror.

"Are you really going to let her die in your arms?" Coyote teased. "If only you were stronger."

"Drop her fast, boy!" a man in the crowd yelled. "Jump upon her and break her neck! Mercy!"

Coyote responded immediately: "If you do that, you will hang from this rope as soon as she is cut down," he warned, and he turned about in the direction of the man who had shouted, scouring the crowd.

A soldier ran over and identified the speaker, and on a nod from Coyote, that man was dragged away, pulled from the square, and from behind the door where he disappeared came the sounds of a whip and screams of pain.

As that commotion died, Coyote turned his attention back to the poor struggling boy, who seemed to be shrinking before his very eyes. Lady Kyrsteen was at the end of the rope once more, then wasn't, then was again, as the poor boy grew frantic, finding his strength only in very short bursts, and openly weeping.

"Are you too weak, filthy boy?" Coyote taunted.

And he was, clearly, the bounces coming less frequently, and poor Kyrsteen hanging more from her neck than being held in his arms at this point. Her tongue lolled out of the side of her mouth, her eyes bugged, unblinking and unfocused.

Finally, the boy just collapsed in a heap of sobs and trembles, helplessly patting at the woman who was hanging beside him. She wasn't even spasming anymore, but wasn't quite dead.

In that perfect moment, Coyote created his big finish. He

first slapped the sobbing child aside, then grabbed the woman and hoisted her, and tossed her straight up so that she actually banged the top of her head on the crossbeam of the gallows.

And down she came, violently, her thin old bones and thin old skin no match for the sharp jerk at the end of the rope, where her head popped free and flipped onto the gallows platform and her decapitated body tumbled below in a heap.

People screamed, people fainted, the boy screamed, and Coyote stood tall, snarling.

"Hear me now, all!" the brutal man shouted. "We are done with your insolence and the cowardice you show by striking in the shadows. From this day forward, any Xoconai killed will have ten sidhe executed, and killed more brutally than anything you have witnessed this day. Know your place! You are beaten, you are conquered. Know your place, sidhe, and live in peace by the mercy of Scathmizzane!"

"Oh, he's quite effective," Grand Augur Apichtli said to Avitl and Melchor.

"Such, every tyrant believes," Viscenti said from within the shadows of the room.

Apichtli turned and laughed at him, then spun on Avitl. "Put forth the word that all magical stones and enchanted items are to be surrendered immediately. Swords, armor, magical rings—all of it! The grace of my mercy to any who possess such items will last only a short while, and we will find them. I assure you of that, so please assure your peasant sidhe.

"And I will have a full accounting of every piece of magic within your dirty and dark monastery, Abbot Melchor," he continued. "You will bring them to me, every one, this very night."

"But Grand Augur, we use these stones to heal and placate the masses you hope to control," Melchor argued.

"You use the soul stone, or the wedstone, or whatever other name you put to that gray rock. Perhaps I will allow you to keep some of those, perhaps not. And perhaps, Abbot Melchor, it all depends upon how quickly you come back to me, and how completely you fulfill my command. I tell you now that I will visit St. Honce in the morning, and if a single item or gemstone is found, St. Honce will be flattened onto all who now reside there."

"Grand Augur!" Melchor gasped, and Avitl, too, stiffened in shock.

"Shut up," Apichtli told him. "A new day is come. The sidhe will be disarmed of their magic—fully so, if your co-operation is not . . . enthusiastic. And not just here, abbot. Oh, no. This edict will go out throughout Quixi Tonoloya, from the sea to the Wilderlands to Otontotomi. Every city, every town, every hamlet, every house will be scoured, the magic secured."

"Does that include St.-Mere-Abelle, Grand Augur?" Master Viscenti said, getting in one last dig, for they both knew well that St.-Mere-Abelle had not fallen and would not fall to the Xoconai, a singular remnant of what had been sitting in a storm of tumultuous change. The taunt was particularly effective at this time, for the Gulf of Corona, too, could not be fully secured by the Xoconai, as the monks of St.-Mere-Abelle crossed it often into the northland of Vanguard, which also remained outside of Xoconai control.

"You overestimate the security afforded you by your stature and reputation," the Grand Augur warned.

"You think I fear your noose or your mad huntsman?" Viscenti returned. "I have found true peace by the grace of Saint Avelyn. I have been to the Sacred Hand in the Barbacan, where rests Saint Avelyn, who showed us the true path. I have witnessed the rise and fall of demons."

"And yet, here you are, a pathetic old man without recourse or agency," Apichtli said. "You need not tempt my wrath, for I'll not make of you a martyr. Oh, no, never that. Are your weak old legs prepared for a long walk, Viscenti?"

The man lifted his chin defiantly.

"There is a road for you," Apichtli explained. "Long and difficult for one your age, but my soldiers will accompany you, and drag you where they must. A road to the north and east. Be happy, old fool. You are going home."

"What is this about?" Melchor demanded. "What are you talking about?"

"He is removing a thorn he dares not publicly pluck," City Sovereign Avitl explained to the abbot. "He is giving Master Viscenti back to Father Abbot Braumin Herde at St.-Mere-Abelle, where he will become no more than another shadow of what was and can never again be."

"Very good, Sovereign Avitl," Apichtli congratulated her. "Perhaps you will yet prove that you can hold control of this place the sidhe call Ursal. Perhaps if you continue to show such insight, I will even have you sit with me when I decide on a more appropriate name for this city."

That news stopped any forthcoming reply, from Avitl or from Melchor, and in the room behind them, Viscenti just scoffed derisively—and helplessly.

"And what of Grand Augur Apichtli?" Avitl managed to say at length.

"I quite like it here, so here I will stay," he replied immediately. "But not as city sovereign, as we have seen other augurs assume in other cities. No, I remain Grand Augur and thus, sovereign of all within Quixi Tonoloya. If you wish to send couriers to the west to confirm this new order, then do so quickly, so we can get on with our tasks."

"And what of him?" Avitl asked, nodding down toward Coyote, who stood on the gallows platform, strong arms crossed over his chest, directing the soldiers who were clearing the square.

"He serves me here in Ursal until I determine that I need him elsewhere. At that time, you will be informed of what is required of you." As he answered, Apichtli led Avitl and Melchor back into the room.

"Required of me?" she asked in surprise, scurrying to catch up. "The city brims with tension, and you do nothing to—"

"Then we will set up a transportation platform of golden mirrors to bring in more macana. Enough of this speculation and banter. Coyote is my agent, my eyes, and my spear. He will help me to bring these troublesome sidhe to heel and teach them the new way of things in this land that is no more Honce-the-Bear."

Avitl turned to Abbot Melchor and offered what seemed almost an apologetic shrug.

Almost.

"As you command, Grand Augur," she said.

"Always," he answered. He turned to the soldier standing guard at the door, a mundunugu of some reputation, a man who had ridden with Tuolonatl when she had begun this great conquest to the eastern sea.

"Get this troublesome animal out of my sight," he ordered, waving dismissively at Master Marlboro Viscenti. "Find a suitable escort and put him on the road to St.-Mere-Abelle, and let me never hear his phlegm-filled voice or his name again."

The mundunugu sentry, Ataquixt, snapped to attention, then nodded, opened the door, and motioned for Viscenti to exit. Ataquixt followed the old man from the room.

"Now," Ataquixt heard the Grand Augur say to Avitl as he left, "what shall we name this capital city of my domain?"

CHAPTER 9

RANGERS

Master Viscenti wasn't bound at all, not his hands or feet, except when his escorts set their camps at night. The monk wasn't being physically mistreated by these Xoconai as he bumped along in the back of the open horse-drawn wagon. Neither was he being made to feel comfortable, nor were they talking to him, but merely at him, with insults and promises that the Xoconai would hold these lands until the end of the world itself.

"You tell your peers who hide in this dark and ugly cage you call St.-Mere-Abelle that they will never again walk freely in the lands beyond their cold stone walls," one of the drivers told him, to the snicker of his partner on the wagon's front bench, a man exceedingly tall and imposing.

"Yes, when we get there," that second driver added unconvincingly.

Viscenti had suspected all along that they weren't really going to take him to St.-Mere-Abelle, but would ferry him far from Ursal and simply murder him, and that snicker and obviously sarcastic remark strengthened those fears. He knew that he would never see his beloved St.-Mere-Abelle again, that his days neared their end—likely this very night, their fourth from Ursal, as they had left the city and the large towns near to it far behind now, moving away from the Masur Delaval to farmlands sparsely populated.

All around him on these lonely roads, there were many places to bury a body so it would never be found, except by the wolves and coyotes.

"What town is marked by those lights down there?" the tall driver asked Viscenti as the sun began to slip below the western horizon, with the stars beginning to twinkle.

Viscenti considered the geography and the time. At twenty or twenty-five miles a day, they were likely about halfway to St.-Mere-Abelle. Dusberry came to mind, but that was along the river, and Viscenti was fairly sure they had gone too far east.

He shrugged. "There are many small towns in these reaches. Could be Lochlin, or maybe Millpeter."

"Small town," the tall driver said.

"Villages that keep to themselves and let the outside world stay outside," said one of the other two Xoconai escorts, trotting his cuetzpali lizard mount up beside the open-backed wagon.

Viscenti shied from the huge lizard. He couldn't stand the things, with their fang-dotted maws and those ugly eyes. Few Xoconai still rode them in Quixi Tonoloya, as they didn't thrive here in the east as well as they had in the western deserts, and for that small blessing, Viscenti was grateful.

He saw the tall, snide driver staring at him with an amused grin as he shuffled across the wagon bed.

"Have you fed your mount tonight?" the tall man asked the rider.

"No. No, he is quite hungry, I fear," the rider replied, turning a sly gaze Viscenti's way.

"Tell me, monk," the other driver asked without looking back, "do you think the people of this town, whether Lochlin or Millpeter, will welcome road-weary mundunugu with proper hospitality?"

"Do either have a proper city sovereign?" asked the tall man.

"Unlikely," the rider answered. "The number of lights shows that to be a hamlet, nothing more, so it is probable that this area is under the stewardship of a regional sovereign, or an augur troupe."

"But surely they would be wise enough to share some food and drink with soldiers of Mayorqua Tonoloya," said the wickedly-grinning tall man.

The other driver pulled the wagon to a stop. "Get out and ready the cooking fire," he told Viscenti, and so the monk did. He had heard this command every night when they stopped to set camp, and cooking their meals was a task Viscenti had been made to perform.

There was something different in the tone of the command this time, however.

Viscenti knew the grim truth, but he knew, too, that there was nothing he could do about it. He moved toward the back of the wagon and reverently made the sign of the Evergreen before his chest, then whispered a small prayer to Saint Abelle and Saint Avelyn to ask them for guidance and courage as he left this world.

The rider's lizard mount hissed at him when he started to move off the back, so Viscenti tucked his legs up and waited for the drivers to come around and help him down.

He did not miss the fact that they were handling him more roughly this time than the previous days. "Set up the camp, then start the fire," the tall man told him, shoving a pack and bedroll into the old monk's arms and pushing him off to the side of the road.

The three began talking in their Xoconai language then, but Viscenti had learned enough of it to follow along.

"Where is Maquatl?" the other driver asked the mundunugu rider.

"Searching a side trail to see if it might bring us down into the valley and that town. He should be along presently. I will go and gather him."

It all came clearer to Viscenti then. His escorts had been told not to return to Ursal until more than two weeks had passed, to make it seem as if they had gone all the way to St.-Mere-Abelle. Now they believed they were far enough out, and with only secluded and scattered villages around, to feel confident in finishing their work and subsequently waiting here in more comfort than the open road.

The lizard rider started off down the trail, and before he had gone very far, Viscenti heard hoofbeats he assumed were from the fourth Xoconai soldier, who was riding a roan mare and not one of those wretched lizard creatures.

"Ah, he comes," the mundunugu rider said, turning back to the soldiers at the wagon.

Indeed, Viscenti thought when the rider came into view down the road, galloping his horse hard. The charging newcomer went right past the mundunugu before the man had even turned back to regard him, and so he never saw that this rider, the man he thought his companion, was wearing a full hood, and never saw the heavy longbow sweeping across to whack him on the head. Off he went, flying to the ground in a rolling tumble.

And up came the bow, an arrow flying away so quickly that Viscenti couldn't even follow the fluid motion. The missile slammed into the back of the wagon, sticking right between the two drivers, who froze with surprise for a heartbeat before breaking left and right around the cart.

Viscenti thought that he too should flee for cover, but he didn't move, trying instead to make sense of the curious discordance here. Surely that looked like the other mundunugu's horse, and the rider was of similar build. But why the attack? And why, then, with the clear hesitation of the drivers, hadn't a second and even a third arrow come flying in to finish the ambush?

The tall driver went under the wagon, while the other ran around and leaped up into the seat, throwing the brake and cracking the whip to get the horses moving.

They'd never outrun the attacker, Viscenti knew.

But the wagon rushed away, the tall driver grabbing the undercarriage, yelling for his friend to stop, as he was being dragged along the dirt road. On came the ambusher, to the spot where the wagon had been, firing another arrow, then a third—both thumping into the front boards of the open back, just below the driver's bench seat.

From the ease of motion in setting and firing those arrows, and the short distance to the wagon, it occurred to Viscenti that this archer could surely have hit the man if he had so desired.

Instead of putting up a fourth arrow or continuing the chase, the mundunugu, if it was a mundunugu, turned his mount to the side and rushed for Viscenti. He went by and leaned low in the saddle, offering the old monk his hand. With frightening strength, he hoisted Master Viscenti up behind him in the saddle and galloped back the way he had come.

They rode down the road for a long way.

"Who are you?" Viscenti asked.

No answer.

"What are you about? Why have you come?"

"Do you wish to die?" the hooded stranger asked, and Viscenti knew it to be a man, then, and one with an obvious Xoconai accent.

"They would have killed you this night," the man went on. "Never did they intend to take you to St.-Mere-Abelle."

"How do you know this?"

"Because I do. Because I was there when they were instructed to take you from Ursal."

"But you are Xoconai! Why help me?"

The rescuer pulled the horse up short, then turned down to a line of pine trees. As they neared the grove, Viscenti saw the missing mundunugu from his escort standing up against a tree, his arms wrapped about it. He was bound, with a hood over his head, and from his posture, it seemed like the only thing holding him up were those bindings.

Some distance away, a second horse waited, a bit shorter than this one, which was indeed, Viscenti realized, the horse of the ambushed and bound mundunugu.

The rescuer lifted his leg over the neck of the horse and dropped to the ground, then handed the reins to Viscenti.

"You can ride?"

Viscenti nodded. The man ran off and leaped onto his own horse. "Stay close, we've a long road ahead."

He trotted by Viscenti, who picked up his pace in the wake of the rider, and the two set off into the night, to the road and across it, then down through the fields and into the trees for safety.

They kept going for most of the night before stopping in a dense copse of maples and river birch near a swift-running stream.

After dismounting, the rescuer at last removed his hood.

Master Viscenti sucked in his breath, recognizing the long-haired, amber-eyed man as one of the guards in the throne room of City Sovereign Avitl, a Xoconai mundunugu—and one of considerable rank and influence, he was sure.

"You . . . you are Ataquixt, the scout," Viscenti stuttered.

"Well met again, Master Viscenti."

"What? Why?"

"I spoke the truth. They would have left you dead in the dark fields for the wolves and buzzards. You would never have seen your beloved St.-Mere-Abelle again."

"In that case, is that not what City Sovereign Avitl wanted?"

The mundunugu smiled and snorted, shaking his head.

"Grand Augur Apichtli, then."

"He is a brutal man," Ataquixt confirmed. "His vision for this land is not aligned with the agreement reached on Fireach Speuer, a treaty destroyed now with the fall of the people of that land. Now, as you know and as we both recently witnessed, Grand Augur Apichtli desires complete subjugation of the folk of Honce-the-Bear, and indeed, he has nearly accomplished that vision, and will before the end of the year."

"But you do not agree with that."

"I can do nothing about it."

"Except to rescue a feeble old monk."

"A small victory. I was there on that distant mountain and partook in the fight with Scathmizzane and his dragon mount. I believed in the treaty, one that obviously cannot be anymore. But you do not deserve the fate afforded you, and so I tried to save you from it, yes."

"To what end, friend Ataquixt?"

The Xoconai held up his hands. "To no end, other than to deliver you to St.-Mere-Abelle, as was promised to you. Go inside, stay inside that fortress—even ferocious Apichtli will not dare to throw his forces against the walls of that powerful monastery again. St.-Mere-Abelle will hold, I have no doubt. The Xoconai have witnessed the power of the brothers and sisters of Abelle within that place, and it's nothing we wish to see again. There you will be safe."

"How can I repay such generosity as you have shown?"

Ataquixt merely shrugged. "You owe me nothing. This

rescue was, too, a selfish act. I needed to do it. I needed to remind myself of who I am and why I so eagerly came to these lands. We are not all of the same mindset, Master Viscenti, much like your own people of Honce-the-Bear. I saved you from your unjust fate as much for my own sensibilities as for your flesh."

"In my heart, I remain in your debt," the monk replied soberly.

Ataquixt nodded. "Then live a good life, and tell your brethren within the fortress of St.-Mere-Abelle not to hate us all. We call your people the sidhe, as you call ours, but we are all just men and women, humans."

"Albeit different-looking humans," said Viscenti.

"Do the brown-skinned people of To-gai resemble the white-skinned, golden-haired people of Alpinador? What of the black-skinned Durubazzi, or the folk of Behren? Or the To-gai-ru?"

"You must admit, your markings are extraordinary even by those standards."

"You think them ugly?"

"Unusual."

"There are more people in the west, in the basin of Tonoloya proper, than in all Honce-the-Bear. Millions of Xoconai. Perhaps your pink and brown skin is what is unusual."

Viscenti considered it for a few moments, then chuckled. "It is a wide world, indeed," he said. "And I expect that we, all of us that we know, have only seen a very small part of the whole."

"Indeed," Ataquixt agreed. "Now eat a bit and sleep. We have four days of hard riding before us, and I expect you to repay me on this journey by telling me tales of your Saint Avelyn and the heroes of the past, Elbryan and Jilseponie."

"You have heard of them?" the master asked with some surprise.

"Quite a bit, but from a source removed, and not from one who was there with them in the Demon War. Tell me about them, I beg of you. Tell me about Elbryan, the Nightbird. Tell me about Saint Avelyn, who, I understand, was your friend."

"A source removed?" Viscenti asked, as much to himself as to Ataquixt. He looked closer at his rescuer then, at the wondrous bow the man had slung over his shoulder.

A darkfern bow.

Master Viscenti had seen one somewhat like it before, and in the hands of a man who acted very much like this Xoconai mundunugu warrior, and he knew where Ataquixt might have gotten it.

"You're a ranger," Viscenti blurted before he could even consider the implications of speaking the claim aloud.

"Take your meal and your rest, Master Viscenti," Ataquixt said. "We've a long road ahead."

It was indeed a long road, full of meandering trails to the north and St.-Mere-Abelle, but to the relief of both men, it proved uneventful. In the end, it seemed, neither the Grand Augur nor anyone else really cared all that much about Master Viscenti.

The two riders stopped on the wide field of deep grass sloping upward to the vast front wall of the gigantic monastery, a structure centuries old. And through all those years, all those decades, the construction of the place had been a continual task of the Abellican brothers, expanding, strengthening, digging deep chambers far underground, all the way down the hundreds of feet of the cliff behind the monastery proper to the salty waters of the Gulf of Corona and the abbey's docks, sheltered in a small deepwater inlet. Ataquixt had seen this place on two occasions over the years, but not for nearly a decade. Looking at it now only reminded him of why the Xoconai leaders had abandoned any hope of ever conquering this last remaining vestige of Honce-the-Bear's previous glory.

If they threw a hundred thousand Xoconai warriors against St.-Mere-Abelle, the result would most likely be a hundred thousand dead Xoconai warriors on this field before St.-Mere-Abelle.

"Will you ride with me to the gates?" Master Viscenti asked.

"No, I must be away. I have pressing business in the far south."

"You are with me and so would be welcomed. Abbot Braumin will be most grateful."

"I would be grateful if my identity is not disclosed beyond a very few at the monastery."

"What is your game, Ataquixt?"

The Xoconai stared at the monk for a long while.

"Why?" Viscenti pressed. "Why save me?"

"You did not deserve your fate, surely."

"Did those who were hanged by the Coyote?"

"I could not help them."

"But you would have if you could?"

"Several of them, at least, and perhaps all of them, committed no crime," Ataquixt explained. "They were hanged as a show of discipline. So yes, of course I would have saved them."

"But what of those among them who might indeed have tried to kill Apichtli?"

"I am not the arbiter of justice, Master Viscenti. Think of me more as a man who will not tolerate obvious injustice."

"How do you know I wasn't the one who released that lodestone at the Grand Augur?"

"I do not, but nor do I know of any evidence that you did. If there was such evidence, do you think you would have escaped Grand Augur Apichtli's vengeance at the gallows?"

"Again I ask, what is your game here? What role do you play in the events of this land you call Quixi Tonoloya?"

"Mostly, to observe, and from the shadows. To watch this land of Honce and help where I may, and to remember always that I remain a small player only."

"A ranger," Viscenti stated, and he had not missed Ataquixt's naming of the land as Honce.

The blunt remark clearly had Ataquixt back on his heels. "I . . ." he started, but paused, staring at Viscenti most curiously.

"A ranger trained by the Touel'alfar as guardians of the world."

"As watchers of the world," Ataquixt corrected. "How do you know this? Of such things as this?"

"I am an old man, Ataquixt. I knew Elbryan the Night-bird quite well. He was trained by the elves of Andur'Blough Inninness as a ranger."

"As a watcher of the world," Ataquixt restated.

"Elbryan was a ranger, and not merely an observer. He saved the world."

"Elbryan was of Honce-the-Bear," Ataquixt reminded him. "I am not. I am of Tonoloya. Do not expect me to lead any revolts against that which is happening in your land, master. Do not expect Ataquixt to fight on your side, should it ever come to that."

"But will he fight against my side?"

Ataquixt just laughed. "I am not the arbiter of politics. Cochcal Tuolonatl, who became the city sovereign of Palmaris, tried to create a just world here and was dismissed back to the west. The powers there, and now at play here in the east, are quite beyond anything I might do."

"But you'll help where you can, individually, as with me," Master Viscenti reasoned and reached out to pat the other man on the shoulder in gratitude. "You give me hope, ranger. The Xoconai are no more uniform in attitude than the folk of Honce-the-Bear . . ."

"Or of the Wilderlands west of Honce-the-Bear," Ataquixt put in. "Or the To-gai-ru or the Behrenese or the Alpinadorans or the Durubazzi."

Viscenti nodded. "We humans are indeed a complicated family, are we not?"

"Only because we are a family who misunderstands our brethren. Willfully so, and particularly so if those brothers and sisters do not look or speak or smell or dress similarly to our own culture."

Viscenti pondered that for a moment, then began to dismount, but Ataquixt stopped him. "Keep the horse, and treat it well. I will consider that your debt paid to me."

Viscenti laughed. "I do hope that the world will allow you to visit us at St.-Mere-Abelle one day, my friend. If ever you come to the gates, tell them that you are my friend, and that you were the rider sitting beside me when I was delivered from certain death. They are watching us now, of course."

Ataquixt nodded his agreement. "I hope I realize that day, in a better time for both our peoples. I hope there will be a day when I can walk the halls with the monks and perhaps learn more of this Abellican religion and magic and way. You go home now to be with your friends and your studies and your god. I will tell you this much: your brothers of the Abellican Order in that monastery have begun sailing more frequently across the Gulf of Corona to Vanguard, which remains free of Xoconai rule, and I doubt the Grand Augur will ever turn his eyes there, since the treasures he seeks are in the south beyond the land of Behren."

"That is good news indeed."

"I wish you well, Master Viscenti."

The monk offered a gracious bow. "Again, I am in your debt. I will deliver that hopeful information."

"One more thing I wish from you," Ataquixt suddenly replied, as he had just thought of it. "You remember the woman, Aoleyn of the Usgar, the witch who fought the Xoconai?"

The monk's expression hardened.

"If someday she comes to your gates, welcome her and accept her for who she is."

"We have rules . . ." Viscenti began.

"Then break them, in your debt to me, and because I tell you without reservation that you and your brethren will learn more from her than she will learn from you." With that, Ataquixt turned his mount and galloped away across the fields.

Viscenti sat there for a long time watching the mund-unugu—nay, the ranger—go. He wondered if the Touel'alfar, the elves who trained these rangers, would come to the aid of Honce-the-Bear.

In the end, Viscenti shook his head and sighed in resignation. Honce-the-Bear was gone, vanquished, and the monk knew that he would likely be long dead before that ever changed.

THREE

NO PLACE TO HIDE

GOD'S YEAR 874
(MAHTLOMEYI XIUITL)

Father Abbot Braumin. I beseech you! Our situation here at St. Rontlemore grows more desperate by the month. The brothers of St. Bondabruce—it pains me, surely, to even call them as such!—have become openly hostile now to we who serve St.-Mere-Abelle. I cannot send my brothers out onto the streets of Entel any longer. They will be attacked!

It is madness. They host our enemies as friends. They celebrate the goldfish! Openly, and encourage the folk of Entel to look past their prejudices and embrace these new people who have come to our land. It matters not the thousands these invaders from the west have killed, or the thousands now enslaved by them. It matters not what these fiends did to St.-Gwendolyn-by-the-Sea!

All they care about is power—goldfish and the brothers of St. Bondabruce both.

The monks of St. Bondabruce openly follow the teachings of Marcalo De'Unnero, curse his name. They know we will battle them for the heart of the people of Entel. This city is the last holdout, save St.-Mere-Abelle, to the goldfish conquest, but I fear that these painted-faced devils have already achieved their conquest here in this city, or at least are nearing that goal. They dominate the docks, the lifeline of Entel. Their warships are moored side by side in Entel harbor, a forest of masts swaying with every roll of the tide. The gold flows from the south. More gold than I have ever seen. More gold than I thought existed. They dominate the waterways from Entel, past Freeport Island, and all the way to the southern lands and the conquered tribes of Durubazzi.

That is truly all that the goldfish Xoconai care about, Father Abbot. I do not believe that they and the De'Unneran heretics are allies in more than convenience. The invaders want the gold that is mined in Durubazzi, and the heretics want power. I declare that it is critical that we at St. Rontlemore are not summarily destroyed. We are the only voice countering the madness.

All is desperate, but all is not lost, I insist. Queen Brynn of Behren is no friend to the Xoconai. They fear her and her dragon. Indeed, the great warships of the Xoconai Armada will not venture anywhere near to the sandy coast of the southern kingdom. There have been whispers of many Xoconai ships burned to husks by the fiery breath of the great wyrm of the desert lands.

They fear her and her dragon, and the armies at her command. That is our hope.

If we hold here in Entel, and indeed, make gains in this south-ernmost port of Honce, then perhaps Queen Brynn will be persuaded to do more than keep the goldfish from her coastline. We can become her anchor here in Honce, that she and her Chezru forces and her mighty dragon might aid us as we push the painted devils back and return these lands to Honce-the-Bear, and defeat the resurgence of the terrible De'Unnerans.

I beseech you, Father Abbot. I pray that my words here are expressed with the sense of urgency that is now needed. Send help. All that you can spare! An army of brothers and sisters armed with the most potent gemstones of St.-Mere-Abelle.

We will strike at them brutally and unmercifully. We will drive them from Entel and send word to Queen Brynn that the time is now for her to join in our battle!

It is our only hope, for if not, I ask, what will be left?

Yours in Blessed St. Abelle,
Brother Edgar Finn, Acting Master, St. Rontlemore
This Wane of Decambria and the Turn to God's Year 874
(May it be a blessed and better year)

CHAPTER 10

THE UNASSUMING
LITTLE FISHER CAT

GOD'S YEAR 873
(MAHTLOMO XIUITL)

"You are too old for such games," the large and muscular man taunted, rolling his staff before him. He let go with one hand and motioned to his two companions, and the three began to stalk in a circle about their target, a small woman wearing robes similar to their own.

That woman, Mistress Elysant, pulled her cowl back from her face to better view those opponents moving to her flanks, but she did not react any more than that, not in hopping about, not in maneuvering her staff, and not in responding to the taunting man, Brother Darius of Dellock.

"What punishment will Father Abbot put upon us when we fall upon you, little woman?" Darius asked, continuing his stalk. He came toward her suddenly, but just a fast step.

She didn't blink, her little grin unchanged. How obvious this one was! He had been taught to taunt, using his barbs as a probe not unlike the feint he had made at her long before he had any intention of actually charging in. Elysant found herself amused as she thought of this, as she imagined Brother Darius being told of these tactics by some breathless Abellican master, puffing himself as some seasoned and skilled warrior, though he had probably never engaged in an actual fight. Most of the monks around her had been bottled up at St.-Mere-Abelle for more than a decade now, and the martial knowledge among the teaching masters was becoming more from secondhand training than from true battle.

She had to work hard to keep her smile suppressed as she considered how to turn the bravado against these three.

Darius started another taunt, this one long-winded, but Elysant wasn't listening, seeing it as the approach ploy, as she liked to call it.

Sure enough, the brother behind her to the right came at her suddenly—another feint, she knew, but this time she issued a little yelp and turned fast. The movement revealed the true attack, coming from behind and to her left, or so it seemed as she stumbled and appeared to nearly fall.

In came Brother Pavarak, the monk behind her left shoulder. In came Brother Darius.

As she bent to the side, Elysant reached her left arm toward the ground, as if to catch herself, her right arm, holding her quarterstaff, flailing up and out behind her.

To their young and proud minds, the trio of attackers believed they had her, she knew, and so too did the many monks around the edge of the courtyard, if their gasps were any indication.

But a turn of Elysant's right wrist sent her staff swinging up and over her shoulder and the back of her neck, its high end coming around and down to be caught by her reversing left as she let go with her right.

Down went the staff tip planting on the ground, Elysant's right coming in to grasp the staff up high.

And up high went the warrior woman, pressing herself into the air and throwing herself into a swinging and twisting flip right over Brother Pavarak as he charged in hard from behind. She landed facing him as he skidded to a stop and spun about desperately, launching a two-handed swing with his staff.

Elysant's staff intercepted, stopping the attack cold and breaking all momentum so that she could retract and jab the tip of her weapon into Pavarak's face. He staggered and tried to resume his swing, but Elysant stepped beside him, ducking low. She brought her staff down and between his legs, then up fast and high, catching inside his left thigh. Her balance was perfect as she stepped under the strike, her feet braced for her to stand and thrust, lifting and twisting the unfortunate young man into a rolling tumble that dropped him hard on his back on the ground.

With Darius bearing in, Elysant slammed her staff's tip into the fallen brother's chest, then up she went, vaulting away at Brother Jingol, the warrior who had faked a charge to begin the exchange.

He wasn't ready for her. He didn't even seem to register that she was there until her staff cracked against the side of his head, sending him stumbling past her, left to right.

Elysant turned only a bit more, enough to throw her staff spear-like into the chest of the charging Darius, taking his breath away and setting him back on his heels—a movement she didn't even witness as she leaped at the staggering Jingol, capturing his right arm under her left and rolling behind him, her weight and angle taking the staff expertly from his grasp. A second turn sent her down low with a sweep of that staff to trip up the off-balance man.

To his credit, Jingol tried to carry through his fall with a roll that would bring him back to his feet, but the staff came down in a powerful strike against the side of his neck, Elysant angling it so that the tip hit the ground just before the shaft impacted, stealing much of its force.

If she hadn't done that, Jingol's neck would have borne the full brunt.

"Defeated!" called the judge of the contest, recognizing that Elysant had scored what would have been a debilitating, and perhaps mortal, blow had she chosen the deadly angle.

She was already turning away from Brother Jingol before the call, fast-stepping to engage the other two, Brothers Darius and Pavarak.

They came at her furiously, staves swinging and stabbing, but she worked the weapon she had taken from Brother Jingol before her in a blur, cracking against the swing of Pavarak, turning vertically to redirect Darius's stabbing staff harmlessly wide.

With a subtle but strong movement, she slid it ahead along Darius's weapon, slamming it against his fingers.

Notably, he didn't taunt as he leaped back from her.

Now she had a few moments alone against poor Brother Pavarak, a skinny scholar whose studies focused mostly on the sacred Ring Stones. To his credit, the neophyte warrior did not run away, but came on with a desperate charge, yelling wildly and missing badly as Elysant sidestepped, let him stumble almost past her, then stepped behind her lead foot and between his legs, locked her staff powerfully under her arm as she slid it beneath his arm and across his chest, then lurched up and back, ending Pavarak's momentum and lifting him up and over her bent leg and hip, dropping him unceremoniously to the dirt.

Before he even regained his breath, she straddled him, her staff tip diving down under his chin, stopping as it came against his throat.

"Defeated!"

Elysant leaped into a twisting back spin, braced staff coming across in anticipation of Brother Darius.

But he had hesitated, and stood back now, eyes darting side to side with obvious uncertainty.

Elysant stood straight, staring at him, and threw Brother Jingol's staff to the floor, then held her empty hands out as if in invitation to the large man.

Darius eyed her curiously.

"It's not a surrender," she assured him.

"Am I to throw aside . . ."

"I do not care."

She watched his expression change as he came to understand that no taunts he had thrown at her or could throw at her had struck as pointedly as her current dare.

At the edges of the ring, brothers and sisters giggled.

Predictably, Darius's attack came straightforward and too powerfully, an overhand chop that might have split Elysant's skull were she a lesser fighter.

Up came her arms in a cross, catching the blow in between them, halting it before Darius could put his full weight behind the strike. She worked fast then in many movements, grabbing the staff with her left, then right. Trusting that Darius was too stubborn and slow to realize to surrender it, she used his solid grip to keep it steady as she threw her legs forward and up, kicking her left foot against his belly, her right against his solar plexus, her left against his chest. She ran right up the man, finally kicking him in the face with her right foot for good measure as she threw herself up and out to the side, over the staff, turning his arm.

He realized then that he should let go, she knew, but too late, for she was already into her second leap and roll up and over the staff, this time forcing the surrender of the weapon, Darius losing all strength in the face of the painful twist to his arm.

Brother Darius was not a disciple of Saint Avelyn, not a gemstone scholar like Brother Pavarak. Like Elysant, his primary lessons came from the teachings of Saint Belfour, a legendary martial warrior of the Abellican Church.

Elysant wasn't going to show him the same deference as she had to Pavarak, she decided as she used her momentum to quickstep away from him with his staff now in her hand.

She turned and threw it into his feet as he turned. She leaped for him, to the side and going past, her right arm stabbing under his right armpit, going in front of his shoulder and up behind his head to grab at his thick black hair, then locking her grip behind him and up high. Her left arm looped over and then back under his bent left elbow, similarly keeping it behind his shoulder, out of his true power range. She continued to drive him backward, forcing him down—but not to the ground, no, for now he was caught, both arms entangled, all balance hers.

She whirled Darius around with shifting pressures, and whenever he tried to resist, she drove upward and forward, bending both his arms painfully and into positions of little strength.

"Witness, brothers and sisters!" she called out. "He stands a foot taller than I, weighs a hundred pounds more, yet he is my doll."

To accentuate the point, she wiggled Darius back and forth.

The humiliation enraged him and he planted his feet, ignored the pain, and stood up straight, taking Elysant right from the ground.

She didn't resist, even hopped a bit to help him, and threw herself over his left shoulder, adjusting her grips and twisting her body perfectly so that her falling weight sent him rolling right over her in a flip that she released at its highest point, leaving him to fall flat and hard to the ground.

And she fell over him, her middle and index fingers stopping immediately before his wide eyes. Clearly, she could have driven them right into his skull.

"Defeated!" called the judge.

The spectator monks shook their heads and mumbled at the stunning display.

"You are good, Brother Darius," the middle-aged Elysant said as she straightened above him and offered him her hand. "Far better than I was at your age."

"How?" was all he could manage, not taking her hand.

"Pagonel of the Jhesta tu," was her answer. "Battle is balance. You will learn."

He stared at her and still hadn't taken her hand.

"Your pride will limit you," she warned, and turned and walked away.

That very same night, Mistress Elysant entered the chamber of Father Abbot Braumin Herde tentatively, not quite sure what to expect. Her nervousness only increased when she noted the select group of other masters standing about the Father Abbot's great desk. None of them had been among the younger masters elevated in the time Elysant had been at St.-Mere-Abelle. This was the old guard, including Master Viscenti, whose hawklike gaze fell over the younger woman as she stepped through the door.

Elysant had been at St.-Mere-Abelle for a dozen years, studying, sometimes teaching, and practicing, always practicing. She had entered the monastery under great acclaim, having returned from a wondrous expedition with a couple of long-lost artifacts from the storied history of the Abellican Church, treasures thought lost to the ages.

She had been awarded the rank of master, or mistress, soon after that adventure, a most remarkable feat considering her accomplishments. There weren't many female monks at St.-Mere-Abelle, though it was more common an event now than before the fall of St.-Gwendolyn-by-the-Sea, a traditional bastion of sisters of the Abellican Church. Fewer still, indeed incredibly rare, was the elevation of women to the level of master, or mistress, at this, the mother abbey. And what had made Elysant's ascension as a woman of the Abellican Church truly remarkable, possibly unique, was that she had almost no affinity for the sacred Ring Stones that channeled the Abellican magic. A lack of ability to empower and use the magical gemstones was not uncommon among the folk of the land, but it was uncommon among those in the Abellican Order, and unheard of for someone who had attained the rank of master or mistress. There were a few notable exceptions in some of the other abbeys, but all had been men, most pointedly the long-dead saint of whom Elysant was a disciple, the great Vanguard warrior Belfour. But nowhere in the almost nine centuries of the Abellican Church, with its detailed histories and logs and tales of brothers and sisters of past ages, had anyone confirmed as mistress a sister without a hint of gemstone affinity.

Mistress Elysant couldn't close a cat scratch with a soul stone, couldn't flick a tiny spark from graphite, couldn't light a candle with the most powerful of rubies.

Viscenti continued to stare hard at her. He had been decidedly against her ascension, but at least he had been honest with her about it.

The masters moved to the sides of the desk as she approached, giving her a straight line to the Father Abbot's desk.

"Mistress, thank you for coming here on such short notice," Father Abbot Braumin greeted her.

His expression remained very serious, she noted—something was going on, and likely it wasn't anything good. She feared for a friend, Brother Thaddius, who had left St.-Mere-Abelle a few years before on an extended scouting mission that, she had heard, had taken him far to the west.

"Have you had a chance to take your supper? I could have some food brought in immediately."

"No thank you, Father Abbot," she replied quietly. The thought of eating in front of this group while they stared at her and waited for her to finish was far more disquieting than any grumbling in her stomach.

"Very well," Braumin said. He fumbled about his desk for a bit, then lifted a parchment and held it out toward her.

"From Brother Edgar of St. Rontlemore," Braumin explained as she took it.

She read the letter slowly and carefully, ignoring the clearly uncomfortable shifting from many of the masters standing about her. None of it surprised her. She had heard the whispers of the Xoconai making a press for Entel, and knew too that St. Bondabruce was becoming more than a nuisance to the monks of St. Rontlemore and the causes of St.-Mere-Abelle.

"The De'Unnerans move more boldly in support of our

conquerors," Braumin said when Elysant looked up from the parchment.

"They care only about power," Viscenti grumbled.

Elysant slowly lowered the parchment. Her relief that this was not about Thaddius proved short-lived under the glares of the masters, the solemn reminder of the dire developments described in the letter. As she considered them more fully, her attention moving away from the relief that no ill word had come regarding her friend, her face tightened into a grimace, one that deepened every time she considered the name of Marcalo De'Unnero. She didn't try to hide it—quite the opposite! Most at St.-Mere-Abelle already knew how she felt regarding the followers of that thankfully dead heretic, but it would be good for these men to have the continuing confirmation. St. Gwendolyn, her beloved home abbey, had been raided and razed by the De'Unnerans. None who had survived that, certainly no woman who had survived it, would hold any love for the De'Unneran cult.

"Unfortunately, it would seem that their power grab is succeeding to an uncomfortable degree," Father Abbot Braumin said. "In St. Precious in Palmaris, the order maintains its loyalty to us in the true Church, but only in secret. The brothers and sisters of St. Precious try not to spit when they praise Saint De'Unnero."

"Saint De'Unnero," Master Viscenti echoed with a snort of utter derision, shaking his head, and grumbles rolled throughout the room. There had been no nomination, let alone any beatification, of Marcalo De'Unnero—the title was a concoction of the Xoconai augurs in league with the De'Unneran disciples still scattered among the many monasteries of the Abellican Church, particularly within St. Bondabruce in Entel.

"In Ursal, the order is greatly reduced and becoming irrelevant," the Father Abbot continued. "Under the merciless judgment and ever-present eye of Grand Augur Apichtli, there is little they can do. And in Entel, that most critical of places, the stirrings are not good."

"I have heard the whispers," Elysant told him.

"Do you know why you were asked to join us this day?"

"No, Father Abbot."

"Because the whispers are not enough," Father Abbot Braumin explained. "They hint at trouble, great trouble."

"St. Rontlemore is far smaller than St. Bondabruce," Elysant agreed.

"If the Xoconai devils are supporting the De'Unnerans of St. Bondabruce, they may become bold enough to openly move against our brethren. That is bad enough, of course—we need no more martyrs. But St. Rontlemore is one of the few places in Honce where a serious cache of sacred Ring Stones remains."

Elysant sucked in her breath. She hadn't known that added layer of intrigue.

"Do you know Brother Edgar?" Father Abbot Braumin asked her.

She shook her head.

"He now leads St. Rontlemore. They have been without an abbot for . . ." Braumin paused and looked to Master Viscenti.

"Six years," Viscenti told him.

Elysant's eyes widened with surprise at that.

"We did not think it wise to call any attention to the abbey," the Father Abbot explained. "It is a small place, after all. Brother Edgar is the senior monk there by many years, and so we trusted in his ability to keep the monastery running as it always has, to serve the poor of Entel. The brethren of St. Rontlemore do not even have a master in their ranks.

"But now St. Bondabruce is growing bolder and showing their De'Unneran fangs," Abbot Braumin went on, his voice rising in tone and volume. "I want you to go there."

"In this very spring?"

"This very day," Braumin answered. "The weather is clear, though I know not for how long. Yes, winter is deep about the lands, but I—but we have faith that if anyone can make this journey, it will be Mistress Elysant."

"Mistress Elysant and?" she asked.

"Just Mistress Elysant," the Father Abbot replied. "If we sent a cadre of brothers with you, the Xoconai would grow wise to our desire to reinforce our allies in Entel, and that is something we surely do not want."

"One traveler," Master Visconti added. "Nondescript. Un-threatening."

"I am . . . flattered," Elysant said, but her hesitance showed that she was more confused and concerned than anything else.

"Have you ever seen a fisher cat, mistress?" Visconti asked, and when she replied with a blank stare, he continued, "A most beautiful creature. Graceful and swift, with fur so thick you want to bury your face into it, and wide, soft eyes. You would be entranced if you saw one—if you found a pup, you might want to bring it into your home and keep it as you might a dog or cat or rabbit."

"Yes, master."

"No, mistress," he corrected. "Fisher cats wish to be left alone. They want no part of you, but if they are forced into a corner by a person, they will begin their attack with a scream, one so high-pitched that it assaults your ears, one so incredibly unexpected that it knots your stomach. And when the fight begins, I assure you that the one who will be screaming will be you, in surprise and in pain. That deceptive little creature is you, Mistress Elysant. You seem so small and gentle, but oh, how the brothers training against you have learned differently."

She didn't know if she was being complimented or mocked.

"We want you to be our unassuming fisher cat," Father Abbot Braumin explained. "We don't believe you will be bothered along the road, but we are confident that if you are, you will be quite capable of getting through the trouble."

Braumin motioned to a brother standing beside a side door to the chamber and the monk pulled it open.

In came another monk, pacing carefully, his hands before him cradling an old monk robe, weathered and frayed.

"I believe that this is yours, given to you by the saint who once wore it," Braumin said.

With trembling hands and her breath caught in her throat, Elysant took the offered garment, one she surely recognized. For this was the actual Robe of Saint Belfour, an item of a time centuries before. Within its cloth folds was a thin coat of silverel, a silvery metal harvested from the rare darkfern plants and touted as the hardest metal known of all. Also within the folds were gemstones teeming with magic. Soul stones and serpentines, to heal, to protect. Simply wearing the robe would help wounds to heal quickly.

Elysant had once "died" wearing this robe, except that its magic would not let her truly expire.

"You wish me to wear this on my journey?" she asked incredulously. She had surrendered the robe to the monks when she had entered St.-Mere-Abelle, that it could be properly encased and protected.

"You are the only one worthy of it," Father Abbot Braumin answered without hesitation. "The spirit of St. Belfour gave it to you, and we think it a wise choice indeed."

Elysant nodded and looked about sheepishly to gauge the expressions of the other masters considering this surprising twist. Her scan was stopped short, however, when she noted another brother entering, this one carrying a quarterstaff—but not her old staff, which had been another gift of the ghost of St. Belfour and was fashioned of polished marble. Her eyes widened as the brother approached.

The staff wasn't of oak or hickory. It was green, and shot with thin lines of silver that flashed in the light of the room's torches.

"This weapon came from the bowels of St. Precious in Palmaris, ushered out of the city along with many more of their treasures when the Xoconai began to change the rules," Braumin explained. "It is an ancient weapon, one fashioned by the Touel'alfar, we believe, and of their darkfern. It is as hard as the staff of stone given you in the tomb of St. Belfour, and the material, the darkfern, is much, much lighter than the stone, or even the wood of a normal quarterstaff. You will find this more suited to your fighting style, and woe to any you strike."

"Father Abbot," she said, barely able to get the words out, "what if I am found out on the road and these artifacts are lost?"

"Better our weapons be used in the fight to save the world, dear mistress, than to have them stored in dark chambers while the people of Honce suffer. You will take them and use them if you must. They will suit you. They are fitting for an abbess of St. Rontlemore."

Elysant was truly overwhelmed, nodding, her expression blank—until she realized what Father Abbot Braumin had just declared. At that point, she nearly swooned, and gasped aloud.

"You will go with the declaration from my pen that you are the abbess of St. Rontlemore," Braumin clarified. "And before you leave, your mission in Entel will be better explained."

"We fear that your tenure will be short," Master Viscenti added. "It is unlikely that St. Rontlemore will hold out for long against the growing tide of darkness. But know that when you return to St.-Mere-Abelle, your title will remain, forevermore, unless you disgrace your office. Should St. Rontlemore become again a functioning monastery of the Abellican Church, Abbess Elysant will there preside."

"And we all know that you will never make us regret our decision, my dear sister," Father Abbot Braumin said with a wry grin. "The Abellican Order will never be disgraced or let down by our unassuming little fisher cat."

CHAPTER 11

PIETY, DIGNITY, POVERTY, CHARITY

The wind groaned and howled, the cold air nipped at her exposed skin, but the sun shone bright on Elysant as she stood in the main courtyard of St.-Mere-Abelle, staring at the huge gates and imagining the wide and dangerous lands beyond—lands she had traversed many times in the past. The magical Robe of St. Belfour kept her warm enough, but she had wrapped a ragged and colorful blanket about her atop it so that she would not obviously appear to be of the Abellican Order to any she encountered. Her darkfern staff, too, was disguised, wrapped in leather and with a crudely carved wooden cap shaped into a wolf's head—or perhaps it was a squirrel's head. Elysant couldn't be sure.

Few were out to see her off, just a trio of young brothers checking the supplies in the oversized pack Elysant would carry. She hardly paid them any heed as they argued over how much water she should carry until it became clear that they were not going to solve the riddle.

"I will drink the snow," she finally said, ending the debate.

The three looked at her incredulously.

"Have you ever traveled the lands?" she said to their obviously-ignorant plotting. "Have you even been out of this prison in the last years, or at any time at all in your adult life?"

"I have rarely heard the mother abbey of the Abellican Order referred to as a prison," came another voice, one a bit scratchy with age. Elysant turned and sucked in her breath to see Master Viscenti shuffling her way.

The old monk waved the attending brothers away and walked up to the mistress.

"I—I apologize, master," Elysant stammered. "I was only . . ."

He laughed. "It is a prison, isn't it? Strange how a place seems so much less so even with the idea that one might leave."

"Yes, but I did not mean . . ."

"Dear Master Elysant, I know what you meant."

She was relieved, then curious, to realize that Viscenti had used "master" instead of "mistress" in addressing her. There had been an ongoing debate in the order regarding the title distinctions, and whether the ranking monk should be delineated based on whether it was a man or a woman. Viscenti, a traditionalist, had not been an ally to those wanting a singular title of master.

Nor had Viscenti been overly supportive of Elysant's promotion to the rank, though he had claimed that was because she was unskilled with the Ring Stones and not because of her gender.

"Do you know your course?" he asked her.

She shook the puzzlement from her expression. "I have an idea."

He held out a scroll tube. "Go south, but turn soon to the southeast," he advised. "I've marked it on this map, one that shows accurate distance and expected travel times from village to village all the way to Falidean Bay."

"I served in the abbey of St. Gwendolyn, which is as far east as one can go without walking on the Mirianic Ocean. The city of Entel is south down the coast from there. I know well the way," she agreed.

Viscenti nodded. "Indeed. And let us pray for a day when we might rebuild that wondrous chapel on the cliffs of the Mantis Arm where our enemies dropped her into the Mirianic. I doubt I will be alive for that groundbreaking, Master Elysant, but I pray that you will be."

Again, she looked at him curiously, caught off guard. "Thank you," she said.

"You doubt my sincerity?"

"You surprise me."

"I am old and set in my ways—to a point. But I am not dead and without the ability to learn. It was my suggestion to Father Abbot Braumin that you be the choice for this task, and my insistence that you would get the job done, that you would survive the road alone more capably than anyone else we might choose. I have watched you, sister."

"You did not wish me promoted to mistre . . . to master."

Viscenti shrugged. "I'm not dead yet," he answered with a chuckle that sounded to her very much like an apology.

"For all my faith in you, though," he added, "I expect that this journey would be much easier if you were proficient with our magic. Father Abbot wanted to send a disciple of Saint Avelyn beside you."

Elysant shrugged and wondered if that might be a good thing.

"I dissuaded him," Viscenti said, stealing the thought. "Elysant won't need any help." He reached into a pocket of his robe and brought forth a dark woolen cap. "Well, no help that she cannot carry." He reached forward and dropped the hood of her cloak back from her head and placed the cap upon her.

Elysant immediately felt something, though she couldn't quite figure out what it was. She reached up to adjust the cap and felt a hard ball in its front fold.

"A cat's-eye," Viscenti explained. "The dark of night will not blind you."

Elysant nodded and understood.

Viscenti looked over at the huge pack the brothers had left on the ground beside her. "I would help you with it, but I doubt I could even lift it," he said. "Can you?"

His laughter stopped short any curt response. "Of course you can, but bearing it over the miles will not be easy."

"It will lighten as I eat."

"It will lighten before that," Viscenti replied, and reached into his pocket once more, this time bringing forth a black leather bracer. He reached for her hand and she held it out for him, not quite knowing what to make of this.

Viscenti pushed up her sleeve and set the bracer, and only then did Elysant notice the gemstones, six bloodstones, set into it under a leathery fold.

A second bracer came from the pocket and Viscenti wrapped it about her other wrist, this one affixed with a half-dozen dolomites, a gem also rumored to be sewn into the robe she wore, and with several prevalent in the staff of stone she had been given in the tomb of Saint Belfour, and that she had wielded in the war with the Xoconai.

"Master, I am not skilled with the Ring Stones. I have no affinity for them."

"That is why we gave you a different staff, yes," he agreed, and continued strapping on the second bracer.

"But these have gemstones."

"As does your robe, and the cap I gave to you," Master Viscenti said. "There are many types of magic in the world, we have come to know. The foul magic of the demon dactyls, the crystal magic used by those like your friend Aoleyn, the magic we are now seeing from the Xoconai. With our magic, we can fashion items, of course."

"Like my robe."

"That robe has more than Abellican magic in it, Elysant. The silverel speaks of elven—Touel'alfar—influence, of course, and the other benefits of the robe are quite beyond our understanding. The enchantments our gemstones can place upon a sword or a cap or these bracers or a multitude of other items come in two forms, enhancement and invocation. You are useless regarding the latter, but the former requires no affinity to the Ring Stones at all. You were not getting the benefits of the stone staff you were given by the ghost of St. Belfour."

"It was a weapon of great power."

"Indeed," Viscenti agreed. "The magical benefits of its dolomite invocation, I mean. Even without the gemstones, that staff was sturdier than any weapon it might face. But so is this one, this Touel'alfar warrior's stave. No sword will chip it, I assure you. And it is much lighter.

"The bracers are enhanced and openly enchanted. Your affinity or lack of affinity for the Ring Stones does not matter. You are stronger and healthier simply by wearing them, as you will see well in near darkness because of the gemstone in the cap, and as your robe will protect you in a multitude of ways. Please, go lift the bag of supplies."

Elysant stepped over and bent low to hook her arm under the satchel, expecting it to be quite heavy. She felt the weight as she lifted it, but it was nowhere near what she had expected.

"If you remove those bracers, you will find that much more encumbering."

"Master Viscenti, I am honored to be entrusted with these valuable items."

"They are nothing compared to that robe you wear, I assure you," he replied. "You are entrusted because you have proven yourself worthy of our trust. Believe me when I tell you, dear Elysant, Abbess Elysant, that you have taught me much in your time with us. I feel quite the fool for ever doubting you."

Elysant knew that she was fiercely blushing. Master Viscenti was as hard as the shell of a Belt-and-Buckle tortoise, and surely not a man of flattery and false smiles.

He wasn't smiling now, she noted, as his expression became quite grim.

"I will complete the mission as desired," she promised.

"Of that, I do not doubt."

"Then why do you fear?"

"I fear for *you*, dear child," he explained. "You are walking into a great battle."

"I have been to war, master," Elysant reminded him.

"Ah, yes, but this is not war, this is worse. This journey you now undertake, at least. You see, you must remain secretive on your way to the city of Entel, but I fear that trouble will surely find you now and again on this difficult journey."

"The snows will be deep, no doubt."

"We should hope so," said Viscenti. "You will survive, whatever the winter throws in your path. No, but I speak of highwaymen and of Xoconai who might find you. I've no doubt that this challenge of enmis, too, will not prove too great for Abbess Elysant. But the true challenge may well come after such a fight, because this is worse than war. This is subterfuge."

Elysant shook her head, her expression puzzled.

"My dear Elysant, there can be no witnesses to your travel. You can take no prisoners. If you are accosted, by the Xoconai at least, you must kill them. If they fall to their knees and surrender, you must kill them. None can know of the great Abellican warrior traveling to Entel and St. Rontlemore, at least not until you are recognized as the abbess within the secure walls of the place."

Elysant wanted to dismiss the words, wanted to believe that she would find no place for the action Viscenti had just described.

But she looked at the old master's face, full of sorrow and

fear, and she understood that such merciless killing would be a distinct possibility.

"Is that truly the Abellican way, Master Viscenti?"

"I do not know what it is, but it is a necessity."

"Piety, dignity, poverty, charity," Elysant recited, the first and most important litany a pledged monk learned.

"Piety, dignity, poverty, charity," Viscenti echoed. "And now add victory, because if we fail and the Xoconai so fully dominate the land, the only part of the Abellican pledge that will be assured for the folk of Honce will be the third, poverty."

Elysant accepted a pat on the shoulder from Viscenti, then gathered up her pack and walked for the gates, which were opened as she approached, showing her the bright and snowy fields beyond.

Redirected after his travels in the west, and now of St. Bonda-bruce, Master Thaddius Roncourt loitered by the door of Abbot Dusibol, whispering to the two Abellican brothers set outside as guards. He had requested an audience knowing full well that he would be denied for the time being.

For the abbot was engaged with City Sovereign Popoca at that time, discussing matters of the rotation of the Xoconai ships, the famed Tonoloya Armada, at Entel's docks.

After charming the pair of guards with tales of his days with Marcalo De'Unnero back in the time before Mayorqua

Tonoloya, Thaddius made his way to the door and even leaned on its frame, offering a soft sigh.

"They could ramble all the day, couldn't they?" he asked, nodding toward the room.

The brothers smiled and nodded.

"Do wake me when I can gain entry," Thaddius said, and closed his eyes, leaning comfortably.

And listening intently.

". . . the only reason I have allowed you to keep your sacred stones!" he heard Popoca growl at the abbot. "Grand Augur Apichtli might well question this decision."

As Popoca lowered his voice, Thaddius dared turn the doorknob and lean a bit, subtly cracking open the door.

"We are allies," Abbot Dusibol returned. "We have helped you secure your power fully, have we not?"

"You have," Popoca admitted. "But I need those docks enlarged. They are building great warships in Amvoy now, a second fleet! They will sail perhaps as early as *tlen yeyi chualoyai*! Do you know what Apichtli will do to me, and to you, if those grand warships have no place to properly and securely moor?"

His voice rose again, alerting the guards, and Thaddius started as if coming awake, then sucked in his breath and quickly moved back, fully closing the door and looking to the brothers as if it had been an accident.

They waved him away.

"Fall in there on those two, and you'll probably not come back out alive, master!" one of them whispered.

Thaddius nodded nervously, as if scared. He moved off down the hall a bit and slid down to a sitting position on the floor, his back to the wall, and quietly contemplated the information. He knew how to speak Xoconai well from his days on the Ayamharas Plateau immediately following the fall of Scathmizzane. When City Sovereign Popoca had said *"tlen yeyi chualoyai,"* or "the third quarter," the context made it clear to Thaddius that he meant autumn.

This autumn. A fleet of new warships sailing to Entel?

Did it mean war with the Behrenese to the south around the Belt-and-Buckle Mountains?

Thaddius shook his head, but he wasn't sure what these adventurous and warlike Xoconai might try. In any case, it was clear that they meant to secure the shipping lanes once and for all, to rid the southern Mirianic of pirates.

Entel would bristle with macana and mundunugu warriors, no doubt, and that would mean no good for the people of this old and unique city.

A short while later, before the abbot and Popoca had finished their conversation, Thaddius took his leave and told the guards he would speak with Abbot Dusibol another time.

He went back to his room and to a hiding place he had fashioned with gemstone magic beneath his floorboards, and there retrieved his journal.

He had some notes to record.

Elysant's journey had gone very well for nearly a week. The days had been cold, the nights wickedly so, but her robe kept her warm. Each day was full of sunshine, each night sparkling with a million stars.

The land was quiet, deep in winter. The two villages she decided to enter were welcoming to a weary traveler, and eager for news of the outside world. When she left that second village on the morning of her seventh day out of St.-Mere-Abelle, turning southeast now for the coastline along the vast inlet known as Falidean Bay, she had still seen no Xoconai.

If that held all the way to Entel, it would be a very good thing.

She didn't expect that, however, as she knew that the weather would shift soon enough, and not in her favor.

The storm roared to life that very afternoon, dark clouds crowding in on violent winds. Pelting sleet drummed on her hood, the ground growing slick before her. She had hoped to travel long into the night, but the swirling winds were soaking her even under her robe, splashing stinging pellets of icy sleet into her face. She turned off the road and crunched through waist-deep snow, moving for a stretch of thick pines not far to the south. She went down into a hollow and had to use her darkfern staff to poke through the top layer of the winter blanket, for the snow was crusted with a hard sheet of ice from the daytime sun melts and now the pelting sleet.

The copse proved farther than it had appeared, and it took Elysant a long while to reach it. By the time she crawled and crashed through the low-hanging branches of a tall pine, the night had deepened, the wind had gone from cold to frigid, and the sleet had become a blinding snow.

R. A. SALVATORE

Miserable and wet, Elysant breathed a sigh of relief as soon as she rolled on the bare ground under the natural tent that was the pine. So thick were the branches that little snow had gotten through, and even the pelting sleet and rain had brought no more than a couple of meager dribbles in the nearly ten-foot patch beneath the drooping, ice-laden limbs.

Elysant brough forth some kindling she had been given in the village, along with her flint and steel. Soon enough, she had a small fire going.

Off came her boots, then her socks, which she stretched out on the branches not far from the fire to dry.

She put her back to the trunk, which was sticky with sap, and stretched her legs out so that her feet were very near the flames.

She reached for some food, but changed her mind and brought forth her bedroll from the large pack instead. She took out some stones as well, placing them around the fire to heat them for later.

Just a quick nap, she thought, and she closed her eyes.

The growl of her own belly awakened her.

Disoriented, she looked around. The fire was long out, and when she picked up the nearest stone she had placed, she found that it was hardly warm. Confused, trying to piece it together, she realized that it was daytime outside.

She got up to her feet, crouching low in the tight canopy, and moved to the edge of the natural tent, wincing when she stepped on a pine cone buried under the bed of needles.

The snow was deeper, she realized as she tried to push a branch aside. At least a foot more had accumulated, and more was falling. She wasn't sure how long it was after dawn—a couple of hours, she guessed, for the sky was thick with gray clouds.

Elysant rubbed her bleary eyes, yawned hugely, and studied the sky, trying to guess when the storm might end.

It didn't matter, she decided soon after. The clouds had come in from the west, and not a hint of blue sky could be seen out there.

Sun or snow, it was time to go.

She dressed while she ate, smiling while pulling on a sock, a hunk of bread in her mouth, as she considered Master Viscenti's lament that the journey would be easier if she were skilled with Abellican magic.

In this moment, she found that she couldn't disagree.

She took great care to leave the natural tent the same way she had come in—she could still see hints of her trail through the heavy and wet snow. Out of the bowl and back to the road, she found the going much easier.

Until the next storm hit, then another after that.

After she had turned to the southeast, Elysant had hoped to make Falidean Bay in a week. It took three. At one point, she holed up in a farmer's barn through a storm, then wound up stuck there with the family for four days, waiting for the weather to break enough for her to resume her journey. They were friendly enough, the three children perfectly delightful.

But the time was passing, and she wondered if St. Rontlemore would still be standing by the time she finally arrived in Entel.

Thus, she was quite relieved when she at last looked down from a high bluff onto the vast and treacherous inlet known as

Falidean Bay. She looked at red mud as far as she could see, for the tide was out—a most tremendous tide here in the funnel-shaped bay. The craggy cliffs and bluffs surrounding the inlet sometimes, as now, towered more than fifty feet up from the mud, but when the tide came in, the water would be up very near to where Elysant was now standing.

How many shellfish hunters had been caught down there and drowned? she wondered.

She had heard many such tales in her days at St. Gwendolyn.

Her course now was southwest along the bay coastline. The snow wasn't nearly as deep due to the relatively warmer winds flowing off the water, and vast patches of open ground were all about. This region was far more populated than the rolling farmlands and forests of interior Honce.

But among those many people were Xoconai.

So many Xoconai.

Elysant did the only thing she could: she kept her head down and kept moving. While she preferred a warm bed in an inn and the company of the townsfolk in these little hamlets and small towns that dotted the Honce landscape, if she noted too many Xoconai faces in one, she turned for the forests and sought out a thick pine grove where she could spend the night.

She was making good progress now, traversing the last seventy miles or so to Entel, when she came into the small town of Fairmount, set out on a peninsula jutting southeast above the bay. Almost as soon as she turned down the main, muddy road in the coastal town, though, she realized her error. She hadn't seen the patrolling Xoconai soldiers from her vantage point on the western road.

They were moving her way, if not for her specifically, motioning other Honce folk out of their path, sometimes with a raised, threatening backhand, and almost always with a taunt or an insult.

Elysant tried to turn away down a side street but realized that the action had only focused the attention of the soldiers on her.

"Hold!" she heard behind her before she took her first full step off the main road. She thought to run, even to step into the alleyway and scale a building.

But they were too close. She stopped and turned about, keeping her head down, gaze to the wet cobblestones, as the soldiers came up before her.

"In a quickness to keep away from us?" asked a woman, her accent thick, her use of the language stilted and uneven.

"No, macana," she answered quietly. "You seemed to wish the street cleared before you."

"So you become afraid of us," she said. "Look at me!"

Elysant started to lift her head, and the woman helped her by cupping a hand under her chin and jerking her face up.

"She tried to run," another of the soldiers said. He was smiling—clearly, they were simply looking for an excuse.

The woman standing before her slapped her across the face. "Who are you?"

"Elise," she said, gasping. "I am Elise of . . ."

Elysant was glad when another started talking, for she

193

wasn't sure how to finish that sentence. Entel, she thought, but then reconsidered, for wouldn't that tell them where she was bound?

Another of the group, another woman, stepped up and grabbed at Elysant's staff. "You carry a weapon," she said. "Sidhe do not carry weapons."

Elysant didn't resist the woman's attempt to take it away.

"Just a walking stick," she explained quietly. "For the mud and the snow and the rocky climbs."

The woman snorted at her. The other woman, still standing right before her, slapped her again, to approving laughter from the others.

"Throw it on the roof and let her climb to get it back," one of the men suggested, and the woman started to do just that, which Elysant thought would be a very good thing.

As she set it atop her atlatl throwing stick, though, a bit of it unwrapped, enough to catch the eye of the nearest man.

He said something to the woman in the Xoconai tongue, and though Elysant didn't know the word, she figured it out immediately, for the woman paused and looked at the staff more carefully, even unwrapping the whole thing.

"Xoxo yotl!" the man said.

"Xoxo yotl?" the woman standing before Elysant echoed, and then asked her, and when Elysant didn't immediately reply, she slapped her across the face yet again.

"I do not know," she said. "Xoxo?"

"Xoxo yotl!" the woman said again, and she looked around to her friends for help.

"The green-stemmed plant," a male soldier answered, and to Elysant, he said, "Darkfern?"

"It is a walking stick," she replied, trying to appear very confused.

"Where did you get such a stick as this?" asked the woman who still held the staff.

Elysant looked over at her, thinking of moves that could extract the staff quickly.

But there were six of them.

"On a field in the northwest," she improvised. "Many months ago, before the first snows."

"A field? Just a field?"

"A field where there had been a great battle, I heard," she answered. "A field south of the great monastery."

"The monastery? The one they call St.-Mere-Abelle?"

"She wears the robes of a monk," one of the others said.

The woman before her grabbed a fold of her robe to look more closely. "And this? Are you a monk?"

"No, this too came from the field."

"From a body?"

Elysant nodded eagerly.

That gave the Xoconai a laugh, with one remarking, "See how much these sidhe respect their holy men? They strip their bodies and steal their clothes!"

"The same monk carried this staff?" the woman before her asked.

Elysant shook her head.

"Drag her back to camp," one other said.

"No," answered the woman before Elysant. "Take the staff back to camp. We can get whatever else we need from this one without bothering our commanders."

Half the group ran off, while the remaining three, the two women immediately about Elysant and one man, pushed her farther down the alleyway, out of sight.

"You robbed the body of a fallen Xoconai macana, one of considerable stature to have a staff of darkfern," said the woman who had been addressing her from the start, the one Elysant had come to think of as the leader of the patrol. "This is no Abellican weapon. Xoxo yotl does not grow in these lands."

"There was no body," Elysant answered, chewing her lip to accentuate her apparent nervousness. Truly, Elysant wanted no conflict here, but given their demeanor and the fact that they had taken her staff, she wondered how she might avoid a fight.

When the woman pushed her yet again and the man told the two women to take her robe, Elysant wondered why she'd want to avoid a fight.

The woman beside her, the one who had taken the staff initially, grabbed for her robe.

Elysant's right arm came up and under the woman's reaching arm, rolling it back and down and leaving her defenseless as Elysant disengaged and brought that same hand shooting upward, fingers stiffened like a knife as they jabbed with sudden and wicked force into the Xoconai's neck.

She fell away, gasping, as the woman standing right before Elysant also gasped in shock.

That surprise cost her dearly as Elysant's right hand came

across, slapping her across the face, then across again for a sting-ing backhand, followed immediately by Elysant's thrusting left hand, palm open and rising under the woman's nose, snapping her head back.

The stunned woman offered no resistance as Elysant grabbed her by the edges of the wooden armor breastplate and turned her to the side. Still holding that armor, the fighting monk dropped low and came up high and hard, lifting the Xoconai from the ground and throwing her brutally into the alley wall.

As the Xoconai bounced off the building, Elysant hopped back just a bit, slugged her in the gut to stop her momentum, then hit her again as she lurched forward with a leaping, down-ward left hook that violently snapped her head and sent her hard to the floor.

It had all happened so quickly that the first woman Elysant had struck was still trying to find her breath and the Xoconai man was only then even registering the scene before him.

When Elysant saw him coming forward, she turned and crouched as if to strike the woman she had just decked, but only to get him to alter his angle, leaning forward.

Elysant exploded out of her crouch, leaping up to the wall, running with three quick steps along it, and flipping right over the man as he tried to skid to a stop.

He swung around, rising, just in time to catch a vicious right punch that stunned, stopped, and straightened him.

Elysant leaped again, this time rising into a circle kick that caught the man on the side of his head and sent him flying into the wall. To his credit, he shook it off, mostly, and swung right around to launch a counterattack.

Except, Elysant wasn't there. He blinked in confusion just once and reached for his macana.

But the tooth-lined paddle wasn't there.

He turned to the side suddenly, realizing his error, and saw the strike an instant before his own macana cracked into his face. Stunned, staggering, he tried to back away, but the diminutive monk was with him every step, battering him, tearing his skin, driving him to the ground with vicious strikes of his own weapon.

The first strike when he was on the ground took his consciousness.

The second took his life.

Elysant didn't linger, as the first woman she had struck recovered and tried to flee. Elysant threw the macana into her legs, tangling them and sending her sprawling forward and to the ground. She tried to rise, but the monk was on her, arms coming around in an unbreakable choke hold.

Elysant glanced over at the woman she had decked, who was not moving. She didn't think that one dead, and hoped she wasn't—not yet—because she needed some information.

She closed her eyes now, not wanting to watch the life leave the woman she now held, tightening her grasp, choking the life out of her.

When that was done, she took a javelin from the body and set it against the wall near the remaining Xoconai, whom she rolled over and slapped back to consciousness.

Roughly, uncompromisingly, she hoisted the woman and slammed her against the wall, settling her into a sitting position.

"Where is the camp?" she asked.

The woman blinked as if not understanding.

"And how many soldiers are there?"

No response.

"Is this worth your life?"

"You will kill me anyway."

"Tell me what I need to know and you can walk away. I just want my staff. My staff!"

It went on, back and forth, for some time, until Elysant shrugged. "I will find them without your help, of course, and now I will do more than gather my staff. I will leave none of your friends alive."

She stepped toward the seated woman and lifted the blood-soaked macana. "You didn't have to die," she said.

"East!" the woman blurted, trying to cover up against the anticipated blow.

"East?"

"The camp is east of town, just a mile out."

Elysant held her strike, even tossed the macana aside and stepped to the woman's right, clearing the way to the alleyway entrance. She nodded toward it.

The woman struggled to rise—Elysant even grabbed her arm and helped her—then started off toward the street.

The javelin entered her just below the back of the skull, dropping her immediately to the ground, quite dead.

Was it a good thing or a bad thing to give her that moment of hope? Elysant wondered.

She didn't know.

She didn't know, and surely hated, all of this.

Indeed, as Master Viscenti had warned her, her current situation wasn't war.

It was worse than war.

Macana leader Teyaoch moved nearer the candles burning on the desk in his tent to better gauge the quality of the stave. He rolled the xoxo yotl item over in his hands, noting the sparkling lines of silverel veining it. Thick lines, and many—there was little doubt of the quality of this weapon.

The Xoconai understood the xoxo yotl, the darkfern, quite well. They cultivated it in the southern reaches of Tonoloya, and farmed it to use in their armor, the wooden breastplates that could stop arrows without encumbering the warrior or hindering movement. He had inspected hundreds of his soldiers wearing such green wood as this. And yet, not really such as this, for this piece was truly exceptional.

Teyaoch was certain that he could crack many types of stone with it.

"So light, yet hardly delicate," he whispered to the trio who had brought him this treasure, standing beside him near the entrance to his tent. He wasn't really addressing them, however, but simply marveling at the stave, thinking then that he would be keeping this treasure for himself. He had no idea of where it might have come from, though, for surely if one of the Xoconai macana or mundunugu warriors had carried such a weapon, it would have been whispered through the military. If the sidhe woman had really found it on the field outside St.-Mere-Abelle, then that battle wasn't so long ago, just a decade and a half.

Was it a weapon one of the monks had carried? Or some other warrior of this land which was known then as Honce?

"Well, no matter," he said, and tucked the stave under his arm as he turned about to the couriers. "It belongs to the proper wielders now . . ."

His voice trailed off as he digested the scene before him: a small sidhe woman wearing a monk robe standing immediately before him and holding a pair of macana paddles, with the three who had delivered the stave to him lying on the floor in a bloody heap by the entryway.

He wanted to ask her how that could be possible. Why had he heard nothing?

He was dead before he got the question out of his mouth.

A week later, Elysant stood on the hillside overlooking Entel, which swept down from these foothills to the great Mirianic, an ocean that she had viewed the vast majority of her days since her childhood.

Not Entel, though. She had only rarely been to this city, which was now considered the second city of Honce-the-Bear, though in truth perhaps even more populous than the first city, Ursal. Entel had surpassed Palmaris in size half-a-dozen years before, and had kept growing. Even aside from its relative freedom from the Xoconai compared to Ursal and Palmaris, Entel was certainly more interesting than either of those walled and dreary places, full of gray stone and solemn people, for Entel buzzed and teemed with the colorful and vivacious culture of the Behrenese people.

Elysant knew this place well enough to spot St. Bondabruce, though, for the giant structure was hard to miss, and St. Rontlemore, her destination, farther along.

Picking her path to avoid the former, the new abbess of St. Rontlemore made her way through Entel.

CHAPTER 12

APICHTLI'S PLAY

M elchor couldn't help but shake his head as he read the edict handed to him by Grand Augur Apichtli.

"Well?" Apichtli prompted when the man had clearly finished, but was still just standing there, staring at the parchment.

"Grand Augur . . ." Melchor said, fumbling for a response.

"It would appear that our dear Brother Melchor does not much like your choices," Coyote said from the side of the room, his voice light and his every word mixed with chuckles.

"Would you allow Coyote to properly express thoughts that are your own, abbot?" Apichtli said. "Are you that much the coward, after all?"

"This is a terrible idea," Melchor replied, lowering the parchment and lifting his gaze to match the stare of Apichtli. He cast a sidelong glance Coyote's way, as well.

"I think it a fine idea," Apichtli countered.

"You are ordering every gemstone and every item enchanted with gemstones to be given over to the Xoconai, throughout all the lands."

"Fool abbot, I know what I wrote, of course. I intend to make this coming summer season of Mahtlomeyi one that will be remembered throughout Mayorqua Tonoloya for all time to come."

"Even the soul stones and the sunstones?"

"Of course."

"The soul stones are how we heal the wounds of our flock. The sunstones cure the venom of serpents and spiders."

"I know how you use them," Apichtli said evenly.

"These sacred stones . . ."

Coyote snorted with derision and spat, "Sacred?"

"Do not ever call them that again, if you have any thoughts of keeping your neck at its present length, abbot," Apichtli warned. "Sacred is Scathmizzane alone in Mayorqua Tonoloya. When our Glorious Gold blesses these items of power, then and only then are they to be referred to as sacred, and never from the mouth of an unbeliever, and particularly not ever from a sidhe."

"This, these stones, are our tradition, the very foundation of the Abellican Church," Melchor protested. "You agreed that we could continue at least some of our practices and prayers."

"You can."

"These are our practices and prayers."

"They are also your weapons."

Coyote snorted at that, then met Melchor's predictable glare with an easy smile.

"Not the soul stone or the sunstone," Melchor said. "They are not weapons."

Apichtli cocked an eyebrow skeptically.

"Not the minor ones, perhaps," said Coyote, who had become very well-versed in the gemstone magic of the Abellicans. "But your strongest brothers can put the more powerful soul stones to use in sending their spirits across the land, and even in stealing control of another's body. I have seen it, Abbot Melchor, so please do not deny it and call me a liar. I do not like being called a liar."

Melchor pointedly turned away from the dangerous warrior and focused squarely on the augur. "You will cause great unrest with this. Not just among the monks, but among the people, who look to us for their care."

"All the stones shall be surrendered," Apichtli replied. "Perhaps if you comply properly and quickly, I will be convinced to return to you the least soul stone and perhaps even the weakest of your sunstones. Perhaps that will be the next edict sent out to the city sovereigns and augurs and the monasteries and abbeys of your church."

"I pray you amend this edict to offer such hope."

Apichtli narrowed his gray eyes and glared at the man. "We have already had this discussion, abbot. I grow weary of explaining the way of things to you."

"You had your executions," Melchor replied in answer to the last time Grand Augur Apichtli threatened to take the stones.

"The edicts are being delivered even now throughout Quixi Tonoloya," Coyote explained rather gleefully. "You are likely among the last of the abbots to receive one."

Abbot Melchor didn't respond, his jaw hanging open. Coyote

liked the look on his face, could imagine the man's thoughts spinning wildly, trying to find some way out of all this, regretting all his concessions here in Ursal, and the many times he had told the rebellious-minded among the sidhe to stand down with his assurances that all would be well.

Truly Coyote's respect of the Grand Augur soared at that moment. The older man was showing true strength here, pushing the boundaries of Xoconai control, tightening the fences around the sidhe into smaller and smaller boxes. Apichtli had seized the moment. From the time the Xoconai leadership had agreed to simply ignore that unbeatable fortress of St.-Mere-Abelle, the Grand Augur had pushed and pushed and pushed.

This was no longer in any sense a cooperative relationship between the glorious Xoconai and the filthy sidhe. The Xoconai armies here in the east were no longer even an occupation in Coyote's eyes. It was a completed conquest. The sidhe of Honce-the-Bear were broken, forevermore, buried under the truth of Quixi Tonoloya. And Mayorqua Tonoloya, the Golden Empire from Sea to Sea, was more than a name.

It was a reality, and almost certainly a lasting one. Cochcal Yaqui, the man named Coyote, smiled in that moment of open proclamation, and silently determined that he would strike terror in the hearts of all who dared try to resist the inevitable dominance of the Xoconai.

"They are no more than days behind me," Ataquixt told Keri. In only a week, the ranger had ridden across the land from St.-Mere-Abelle to this hillock outside of Whispervale.

"You're certain of this?"

"My contacts to City Sovereign Avitl of Ursal hinted to me that the order to march will begin very soon. The edict for the removal of every gemstone and every item made magical by them has already traveled the lands, to all the larger towns and cities. That is done. And now, it seems as if the Grand Augur Apichtli turns his eyes to the smaller villages, including Whispervale and her five sisters."

Keri sighed and cast her gaze to the northwest, toward Ursal, unseen in the distance. "Perhaps the Xoconai who come here will understand that we're best left alone and pose no threat to their empire."

"I expect that Avitl may be sent here eventually," Ataquixt replied. "Apichtli has hinted rather overtly that he will assume the post as Ursal's city sovereign in addition to his oversight of the whole of Quixi Tonoloya as Grand Augur. He does not much care for Avitl, and relegating her to a handful of communities that matter not at all to him would be one of his typical plays.

"But that will be in the future, no doubt," Ataquixt warned. "Apichtli will want to know that the land is fully tamed. It will be Cochcal . . . General Yaqui who leads the macana and mundunugu here. Beware that one, my friend. He is called the Coyotl by Apichtli—Coyote in your tongue—and he earns the name with ferocity and cunning."

Keri's face tightened. The fingers on her right hand began

to roll and flex, and she felt the call of her magical tattoo, one she had given herself with gemstone powder, tiger's paw and wedstone, to transform her arm into that of a cloud leopard just to remind Ataquixt and herself that she could.

"Coyote understands Abellican magic as well as any of the Xoconai," Ataquixt warned.

"I will not ever be confused with an Abellican."

"But your magic is much the same—indeed, the most notorious villain in the recent history of Honce-the-Bear was a monk known for transforming his limbs into those of a tiger."

"Marcalo De'Unnero, aye," Keri said, and relaxed her hand. "They sing of him in the taverns in their ballads of the DemonWars. De'Unnero is not cast in a favorable light."

"Beware Coyote," Ataquixt insisted. "Promise me that."

Keri nodded her agreement. "I'm done with battle, done with murder, done with blood."

"That is good, but understand in your heart and soul that Coyote most certainly is not. Give him a reason to make examples of the folk of this area, and they will hang by the dozen or melt to gel within the golden mirrors, or face death in an even more dishonorable and painful manner. Coyote's only play is brutality."

"We will give him no reason, then."

"Thank you." Ataquixt came forward and reached out to hook his hand over Keri's shoulder, pulling her close for a hug. "We were so close to having a better world for all," he whispered when he had her tight.

Keri kissed him on the cheek and pulled back to arm's length.

"I'll settle for peace in my little corner of it," she said. "For me, for Connie, for our boys, for our friends."

"And for Kenziel?"

Keri laughed at him. "You still can'no say it right. Kenzie."

"Such a silly name."

"The one time we ever discussed his name, you asked me to change it to Tlazohootaloni!" she said with a laugh, purposely mispronouncing half the syllables.

"One who is loved!" Ataquixt protested.

"Aye, and a true Bearman name, if e'er I heard one!" Keri proclaimed with great and exaggerated sarcasm.

"You are not Bearman."

"Even in my homeland, such a name'd bring giggles and slings, and then, oh to be sure, would bring suspicion," Keri reminded him. "And how might this Coyote view the child of a woman who was not Xoconai wearing such a name?"

"How will Coyote view Kenzie in any case?" Ataquixt asked seriously.

Keri, too, sobered at the unsettling thought. "He is still a boy," she replied. "His voice is that of a young girl. He has no hair on his chest or face."

"It is not the hair that worries me."

"No Xoconai coloring, either," Keri assured him.

"It doesn't show until . . ." He paused, fumbling for the word. *"Manayot."*

"The beginning or the end of the change?"

Ataquixt stared at her curiously.

"The change from boyhood to manhood," she clarified. She thought of her earlier conversation with Connie. Kenzie's colors were coming in, hinting of them at least, undeniably—she could only hope that he was near the end of their process.

"During the change, yes," Ataquixt confirmed. "The shades will probably be subtle at first, mostly in the reddening of the nose. By the end, he will have full plumage, and I would be surprised if Kenzie's colors are anything less than glorious."

Keri smiled at the not-so-subtle boast, but it was short-lived, as was Ataquixt's wry grin.

"Kenzie will never pass as full Xoconai," she said. "His skin is not golden, but darker. Olive, like mine. His hair not flaxen, but black like mine."

"His eyes are light, though, and amber, unlike yours. Indeed, unlike any person I have seen in this land."

"Aye, 'tis a source of many whispers in the village," Keri admitted. "If his color comes in, even if his eyes shine brilliantly as you're hoping, Kenzie won't pass as full Xoconai. That I know."

Ataquixt rubbed a hand over his cheeks and chin pensively and worriedly. Such children as Kenzie were not unknown in the region, as some had been conceived in the earliest days after the battle on the mountain and the truce of cooperation between the Xoconai and the folk of Honce.

"Children like Kenzie were welcomed once," the ranger said. "They were seen as a sign of a better future for all, for both our peoples."

"Was that not our hope?"

"It still is."

"Kenzie's been treated the same as any other boy in Whispervale," Keri assured him. She felt like she was replaying her conversation with Connie, only with her taking Connie's role—only then did she come to understand how fearful she truly was for the future of her dear Kenzie. "I do not believe for a heartbeat that treatment here will change, colors or not."

"Things are changing in the wider world. For people like Grand Augur Apichtli, there is no place for half sidhe in his beautiful domain of Quixi Tonoloya."

"Sidhe," Keri mouthed quietly. How the remark pained her! She had used that word when she was young to describe the vicious mountain goblins, but to hear the pejorative used to describe her beautiful boy was particularly galling. She knew that Ataquixt was just being honest with her—he was always honest with her—and telling her the truth of how this Apichtli person would view things.

"No place or a lesser place?" she asked.

"Lesser, but perhaps even least."

"I will make a place for him, then," Keri said defiantly. "That was my promise to you those years ago, and it is my promise again, for Kenzie."

"I do not doubt you at all. But take care and beware Coyote. If you can get through his reign here, should he indeed come to Whispervale, the transition to Avitl will be far easier."

In reply, Keri lifted her shirt to show her belly ring, set with magical gemstones, and said, "I do'no think anything will be easy."

The ranger's expression acknowledged to her that he understood the depth of Keri's dilemma.

"How long?" Keri asked, dropping the shirt.

"I do not believe they have left Ursal quite yet. Even if the order is given this day, as was hinted, you will have a few days."

"Have you looked upon Kenzie?"

"I will, if you are agreed, from the hillock behind your home, as I've done before."

"I will set him to work in the garden, but perhaps it is time for you to come down from that hillock."

He stared at her as if frozen.

"Perhaps it is time for him to meet you. Perhaps it is time for him to go with you." She felt her knees wobbling as she spoke the words, heard the quiver in her voice. She desperately wanted to retract that second statement, even the first. But how could she in the new reality of Quixi Tonoloya?

"Go with me where?" Ataquixt asked. "I must return to Ursal and the side of City Sovereign Avitl. My oath does not end, however the world spins about me. I told you this when first we spoke of—"

"I know," Keri cut him short. "I know. 'Twas our agreement, on my demand as much as your own necessity. And you're doing more than ever I could have asked of you. I am just so terribly afraid."

He pulled her close for another hug, one they both needed. "As am I," he said quietly. This time, he pushed her back to arm's length and stared at her earnestly. "But I have no doubt that you, the brave and powerful hero of that distant land, of all the lands, will do whatever needs to be done."

Keri smiled and winced all at once. She felt like dark shadows were rising around her, pushing her back to a place of anger and fear. She thought of a long-ago day, a dark moment, when she discovered the lair of the demon Fossa, and could smell the stench of death so thickly that there seemed no end to it, no escape from it.

As, she feared, there was no escape for her from who she was and what she was.

She knew what she had to do first, in any case.

She had to dance.

The ranger crouched in the brush atop the hillock, unable to contain his smile when Kenzie walked around the side of the house, pushing a wheelbarrow full of dirt and manure. The boy moved to the garden, whistling a happy song.

He was a slight thing, to be sure, but there was no missing the budding strength in his arms when he lifted the shovel and began his work.

It took all Ataquixt's willpower to stay low and out of sight, for he desperately wanted to run down and introduce himself, to pat this boy hard on the back, to give him a great hug.

But he could not, and he should not, he knew, for all their sakes—even above the agreement he had made with Kenzie's mother those years before. If the world had continued along its expected course after the treaty, then things now might well be different, the ranger knew. But the world spun of its own accord, and had now circled into a reality that Ataquixt had feared since the Xoconai had crossed the mountains.

As it stood now under the auspices of Grand Augur Apichtli, the fewer interactions Kenzie had with the Xoconai—with *any* Xoconai—the better.

Even with the disappointment, Ataquixt retained his smile as he crouched there behind the milkweed and watched the graceful movements of this boy, this young man, shoveling cow pies.

"Someday," Ataquixt silently mouthed, silently vowed, and he melted away into the shadows without a whisper of sound or the flutter of a leafy branch.

CHAPTER 13

THE STORM FRONT

"You know my demands of you," Grand Augur Apichtli told Coyote. "Gather an entire brigade, one heavy with mundunugu. Take them to the south and tame all the towns between Ursal and the mountains. Collect the gemstones, as I have decreed, and make sure that those few villages offer no resistance to the changes that have come to Quixi Tonoloya. Collect servants, young and strong sidhe. Press them into service and secure the towns fully. Tame them without mercy, but try not to kill too many, as those farmlands will be needed. Hold through the winter and meet me in Ursal when the snows recede."

"With great pleasure, Grand Augur," Coyote answered, and his smile confirmed that he had been waiting for this order for a long time, waiting for the reins to be thrown aside. "What latitude have I?"

"Full. Except, no children," he told the fierce warrior. "Press into service those betwixt and between, not yet adult enough to cause problems for our captains, not too young to be useless aboard."

"How many?"

"As many as you need. I am sure that you will use your best judgment."

An entire brigade, Coyote mused. Fifteen hundred mundunugu riders and macana foot soldiers. He would sweep the small towns in the southland in short order.

"I will send along augurs to follow your glorious march and tend to the tedious work of governing these hamlets. I trust you will mark your progress appropriately. Appoint from those augurs city sovereigns to take control of each town," Apichtli told him, answering the question before it was asked. "And leave them enough macana soldiers to keep the sidhe properly cowed."

Coyote smiled at that, understanding the Grand Augur's meaning all too well.

He would mark his trail with crucified sidhe, with great pleasure.

Soon after, Abbot Melchor stood quite still, trying to hide his nervousness. He was alone in the room with Apichtli and Coyote, and no good had come from the meetings with these two on the previous few occasions.

"I am told that you have identified a handful of Xoconai who might become proficient with your magical stones," Grand Augur Apichtli said.

Melchor sighed and nodded.

"Then they will go with Coyote, and with you," Apichtli announced.

It took Melchor a moment to digest that before he looked up, his eyes wide with surprise.

"Oh yes, abbot . . ." Apichtli paused and assumed a pensive pose. "Hmm," he said a few times, before clarifying, "Perhaps we should simply call you Brother Melchor now, for I have decided that you are formally relieved of your post as Abbot of St. Honce."

"Only Father Abbot can—" Melchor started to protest, but he stopped short under Apichtli's withering glare.

"Do I really have to explain to you yet again how all of this works?" Apichtli asked.

"No."

"No? Just no?"

"No, Grand Augur," the suddenly former abbot replied.

"Good. You serve Coyote now, and you will do so loyally, and with the recognition and understanding that your work here will help lead to a better end for your people than they deserve. Perhaps it will even deliver to us a day when your people are no longer simply filthy sidhe in the eyes of my people. Perhaps one day far ahead, we will even come to think of you as humans like we Xoconai, though surely of an inferior breed. But this is your path, and you have no other, and not just for your own sake."

Melchor swallowed hard and considered the last interrogation Coyote and Apichtli had put him through, one that had become quite personal, and during which, under the press of that terrible golden headband, he had been forced to admit his own deceptions and sins.

"Your mistress will be well cared for," Apichtli assured him. "Your two daughters will live as freely and happily as any sidhe might know in Quixi Tonoloya. Unless you cross me. Unless I am informed that you did not serve Coyote with all your heart and your magic. Do I need to describe to you what will happen to them if I am informed of any mischief on your part?"

"No, Grand Augur."

CHAPTER 14

BURIED TREASURE

K eri fell into the dance as completely as she ever had, her mind slipping the bonds of the troubles brewing all about her and becoming clear within the notes of the communal song of the witches. She didn't see the individual lanterns burning, just the maze of lights turning circles within the perimeters of the others.

She felt light in her heart, as if no darkness could follow her to this place. She felt removed from the world, and basked in that sweet dream.

She felt as if she was a young girl again, being taken away by the mood and the breeze and the sounds of the night.

But she didn't fall into the magic.

She didn't bring forth the heat or the cold, or the magical lightness of being, of floating, of flying.

The witches sang and danced in circles of their own, and rotated in a larger circle altogether, the seven women twirling, arms out wide as they held small lanterns in each hand, the light and sheer fabric of their loose smocks flying about them in ghostly fashion.

Beautiful and harmonious, lifting the spirit and the heart, the music and the weaving lanterns carried the night, and carried the seven dancers for a long, long while.

Until they neared the end of the last dance.

Then it was just a common sense of pervading sadness, for all seven, for Keri had informed them that this would be their last dance for the foreseeable future, perhaps forever. To a one, they viscerally felt and understood that which they were about to lose. For all of them—for the women born in Whispervale who had known nothing but this village for their entire lives; for the woman known to the village as Keridven, who had lived in Whispervale for a dozen years now, and had been dancing like this since she was a child decades before; for Connie, who had come to Whispervale less than three years after Keri, guided by a friend to find the woman she had known in another place long ago—these dances under the moon and stars had been a true blessing, as holy and spiritually uplifting as any meeting the Abellican monk serving Whispervale had organized in his tiny chapel in the town, as much a blessing as a good harvest, as pleasurable as lovemaking.

Because this dance Keri and Connie had taught to these village women was just that, lovemaking to life itself.

There were many tears when the dance ended, with hugs all around and promises that they would find a way to do this again, and assurances that the new Xoconai city sovereign coming to claim Whispervale for this proclaimed empire of Mayorqua Tonoloya surely wouldn't be as nasty as his reputation.

No, of course not. He couldn't be.

"It was not as . . . magical as our last dance," Keri admitted, her voice breaking the quiet of the night so suddenly that it surprised even her.

"Why was that?" asked Ethedred, the oldest of the village women, a sweet widow only a few years older than Connie. She was barely into middle age but had completely white hair, though it was still thick and lustrous.

"Aye, why were we earthbound and without changing winds?" said young Shivahn, always light-footed and always smiling.

"And where was the music?" Ethedred asked.

"I heard the music," Molle, who was one of the twins, and Connie said together.

"The dance is different of its own accord," Keri answered firmly, and she held up her hands to prevent interruption. "We do'no know what will happen up here when we call to the spirits of the night—and that is our mystery and our secret. I do'no know why our last dance was so special, almost as if a web of magic fell upon us and lightened us in our every step, and lifted us higher in every jump, and guided us so perfectly. I do'no know, but this I do know: we mustn't be telling of our dances, and mostly, we mustn't be telling of that last dance. Aye, there was something special about it. We're all knowing that. But it's something that none who weren't here would understand, or likely accept."

"I want to feel it again," said Ethedred, brushing her white hair back from her face. "Like this night, aye, but more so, like the last one."

"As do I," Keri answered.

"Aye," Molle and Malle chimed in agreement, a sentiment echoed by the one remaining Jilly in the troupe, a woman who had been dancing with Keri for most of those dozen years now.

"As do we all," Connie cut in. "But hear me well, my sisters of the dance. I've been twirling under the moon and the stars all my life, and only once have I felt as if some great magic had fallen over me, over us all. Only that one dance we all last shared. Hold the memory, I advise. Hold it tight in your thoughts and your heart, and make of it a part of yourself that'll not ever fade."

"I know I will," said Keri.

Connie moved over to Keri and took her hand, and Keri flashed her a smile of gratitude. The others milled about, collecting their clothes, then walked from the small lea, saying their goodbyes and words of appreciation for these two women from another land who had led them in this joyous experience.

"Aren't you coming, then?" the white-haired woman asked over her shoulder when she and the two walking with her were a few steps away.

"Presently," Keri answered. "I just want to enjoy the quiet."

"We just want to enjoy the quiet," Connie corrected suggestively, pulling Keri close and resting her head on her partner's shoulder.

"Well played," Keri whispered to her when the others nodded and giggled and moved off into the darkness, down the trails leading to the night fires of Whispervale.

"You are really doin' this?"

"Have I a choice?"

"Even the wedstone?" she whispered to her old friend from another place, another world, it seemed.

Keri nodded. "You heard well what Ataquixt told me. We mustn't take this Coyote lightly. Carelessness'll bring catastrophe."

"I wish they were all like Ataquixt."

Keri just smiled and nodded, though she knew something Connie did not: Ataquixt was a ranger, trained by the Touel'alfar. Keri knew about rangers—she was probably the only person from the distant lands of the Ayamharas Plateau who did—and so she understood the depth and truth of Ataquixt's motivations here. He was Xoconai, his bright red and blue and white face markings as clear as any other, but his loyalty was to no particular culture, but to the wider world about and all the sentient peoples who inhabited it.

Connie continued to smile at the mention of the Xoconai scout, and Keri surely understood her feelings here. Ataquixt had saved her after the fall of the crystal cave on Fireach Speuer. Connie had been in full flight from the battle that had seen her mountain village destroyed and her sisters of the Coven slaughtered, and the ranger had found her and guided her to Whispervale to be with her old companion.

Even back then, Ataquixt had warned the two women of the coming darkness, and now, it seemed to be reaching its inevitable state, its dark tendrils stretching even here in the remote villages of the Belt-and-Buckle foothills.

"All those years ago, he told us," said Connie. "I believed him, surely, wary as I was then with the war so fresh in all our minds. That edge has dulled with the passing years. I hope that I can gain that edge again now."

Keri didn't disagree. Even after the whispers of the Xoconai consolidating their victory had begun filtering into Whispervale in recent years, and more particularly in recent months, nothing had really changed here in these villages. Even Manowhey, the then-young and studious Abellican monk who served the folk of the six small foothill towns, had been able to keep his chapel operating without much worry.

But now the whispers were growing more and more troubling. Bad news came continually from Ursal, stories of an army gathering and marching, a formal decree regarding the Abellican gemstones, word of new and severe leadership in the great city not so far to the north.

The thought of it made the hair on the back of Keri's neck stand up. She had seen the truth of Scathmizzane, the Glorious Gold of the Xoconai. She had seen the shadows beneath that shining exterior of Scathmizzane, the blinding rot of a demon posing as a benevolent god.

Indeed, she had rent that shining exterior to shreds, revealing and destroying the façade of a god who was truly no more than another of the many demons that haunted the world of Corona.

But she hadn't destroyed the demon itself, apparently. Nay, for the demons of this world were eternal. One of the monks at St.-Mere-Abelle had told her that demons were the physical manifestation of the evil that was in the hearts of men.

She knew well that there was no shortage of evil in the hearts of men.

"You heard Headman Broadshirt's reading of Grand Augur Apichtli's decree declaring that the magic Ring Stones of the Abellicans be confiscated," Keri reminded her friend. "You know well that the Xoconai would consider my own cache contraband under that order. I fear not what they would do to me if they found them, but . . ."

"But our children," Connie finished, and Keri nodded grimly.

All three were prime age for impressment into the Xoconai service, something else Ataquixt had warned. Keri wasn't about to give this new overlord any excuse to harm her children.

She fished about under her pile of clothing and produced a small wooden box she had concealed there, then began reverently removing her jewelry, her rings and earrings, ear cuff, and anklet. Last came her belly ring. She felt naked when she removed that last piercing, when she severed contact with these magical pieces that had become as second nature to her, a part of her.

On impulse, Keri reached back into the box and collected the belly ring. She carefully removed the external strands holding the gemstones, then put the wedstone base back into her navel. She slipped it in deeper, then closed her eyes and called upon the healing magic, sealing the skin above it. The wire was fully inside her skin now, and she could feel it, could feel the magic keenly.

The wedstone, the stone of healing.

She hoped she wouldn't need it, but given the circumstances, she couldn't dare to be without it.

Carefully, she buried the box under the exposed root of a tall oak.

"Remember this place," she told Connie. "If something happens to me, if I am lost to you and to our children, then these precious jewels all fall to you."

"Nothing will happen to you," Connie replied, but both knew that she was only saying it as a measure of comfort that they both needed to hear.

They dressed quietly and started away, but Keri, for some reason she didn't know, thought to hide her shift in a knothole in the oak.

"If we can'no come back here, I'd prefer not to have the reminder so close at hand," she explained.

Connie nodded sadly, then moved up and stuffed her shift into the same hole.

Arm in arm, the two women went home.

The echoing calls of golden horns shattered the morning hush in Whispervale, rousing the citizens, many from their beds, and bringing them running to their windows or out onto their front porches. Excited children rushed out to the streets to see what was happening, and fearful parents chased them and dragged them back.

Mundunugu warriors appeared, trotting up the road, then

turning their lizard mounts left and right to flank the town. On and on they came, encircling the main village wholly, and up the road came the macana marchers, all splendid in the gold-painted darkfern breastplates and feathered helms, javelin tips gleaming in the morning light. Three squares of several score of soldiers in each marched right down the main road of the town, breaking with great symmetry to line the streets, thus putting themselves between the townsfolk and the wagons rolling in from the north. These were mostly packed with kegs and sacks, but with one driven by Xoconai drivers and carrying a group of six, three in Abellican robes and three in the decorated red robes and gold shirts of Xoconai augurs.

That wagon was preceded by a lone rider, tall and lean. He had the hood of his cloak dropped back onto his shoulders, his bald head shining in the sunlight, and a pair of thick curved-blade swords crisscrossed on his back.

His clothing was nothing special or ornamental, his boots muddy from the road, his long brown cloak threadbare, but the way he sat in the saddle and the way the macana warriors to either side about him stiffened as he passed left little doubt to the onlookers that this man was in charge of the force that had come to their town.

From the porch of a small cottage off to the side of the main boulevard, behind the planters that covered the railings of the decking, five such witnesses understood the gravity of the moment more, perhaps, than anyone else in Whispervale.

Forewarned by Ataquixt, Keri watched with great interest.

Connie kept glancing at her for support, she knew, and she offered many comforting nods and whispers of "It will be all right."

She squeezed the shoulders of Kenzie, who stood before her, then reached out to the side to do so to Dafydd, while Connie wrapped her arms around the broad chest of the older son, Carwyn.

"In the wagon, those are holy men, like Brother Manowhey," Dafydd noted.

"Abellican brothers," Keri said. "From St. Honce, likely." She started with surprise when the wagon crossed the entry to the side street, barely twenty steps from their porch, for she recognized one of the brothers as Abbot Melchor. She thought of Ataquixt's information and the decree read by the headman of Whispervale, and was glad indeed that she had buried her precious gemstones far from the town.

The rider leading the wagon held up his hand and the soldiers, all of them, rider and marcher alike, came to an abrupt and complete halt.

"Remain in your homes this morning," he ordered the townsfolk. "I am Coyote, now sovereign of this town and the five sister villages. Go in and consider this truth above all else. Expend your curse words and spit your complaints to one another, this very morning. Get them all out, sidhe. Throw them from your lips and from your thoughts, because they will not be tolerated when the sun begins its descent. From this moment forward, you will recognize that you are subjects of Mayorqua Tonoloya, the Golden Empire of Scathmizzane." He paused and looked all around, and every person who fell under his gaze, even the five on the porch in the back of the side street, felt as if he was speaking to them personally.

Keri felt the hairs on the back of her neck standing up. Again, Ataquixt's warnings echoed in her thoughts.

This one was formidable.

"Who leads this town?" he demanded.

Eyes shifted, heads turned, looking to a porch on the grandest house, a two-story affair, on the main boulevard, where stood an older man with a finely trimmed white beard and thin white hair.

That man, Headman Paddy Broadshirt, glanced about, composing himself, then replied in a solid voice, "I do."

Coyote looked around, nodding, then settled his gaze back on the headman. "Vacate your quarters at once," he ordered. "Take nothing, just leave. Your house will serve as my own."

"Le . . . le . . . leave?" Paddy stammered. "Where am I—"

"I care not at all. Take your family and leave the house. Now."

Paddy harrumphed and crossed his arms over his chest, which was still broad and strong despite his age.

Coyote raised his hand, and every macana warrior near to the headman's house grunted "Hoi!," shifted their left leg forward into a readied crouch, shields coming before them, javelins dropping into notches on those bucklers, and all aiming straight at Headman Paddy Broadshirt.

"Need I ask again?" Coyote warned.

He didn't need to, no.

Early that afternoon, Paddy Broadshirt was escorted back to his house by mundunugu riders, lizards flanking him and hissing at him every step of the way. The shaken Whispervale headman was shoved roughly across the front threshold into the sitting room of the large house, where Coyote, Abbot Melchor, and the three Xoconai augurs were waiting, sitting in a semicircle of chairs, facing a sixth seat that was empty. Paddy took a step toward it, but stopped under the withering glare of Coyote.

"You have not yet earned that seat," Coyote told him. "Perhaps someday."

Paddy glanced around nervously.

"You have not earned the right to look away from me for even a single heartbeat," Coyote said.

Paddy stood very still and stared at the imposing warrior.

Coyote turned to Melchor and nodded, and the monk produced and read the edict of Grand Augur Apichtli.

"Who in this town possesses Abellican magic?" Coyote asked with great calm, unnerving calm.

"Brother Manowhey has a chapel here," Paddy explained. "He has a soul stone and one other . . . one for poison, I think."

"Sunstone," Melchor quietly told Coyote.

"He travels the six villages, tending the wounds of . . ."

"Did I ask that?"

Paddy shut up.

Coyote leaned forward, locking the frightened headman's gaze. "Is he here in Whispervale now?"

Paddy's head began to nod rapidly. "He . . . was. Yes."

"In the chapel?"

The headman's head bobbed even faster.

Coyote placed his hands on the arms of his chair and shot up from his seat, the others fast following. The great warrior held out his hand toward the door, inviting Paddy to lead the way.

Many of the villagers watched the procession to the chapel, none more intently than Keri. It wasn't hard for her to figure out that this was no benign visit, no meeting of etiquette. The look on the face of the Abbot Melchor alone had made that quite clear. She didn't really know Melchor, and hoped he knew nothing of her true identity, of who she had once been, and hoped even more that he wouldn't recognize her. She had seen the young monk many times when she had been in Ursal in the early days of cooperation between the Xoconai and the folk of Honce. He was known as Master Melchor then, not the abbot of St. Honce, but very young for such a lofty title. Even then, it was clear Melchor would succeed Ohwan as the lead monk in Ursal.

She had met him formally only once, when Master Marlboro Viscenti had introduced them, and Keri breathed a great sigh of relief recalling that now. For Viscenti had introduced her as Keridven of Whispervale, and not the identity she had abandoned—and at that time, had abandoned for only a couple of months. Viscenti had not much liked Keri when she had gone to St.-Mere-Abelle that one time during the war, even demanding of the Father Abbot that she be stripped of her gemstone jewelry. But as the events had unfolded, she came to believe that the monk was coming to appreciate her, somewhat at least. He had introduced her to Melchor with high praise, and had whispered high praise of Melchor to Keri, as well.

But that young master had been full of smiles, Keri recalled, as she thought back and considered how pleased she had been to hear of his ascension to abbot of St. Honce. The man she had met had not worn any scowls like the one now upon his face as he determinedly pushed Headman Paddy Broadshirt toward the chapel door, ordering him to gain entrance.

When the group disappeared into the chapel, most of the onlookers went about their business. Keri spent a moment letting them disperse to their duties, then collected her basket, glad that she had brought it with her this afternoon, for she had come out to pick some blueberries.

And the blueberry patches were to the side of the village chapel, lining the graveyard.

All smiles, acting carefree, the small woman skipped along, nodding at anyone who noted her. She moved past the front left corner of the chapel, then halfway along the jagged side of the building, which was constructed with overlapping angled walls, so that the whole of the building somewhat resembled an evergreen tree, the symbol of the Abellicans, lying on the ground.

Keri glanced back to make sure that no one—no Xoconai soldiers, at least—was watching, then rushed up under a slightly opened window. Before she even got there, she heard the harsh words being thrown at Brother Manowhey by the man called Coyote.

"Good abbot, reason with him. This is my charge here in the six villages," Manowhey responded.

Keri went up to her tiptoes and peered in. The interior nave was fairly narrow here, as they were near the back of the building—the top of the tree. Manowhey stood with his hands folded before his sternum, shuffling nervously, his back to the altar. Before him stood Coyote, and only then did Keri appreciate the gravity of the warrior. He was tall, but the way he hunched up his shoulders to tower over another made him seem even taller. For his shoulders were very wide, and seemed even more so because of his narrow waist. His arms were chiseled as if from stone, muscles taut, perpetually clenched, and his face remained locked in an endless scowl in the shadow of a thick and protruding brow below his bald pate. His large nose angled forward from that brow, then dropped straight, beaming with bloodred intensity, and his eyes were set so severely that it occurred to Keri that the man never blinked.

He was ever on his guard, always set in the moment before a battle.

Behind Coyote, Paddy Broadshirt sat on one of the benches,

head down, hands in front of him as if in prayer. Next to him in the aisle between the benches stood Abbot Melchor, his face impassive, his right hand up before him, palm up, cradling a red stone that Keri believed to be garnet, which he tapped with a golden wand held lightly in his left hand. Back toward the wider hall, three Xoconai augurs moved about the benches and the anterooms, and to Keri's surprise, they too were holding similar red gems and golden wands.

The woman remembered Ataquixt's warnings regarding the confiscation of all magic. A person trained in using the gems could sense the vibrations of magic through a garnet as clearly as they might see a tree in the sunlight or hear the call of a night bird. Were these Xoconai augurs learning to use the Abellican Ring Stones?

But still, she didn't quite understand what she was seeing. She had thought that magic could be detected only when it was in use—at least, she herself could only sense it through a garnet at those times.

She thought of the mirrors used by the people of the west, polished golden sheets through which armies could march to far-distant locations. Xoconai magic was based in gold. Was it possible that the conquerors were combining the powers of their two schools? Keri had to work hard to steady her breathing, and was glad indeed that she had buried her cache of enchanted jewelry.

"Just these two gems? That is all you possess?" Melchor asked, holding his hand toward Manowhey.

"Abbot, please. Without the soul stone, how am I to treat the wounds so often seen among the folk? Or the illnesses? Without the sunstone, how am I to cure the venom from the snakebites and spider bites that are all too common here where the hill vipers and hourglass blacks are plentiful?"

Keri ducked down below the window, her hand moving reflexively to her belly, where she had kept her own soul stone, tucked under the skin of her navel. Certainly, she understood the benefit of such a gem to the folk in these secluded villages, where injuries and disease were indeed common occurrences. Brother Manowhey, feeble as he was in the use of the magic, was seen as a hero in all six towns.

"Just these two?" Melchor asked again.

As Manowhey began to respond, he was interrupted by one of the Xoconai augurs, calling out in the language of the west, which Keri had learned to speak quite fluently, "There is more here."

"He lies," Coyote accused in the common tongue of the land.

"Brother?" Abbot Melchor said.

Keri went back on her tiptoes and peered in. Manowhey looked confused, his arms out wide, palms up, as if to show that he had nothing more.

"Just the two," he stammered.

"Search him," Coyote ordered.

"Not on him," the augur explained, again in the western language. "Over to the left, by the wall." That man pointed his golden wand toward the wall, in Keri's general direction.

The woman dropped immediately, panic rising, her hand going reflexively to her belly and the wedstone. She realized then that she was likely the source being sensed by the augur! She paused only for a moment at the base of the wall, then slipped along it toward the head of the chapel.

Brother Manowhey cried out suddenly and sharply, followed by the growl of Coyote. Then came the screaming and the beating.

Keri ran full-out to the back corner of the building and turned behind the gardens to flee into the shadows of the tree line.

She didn't stop running until she was back at her house.

"I must be gone," she told Connie, who was the only one there at the time, the boys having gone to their daily work.

"Be gone where?"

Her shaky voice and movements told Keri that she understood the seriousness here.

"Anywhere. I'll not be far. But they will find me if I remain. They can sense the magic."

"You buried the jewelry."

Keri shook her head, lifted her shirt, and tapped her belly. "My wedstone."

"Remove—"

"And even this, perhaps," Keri interrupted, holding forth her hand to display the leopard-paw image tattooed there.

"They can sense it even when you're not using it?"

"I do'no know, but I believe they can."

"Keri!"

"Yourself and the boys—but not Kenzie—need to be out and about the town, listening to all the whispers."

"Not Kenzie? He's not really showing his colors yet."

Keri replied with a look of fear, and was glad indeed when Connie didn't press the point; the woman just nodded her agreement.

"I can'no risk being around, for all your sakes. I'll not be far, and I'll be watching, but you tell any and all, even the boys, that I've gone away for a bit." She considered it for just a moment. "To Ursal, tell them, to trade some food for new blacksmithing tools as a summer solstice gift for Carwyn."

Connie rubbed her face and looked around as if expecting the Xoconai soldiers to burst into the room at any moment.

"I'll not be far," Keri promised again. She came forward and kissed Connie on the cheek, then hugged her close and whispered, "Keep our boys safe," into her ear.

Then she was gone, running out behind the house and through the woods, up to the same hillock where Ataquixt had viewed his son. She paused there, wishing the ranger was still about, again thinking that it would have been better for him to take Kenzie far from this place.

She didn't really know her next move. Should she go and retrieve her gemstones, arm herself with the full breadth of her formidable power? If it came, at last, to a fight . . .

Keri sighed at the mere thought of it. Yes, she was powerful. But there was an army of enemies here, including the dangerous Coyote, trained Xoconai mundunugu and macana, and at least augurs and an Abellican abbot with magical powers beyond her understanding.

She melted deeper into the forest to think things through. She didn't know what to do, and the mere thought of becoming again that woman who had spent years battling demons and waging war, who had killed so many with her terrible magic, left her slumped against a tree, shaking and crying.

CHAPTER 15

THE EXCUSE

The summer sun was still warm, the sailing pleasant enough, and Grand Augur Apichtli was in fine spirits indeed when his boat slid into the Palmaris dock, where he was greeted warmly by a large entourage of augurs and mundunugu. The lizard riders formed a line down either side of the dock, their atlatls loaded with javelins and held at the salute position atop their non-throwing shoulder.

At the end of the line waited the augurs, standing solemnly—quite unlike the obvious enthusiasm shown by the mundunugu, Apichtli noted. He noticed, too, that City Sovereign Necanhu was not among the reception party—quite a slight, and one the uncompromising Grand Augur vowed to remember. He said not a word to the waiting augurs, just offered a slight nod of his head to acknowledge them as he climbed up onto the decorated palanquin and waved for the sidhe bearers to go.

Across the city they marched, Apichtli's mood improving once more as he learned that the city of Palmaris had turned out for him, with thousands lining the streets all the way to the seat of power.

He stepped down from his palanquin onto the back of a kneeling sidhe, then entered the fortified keep of Palmaris that served as the city's governing chamber. Through a short corridor and past several grim-faced sentries he entered a large room with a high ceiling, vaulted and decorated. Apichtli's mood changed yet again, this time to apprehension. City Sovereign Necanhu sat upon his great throne of red silk, his expression pensive, his chin resting on one hand. It took him a few moments to notice the approaching GrandAugur, and then he leaped from his seat and stepped aside, offering the throne to Apichtli as demanded by Xoconai protocol.

Apichtli settled in the high seat and looked around the room. Necanhu's guards stood impassively at their posts. The augurs remained at the entryway of the throne room, mixing comfortably enough with Apichtli's entourage.

But something was clearly troubling the city sovereign, as well as one other, a mundunugu warrior dressed in a filthy uniform.

"We are honored to have you, Grand Augur Apichtli," Necanhu said.

"You don't look very honored, Necanhu. Is there a problem here in Palmaris?"

"The city is in firm control and operating smoothly, I assure you. Our shipbuilding is increasing beyond your demands and—"

He stopped as Apichtli held up his hand. "Then what is wrong?" the Grand Augur demanded.

City Sovereign Necanhu looked to the dirty mundunugu.

"This courier has come across the breadth of Quixi Tonoloya, Grand Augur, from Entel up the coast along Falidean Bay and across the miles to Amvoy, and across the river to Palmaris."

Apichtli fixed his glare on the mundunugu, who was shifting nervously from foot to foot. When Necanhu continued his tale, Apichtli held up his hand again, motioning him to silence.

"Quite a journey," the Grand Augur said to the woman.

The woman cleared her throat.

"Speak!"

"I was trying to find you, Grand Augur Apichtli," she explained. "Port to port and city to city."

"Sent by?"

"City Sovereign Popoca of Entel, Grand Augur."

Apichtli cocked an eyebrow and looked over at Necanhu, who opened a dirty scroll case and produced a parchment, then handed it over to Apichtli.

Apichtli let his imposing glare lock onto Necanhu as he unrolled the parchment. As soon as he glanced down at the writing, though, his eyes widened and the set of his jaw softened to near slackness.

Grand Augur Apichtli:

We have suffered a great loss. I dare not write it down. The courier will detail.

Yours in Scathmizzane,
Your humble servant, City Sovereign Popoca

"What loss?" Apichtli asked the female mundunugu, though he feared that he already knew the answer.

"The MTS *Uey'Lapialli*," the messenger answered nervously.

"The *Uey*?" Apichtli asked flatly. "The best cargo vessel in our armada?"

"Yes, Grand Augur."

"Lost? The *Uey*, our best ship in these waters, is lost? The best ship in all the east, is lost?"

"That is the fear of City Sovereign Popoca, yes, Grand Augur," the woman replied. "The ship was very late back to Entel. There was a great storm, and there are whispers of . . ."

The courier's voice trailed off.

"Very late? What do you mean by that?"

"She was due back in Entel long before midsummer's day." The woman swallowed hard.

"The storms in the South Mirianic blow fiercely," Necanhu put in, obviously trying to take some of the pressure off the poor common soldier.

Apichtli understood Necanhu's intent, but that did little to calm him. "Just a storm, so you think?" he asked with dripping sarcasm. He looked as if he wanted to murder the poor woman then and there, because those thoughts were flashing through his mind, indeed.

"The pirates," she stammered. "They are many and swift, sidhe and tepit."

"Tepit? Powries? The *Uey* is gone weeks!" Apichtli said. "Weeks! Why am I only reading this now?"

"City Sovereign Popoca wanted to make sure . . ." Necanhu

started to say, but he shut his mouth abruptly when Apichtli glared at him.

The Grand Augur snapped his gaze back at the mundunugu woman.

"I do not know," she admitted. "I was sent forth when hope was lost. I have not stopped . . ."

"Shut up," Apichtli told her. He settled back in Necanhu's chair and considered the implications here. He had spoken with his friend Popoca in Entel early in the year about the *Uey*'s mission, one great and glorious. Popoca had decided to increase the flow of gold with deception, to secretly smuggle a vast quantity of the precious metal from the southern lands to Watouwa, an island known for sugarcane, using the magical teleportation mirrors. Pirates would not bother to chase a ship of the *Uey*'s size and power for mere sugarcane.

"Where?" he demanded.

"Somewhere along the coast of Behren."

"Sailing north or south?"

The woman swallowed hard again. "She was sailing north when she was lost, Grand Augur."

"Laden, then?" Grand Augur Apichtli closed his eyes and folded his hands before his face. Thinking back to that conversation with Popoca. The city sovereign had cautioned patience to Apichtli regarding the bold plan to collect the gold in Watouwa and ship it north. More mirrors were being set up on other islands. Within two years, they might have the teleportation infrastructure in place to avoid using their ships to move the gold altogether.

Apichtli had brushed aside that caution, though. He couldn't wait another year, let alone two. He slowly and menacingly raised his scowl, aiming it at the road-dirty mundunugu.

The poor woman looked as if she might simply topple over.

"Laden with gold," Necanhu answered for her. He too was aware of Popoca's plotting, since Entel would be the destination of the *Uey*, to off-load the treasure. The city sovereign of Entel had promised a great haul of Durubazzi gold to accompany the bold moves Grand Augur Apichtli was executing about Quixi Tonoloya. Gold was the currency of the Xoconai.

Apichtli had come here, finally and after months of traveling the lands, expecting to hear the enormous count of that most-prized cargo off-loaded and sent on its way to Otontotomi and beyond. He had no idea of the disaster.

And truly it was a disaster! Gold was the primary conduit to the magic of the Xoconai.

And now, apparently, much of that precious metal had been lost.

"A storm?" Apichtli asked.

The woman shifted nervously yet again. "Whispers of a pirate band pursuing the *Uey'Lapialli* have been heard about the docks of Freeport Island."

"I would believe that City Sovereign Popoca wanted to learn as much as he could before he troubled you with the news," Necanhu got in before the withering gaze silenced him once more.

Apichtli turned back to the courier. She seemed as if she wanted to bite back every word of that admission, he recognized, and it was all that he could do not to laugh at the pitiful woman in that tense moment.

"There are more couriers on the way with every whisper that clarifies this?" Necanhu explained the moment he was freed of that glare.

"Of course," the courier replied sheepishly.

"Get out," Apichtli yelled at her. "Out of this audience hall, out of this keep, out of Palmaris, and all the way back to Entel before you stop running. And do not ever return to me unless it is with better news."

"Of . . . of course, Grand Augur," she stammered, then bowed and ran away.

"Well, this is a disappointment," Necanhu said when the room's large door slammed closed behind the departing woman. "Indeed, a disaster."

"A disaster for Popoca, perhaps," Apichtli replied, clearly surprising the city sovereign. "Gold is replaceable, though costly, and we are building many ships for our cause. These pirates are a menace, but they are also an excuse to tighten our hold on the land. Come, my friend Necanhu, let us go and plot. We will not let this heinous act go unpunished."

"Popoca has vowed to be rid of the pirates."

"Forget the pirates! I will deal with them. They are gnats. The prize is here, this land, Quixi Tonoloya, and the sidhe here will pay dearly for the crimes of their kin on the sea. This is our final excuse to take complete control, don't you see? We will let Popoca worry about his troubles on the waters and we will close our fist fully about the lands and fully about his city."

City Sovereign Necanhu stared at the other man unblinkingly.

"You seem surprised."

"I expected you to be angry."

"Oh, I am indeed, do not doubt. Do you expect me to flail and whine? This is a great loss, and so we must work hard and work well to turn it into a great benefit."

"I did not—"

"Of course you did not. I speak of vision, and not mere administration. You make the harvested trees flow to Palmaris and you make the shipyards run, while I tame the world for Scathmizzane. This is why I am the Grand Augur and you are a mere custodian."

"Yes, Grand Augur."

"Send your fastest riders with your best horses to the transport mirrors and have your augurs teleport them at once to Ursal."

"Grand Augur, the mirrors?" Necanhu replied. "We were told that the Palmaris station was to be used only for gold transport, and only to the west, to Otontotomi. The magic in them has thinned and they will need massive infusions of . . ."

"And now with this news, you will have less gold to teleport, and thus you are instructed differently. By me. Send your riders to Ursal. Do you wish to question the order?"

"No, Grand Augur!"

"From there, our couriers ride south with all speed to the villages in the mountain foothills to find Cochcal Coyotl. I will write his orders. You see, Necanhu, it is time to tame this place fully, and it is time for you to build such a fleet that these troublesome pirates will come to regret their actions."

Necanhu bowed deeply. "At once, Grand Augur!" he replied and rushed out of the room.

Grand Augur Apichtli smiled when the city sovereign was gone. This was an opportunity, he knew. Entel had been one of two thorns remaining in his desire to exert full control of all Quixi Tonoloya south of the Gulf of Corona. Perhaps St.-Mere-Abelle would remain out of his grasp, but Entel?

No more.

CHAPTER 16

THE IRRESISTIBLE BEAST

She watched the movements in Whispervale from a perch high in a tall pine hundreds of steps from the village. She didn't dare move closer, for Keri remained terrified that the garnet-wielding priests would discover her secret from the magical emanations of her tattoo or from the wedstone post in her belly. She wasn't close enough to even discern Xoconai facial coloring, but fortunately, the gold-painted armor of the soldiers and the shining golden robes of the augurs gave them away. That was her focus, of course. What were these conquerors about? She remained particularly interested in the comings and goings from the house of Paddy Broadshirt, which was now the headquarters of this warrior named Coyote and his closest aides. He was her primary concern, along with the augurs and Abbot Melchor—why was Melchor even here?

Her frustration grew as the morning wore on, as a wall of heavy clouds came in to blanket the sky. The dimming daylight made it even harder for her to discern who was who, Xoconai or Bearman. She was even having a difficult time figuring out which house belonged to which villager, because she had never really looked at Whispervale from this angle before.

How Keri wished that she had her gemstones, or at least the turquoise ear cuff! Instead of watching the town from afar, she could use that one to get into the mind of a bird or a squirrel and could move down closer to see, perhaps even to hear, all that was going on.

Her nerves had her glancing across the village to the north-west repeatedly, to the hill where she had buried her treasures. More than once, she almost started that way.

She took a long and deep breath to settle herself on that high perch, and focused on the task at hand. As one group moved along the roads of the nearest corner of Whispervale, the south-eastern region of the village, she gained confidence that Abbot Melchor was among them, along with two of the augurs and a quartet of soldiers. And Keri knew, too, that Molle and Malle, the twins from her Whispervale coven, lived on this nearest street as well.

Would the conquerors keep the interrogation solely about the possible location of any wayward gemstones? Even were that the case, Keri recognized the youthful naivete of the twins and feared that Abbot Melchor and the others wouldn't leave that house without learning something about the dancing. Or maybe they already had heard some whispers. The only question, then, was whether or not the answers of Molle or Malle, as well as the other village witches, would allow the priests to connect that dance to the magic that was to be confiscated.

Keri held her breath when the group entered what she was

fairly certain was the house of the twins. She didn't move and didn't turn her gaze for what seemed like a long, long while. Her fears were only magnified when Melchor and the others came back out, for they didn't travel to the next house in line, but moved with seeming urgency back up the street, a very different cadence than they had been showing in their methodical searching of the village to this point.

Keri sensed that something had changed. But what?

Should she go back to her own home and get Connie and the boys out of there? But the boys weren't even at home, likely! She could see the smoke coming from the smithy across the town, and Carwyn, at least, was almost certainly there. She was shaking her head even as she considered a plan, for she could not forget that going too near to those garnet-wielding augurs and the abbot might well alert them to her magic.

Again, she looked to the northwest, to the far-distant hill that held her buried jewelry. Again, she thought she should collect that magic and flee.

She hated this indecision, but she simply could not gather enough information to make any decisive move. She decided to travel closer to home, and then try to sort things out from there—her house was on the way to the distant hill, in any case.

Yes, she'd feel better there, because above all else, Keri wanted to protect those she loved.

She dropped down branch to branch and finally to the ground, got her bearings, then sprinted away, not slowing until

she came once more to the hillock overlooking the garden behind her house.

There, again, she was caught by her impulses. She desperately
wanted to go down to the cottage and find Connie.

But why? What could Keri even tell her partner with any
certainty? She didn't know what had happened at the house
of the twins, didn't know if the departure of the Xoconai and
Melchor had anything to do with Molle and Malle, or with the
dance at all. How much was based on actual evidence, and how
much came from a place of fear?

So Keri settled in and she watched, looking for hints, trying
to discern who, if anyone, was even home. And looking beyond
this quiet side lane to the wider village beyond, seeking hints of
the next moves of the Xoconai.

The day dragged on. The cloud cover became heavier, and a
light drizzle filled the air. Keri began to believe that she should
have gone to collect the jewelry, to have the pieces ready for now
at least, with her suspicions of budding trouble. She only came
to believe that more when she saw two forms hustling down the
quiet lane, Carwyn and Dafydd moving swiftly, with Dafydd
repeatedly, and clearly nervously, glancing back over his shoulder.

The two disappeared behind the roofline of the house, and a
moment later she knew they had entered when Carwyn rushed
by one of the windows below her, calling for Connie.

Keri rose and brushed the dirt off her clothes, gathering her
courage, trying to formulate some plan at least.

Whatever her better judgment might be, she simply couldn't

take the tension, and so sprinted down the little hill and past the garden to bang on the back door.

"Connie!"

The door opened and burly Carwyn stepped aside to let her in. In the main room, just beyond this small foyer and short hallway, Connie and Dafydd looked to her with surprise—but more than startlement, Keri surely saw the fear on Connie's face.

"They know of our coven," Connie told her.

Keri rushed into the room, glancing all around.

"Where's Kenzie?" She looked to Connie, who led Keri's gaze toward Dafydd with her own.

Dafydd shrugged and shook his head.

"He was working with a young stallion over at farmer Rybald's," Carwyn said, coming into the room. "But that was early this morning. I've heard nothing of him since then."

"What do they know?" Keri asked all three. "They know of our dancing, certainly. Anything more?"

Connie held up her hands helplessly. "Who else knows more who's not in this room?"

"They know you have sometimes helped Brother Manowhey in his rounds of healing through the six villages," Carwyn put in.

Keri nodded, but she wasn't too concerned about that. Always had she covered her magical healing by using fake salves and brews.

"We should be gone," Keri decided.

"Yourself should be gone, and now," said Connie.

"All of us," Keri insisted. "We will go and find Kenzie and the five of us will—"

"Will be hunted and caught," Connie cut her short. "The Xoconai are all about the hills, and they ride swift lizards. You get yerself gone, and be quick, for all the reasons we talked of earlier. We'll handle all that comes this way, and you'll return when the trouble is past."

"They approach!" Dafydd called from beside the front window overlooking the porch.

"Quickly," Connie told Keri, motioning to the back door.

Keri hesitated only a moment, knowing her friend to be correct. Having her here could lead to no good. She moved out the room's back door, down the short hallway, and into the rear foyer.

Loud knocks hit the front door.

"Open!" came a loud call.

Keri froze. She recognized the voice.

She rushed for the back door, even began pulling it open, before shutting it fast and falling against it. The garden crawled with mundunugu warriors riding their colorful lizards.

The front door was pushed in, and through a small crack in the wall, Keri could see soldiers entering, the augurs and Abbot Melchor entering.

Coyote entering.

Keri didn't know what to do. She had erred in coming here, and now she had waited too long. She breathed deeply, forcing herself to calm down and focus.

"Where is your partner?" she heard Coyote ask Connie.

"My partner, you say?"

"The woman who lives here with you. The one you dance with on the hill. Where is she?"

"Is there a problem, milord?" Keri asked graciously, stepping back into the main room.

Coyote's eyes narrowed, and he couldn't keep the grin off his face. "That is what I am here to find out."

"Do tell your soldiers not to trample our garden, I beg," said Keri. "Their lizards . . ."

Beside the warrior, Melchor was subtly shaking his head at Keri, obviously begging her to stop.

Coyote turned to one of the augurs, who held a golden wand in one hand, a garnet in the palm of the other. The second augur stood beside the first, one fist up beside his jaw, and it seemed to Keri as if he was whispering, or chanting.

Keri cursed under her breath.

"Your magic," Coyote snapped suddenly at Connie. "Hand it over. All of it!"

"Magic? Milord, we have no . . ."

She stopped when Coyote nodded to the soldier standing beside Connie, who immediately smacked her across the face.

Carwyn yelled and started for her—or tried to, until a pair of Xoconai warriors grabbed him and yanked him back, holding him fast.

"Mother!" Dafydd yelled, and grabbed a small gardening spade from a hook on the wall, then suddenly leaped for the man who had struck Connie.

"Dafydd, no!" Connie and Keri shouted together, but too late.

Everything seemed to slow down for Keri then, terribly so. Dafydd sprang from the front wall, the spade lifted beside his head.

The macana warrior beside Connie shoved her hard and turned to meet the charge.

Carwyn screamed.

Connie screamed.

They all screamed in helpless denial.

The Xoconai augur threw his fist forward and opened his hand, and something shot forth, instantly ringing as it struck the spade's blade, chipping the iron and driving through, the broken bit and the missile exploding into the side of Dafydd's head, blood and bone and brains spraying. The poor boy flew to the side into the wall and there crumpled.

Keri saw nothing then but a wall of angry red. She heard a sound escape her lips that seemed not at all her voice. She felt hands grabbing at her from behind—a pair of soldiers who had entered though the back door. They took her by the arms and the collar of her shirt, tried to hold her back.

A roar of protest erupted from Keri. With strength that surprised her captors, she tugged her right arm free and rotated to the left, bringing that hand—nay, that paw!—up and across in a powerful swipe, her leopard claws extended, ripping the face off the nearest man. Hardly noticing, she followed through, her arm, now the thick and powerful limb of a cloud leopard, catching the second soldier on the shoulder, digging down and across, tearing the ties from his wooden breastplate and driving him down, howling in agony, to the floor.

Keri continued her turn, losing herself in anger, trying to sort it all out with human sensibilities that seemed to be fast leaving her. She noted Carwyn, screaming for his brother, trying to pull forward as the two soldiers continued to hold him fast and now began pulling him down to the floor.

Around Keri went, and she felt as if she was sinking as she turned, falling even.

She saw the two augurs staring at her wide-eyed, saw Coyote, who seemed to be quite pleased by it all, saw Melchor to his right, waving his arms and shouting, shocked and desperate.

Connie lay tangled with a chair she had fallen over onto the floor. She was up on her elbows, yelling, howling, as she looked at the bloody Dafydd, lying so very still with the side of his head blown away.

The soldier who had shoved poor Connie pulled a javelin over his shoulder, going for her.

Keri wanted to go to Dafydd and call upon her embedded wedstone, but she knew without doubt that he was already dead. She needed to get back up, and was even trying to do so before realizing how completely the magic of her tattoo had come upon her.

Her clothes tugged at her strangely, for they were made for a human woman, not a leopard.

She felt a stab in her haunch and spun about with lightning fury, her front paws batting at the macana paddle of the soldier with the torn shoulder, yanking it from his grasp, tearing his hand and forearm. Back and forth, she swatted, and the poor man couldn't hope to keep up with the animalistic speed of the barrage.

She could have easily killed him, and perhaps she did, but

she spun about again, trying to find some way out of this, some way to put it all back to normal.

But the pain . . . but the horror.

Her son Dafydd was dead.

They were lost, all of them.

Before Keri even understood the movement, she sprang into the air at Coyote. Up came his twin long blades, stabbing at her, cutting her.

She crashed against him, turning as she went, planting her back claws against his chest as he fell back, and springing away again, flying for the open door, soaring through the open door.

Soldiers were all about the street before the house, all calling, lifting spears.

She had to get away. Nothing else mattered. She had to get far from those she loved, that they would be less connected to her, and to the carnage she had done here.

She darted around the corner of the house and felt something against her hip, as if she had been kicked. She saw a young Xoconai macana warrior blocking her way, a woman, her face a mask of shock and terror.

Up leaped Keri, and the woman cried out and tried to cover up against the charge.

But the leopard went right over her, landing awkwardly and stumbling, but righting herself quickly and sprinting away, up the hillock behind the house.

Mundunugu called out and took up the chase, but their lizards couldn't hope to keep up with the speeding cat.

And Keri ran for all her life, for the lives of those she loved.

But Dafydd was dead.

It took her a long time to realize that there was an awkwardness to her gait, and even longer to finally look back and see that she was carrying a javelin in her haunch.

It hadn't been a kick, after all.

Somewhere deep inside, the woman thought she should come out of this animal form and use the wedstone secured under the skin of her belly button to heal that wound.

But Keri was lost in the transformation, and the leopard knew it could not stop and could not slow.

She ran on.

At one point, the javelin clipped a tree trunk as she veered about it. The javelin went went flying free, tearing her skin, bringing more fire and pain.

She ran on.

Then stumbled on.

How far had she gone? How near was the hill?

She thought to come out of this leopard form, for it was truly exhausting her, and she knew that she was losing a lot of blood and needed to fall into her wedstone and heal. But when she slowed, she saw movement to the side, the flash of a Xoconai face.

They were still with her!

How was that possible?

Too desperate to try to sort it out—perhaps they had widening perimeters of warriors and scouts, or maybe she had run in a circle—Keri only knew that she could not stop. They would find her, naked and with minimal magic, and no energy left to even use it in any case. They would catch her and would surely kill her.

She couldn't stop, so she loped along. She tried to climb a tree, thinking that perhaps she might hide on a high bough, but she wound up hanging by her front claws, for her rear legs hadn't the strength to lift her.

She dropped to the ground.

She stumbled some more.

She noted movement, saw it to be a Xoconai soldier fast approaching.

She fell away into darkness, lost, doomed.

"What do you know?" Coyote yelled at Connie.

The man was healing himself as he spoke, using the magical stones hanging on the necklace he wore. Despite her predicament, Connie's mouth dropped open as she saw the warrior's wounds closing as surely as if Abbot Melchor or Keri was magically mending them.

"Yes, foolish witch, I am versed in the Abellican magic," he said, obviously noting her surprise. "And I have heard stories of what I just witnessed, but not many. There is a secret here, and you know it, and I will have it."

"I . . . I know nothing. I came here a dozen years ago, and Keridven took me in."

"You dance with her!"

"Yes."

"And with the others. Five others!"

"Yes." Poor Connie tried to catch her breath, tried to digest it all—but her son was lying dead on the floor and her other son had been severely beaten and bound and dragged into another room. And Keri, her dear Keri, her best friend and partner, had been chased away. She knew that they would hunt Keri forever if they learned the truth of her identity, if they learned that she was Aoleyn of the Usgar, who had destroyed the avatar of their god, Scathmizzane! Aoleyn the witch, who had driven the Xoconai invaders into a draw and a truce. Now that they had abandoned that truce and decided to become conquerors, was there anyone alive in all the world more dangerous to their designs of complete domination than Keri?

Coyote nodded to the one augur who had remained behind when so many had gone in pursuit of the leopard, and the man produced a large golden circlet. He motioned to two other soldiers in the room, who rushed over and further secured the trembling woman, then the augur moved up to her and placed that circlet onto her head.

Clearly, it was magical, for when he whispered to it, it shrank in size to fit her snugly.

"Now," Coyote said when the augur stepped away, "tell me about your lover."

"We are a family. She is my partner."

His questions came at her hard and fast. "Where are you from? What is your true name? What magic is used in your dance?"

"The west. I am Connebragh, just Connebragh. We do not use magic . . ."

Coyote's expression soured at her first answer, but it was the third that brought the biggest response—not from Coyote, but from the thick and heavy circlet on Connie's head, for it suddenly and uncomfortably tightened.

Connie grimaced and reflexively tried to reach up to adjust the headband, something the two soldiers would not allow.

"And now you understand," Coyote said wickedly. "We, too, have magic, and not just that which we are learning from the Abellican brothers. That ring upon your head will reveal your lies by creating pain upon your face. You will notice, 'Just' Connebragh, that it has not loosened. It won't, and every lie tightens it more. Tightens it until your skull cracks and implodes. Until you can no longer lie only because you can no longer speak, because your mind is ruined. If you are lucky, you will die. If not, you will sit and drool and little more."

Connie looked to the augur, who stood impassively. Beside him, Melchor was praying, appearing very distressed.

But he was saying nothing—he wouldn't even look her in the eye.

"Now, you say that you are from the west," Coyote continued. "What is the name of the place you called home?"

Connie grunted and grimaced, searching for some evasive way to answer without lying.

But the band tightened again, not as powerfully as the first time, but without any doubt.

"Did I mention that every passing heartbeat without an answer is unacceptable?"

"Fireach Speuer!" Connie yelled out, and gasped.

"Your lover is from this place?"

"No."

The gold dug into her scalp. Connie found it hard to fully open her eyes.

"What are you doing to her?" she heard Carwyn yell out from the other room, followed by the sound of her eldest son being beaten yet again.

"What is your lover's name?"

"Keridven," Connie replied. "I call her Keri."

The band didn't tighten further, giving her hope that there was a way around this deadly trap.

"Her true name! Her given name!" Coyote demanded.

"Keri!" she yelled, and she began thrashing as the band closed in.

"What is her true name?"

She clenched her jaw and wasn't sure that she could reply even if she wanted to.

"What is her true name?" Coyote battered her, asking over and over again, looming over her, his face a mask of outrage.

The band slowly tightened.

"Your head will collapse! Tell me!" the ferocious warrior demanded.

Connie heard the crack of her skull—she wasn't sure if she actually heard it externally, or simply felt the sudden jolt of agony.

Melchor said something, she thought—perhaps something about her being useless if dead.

Coyote spoke again, but his voice seemed distant.

The world spun. Connie felt the drool running freely from her mouth, or maybe it was blood. She tried to look, but couldn't see. She tried to listen, but couldn't hear. She was on the floor, then, she thought, but she couldn't be sure—but she was certain when the band was pulled off her broken head.

Then she did hear Coyote's voice, right before her consciousness flew away, "Do not let her die."

FOUR

THE WITCH AND THE ABBESS

Summer, God's Year 874

(Mahtlomeyi Xiuitl)

—— ∞∞∞ ——

My Great and Mighty Cochcal Coyotl:

All glory to you and all glory to our holy cause. I trust that you are well and that the settlements in the southern foothills are well in hand now. I have dispatched City Sovereign Avitl and some further reinforcements to your side.

Your orders, my glorious and mighty general, have changed. Turn the lands you have tamed over to Avitl. Leave to her whatever forces she will need to hold those villages in her golden fist. Gather your remaining forces and whatever indentured sidhe you have collected and go at once and with all swiftness due east to the city of Entel and the hall of City Sovereign Popoca.

Tell him that he is out of excuses, and soon out of time, my general. Tell him to tame the coast and to assist you in fully bringing Entel under our complete and unquestioned rule. Do whatever you have to do. Destroy those pockets of sidhe resistance. Lay flat the monastery called St. Rontlemore and show no mercy to those sidhe monks who did not bow to the light of our Glorious Gold, Scathmizzane. Take greater care, but only as much as you can without endangering your mission, for the ships and people of the Kingdom of Behren. Banish as many as you must, hang none, but, my general, take that city fully. Fear not any reprisals from this Chezru Chieftain sidhe named Brynn. Nay! Entel is within the borders of Quixi Tonoloya. It is our city, not the Chezru Chieftain's.

You will find warships moored in Entel harbor, of course, with others coming and going as they patrol our coasts and the southern seas. Expect many more to sail your way! Palmaris and Amvoy will work tirelessly to supply a great fleet, with the first warships arriving to Entel in the spring—and they will be the greatest vessels in these eastern waters, do not doubt! I will have that train of gold sailing smoothly from those southern jungles to Entel's shores, and across our kingdom. All the gold that our leaders in the west demand and enough still for us to make this region we rule worthy of the empire of Mayorqua Tonoloya.

My friend, my general, I cannot tolerate the sheer ugliness of these sidhe cities and squat structures much longer. We will make Quixi Tonoloya as beautiful as our land in the western basin.

We will make of our lands beauty that will bring the leaders of our people here with pride and true joy!

You have all power in Entel, Cochcal Coyotl. Remain behind the shadows of City Sovereign Popoca's curtain, I advise. Entel is yours, but let the reign of Popoca wear the mantle of glory.

And thus, in the event of failures, the mantle of blame.

Your in Glorious Gold,
Grand Augur Apitchli

CHAPTER 17

BROKEN

A single speck of light entered her consciousness, or perhaps it was just a flicker of that very consciousness, awakening anew. It grew gradually, becoming a duller blur instead of a pinpoint of light, then began to sway.

Somewhere deep in the blackness, Keri thought it was a candle.

A candle?

Its glow widened, revealing a blockade of stone—a wall?—behind it, reflecting the meager light in small dancing shadows. Not a worked wall, no, but an uneven, natural stone formation dancing with the shadows.

Each revelation brought words to her mind, and every word awakened her more to the world around her.

She wasn't dead.

She tried to remember what had happened to her, but she wasn't ready for that yet, still too intent on simply trying to make sense of her surroundings.

She heard herself gasp when a face came into view, hovering over her suddenly, startlingly.

She thought she recognized the person. Blinking rapidly, trying to sort out so very much in a short time, her vision cleared and she was, surprisingly, less sure of the identity.

"Connie?" she asked, but so weak was she that she didn't even hear her own question. She thought it was Connie, but . . . different. It looked like the woman's face had been warped somehow, asymmetrically, and the left eye was glazed over, gray and dead.

"Shh, Keri, be calm," she heard. "You've been asleep a long time and you've still a long way to go."

"Connie?" she asked more insistently, the effort causing a burning pain in her throat.

"Aye, it's Connie, your own Connie, and you're safe. But you're needing sleep."

She felt some liquid on her lips—Connie giving her something to sip—then a very short while later, heard Connie chanting and felt a slight wave of warmth flowing through her.

Connie was healing her with a wedstone.

But Connebragh of the Usgar, her dear Connie, had never been known to have an affinity to magic.

Darkness swirled about poor Keri and she fell away once more.

She woke up several times over the next few hours, or days, or weeks, or . . .

She simply had no concept of the passage of time. Each incident, she found herself alone and in the dark—pitch-blackness. She whispered for Connie, but no one answered.

Maybe, she thought, she wasn't even really awake.

Finally, though, a speck of light beckoned to her, and Keri watched it grow into a candle, and saw the wall, then the ceiling— she was in a deep cave, she realized. And she was not alone.

"How are you feeling?" Connie asked her from the side, and this time, she was able to manage to turn her head as she lay there on her back to see the woman. Connie was in a chair—why was there a chair in this cave?—and knitting.

Knitting?

Keri's vision wasn't rolling in and out this time, and she didn't fall back in pain when she propped herself up on her elbows.

"What are you doing?" she asked Connie.

"Killing the hours," she answered. "Summer's not staying here forever, and we could both use some warm mittens."

Keri tried to process that, tried to use the mention of passing time to find some way to ground herself in whatever this reality might be. But the second part, about the two of them, distracted her.

There were five in the family, not two.

A gasp caught in Keri's throat as she remembered Dafydd!

"How long've I been . . . here?"

"A month and more."

The reply nearly knocked Keri back flat on her back. "But you're gettin' there," Connie added hopefully.

"Where're our children?"

271

Connie paused, then set her knitting down, rose from the chair—and Keri recognized the chair as Connie's favorite rocker from the porch at the house—and slowly approached.

"Where're our children?" she asked again, more insistently.

"Easy, my friend."

"No! Where are they?"

"You'll put yerself back to wherever you've been," Connie warned. "You'll get all your answers when you're strong enough to hear them, and to do something about it all, perhaps. But now . . ."

Keri had a hard time arguing with that, but she intended to. Simply becoming agitated was draining her—she could feel the bite of her wounds and knew they had been considerable, mortal likely, except here she was, still alive.

"Where am I? Connie, where are we?" She looked all around and sat up quickly, then nearly fell back as a wave of dizziness overcame her.

"In a cave in the mountains. Very deep, very safe."

"And you healed me? How? When did Connebragh become so powerful with magic?"

"I am helping," the woman said. "Now, please, you lay yerself back down and close your eyes."

Keri started to relax just a bit, but she wasn't going to let the obvious diversion by Connie delay her. "Dafydd?" Keri demanded.

Connie's one remaining good eye dilated—even in the dim candlelight, Keri understood the emotional reaction just mentioning Dafydd's name had caused.

"He's dead," Keri stated flatly.

"We buried him on the hill behind the garden," Connie confirmed, choking back sobs. "A pretty place. He'd have liked..."

Keri came up from the bed and fell into her arms, crushing them together.

"We? Yourself, Carwyn, and Kenzie?" she asked.

She felt Connie stiffen. The woman pushed her back and stared into her eyes, slowly shaking her head.

"They are gone," came a different voice, so unexpectedly from the side, and so, too, came a second light. Not a candle nor a torch, but steady and white from the light of a magical diamond.

Keri pulled back fully from Connie and spun around, on guard so suddenly. They were discovered and in for a fight, she feared.

Or were they? Her face screwed up with confusion to see Abbot Melchor walking toward them from the natural corridor, the diamond light source hanging on a chain about his neck.

But behind him came a Xoconai! Keri began to call to her tattoo, the effort painful and strangely discordant. She released it abruptly, though, when she recognized the man.

Ataquixt.

"Abbot Melchor is the one who healed you," Connie told her quietly. "Most of your wounds, at least. He left me here with a wedstone to continue the tending, but you'd surely be dead and buried with Dafydd if not for him."

"If we were somehow able to sneak you back into Whispervale to bury you," Ataquixt said.

"What's it all about?" Keri demanded, looking from the two men back to Connie. "Where are my boys?"

"Coyote has pressed many of the young men from the six villages into service. They all departed a week ago, bound for Entel and the coast," Melchor told her. "I believe that they intended to stay through the year, but a courier from Grand Augur Apichtli arrived unexpectedly and sent them quickly on their way."

"And my boys?"

Their lives will be hard, but they should be safe for now, at least."

"We have to go get them!" Keri insisted.

"You cannot," said Melchor. "Coyote has an army with him, and one thick with augurs versed in their own magic *and* that of the Abellican monks. They carry many powerful Ring Stones with them, and they know how to use them."

"Coyote, too," Ataquixt said. "As I warned you before, take great care with that one."

"You . . . the leopard you became hurt him badly," Melchor told her.

"And he healed himself," Ataquixt added. "He possesses many magical items. I suspect he has been collecting them from around Honce for years now, plundering the monasteries and the palaces of the lords who had favor with the church and thus had been gifted with marvelous and powerful items."

Keri remembered her leap, the raking of her claws across Coyote's chest as she sprang away.

"He knows who you are, or suspects, at least," Ataquixt continued. "He tried to get Connebragh to tell him."

"But I did'no," Connie said quickly when Keri turned to regard her. "They broke my head, but I told them nothing."

Keri reached back and pulled Connie to her in a side hug, and took comfort when dear Connie rested her head on her shoulder.

"I almost killed him and he knows who I am, but he left?" Keri posited with clear skepticism.

"He thinks you are dead," Ataquixt said.

"Why would he think that?"

"Because we faked it," said Melchor. "Ataquixt told him that he found you dead in the mountains and built a pyre for you—we claimed we didn't know at that time that you were an outlaw."

"I found you when you fled the fight at the house," Ataquixt explained. "I came upon you when you fell to unconsciousness."

Keri nodded, thinking that perhaps she remembered someone coming upon her in that terrible moment—a Xoconai soldier, she had thought.

"From the churchyard in Whispervale, we exhumed a body of a woman recently dead and burned it on that pyre right before Coyote arrived there," Melchor continued. "He thinks you are dead, and better for you, better for all of us, for him to continue to believe that."

"City Sovereign Avitl has arrived from Ursal to take control of the six villages," Ataquixt added. "She is fair and not unkind, but you must take great care that she never learns that you are alive. Coyote very much suspects your true identity, and the whole of Grand Augur Apichtli's forces would fall upon you if he ever heard a rumor that Aoleyn of the Usgar was lurking about this land he now considers his domain. There would be no mercy for the woman who tore apart the avatar of Scathmizzane. When you are rested, I will get you out of here—Connie, too—and we'll find a new home for you two where you can live in peace."

"Peace? My child is out there!" She almost said "our child" to Ataquixt, and only changed it at the last moment.

"That man murdered my son!" she went on, growing more agitated, and again feeling the pain and weariness creeping up around her. "Peace? If you're thinking I'm to let this all flow away from me, then you're thinking wrong! How can you suggest that I run and hide somewhere else when Coyote holds Kenzie and Carwyn in his murderous hands?"

"They will be pressed into service on ships, most likely," Abbot Melchor said. "Coyote will have no need of them in the court of City Sovereign Popoca of Entel, who allows few sidhe into his palace, and none other than those traitorous monks of St. Bondabruce, I am told."

"Traitorous?" Keri asked with a snort. "What d'you call yerself, then? Why would one such as Abbot Melchor use that word in a disparaging manner? You came here beside Coyote. Melchor was with him, aye, he interrogated Headsman Paddy, and when he attacked . . ."

Her voice trailed off.

"Abbot Melchor is the reason you are still alive," Ataquixt calmly interjected.

"Still, he has the gall to call others traitorous?"

"The brothers of St. Bondabruce are De'Unneran heretics and traitors to the Abellican Church," the abbot retorted.

"To the church?" Keri echoed incredulously. "What about to the people of Honce? What about yourself, Abbot Melchor?"

"I am about trying to keep as many people alive as I can," he replied without hesitation. "I try to mitigate the fights. I tried to keep the peace and serve Avitl, who was the city sovereign of Ursal, and who is no tyrant, in a way that would show the folly of Grand Augur Apichtli and his ilk."

"But they won," said Keri.

"They are winning," came the correction. "And I will continue to do what I can, where I can, until it all sorts out."

Keri wanted to snap back at him, but she hadn't the heart—or the strength. She understood Melchor's attitude all too well. She had once been the most formidable witch in the world, with the power to destroy perhaps hundreds of her enemies. But she hadn't. She hadn't used her magical powers to harm anyone in the fifteen years before the exchange in the little cottage back in Whispervale. She had killed before, many people, Xoconai and even members of her own tribe. She had fought for what she believed in and had felt the warmth of the blood of her enemies on her hands—or paws.

She had no heart for it anymore, and hadn't for a long time. She was Keridven now, a healer, a dancer, who sang and listened to the music of nature. The woman she had been, Aoleyn of the Usgar, had died when she had settled in Whispervale more than a dozen years previous, so soon after the moment when she and Ataquixt had conceived her beautiful Kenzie. Ah, Kenzie, to be the hope of the world!

Kenzie and his mother Keridven.

But not Aoleyn.

Aoleyn was gone, killed by Keridven.

But now one of Keridven's children had been murdered by Coyote and his augurs.

And Keridven's other two children, including her own blood, Kenzie, had been dragged away.

She didn't know what to do.

She fell to the floor, exhausted, and the darkness closed around her once more.

When she awakened again, Keri was back on the cot in the candlelit cave. She must have stirred before coming back to consciousness, because she found Ataquixt hovering over her, looking down with concern. Connie, though, was nowhere to be seen.

"Welcome back," he said with a smile, but immediately changed his tone to something more somber when he added, "You need to understand that you are not nearly fully recovered, my dear friend. You were on the edge of death. The very edge. When I found you in the forest outside of Whispervale, I thought you were already gone. Even after Abbot Melchor began his healing rituals on you, he gave little hope that you would survive. And do not fool yourself into thinking that the danger is past for you, please. We almost lost you again right after our last talk."

"How long?"

"Since?"

"From the beginning. Since I have been here? Since Coyote ran off with my children—ran off with *our* child?"

"Summer is nearly gone, autumn coming fast. Abbot Melchor has tended you no less than a dozen times, leaving exhausted after each session, and Connebragh, dear Connebragh, has been at your side for all but the first two days and the last two."

"It is daylight outside? Take me there. I need to feel the wind and sun on my face."

To her relief, Ataquixt agreed. He pointed to the side, where some clothes and shoes had been left for her, but Keri shook her head. Ataquixt led her up the tunnel to a small cave, and beyond it, the wide world. They were in the foothills, due south of a small village—perhaps Whispervale, but she couldn't be sure from this distance and angle.

She pointed to the village, aiming a questioning expression at Ataquixt.

"Three miles," he said.

"Whispervale?"

"Yes."

"And Coyote has not returned? He is long gone from there? With our child, my children?" She wasn't about to let this drop, but tried to hide her anger—anger also pointed right at Ataquixt for allowing it all.

"He will not return."

"And you let him go. Why did you not send Melchor to me immediately to stand me up that I could . . ."

"Die? Or, perhaps worse for you—for I understand you quite well, my dear Aole . . . Keridven—to confirm to Coyote your true identity and thus doom Kenzie to a fate worse than indenture? As I told you, Coyote suspects you to be Aoleyn of the Usgar, the powerful and dangerous witch who tore the very skin from his god. The only way to protect Kenzie was to make sure that Coyote thought you dead. The only way to continue to protect him—and Carwyn!—is to make sure that Coyote still thinks you dead, and therefore cannot, can never be, certain of your true identity. With Aoleyn dead and burned to ash, he has no reason to care at all about your children—they are no more a threat to him than any other unfortunate young person impressed into the Xoconai armada. Can you not see that?"

Keri took a few deep breaths to calm herself. Logically, she understood that Ataquixt was probably correct. He knew the Xoconai in general, and Coyote in particular, much better than she ever could. "Why bring in Melchor, then? Could he not betray me, betray us? He was with Coyote when Dafydd . . ."

She couldn't finish that thought aloud.

"Abbot Melchor is a good man, but a complicated one in a world more complicated still. His allegiance is to the Abellican Church—he is a true Abellican, though that was not always the case. Once, he was seduced by the simple worldview of a monk named Marcalo De'Unnero, who created a fanatical following that tore the religious order apart. Now, the De'Unnerans raise their heads again, so it seems, in favor of the conquering Xoconai."

Keri thought of her days in St.-Mere-Abelle, of her time with a monk named Brother Thaddius, who had traveled a similar path in his shifting allegiances within the church. She understood what Ataquixt was saying here, but still, the image of Melchor standing beside Coyote remained thick in her thoughts, and inspired her fears.

"I brought Abbot Melchor here because if I had not, you would have died. It was not a choice of who to bring in—it was him, or let you die. He is formidable with the gemstone magic, and even so, you barely survived. The wounds you took in your flight from the battle were deep and mortal, no doubt. Connie could not begin to heal you. Abbot Melchor is a man trying to do good in a very dangerous situation. He served Ursal well under City Sovereign Avitl, who is not like Coyote and Popoca and Grand Augur Apichtli. Abbot Melchor is fighting two wars, the first in trying to mitigate this deadly shift in the leadership of the Xoconai, where he has few allies. He counts Avitl as one, or at least, she is not an enemy. But even she is very cautious when going against the Grand Augur and that fierce man's vision for Quixi Tonoloya.

"And Melchor is also trying to keep his beloved church from falling into darkness, and again with few allies—or at least, where most of his allies are holed up in the great monastery of St.-Mere-Abelle in the north, or beyond that, across the wide Gulf of Corona in a land called Vanguard. The lesser monasteries scattered throughout the lands are almost all under siege, politically if not militarily. Those who cater to the vision of the heretic De'Unnero are gaining favor with the severe augurs and city sovereigns—perhaps these zealot monks view accepting the Xoconai as conquerors as their way to ascend to dominance within the church that had for so long been so very important in this land. Perhaps they seek to pervert the Abellican Church to become one with those who worship Scathmizzane."

"Opportunists who care only for their own power and nothing for the people they pretend to serve," Keri remarked. "They ride the chaos for their own ends."

"That is the oldest story in the history of our race, and the seemingly eternal battle in the societies of humankind."

"You think I judge Abbot Melchor too harshly, then," Keri stated instead of asking.

"If I agreed at all with your suspicions that he would betray you, us, I would go into Whispervale and kill him this moment. But no, my dear friend, he will not betray us. But neither should you expect any support from him beyond this healing he gave to you. He and I have spoken many times about this. Abbot Melchor believes that you should go far from this region, to the Mantis Arm coast in the northeast, where the Xoconai remain few in number, or back to the Wilderlands in the west, or perhaps even to St.-Mere-Abelle. Surely, Father Abbot Braumin and the monks will welcome you back in after your heroics in the war."

"I have two sons out there in trouble," Keri reminded him through gritted teeth, hissing the words as much as speaking them. "You're asking me to run and hide? You're asking me to abandon—"

"What do you think you can do?"

She wanted to respond, but couldn't quite find the words.

"If you reveal yourself, you should expect that Kenzie is doomed," Ataquixt said flatly.

"I understand your thoughts, but can'no leave them to this fate."

Ataquixt sighed, and Keri could tell that he was as pained by it all as she. "They will live the next years of their lives as sailors."

"They will live as enslaved men on a sailing ship, nothing more—and that is only if you are correct in your guess as to Coyote's designs on them. And when they are no longer of any use, they will be replaced, and what? Set free? Will it even get to that point? I have heard that many ships sailing the Mirianic in the east find a watery death. Pirates and storms and powries and . . ."

She stopped when Ataquixt came forward and hugged her.

"The whole world is dangerous," he whispered in her ear.

"They are just children."

"They are young men. Hold faith."

She wanted to tell him that she simply didn't know what to do, but instead just melted on his shoulder and sobbed, as did he.

When they were done with that cathartic cry, the two shared a long and loving look. They were friends, true friends. So dear that Keri had trusted Ataquixt enough to tell him the truth of Kenzie, even knowing that the Xoconai mundunugu couldn't, and shouldn't, be much a part of Kenzie's life. For Ataquixt still had his life and his responsibilities as a ranger, and as an insider in the Xoconai societal structure.

What did she have? Who was she now? Where would she go?

Only one thing came to mind at that moment, but it was something she didn't want to share with Ataquixt or anyone else.

"Abbot Melchor and Brother Manowhey have brought Connebragh and the other dancers into the church," Ataquixt said.

"To stay? Are they in danger?"

"Into the Order of St. Abelle, I mean. They are now sisters of the church. And yes, they were in danger. Before he departed, Coyote had set up golden mirrors to incinerate them, but Melchor convinced him that such an act would anger all the villages and leave them in turmoil before Avitl could take command, which, of course, would make things difficult for Grand Augur Apichtli. Melchor also convinced Coyote that it was you, Keridven, who had instigated the dancing, and since you were dead now, he had nothing to fear from the six pathetic and broken women. They were just folk seeking more meaning in their lives in a world gone mad, he told Coyote. When City Sovereign Avitl arrived to take command of the villages, she allowed Melchor to end any discussion of their possible crimes by bringing them into the church, and he and Manowhey were happy to agree."

"That is good."

"You'll not find the same leniency for yourself, in any of the villages."

"I know."

"The day is late," Ataquixt said. "I expected Connebragh before now. Go back in and rest, my friend. Take the time you need to heal and we will help you to find your way."

She agreed with a nod and turned back for the cave, pausing just a moment to bask in the long rays of the lowering sun.

"I'll return in the morning. Perhaps Connebragh can free herself of her duties and join me."

Keri gave him a hug, then went into the cave and down the tunnel to the room below. She lay on the bed for a short while but had no intention of sleeping. Finally, she summoned enough nerve to put her hand over her belly, to reach for the magic of the wedstone set there. She felt the healing warmth . . . physically, but then came a sharper pain, sudden and terrifying, like the shadow of a serrated blade flashing before her eyes, flashing into her heart.

Gasping, she fell back onto her cot.

She took a moment to steady herself, telling herself that she had been caught off guard, and that it would not happen again.

She collected a pair of shoes but didn't bother with the other clothing—the day was warm and her shift and light breeches would be enough, and besides, she intended to make her journey in a different form than that of a human woman.

She went back outside, delighting in the sounds of the crickets and the tree frogs and all the other wonderful creatures that gave music to the night. She nearly giggled when she heard the hoot of an owl, the melodious call taking her away from her pressing worries and grief, albeit for a short moment only.

Keri stripped down to nothing, then looked at her palm and

nodded. She fell into the magic of the tattoo, trying to shift into the form of a cloud leopard.

Trying.

She felt a pang within her chest again, then another, as if someone was flicking her heart with their finger—no, not with a finger, but with that shadowy blade.

She heard the music of her beautiful tattoo, but it was distant.

Keri focused more intently. The sounds of the night faded a bit as the music of the magical stones increased.

A memory flashed in her mind, as clear as the scene before her when it had actually happened. Rocks tumbled under the power of her magic in that faraway place, dropping the leader of her Usgar tribe into the piling rubble before her. She saw his last breaths, savored her own claw ripping his face away.

Another image flashed in her thoughts: a boat sailing for her and the others fleeing the Xoconai, when she raised an iceberg before the craft, scuttling it. She heard the screams of the splashing and drowning sailors—screams that overwhelmed the magical song.

And then she saw and felt again her fleeing pounce back in the cottage, the clasping of her claws to gash and rip the man, Coyote. A spray of red mist filled her mind's eye. Destruction, death, murder.

Keri fell to her knees, clutching her chest. The pain was constant now, so suddenly.

It subsided a few deep breaths later, when all thoughts of becoming a leopard had flown from her mind.

She put on her shoes and began to walk, picking a course west of Whispervale.

The moon hadn't yet risen when she set out, but it was thin and high in the sky by the time she at last came to a small clearing on the hillock. She spent a few moments getting her bearings, and recalled again the dance when she had used her magic—it seemed like years ago!—to lift the other six women from the ground, to make the wind hot and cold.

She rushed for the exposed tree root, the spot where she had buried her treasures, and was relieved indeed to find that the ground had not been disturbed. She looked around for a stick, but seeing nothing nearby, just fell to her knees and began to dig at the grass and earth with her hands. Again, she thought of the leopard, thought to turn her arm into that of the great cat.

But no. She could not.

She felt the box soon enough and dug it out fully, then put it on the ground beside her. She wiped her hands on her pants, took a deep breath, and carefully reached for the cover.

A footstep sounded behind her, freezing her in terror.

"I knew you would not remain within the cave this night," came a voice.

Ataquixt's voice, which was indeed a great relief.

"You are so restless," he said.

She turned around to view him as he walked toward her. "You knew of this?"

"Of this place? Of course. I followed you here, but not closely, as I suspected your destination as soon as you passed by Whispervale."

"And o' this?" she asked, reaching back and bringing the box around. She pulled open the cover, the jewelry glistening in the moonlight.

"I wondered what had become of your treasures. Now I know."

Keri let that sink in for a few moments. Connie hadn't told him. Dear Connie!

"You should be very careful," Ataquixt warned. "Those items are contraband, expressly forbidden now. The Xoconai have ways to detect them."

"I know all about that."

"Simply possessing them is now punishable by death in most places."

In reply, Keri held up her palm in the moonlight. "And this?" she asked. "They can detect the magic imbued in this tattoo, I am sure. Will you be flaying my skin now to save me?"

He sighed and shook his head. "You should go back to the cave. You are not fully recovered—you should not even have come out this far this night."

"Had I not, I would remain vulnerable and in need of your protection, and perhaps still dependent upon the healing of Melchor and Connebragh. Now, I don't. If I am discovered by the Xoconai, weep for your own people, not for me." Even as she offered the boast, she felt the sting deep inside. She could talk of the fight, but could she really wage it?

"Discovered in the cave, you mean?"

"I do'no know."

"Please, I beg of you. Now is not the time for you to come forth. There is much . . ."

"My children are out there."

"You are not ready, and you don't even know where they might be."

"Coyote went east to Entel, so you said."

"He is already likely there."

"Then my boys are there."

Ataquixt shook his head. "Likely aboard a Xoconai ship. Perhaps out at sea, perhaps headed to another port—along the Mantis Arm, or all the way around the coast to the river called the Masur Delaval. To Palmaris, or Ursal, even. You cannot know."

"Then the longer I wait, the less I will know."

"No!"

"Do you think you can stop me?" Like the previous threat, it was a bluff, for Keri wasn't sure she could begin to resist the ranger at that time. Her chest was beginning to hurt simply thinking of calling up some magic.

"Go and heal. Show patience, I beg. Let me escort you back to the cave, and then, on my word, I will try to find more information for you about your boys . . . about our son."

"Promise me that you'll find out what happened to them."

He nodded.

They were only a few miles from the cave, but it took the rest of the night to arrive, and if Ataquixt hadn't been there to support her, Keri doubted she would have made it.

I need to sleep, she told herself, silently promising that she'd use the wedstone in the morning and fully rid herself of her maladies.

It was a promise she would make every day for the next two weeks.

Her wounds, she came to realize more fully with each attempt, were more than physical. Much more.

Every memory that came to her when she began to listen to the song of the magic was one of blood and death, bringing waves of guilt and horror. Even the song of the wedstone under her belly button could not avoid that festering wound, as if she had somehow injured her very life force.

So much of the troubles and death that had come to the world lay at her feet, the blood on her hands, and she could not escape it.

CHAPTER 18

THE MELTING POT

D ays passed before Keri came out of the cave again. She spent her waking hours trying to call upon her enchanted jewelry to heal her wounds, but found every time that the deleterious effects, the exhaustion from trying to fall into those magical vibrations and the haunting memories they aroused in her, were more acute than the benefits she gained from the magic.

She was full of grief, full of pain, and full of guilt, like three black wings weighing her down both physically and emotionally. She mourned the death of Dafydd alone in the dark, and every thought, every flashing image, of that tragic moment led her into a spiral of guilt and fear over the many battles she had waged, the people she had killed.

The war that she, for all her good intentions, had facilitated by destroying the demon Fossa, which had plagued her homeland, the demonic entity that had kept the ambitious Xoconai west of the mountains. In her despair, lost was any notion that she had been justified in her actions. She simply could not bring herself to see any mitigating reason in this dark time—for wouldn't that be exactly the type of excuse-making the brute named Coyote might do to excuse murdering Dafydd?

The descending spiral imprisoned Keri in that cave and held her back from accessing the magical powers that had previously come so easily and joyously to her.

Connie visited her a couple of times in the next few days, but Ataquixt, she learned, had departed Whispervale. He had promised to get her some information regarding Carwyn and Kenzie. She could only hope that he would come through for her.

After another middling attempt with her gemstones one day, the exhausted Keri finally reached her breaking point. Anger and frustration drove her out of the cave and into the morning sunshine. She lay down on a rock near the cave entrance, basking in the surprisingly warm late-summer sun—or perhaps it was now past the solstice. She could not know. She lost herself in its glow, which contrasted so wonderfully with the chill edge carried by the mountain breeze.

She would do this every day and forego the magical healing, she told herself, and she did, even coming out in the rain on more than one occasion just to breathe the open air and hear the songs of the wildlife around her. So tempting was it to find an animal and enter its mind, to see the world through its eyes!

But no.

She decided that she would forego all thoughts of her magic for now. She would let the wounds heal, let the grief diminish somewhat, at least, and let the guilt fall further and further into her past. If she never had to call upon the magic again in her lifetime, that would be a blessing to her, she believed.

"It is a lovely day indeed," she heard from afar one bright morning, the voice stirring her from a nap on a rock she had come to think of as a bed. Keri opened her eyes a bit, felt the sting of the brilliant sun in the deep blue sky on a chilly, breezy day.

Leaves showing the first hints of brown and golden and red rustled in the wind, fluttering in a synchronized dance like a flock of excited birds. Keri watched them, entranced, then started fully awake, at last registering that someone had spoken to her!

She bolted upright to see the approach of Ataquixt, the ranger's pinto shuffling noisily through the leaves. Connie sat behind him astride the mount, holding the long reins of a donkey that walked behind.

Ataquixt paced his mount up beside Keri and flipped his leg over the saddle, dropping easily before reaching back to help Connie down.

"How are you?" Connie asked, moving quickly up to her friend.

Keri nodded and accepted the woman's hug, then her hand in helping her to her feet.

"I am well," she replied, looking at Ataquixt as she did. "Better than last we spoke, and ready for the road, if I know which road to walk."

"It is not so simple as that," Ataquixt replied. He offered a disarming smile, but Keri would have none of that, her scowl telling him to get straight to the point.

"Kenzie and Carwyn traveled to Entel with Coyote's group,

as we believed. But from there, I cannot be sure. Carwyn, at least, was apparently taken by a press-gang onto a warship. I heard the name *Lauilli* mentioned, but I cannot be sure. The ship was no longer in port, nor was there any timetable for its return. I waited a few days, trying to confirm that your boy had been put aboard, and perhaps find a proper schedule for the vessel, but there is much happening in that city right now, none of it encouraging, and there was nothing more I could garner."

"What more is happening?"

"Entel has two monasteries, St. Rontlemore and St. Bondabruce. Rontlemore, smaller by far, remains loyal to the Abellican Order, to St.-Mere-Abelle and the Father Abbot. But the brothers of St. Bondabruce had walked far from the Father Abbot even before the war, preferring the teachings of a monk long ago declared a heretic by the church powers. Now they have fallen in fully with City Sovereign Popoca, and I could not dare allow him or Coyote, who remains in Entel, to find out that I was in the city, let alone that I was looking for a pair of young men taken from Whispervale."

"The Xoconai suffer St. Rontlemore to survive?" The notion surprised Keri, given how forceful they had become here in the midlands.

"Entel is unlike any other city of Honce. The bonds with the Chezru Chieftain and the Behrenese people south of the mountains are considerable. Even so, the city is fraying now. There have been reports of battles between the rival monks, and it is no secret that Coyote and Popoca spend many hours in St. Bondabruce, which is a quite formidable place, holding many more monks and many more gemstones than the old St. Rontlemore."

"What does this mean for our sons?" Connie asked.

"It means that they are safer out on the seas, so I hope the rumor is proven true." Ataquixt turned a sorrowful stare on Keri. "But it means that finding them will be no easy task, likely an impossible one."

"You should stay here with me," Connie told Keri. "They are not mere boys anymore. They are men, young and strong. Ataquixt has told me that most who go into servitude with the armada eventually buy their way back out."

"Kenzie is not yet twelve," Keri argued.

"But he has the experiences of one much older," said Connie. "Trust him."

Keri stared at her hard.

"She is not staying," Ataquixt said before Keri could answer. "She cannot. Your enemies think her dead, on my word and Abbot Melchor's word."

"Then let us go somewhere far from here," said Connie.

"I intend exactly that," Keri replied.

Ataquixt nodded.

"But not you. No, Connie," she said, moving close and gently stroking the woman's hair. She tried to hide her grimace when she felt the extent of the damage to the woman's head—she could only think of the tribesmen about the lake in her homeland, who wrapped the skulls of their children to purposely misshape them.

"Connie, I'm going to find them," she promised quietly.

"And when I do, and bring them back, then we four will all go off together to find a new life."

"Promise me," Connie demanded, tears flowing, showing Keri that for all her talk to the contrary, she really wanted Keri to rescue the boys as badly as Keri wanted it herself.

"I am ready," Keri announced to Ataquixt. "I am leaving, bound for Entel, and for wherever the trail leads me from there."

"I know," Ataquixt said, flashing that wry little grin of his that Keri found so attractive. He held out a small pouch for her. "Gol' bears, the currency of this land when it was called Honce-the-Bear. The Xoconai treasure them, both because they wish to collect them all to get them out of circulation, where they remind the people of what they had before, and because, well, they're gold. Those unfortunate folk pressed into service can be bought out of their indenture. Take care your identity, or why you are so interested in these two young men in particular—if you do find them, I mean—and perhaps this gold will suffice. You'll need little else, for the donkey is loaded with enough supplies to get you much of the way to Entel."

Keri sighed in great appreciation. She bent in and kissed Connie on the cheek, then walked across for a hug and kiss from Ataquixt.

"You take great care," he whispered, and Keri, her head on his shoulder, nodded her assurance.

After he had drawn her a crude map of the trails to get her out of the mountains east of Whispervale and on the road to Entel, Keri said her goodbyes to Connebragh and Ataquixt, promising to return soon with the boys. She waved them away, watching them until they were out of sight down the mountain trail.

The only one of the three who thought they'd ever see each other again was Connie, Keri realized, for in her heart, Keri knew she'd probably never return, and Ataquixt's tears belied his confident nods and smile regarding any future meeting.

Keri waited a long while for the two to be far away, and to be sure that she was not being followed by Ataquixt, after all, before she started out. She found a suitable walking stick, took up the reins of the donkey, and quietly stared at distant Whispervale for many heartbeats, mouthing a sincere goodbye to all the folks she had known there. And to say goodbye to the town itself, as well, for it had been her home for nearly as long as the settlement atop Fireach Speuer far to the west.

And a better home it had been.

CHAPTER 19

BLACK WINGS AND RED BLOOD

Her journey started slowly, hesitantly, full of worry and second-guessing. Maybe she should have Ataquixt collect Connie and take them both far from this place. Perhaps the boys, particularly Kenzie, would indeed be better off without her help—she could have Ataquixt use his connections to locate and watch over their situation. Maybe he could even get this woman named Avitl, if she was as fair and just as he claimed, to buy out their service and bring them back home.

Indeed, grand fantasies played through Keri's head as she walked along the descending trail that chilly morning.

No, it was no longer summer, she realized. The autumn had begun.

She recognized her hopes for exactly that, unrealistic fantasies, but still, there came to her a spring in her step that she had not known for a long, long time. She simply couldn't bring herself to admit there was no possibility of realizing those fantasies and thus dismiss them, but it didn't matter, for she put them out of her thoughts, turning instead to the sights and sounds and smells about her. She attuned her senses into the beauty of the mountain as it prepared for sleep, with leaves dancing on the breeze, squirrels and other small critters rushing all about to collect their winter stores, and birds, so many birds, flying from tree to tree to complete their nests, while larger hawks and eagles waited for their opportunity to catch a morning snack.

Something had already found a meal, Keri noted when she broke for lunch and caught sight of a wake of vultures patiently circling on high, not so far away. A fallen deer or elk, or long-horn sheep, she figured, for the foothills of the Belt-and-Buckle were thick with them.

She sat there for a long while staring up at the great birds drawing a circle in the air, envying them as the breeze tickled her face. Of all the magic Keri had ever known, flying was by far the most satisfying to her—and not her own flights with her magical moonstone (which were really little more than extended hops, or falling glides, in the case where she had soared down the mountainside), but the true flying she had experienced by sending her sensibilities into the body of a bird.

That, more than anything Keri had ever experienced, was true freedom.

She almost felt like she was up there with them—almost—when the breeze blew stronger across her bare skin. She was hardly aware that she had called up to them through the magic of the turquoise ear cuff she wore, until one of the birds circled lower.

Smiling, the woman watched the vulture's turns above. It wasn't high up now, and she could make out the featherless black head and the silvery patches on the underside of its wingtips, stretched like the fingers of an open hand.

It was looking for her, answering her call, she knew.

Keri swallowed hard. She was afraid to try it, to call upon the magic, but the temptation proved simply too delicious.

She sent her spirit through the ear cuff, reaching out again, and this time with more than a simple call to the graceful creature.

The world seemed to shrink, then, as she attuned to the sensations within the corporeal form of the vulture. She felt the wind so much more clearly, tickling the undersides of spread wings—of *her* spread wings! The change in vision jarred her initially, for she could look down at her abandoned corporeal form and see every detail, every eyelash, as if she was staring into a mirror right before her face instead of a figure a hundred feet away.

How brilliant! How magnificent this vision, so many times keener than anything a human might ever know—unless that human knew how to use this turquoise magic.

She bade the winged form to climb. She took control, and so up, up went the large bird. The world widened below her, but if she focused, the details of it became no less clear. She quickly spotted the carcass of a dead skunk that had lured the group here.

She wondered at the smell. Wouldn't it be off-putting? Would a vulture really eat a dead skunk?

She swooped lower to learn if she could catch any hint of that rotten-egg stench.

Nothing really assaulted her. The smell was mild, at most.

Down she flew, gaining speed, feeling the wind, seeking the scent.

Falling, she thought, as Tay Aillig had fallen . . . to his death.

The demons reared—Keri wasn't in her own body, so she couldn't crouch over at that sudden shock.

But she did, or the vulture did, weirdly, and thus lost control as it plummeted!

Keri noted the details in the bark of the oak a moment before a bright and hot flash expelled her fully from the flopping avian beast.

She was back in her body just in time to hear the loud squawk, the dying shriek, of the black vulture. She leaped to her feet and started running in the direction of the oak, but found that she couldn't easily get there across hidden ravines.

She would need to use her magic to get to the bird. She would need her magic to heal the bird, if it wasn't already dead.

She focused on the ear cuff, fought through the sudden, sharp pain, and tried to reach out, and she knew.

It was dead.

She had killed it. She had doomed it by bringing her turmoil into its form.

The woman gasped in horror. Her mind continued down a path, rolling like a stone down the side of a mountain. She imagined that the vulture had a nest of fledglings—all would starve because of her selfishness, her need to satisfy her own senses at the expense of the poor bird.

Keri rushed back to the donkey and walked away, not

looking back. And she kept walking through the day and long into the twilight, chased by guilt. She heard the wolves and coyotes when she set her camp every night and prayed that they would stay away.

For if they came for her, she would have to use the magic to fend them off. She didn't want to do it. She wasn't sure she could do it.

Truly, the woman was lost, not with regard to *where* she was, but with regard to *who* she was.

She fought through the demons and kept going, down from the mountains and across the foothills to the eastern road. Doubts followed her, the demons came with her in the form of brutal memories, haunting her thoughts, tearing at her heart and soul.

So often through the next few days did she find her cheeks wet with tears, and they weren't from the chilly wind sweeping down off the Belt-and-Buckle range.

She thought of Dafydd, and she cried.

She remembered those she had killed with her magic, and she cried, and she was angry, both at herself for doing it, and at herself for not being able to do it now!

That was the diabolical paradox that chased her. She needed her magic in this troubled time as much as ever, she believed. The fate of her two remaining sons very likely depended upon it. But the focus would not come.

She thought of the vulture, and she cried—she cried for it, and she cried for herself.

As the days passed, she came into more populated lands,

with small settlements sprinkled about the clear trail. Entel was less than a hundred miles from Whispervale, and with the mountains behind her and the weather still holding on to autumn, she knew that she was nearing the place after only a few days on the roads—had she gone straight north through Whispervale to the eastern road, she might already be there.

If she could trust her magic, if it didn't exhaust her with every use, she could have been in Entel the same day she had left the cave! Even as it was, she could have used it to lighten the load on the donkey, even lighten the donkey itself, to allow for a faster passage. But no, she could not bring herself to try.

People now passed her on the road, but she did not engage, did not even make eye contact. When she neared a village, she went off the road and circled it with a wide berth.

Except for the sixth day, when dark and ominous clouds began rolling over the mountains to the south, bursts of lightning showing over the high peaks. The wind was blowing harder, and Keri knew the land well enough from these last few years to understand that a great storm of wind and rain, sheets of rain so thick that she would hardly see the road in front of her, was fast approaching. She looked around for some cover, but this far east, few trees stood about the tended fields—this was the farming region of Honce, with wide, cleared meadows sectioned by low walls of piled stones.

Seeing little choice, Keri spotted a barn in a field and made for it, pulling the increasingly nervous donkey behind her. At one point, she had to dig in her heels and tug with all her strength, then coax and cajole and try to push the damned jenny!

How easy it would be to just go into the creature's mind and coerce it forward with her own thoughts.

But the black vulture . . .

The storm broke before she reached the barn. She finally had the donkey moving, at least. Still, when she slid the door open and entered, she was soaked to the bone, her equine companion dripping lines of rainwater.

A horse whinnied from a stall at the far end. A pair of cows were tethered closer to the door, but they paid her and the donkey no heed. Even the pigs had been brought in, a trio of them snorting and snoring in a muddy stall.

She thought she should go to the house to ask for permission, but dismissed the idea. She was too tired, too wet, and just didn't want to see anyone.

"Do'no make a mess of the place," she told the donkey, and she brought it to the side and tethered it to a post, then dropped some hay before it.

Back across the floor near the hay bales, she stripped down to her shirt and breeches, tossing her cloak and overshirt to the side, spreading them out that they might dry. She found one of the horse blankets and spread it over some straw, then fell upon it, exhausted.

Some chickens moved about to the side, and she spotted a rooster up on the edge of a loft. "Pray ye wake me with the sunrise," she told the bird. Yes, she wanted to be far away before the farmers awakened and found her.

She didn't get her wish, for not long after she fell asleep, the barn door slid open and a group of five entered.

"Hey now!" a man said loudly, waking her.

Startled, Keri rolled right up, shielding her eyes from the lamplight.

"Who might ye be, lass?" the man said.

"This be your barn?" Keri stumbled in her reply. "I'm sorry. I just . . . I came in . . . the storm. I want to be no bother . . . I mean, I'll not take . . ."

She stopped blabbering when she noted the old farmer patting his hand in the air to calm her.

"Who might ye be?"

"I am . . ." She hesitated, looking past the man to the other four, two men and two women. Younger, perhaps in their twenties, and dressed like travelers, not farmers.

"I be Connebragh of Ursal," she lied, and she tried not to wince. She also tried to emulate the thicker accent of the Whispervale region, but feared that she was failing, both in accent and in improvisation. She should have used a different name than poor Connie's!

"Ye're a long way from home."

"Entel," she stammered. "I'm on my way to Entel."

The man nodded. "Well, ye're welcome to stay the night. Storm will break before dawn. These four are same as yerself. They've some food from my table that they'll share." He looked back at the travelers, who nodded. "If ye're hungry in the morning, you come and knock. If not, well, fare well, Connebragh o' Ursal. And take heart, for ye've less than two days more walking."

He moved off and hooked the lantern on a bent nail. "Ye

keep care with this," he told them all. "When ye settle for yer sleep, then put it out, aye?"

They all nodded, and the farmer took his leave.

He wasn't gone long before the mood in the barn changed.

"Entel?" one man said with a snort. "Why're ye bound for Entel?"

"The place's in chaos," a woman added. "Monks fighting monks, goldfish chasing people from their homes. Beating anyone who darest argue. Half the south ward was burned to the ground in a fight of fireballs."

"Goldfish?"

"The pretty-faced invaders," the other man said, and spat on the floor. As he did, he paused, then walked over near to the donkey, to the saddlebags Keri had placed over a rail.

"My clothes and supplies," Keri said. "Please do'no—"

"Easy, lady," the first woman said. "We ain't to hurt ye. We ain't highwaymen or killers. Just plain folks chased out and with nowhere to—"

"Hey, now!" the man at the now-opened saddlebags said, and he lifted a small sack and jiggled it.

"No!" Keri demanded.

He opened the sack, peered in with a wide grin, and pulled forth a few large golden coins. "Well, someone's more'n she's saying, eh?"

"No, that's mine. I need it."

"Need it?" the first man said, looking to the other.

"Twenty and more gol' bears," the second man replied breathlessly to that glance.

Keri started for him, but the first man and woman grabbed her, the other woman drawing a dagger.

"So, ye're thieves, then," Keri spat at them.

"No," the first man insisted. "But might ye be telling us how Connebragh o' Ursal holds a treasure like this in her pouch? And why she's in a barn, uninvited, when there's a tavern and an inn not fifty yards farther along the road?"

"Maybe she's the thief, eh?" the woman with the knife said.

"I'm no thief!" Keri replied, narrowing, then closing her eyes, trying to keep her calm. "The gold was given me by a friend."

"Good friend," said the woman holding her.

"For my sons!" Keri said. "For me own boys. Taken by the pretty-faces, they were, and put aboard a ship. I'm meanin' to buy 'em back. Please, I beg, do'no take it."

The four looked around to each other, shrugging, nodding, shaking their heads.

"Half of it," said the man holding the bag.

"That sounds fair," said the other man.

"No, I need . . ." Keri stopped and felt the tension and strength flowing out of her. She saw the desperation on the faces of these four dirty travelers, poor folks rendered homeless and chased out.

She knew keenly what that felt like.

She had twenty-six gol' bears in the sack. Would thirteen be enough?

"Half," she agreed. "I'll let ye take half."

"Let us?" chuckled the woman holding her roughly by her left arm. "Leave her five and take the rest! Lying wench."

"No, no," the man said.

Keri started to breathe a sigh of relief, but then she felt the man brushing back her thick black hair over her ear. He looked at her hands, even glanced down and noticed a sparkle from her gem-studded anklet.

"She's bejeweled," the man laughed.

"Poor peasant from Ursal?" the woman scoffed at her.

"Leave her half the gold and we'll take her jewels instead," the man holding her said, and he grabbed at her right hand, at her citrine and bloodstone ring.

Citrine, the gem of stone.

Bloodstone, the gem of strength.

He grabbed for the ring and Keri clenched her fist, rolling her fingers. A wave of panic hit her—whatever her present concerns, whatever demons haunted her, she simply couldn't surrender these gems.

The man, who was large and quite strong, grabbed her wrist with his free hand, squeezing hard, and pried at her fingers to straighten them, never letting go of the ring.

Desperation flowed through Keri, indeed, as did something else.

The bloodstone called to her. It almost seemed like that to her, as if the stone was screaming out to her, as if she was its mother, for protection from the thief.

And in its call came magic, the magic of strength. The woman growled, too frantic to worry about the fall of Tay Aillig, or the wrecking of the Xoconai boat on the lake outside Oton-totomi, or the fight with Scathmizzane. Too frantic, then, to even think of the fight in Whispervale or the poor black vulture.

308

Too desperate to think of Dafydd.

No, none of that was there. None of the black wings of grief and guilt and fear. Just the present and the desperate moment. Just this attempted theft of something she could not lose, and the sense of strength flowing up her arm. She locked her hand into a fist, pushing aside the prying fingers with ease, and bending one in the process—painfully so, if the thief's yelp was to be believed.

A second magical sensation joined the first, and she felt her hand hardening.

Hardening?

The man fell back, shaking his wounded hand, then stepped forward and slugged Keri on the side of her face, staggering her to the side, pushing her deeper against the clutch of the woman there.

That woman grabbed her by the hair.

Instinctively, Keri's right arm came across, that balled fist slamming the woman in the chest.

Her breath blasted out violently. She let go of Keri and reeled, her face a mask of confusion, her hands grasping at her chest until she simply fell over.

Keri felt the man coming in at her from the other side and instinctively swung her right arm back the other way. She was shocked when her eyes followed that movement, when she saw that her backhand was still with a closed fist, and more so, that her fist, even in the meager lamplight, did not appear like a human hand at all, but like a block of stone.

Stone!

And when it connected on the leaping attacker, it felt like that, as well, for she batted the man aside with ease, launching him over a bale of hay to go crashing through the rails of the fence of the stall holding the pigs.

Keri brought her hand in to study it. She was shocked by the transformation, but only to a point—hadn't she repeatedly turned that arm into a leopard's paw, after all?

She looked up to see the other two thieves staring at her, mouths hanging open. The woman to the side groaned and showed no signs of rising. The man lying with the pigs was making not a sound.

The standing woman cried out and flung a knife at her.

Keri threw her right arm up to block, and the blade hit her stone hand and bounced harmlessly away!

"Drop the bag," she told them. "And get out."

The two continued to stare. "Shoot her," the woman told the man, who had a bow slung across his back.

"Get out," Keri repeated.

They glanced back and leaned toward the barn door, even took a step.

"The bag!" Keri yelled. The two broke and ran, taking the gold that would buy back her sons.

Keri stamped her foot, calling upon the graphite bars of her anklet.

Her lightning bolt caught them as they reached for the barn door. It lifted them from the floor to slam them into that closed portal. Keri was there before either got up from the dirt, warning them to stay down or face her wrath as she collected the sack of gol' bears.

Both cowered, hair still flying wild and teeth still chattering from the energy of the lightning bolt, shying and staying low whenever this powerful witch even looked at them.

"Go and see to your friends," Keri instructed, and, for some reason she wasn't sure even she understood, she handed each of them a gol' bear. Then she went and gathered her belongings and her donkey.

"That gold I gave to you buys my silence of your crime," she told the four, who were then together against the hay bales, staring at her in obvious terror. "And buys your own silence for what happened here. I am a sister of the Abellican Church," she lied. "I am trying to find a way to better the lives of people like you and all of us suffering under the changes wrought by Grand Augur Apichtli and Xoco . . . the goldfish. Do'no compromise me and my mission, I warn you."

She moved for the door, pulling her cloak tight as she heard the storm still howling outside. She paused when she got there and looked back at the four, who hadn't moved an inch.

"I hope that gold helps you," she said sincerely. "I'm not blind to your plight, for 'tis one common about the lands."

Keri noted that the woman she had punched with her stone fist was struggling to breathe. She looped the donkey's rein over the door handle and walked over to the group, hands up unthreateningly.

Slowly, she placed her hands on the woman's collarbone and

called upon the magic of the wedstone, sending forth waves of healing magic. Almost immediately, the woman's breathing steadied.

And with the moment of desperation past, Keri felt the pangs of her history, heard the screams, felt the warm blood.

"Forgive me," she whispered to the woman, and she turned and rushed away, not even looking back (where she would have seen four stunned expressions staring at her) as she tugged the donkey's lead and went out into the storm.

She started for the road but veered to the farmhouse. She fished about for a gol' bear and slid it under the front door, then pulled up her collar and went on her way, pelted by rain, buffeted by wind, and with shocks of lightning a thousand times more powerful than anything she could ever hope to summon crashing all about her.

She didn't get far in that storm, cowering in a hollow beneath a large stump, trying to calm the poor drenched donkey. How she wanted to venture into its mind and steer it somewhere drier and safer, and calm the fraying nerves.

She didn't dare. She couldn't dare.

She fell asleep only briefly, waking to a nightmare vision of the woman in the barn with her chest crushed in, gasping her last while the ghost of a torn Tay Aillig, his ripped face hanging by a strand of skin, hovered over her, laughing manically.

She was out of the hollow as soon as the storm broke, before the dawn even, moving her tired legs along down the road as fast as she could manage. She steered far from the next village in line, and a small cluster of farms the next day, and finally came upon a foothill to see houses scattered along the slopes before her to the east, all looking down to the northeast, to a large city dominated by the giant structure of St. Bondabruce, with its soaring spires and wide courtyards and gardens. The place was full of color and great windows shining in the sun, and pennants waving in the sea breeze above tents of bright cloth. It appeared very different from any other large structure she had seen in Honce—because of this monastery's long ties to Behren, she presumed.

She was wounded by the thought that an architectural creation of such masterwork and beauty now housed an order falling in line with the iron authority of the Xoconai, but when she thought about it, it made sense to her. The Xoconai were beautiful, she thought, their clothing and armor splendid, their architectural structures similarly shining (though overwhelmed with gold).

She scanned farther to the southwest, farther from the coast, and noted a singular keep, impressive but not so huge.

St. Rontlemore? she wondered.

She couldn't be sure.

She spent a long while there studying the city, noting the scores and scores of masts in the wide harbor, the great variety of ships anchored out there, or pulled up along several long wharves. She guessed easily which were ships of the Xoconai fleet, large and thick, with banks of square sails. She noted some ships that seemed very different from those, and guessed them to be Behrenese craft. For this was Entel, where Behren met Honce-the-Bear, where the influences of the southern kingdom were said to be extensive—and apparently so, she noted, looking again at St. Bondabruce, and listening carefully to the strange music that seemed to be flowing from many places along the streets of the city, featuring notes and sounds very different from the dour dirges and lamenting melodies she had heard from the street musicians in Palmaris, in Ursal, in Whispervale, and even when she was at St.-Mere-Abelle. These songs were fast and happy. Simply listening to them lifted Keri's spirits and made her want to dance.

"All right, then," she told the donkey. "Let us go and see this place where the cultures of the two lands are said to join and form arts and foods and joy unlike any other."

CHAPTER 20

ENTEL

That afternoon, Keri walked into the sprawl of Entel along a wide cobblestone street called Falidean Way without incident, without even a question from a guard, Bearman or Xoconai.

The sheer size of Entel surprised her. She had been in Ursal for years, so she was not unused to crowds and the bustle of a city, but Entel was very unlike Ursal. Ursal was much more vertical, with three-story tenements, a huge keep and palace, large homes, and, of course, St. Honce. Most of the people who were considered citizens of Ursal actually lived outside the city's tall walls. Entel, though, really had no clearly defined walls at all, and no gates to control the influx and outflow of people, citizen or not. It was a sprawling mass of houses and tents and long low warehouses down by the enormous docks. Entel stretched to the sea, and to several small islands out there in the east, and up the mountainside to the south and west, with a forest of houses climbing higher and higher, each afforded grand views of the city proper and the endless Mirianic beyond.

The influences of Behren were everywhere, and now two cultures who had shared Entel for centuries had been joined by a third, as the Xoconai had flocked to this unique city in great numbers, bringing their own ways and colors and sounds. When Keri had come to live in this land called Honce soon after the war had ended, Ursal was still the most populous city in the land, with Palmaris and Entel considered second and third, in varying order depending upon whom you asked.

Now, simply walking the streets, Keri had no doubt that Entel's population was larger than any other, including Ursal, and it wasn't close.

From what she had learned from Ataquixt, it made sense to her. This was the largest port, bringing goods from all the lands to the south. From the south now came the gold, the most treasured metal of the Xoconai, the source of their magic and their power. Wealthy Xoconai had come here to grow wealthier.

From the south, too, came exotic trade.

Keri was hardly interested in such things, but even as disinterested as she was in anything but finding her sons, she could feel the difference of this place, the possibilities, the varying sorts of beauty.

That all occurred to her, but she kept such distractions far to the side, her focus leading her to the dock area of the city, and to a lane full of taverns and inns servicing the port.

Door-to-door she went, from one tavern keeper or bartender or waiter to another, playing the role of a poor traveler, claiming her family all dead, leaving her out of luck and out of money, and begging for work.

And so, on the very first day that she had entered the city, Keri found herself in the back room of a famous, or infamous, large tavern and boardinghouse, One Last Before the Sea, sitting on a cushioned couch before the proprietors, a husband-and-wife team known throughout the dock ward for their tight ship, fair drinks, and their perfected use of hard wooden batons to control the unruly. The main proprietor, Katatina, was a tall woman with very broad shoulders and a huge chest—Keri wondered if someone had taken the ribs of a giant and stuck them into a human woman. She looked . . . off, and yet was quite handsome, with dark eyes always opened so wide that the white could be seen all about her pupils at all times. And did she ever blink? Her hair was dark and long, thick and wavy, and her smile enormous, even if it showed as much gum as teeth. She was Behrenese at least in part, obviously, tan-skinned. Keri thought her older, but her skin certainly didn't show any signs of age, for it was smooth, and her muscles showed no slack. Individually, none of her features seemed to work, but somehow, together they formed a lovely, if formidable, presentation.

Her husband, Hodner Brewster, was not from the kingdom south of the Belt-and-Buckle Mountains, his features Bearman through and through. He was shorter than Katatina by a few inches, and slender, but not skinny. He moved with the ease of

317

a fighter, and his blue eyes never stopped surveying all about him. He had a ready smile and a hearty laugh, Keri soon enough learned, but she didn't doubt that this was a dangerous man to anger.

Doubly so if his wife joined in.

"You have blood from the desert, yes?" Katatina asked her when the interview began. "A father or mother from Behren?"

"No."

"To-gai, then?"

"No, I'm from the west." Keri noted the two sharing a glance at that, and she understood their surprise, surely.

"Not that far west," she added. "Not over the mountain divide. Not from the lands of the Xoconai."

"The Wilderlands?"

Keri decided that was close enough, and nodded. "I've been in Honce . . ."

"Quixi Tonoloya," Katatina quickly corrected, and she wagged her finger at Keri. "If we take you on, you will be serving many Xoconai—sailors, warriors, augurs. Any reference you make to this land as it was named before their arrival will bring consternation, at the least."

"Quixi Tonoloya," she replied with a nod. "I been here for fifteen years, since the war. My family lived in Ursal, when last I had a family. But they're dead many years now and so I've found myself wandering. Too painful to stay, and alas, but I've found no new place yet to call home."

"Then you will just leave us one day?" Hodner interrupted. "We will spend days and days properly training you and you will just leave us?"

"No, no." It was all a lie, both this response and her history, of course, and Keri could see from the expressions worn by the pair that they saw right through her.

"Are you running from something or to something?" Katatina asked.

"Neither and both."

"And when are you running again, Connebragh of Ursal?" the woman pressed, and the way she spoke the name told Keri that she didn't believe that, either.

"Connie," she said sweetly, flashing a disarming smile, or so she hoped. "Please call me Connie."

"And when are you running again, Connie?" Katatina restated.

Keri's face turned serious. She was playing with a couple who survived and thrived because they understood the truth of those they met. These two dealt with transients, sailors, pirates, Xoconai soldiers, rogues, every single day.

"I do'no know," she answered honestly.

"There's the Wilderlands accent," Hodner noted with a sudden and sharp laugh. "Well, it would be better if you were a better liar, but you seem strong enough and quick enough with your wits to survive the floor."

And so, Keri became Connie the barmaid at the sea-sprayed One Last Before the Sea, thick with mildew, loud with song and swears, with weather-warped walls and slanted floors that grabbed at her shoes from the sticky remnants of too many spilled drinks, both pre- and post-consumption.

She took well to the job, milling about the patrons, listening to their conversations. She even used her bloodstone, just a bit each night, to strengthen her arms, which were aching under the weight of trays laden with glasses and plates. For the first few nights, she found herself quite nervous around so many Xoconai, but she kept reminding herself that these were sailors coming in from the ocean to the east, with little knowledge of minor events in a small village a hundred miles inland. After a week or so, she finally managed to settle in and relax.

She also came to think of Katatina and Hod, as Hodner told her to call him, as friends. Each night after the common room had finally cleared out, the three and a couple of other servers sat around enjoying a meal and some drink of their own.

Never once did she feel threatened or afraid.

If her business to find her sons weren't so pressing, a great weight hanging over her head, Keri considered that she could stay here and be quite happy. She even fantasized about eventually settling in Entel, maybe working this very job, with Connie and the boys, quietly, away from the troubles of the wider world.

For all of that, however, Keri was also growing anxious with each passing day. She spent her off-hours walking the docks and the beach near it, sometimes hunting quahogs or dropping a fishing line from a wharf, but always watching the ships, so many Xoconai ships! Dozens of warships were in port, and whenever one sailed away, it was quickly replaced by another, and with every new carrack or frigate or schooner coming in under the golden flag, her heart leaped with anticipation.

But none were named *Lauilli*.

At the end of her second week, on a bustling, brilliant sunny morning, Keri grew frustrated at the docks. The Xoconai warships were all quiet, the only turnover being the Honce and Behrenese merchant vessels coming and going.

Glancing back nervously with every step, the woman moved down the roads toward the heart of the city. She knew she'd be more likely recognized among the Xoconai soldiers or discovered by the ever-vigilant augurs than by anyone at the docks, but she had a possibly desperate play that she needed to try, for her sons.

She passed St. Bondabruce, huge and colorful and reputably inviting—except that now the place teemed with Xoconai warriors and augurs! They tried to be inconspicuous, keeping low on the parapets, seemingly relaxed and leaning against the walls near the wide-open gates. But Keri knew better. They were watching everything.

This Abellican monastery was now dominated by the Xoconai.

She picked up her pace, veering south, trying to put distance between herself and St. Bondabruce, and then shuffling even more urgently when she crossed a side street to see a trio of augurs holding their golden divining rods out before them, their other hands raised, palm up, showing the red sparkle of magical garnets. One glanced her way, curiously, suspiciously, but fortunately, she was in a bit of a crowd and doubted that the man, had he detected some magic from her jewelry or tattoo, could single her out. As soon as she was out of sight of that trio, she picked up her pace, fast-walking, even trotting, turning down the next side street to the west, then back again to the south at the next intersection.

Still hustling, she passed two more blocks before coming up on a line of people, some sitting, some even lying on the cobble-stones. When she glanced again to the west, she understood: these poor folk, injured or sick or maybe just hungry, were waiting for an audience in St. Rontlemore, the large square keep in sight only two blocks to the west.

Keri glanced back, fearful that the augurs were still sensing her magic and perhaps closing in. She decided not to wait her turn—who knew if she would even be seen by the brothers of St. Rontlemore that day with so many other needy folk before her?—and instead pushed ahead along the line, walking deter-minedly for the monastery.

More than a few sour looks came her way, and more than a few muttered curses, but she kept her course, finally arriving before the entry stairs, where a handful of monks were trying to manage the crowd by running a triage on the common folk. She felt better, reassured, when she saw one brother cast some healing spell upon the arm of an older woman, who smiled in reply and kissed him on the cheek before hustling away.

Another monk, a sister, walked the line, handing out food and drink.

"May I help you, good lady?" she asked of Keri.

"I need to see someone in the abbey."

The woman shrugged sympathetically, but turned her gaze down the line and nodded her chin.

"Please, it is urgent, and it is important."

"No one would be here if they did not feel the same."

"It is important to St. Rontlemore," Keri pleaded.

The monk just looked at her, half shrugged, and shook her head. She didn't refuse outright and seemed confused as to what she should do, so Keri tried to formulate a more urgent plea.

Another monk, an older man with gray stubble, sunken eyes, and the ruddy face and weather-beaten wrinkles so common here near the ocean, walked over to ask if there was a problem.

"She says she has something important for St. Rontlemore," the sister reported.

The man looked at her, then back at the stairs, where another pair of monks were watching closely. He paused for a moment, then motioned for Keri to follow him.

"You will have to explain more than that if you wish to be placed before those who have been waiting longer," he said to her as they walked.

Keri hardly heard the man, her eyes fixed on the two brothers who were watching her approach. One broke away and rushed back in through the abbey door.

A moment later, the brother on the stairs turned back only briefly—someone was calling to him from inside, though Keri couldn't make it out—before turning back and motioning Keri and her escort to hurry along.

She wasn't stopped at the stairs, but went right up and into the monastery, unsure but hopeful.

But less hopeful by far when she entered an empty anteroom, a short and narrow corridor with a closed door on the other end. She turned to her escort, who had slowed for some reason, but he was already shutting the exit door behind her, while he remained outside, leaving her alone in the darkness.

"Who are you?" came a voice from the side, beyond the wall.

Keri shifted nervously, realizing as her eyes adjusted that these narrow walls had small slits in them. "Murder holes," she had heard them called in Ursal.

A moment later, she was bathed in dim, magical light, and she was able to confirm that both walls were indeed lined with the small holes, waist high. The monks she had known in St.-Mere-Abelle were skilled with crossbows, she recalled.

"My name is Keridven o' Whispervale," she replied, "a small village a hundred miles to the west."

"You have come a hundred miles to tell us something?" There was no missing the skepticism in the question.

"For my own reasons, I've come, but aye, I've information that the monks of St. Rontlemore might find interesting, even important."

"We find your possession of Abellican Ring Stones both, I assure you."

Keri glanced reflexively at her ring, then tucked her hand under her cloak, then realized that she had just identified a magical item for them!

"Oh, but they're no' Abellican Ring Stones. I'm no' of this land. I've come from the—"

"Heresy is swiftly and eternally exorcized," the hidden interrogator said.

"I'm from the west, beyond your church," Keri quickly replied. "Brother Thaddius?" she asked, referring to the powerful monk she had come to know in her exploits in ending the war.

"Are you knowing of Brother Thaddius?"

She heard more than a few gasps, even a growl, at the mention of the monk, and she became suddenly unsure. Had she erred in coming to St. Rontlemore? She had thought—Ataquixt had told her!—that Rontlemore was allied with St.-Mere-Abelle. If that information was wrong, she was in dire trouble.

"Do tell us about your friendship with Master Thaddius of St. Bondabruce."

Keri felt her breath blow out. Thaddius in St. Bondabruce? Had she misunderstood Ataquixt? Had she walked into the wrong monastery? Was Coyote in the room behind these walls?

"Must be a different man," she stammered. "I've not seen Brother Thaddius in a dozen years and more, in the west . . ."

A commotion behind the wall interrupted her. She heard several voices, some excited, but she couldn't quite make out the conversation.

The entry door at the end of the hall swung open and a woman wearing an ill-fitting weathered robe came into view.

A small woman, no taller than Keri, who herself barely topped five feet. Her hair was long and light brown, with a bit of gray mixed in, and her grin toothy and bright, her light brown eyes smiling as fully as her mouth.

"Elysant?" Keri mouthed silently, for she had no voice.

"By Saint Abelle," the woman said, and came forward to wrap Keri in a tight hug. "Aoleyn," she whispered. "I feared you long dead since the breaking of the truce. There are whispers . . ."

"They're not true," Aoleyn answered. "For I'm quite alive." Moving closer, she whispered into Elysant's ear, "Please call me Keridven, or Keri, if you would."

"You are among friends here," Elysant whispered back. "But as you wish." She pushed the unexpected visitor back to arm's length, staring at her, studying her, then asked, "What magic have you enacted here?"

"None."

Elysant escorted her into the main entry room, where a cluster of monks stood. "Brother Edgar," Elysant said to one older man, motioning to Keri.

"Of course, abbess," he replied, and held up a red garnet and, surprisingly, one of those golden rods used by the Xoconai augurs. At the sight of it, Keri turned a surprised look to Elysant.

"They learn our magic, we learn theirs," Elysant answered. "Or we try to, at least."

Bother Edgar moved closer cautiously.

"She'll not harm you," Elysant assured him, and then to Keri, "Show your jewelry."

Keri shrugged and held up her hands to display her rings, then pointed to her earring and the turquoise cuff on her other ear. She opened her cloak and lifted her shirt to reveal her belly ring, hiked her pant leg to uncover her anklet.

The monk shrugged, clearly frustrated. "I sense magic, as I did when she climbed the stairs of St. Rontlemore. And again in the foyer."

"The murder hall, you mean," Keri remarked, and the man looked shocked.

"These are dangerous times," Elysant reminded her. "St. Bondabruce has openly attacked brothers of St. Rontlemore on the streets, and we have caught more than one of their agents posing as desperate peasants in the charity line. And surely our Xoconai occupiers hold no love for St. Rontlemore, as we have not disavowed our ties to St.-Mere-Abelle."

"Come now with me to more private quarters," she bade her old friend and led the way, Keri and a group of monks following closely. When they reached the private audience chamber of the abbess, Elysant allowed only Keri and Brother Edgar inside, however, much to the chagrin of the others.

"Trust me," Elysant begged after she had shut the door in the face of the protesting monks. "Please remove all your jewelry."

Keri looked at her skeptically for a moment, trying to replay all their interactions those many years ago, and trying to make some sense of how Elysant might be acting as abbess here, but with Brother Thaddius serving as a high-ranking master in the hostile St. Bondabruce. After a few moments, her expression softened and she came to trust that the abbess had her best interests at heart, or at least, that Elysant wouldn't use such trickery to betray her. She carefully removed her rings, her earring, her ear cuff, the anklet, and last, her belly ring, placing them all within easy reach on the edge of Elysant's large desk.

"Move to the side," Elysant instructed, waving her away from her jewelry.

Again, Keri wore that suspicious and skeptical look.

"First, you both move to that corner," she answered the abbess, pointing to the opposite wall near the door, which would leave her closer to her treasured items than they.

Brother Edgar snorted, but Elysant grabbed him without hesitation and pulled him along.

Keri stepped away from the desk, and the old brother lifted his garnet and the Xoconai rod.

"It is not the jewelry," he assured his abbess. He was shaking his head, his expression a mask of confusion. "Or not just the jewelry, at least. It's her. She glows of magic, subtly, but without doubt."

In response, hardly caring, Keri pulled up her shirt quite high, drawing a gasp from the embarrassed Edgar and a surprised look from Elysant. Defiantly, she stripped off her shirt and her breeches, leaving her in her undergarments alone. She showed them her work, her marvelous tattoo, the paw pads on her hands, the markings on her sides and legs and back.

"Woman!" Brother Edgar begged, averting his gaze, to which Keri snorted with amusement.

Elysant, though, approached, her eyes wide, her jaw hanging open. She reached a hand forward tentatively to touch the cloud leopard markings on Keri's side.

"Brother Edgar, use the stone," she instructed.

"But . . ."

Keri chuckled again and felt quite relaxed now. If these two were planning to disarm and harm her, they had certainly failed in their play. "He needs to spend more time outside these dark walls," she whispered to Elysant, who laughed along with her.

But the abbess cut it short and shook her head, waving her hand to force herself back to the seriousness of the moment. "Brother Edgar, use the stone now. What do you see?"

The monk held up the garnet and looked at Keri through its magic. "I see magic," he said after a few moments. "She is a magical creature!"

"A fine compliment," Keri said.

"She is indeed, and more than you can begin to guess," Elysant said with a wide smile. She had seen Aoleyn's tattoos before, though not this much of them, and more than that, she had witnessed the power of this magic-using witch from the Ayamharas Plateau in all its glory.

"What exactly did you use to create this?" Elysant asked, rubbing her fingers over the delicate lines of the markings along Keri's side.

"They are made with tiger's paw and wedstone, which you call soul stone," the witch answered. "The dust of both. I needled them under my skin."

"And they retain their magic?" Edgar asked.

Keri thought to turn her arm into a leopard paw, but even the notion reminded her of the pain and anguish such an action would bring to her. Now she did a bit of self-reflection. The magic was constant within her, and the magic, the thought of it, was bringing her great pain.

In that telling moment, she finally understood why she couldn't escape the black wings that fluttered up inside of her, the pain of memory, the paralyzing, debilitating shock every time she called upon a power.

It was always there. She hadn't fully realized the implications of that truth until here and now.

She swallowed hard and nodded to answer Brother Edgar.

Suddenly, she felt naked. She grabbed up her pants and put them on, then her shirt, and moved for her jewelry.

"The markings," Edgar told Elysant. "They are the source. The magic is there, as within the Ring Stones, as within her jewelry, but the magic is in use in those markings, a constant vibration and song."

When she looked back at him, Keri saw him staring at her quite differently now, almost in awe.

"You are a godly being," he whispered breathlessly.

"Never say that," Keri shot back sharply, startling him from his trance.

"You cannot blame him for his amazement," Elysant said.

"We of the Abellican Order have never heard of such a thing."
She looked to the brother and said, "Leave us. And say nothing
of this to anyone, on my order and on your word."

"You cannot stay alone with . . ."

Elysant's glare shut him up and he scurried out of the room,
where the others were huddled and questioning him before he
even shut the door behind him.

"How I wish Thaddius were here," Elysant said.

"Wouldn't he be fighting against you if he was?"

The abbess chuckled. "Not everything is as it seems," she
assured her old companion. "I am here for a specific reason, on
order from St.-Mere-Abelle. Father Abbot Braumin assigned
me to St. Rontlemore only in the beginning of this year, and it
will not prove a long stay."

"And Thaddius?"

Elysant merely smiled and shrugged, but she didn't have
to state it openly for Keri to figure out some possibilities here.
She knew that Brother Thaddius had been a supporter of the
heretic Marcalo De'Unnero before the great battle over the soul
of the Abellican Church, at least at one point. St. Bondabruce
had remained supportive of the dead De'Unnero's principles,
so Ataquixt had told her.

Thus, Brother Thaddius was well-known, and quite likely
regarded as an ally, among the cult of heretics, of course, and
so perhaps it was something else that had placed him in St.
Bondabruce than any fealty to that lost cause.

She hoped she was right—she had come to respect Thaddius
in their time together. The idea that he would throw in with

331

the Xoconai after the betrayal of the treaty he had helped to forge truly pained her.

But she pushed those troubling possibilities out of her thoughts, for those were the concerns of a past time, a time when her name was not Keridven of Whispervale.

A time she had thrown far, far behind.

"You must take great care," Elysant said to her.

"They can find me with their golden rods and a garnet stone," Keri agreed, nodding. "I know, and I do not know what to do about it."

CHAPTER 21

A GATHERING OF ABSOLUTISTS

M aster Thaddius Roncourt of St. Bondabruce sat in his assigned seat at the side of Abbot Dusibol's audience chamber. Thaddius wasn't impressed with the man, wasn't impressed with any of the brothers here, and he truly wondered how he had ever fallen under the spell of the De'Unnerans. For he was easily the most powerful monk in the monastery in using the sacred gemstones, but no one else knew that, and he had no intention of telling or showing them.

But one man now in this very room, a puffing rooster with a face, arm, and shoulder scarred by the flames of a vicious fireball, suspected that Master Thaddius's story of minimal magical powers was at least underplayed.

Thaddius watched that man, Brother Glorious, very carefully now. Had he known that Glorious was still alive and here serving as Abbot Dusibol's right-hand man, he wouldn't have agreed to come to this monastery. He had tangled with Glorious the De'Unneran before—it was Thaddius's own fireball that had so scarred the vain rooster.

Fortunately, so much was going on at that time that Glorious's obvious suspicions weren't going to get much play. The other men in the room had no interest in such personal squabbles, or grievances such as Glorious held against Thaddius.

For these were the men—Abbot Dusibol, City Sovereign Popoca, and the newcomer, this warrior named Coyote, who was the personal envoy and champion of Grand Augur Apichtli—the leaders of the Abellican Church had labeled as the Absolutists: the would-be absolute and unquestioned lords of the lands known as Honce-the-Bear.

Surely, they sounded as such right now—and Thaddius found it quite notable that they were speaking exclusively in the language of the west, Xoconai. Thaddius spoke it as well as the Xoconai in the room, of course, and it amused him more than a little that Brother Glorious quite often seemed lost and confused, and could contribute almost nothing to the meeting. The man had tried desperately to learn the language, at Dusibol's command. Thaddius had even been assigned to teach him. But, alas, such intelligence wasn't one of Brother Glorious's strong suits.

"When we have cleared the coast and taken full control of the seas, only then will our hand against Chezru Chieftain Brynn Dharielle be truly favorable," Abbot Dusibol explained to the two Xoconai.

Thaddius rubbed his forehead and eyes, using it as cover to prevent anyone from noting his scowl. Only the day before, Dusibol had been entreating some emissaries from Behren to give him time to settle the city from the recent Xoconai advances.

He would return Entel to the same state it had known before the war, he had assured them.

And Dusibol had entreated such nonsense so convincingly, as he was doing here and now, albeit in exactly the opposite direction. If Thaddius hadn't been in Dusibol's inner circle—something that had happened only because of their relationship decades before in the time of Marcalo De'Unnero—he would have no idea which side Dusibol was playing, and which side he intended to truly support.

"The pirate ships are fast and run to the coast of Behren," City Sovereign Popoca noted. "They will engage a superior ship only momentarily before turning and fleeing to the shallower waters—and in sight of the infernal beast that is rumored to be ever patrolling the coast of the southern kingdom."

"Because you cannot do enough damage to them quickly enough to prevent their flight," Abbot Dusibol countered.

The two Xoconai looked to each other, arching their eyebrows. They were not used to being corrected by a sidhe, Thaddius knew, even though they were trying to form a very tight relationship here with St. Bondabruce. Even though they were asking the monks to teach them about Abellican magic, and incorporating that magic into their own arcane powers, they still considered Dusibol and all the others here to be exactly that: sidhe, goblins, lesser than they.

"You are well aware of the gemstone we call the lodestone, yes?" Dusibol pressed, clearly also recognizing the same disdain dripping with every word from the two powerful guests.

Popoca looked to Coyote, who grinned wryly and drew forth

his long, slightly curved swords. He held them parallel before him, then nodded and greatly loosened his grip.

A heartbeat later, the blades slapped together tightly, tip against tip, and with such force that the strong man had to grasp them more tightly to prevent them from jolting right out of his grasp, for the sabers flew apart, rolling Coyote's hands outward.

"Both of his weapons are powerful with lodestone, or as we call it in our language, magnet," Popoca explained.

"I can deflect any strike or aim more completely," Coyote bragged.

"If it is an iron-based target," Thaddius muttered under his breath. Lodestone was situational, but extremely powerful in those select instances.

Coyote continued to smile, his expression unchanging, his eyes locked on Dusibol. His left-hand blade suddenly shot forward and to the left, stabbing precisely against a small and ornate clasp with which Brother Glorious adorned his Abellican robe.

The large monk gulped at the sudden shock, and looked down, clearly horrified. For not only had the strike marred his fancy and expensive clasp, it had torn his meticulously fitted robe, and now, worse, a bit of blood was leaking forth.

Brother Glorious cried out in protest, obviously more concerned with the tear and the stain and the damage to his items than he was with the gash in his chest.

"Oh, shut up, brother," Dusibol told him.

"You were lecturing us on the powers of lodestone, I believe," City Sovereign Popoca interjected.

"Lecturing? No, of course not. I was merely making sure that you were aware of this particular Abellican magic."

"Magic is not only the province of your little church," Coyote put in. "We know magic. The witches in the west know magic, perhaps more intimately than your clergy. The Samhaist shamans know magic. Even the sidhe of To-gai and Behren and Durubazzi know magic, akin to your own, and our own, to be truthful, though with their own particular style placed upon it."

"The Abellican Church—" Brother Glorious began to argue.

"A little humility would serve you well, Brother Puffer," Coyote said, using the derogatory moniker he had placed on Glorious on the first day they had met.

Abbot Dusibol held up his hand, a small gray stone pinched between his thumb and forefinger. He motioned to a brother standing guard at the main doors, who reached his arm out wide, holding forth a metal pan with a long wooden handle.

Dusibol clenched his fist around the stone, closed his eyes, and began to chant softly. His outstretched hand began to tremble, and the abbot growled and tried to hold on, chanting still, building the magic.

He let go, finally, the released lodestone crackling the air as it zipped across the room to clang loudly into the pan, where it stuck fast.

Brother Glorious giggled. The two Xoconai seemed less amused.

"We all know this more common usage of the lodestone," Dusibol said. "An assassin's bullet."

"An assassin's strike that is well-known to Grand Augur Apichtli," Coyote reminded the abbot threateningly.

"We in the Order have our own marshals, hunters we dispatch to bring heretics and outlaws to a just end," Abbot Dusibol continued, though there now was a hint of nervousness in his voice. "We call them Brothers Justice, and in recent years, those brothers were well-trained, and well-equipped with these gemstones. Fortunately for us now, after the schism within the Abellican Church, most of the Brothers Justice flocked to St. Bondabruce."

"So St. Bondabruce has a cadre of assassins," said Coyote.

"No," the abbot replied, then paused. "Well, yes, but more fortunately, we were blessed with many lodestones." He pointed to the pan across the way. "You have witnessed the attraction power of the stones—using them as I just did is quite limiting, of course, because you have surrendered the gemstone with the shot. But you have also shown us the repulsion powers of the stone, master Coyote, and that would make the shooting far less limited, would it not?"

Coyote narrowed his eyes, considering. Thaddius watched him intently. Popoca seemed lost, but this one, this cunning and dangerous Xoconai warrior, was figuring it out.

"You would sacrifice accuracy," he said.

Abbot Dusibol nodded.

"The stone guides the shot, not the assassin," Coyote explained to Popoca. "The assassin simply brings forth the magical energy and locks the stone onto a target. That is the aiming, and the assurance of a strike, as with my blades." He turned back to Dusibol. "You cannot do that with repulsion."

"True enough. The accuracy is diminished. Nor could one take up a stone such as the one I just launched and send anything flying with any real force."

"Then what is this about, Abbot Dusibol?" Popoca demanded. "I have a fleet in my harbor and shipments of gold waiting for them in the south. My time is precious."

"Come," the abbot bade the others, walking toward a side door in the large chamber. Brother Glorious rushed ahead.

Brother Puffer, indeed, Brother Thaddius silently noted, for it was clear that the man wanted to be the one to do the reveal. Shaking his head at the predictable fool, Thaddius fell in at the back of the line.

Through the door, the group traveled down a circular stairway to the first floor, and to a large chamber where a group of monks and civilians were hard at work, some looking over papers at several desks, others assembling racks. An open door across the way led outside, and there, a handful of forges had been fired, blacksmiths laboring.

Along one wall stood racks of piled metal balls of various sizes, some as large as Coyote's massive fist. Other racks held coiled chains—and near that one, some men and women were working files to put edges at every possible place and angle on those links.

In the middle of the room sat a large object under a blanket, and to this marched Brother Glorious. He grabbed a corner of the wrap and looked to his abbot.

Dusibol nodded and Glorious pulled the blanket free, revealing a truly strange-looking object—from the Xoconai perspective, clearly. Coyote walked toward it as if compelled by some unseen magical force, while Popoca hung back, staring intently.

Most startling of all, the centerpiece of the contraption was covered in gleaming gold!

"I give to you the St. Bondabruce *cannon!*" Brother Glorious proclaimed, and in the language of Honce, not Xoconai.

"Cannon?" Popoca echoed, looking to Dusibol.

"An armagrande," the abbot explained, translating to Xoconai.

Popoca held up his hands in confusion.

"A divine thrower," Coyote said quietly, and Popoca's eyes widened.

The warrior had already figured out the war machine, Thaddius realized when he heard Coyote's reference. In the invasion of Honce those years before, the Xoconai had used similar cannons—divine throwers, they called them—powered by the great crystal above the magical caves in far-off Fireach Speuer. Scathmizzane's avatar had channeled that power to the war machines to devastating effect, particularly upon the city of Ursal, which had been breached with those magical cannons.

"This is not possible," City Sovereign Popoca stammered. "Scathmizzane alone delivered . . ."

"We indeed fashioned our design upon those weapons of old," Abbot Dusibol explained, "using our magic now instead of the powers granted by the God Crystal of the western mountain and the channeling brilliance of Scathmizzane."

His voice trailed off at the end, for Popoca's face was turning a bright shade of red and the man seemed ready to explode.

"Sacrilege and blasphemy," Popoca squeezed out through his gritted teeth. He started forward, but Coyote intervened, lifting his hand before the man to hold him back.

"You thought to emulate a god?" Coyote asked. "Our god?"

"No, no, of course not," Abbot Dusibol said. "Our magic is not nearly as glorious, of course."

Beside him, Brother Glorious harrumphed and seemed quite taken aback—until he looked at the scowling Coyote and deflated.

"But the magic of the Abellican Order and that of your augurs is . . . complementary, at least, as you've shown with your augurs using golden wands and garnets together to root out illicit gemstones and magical items," Dusibol quickly explained. "This is our Abellican version of a Xoconai divine thrower, and while nowhere near as effective, I am certain, it may be of great use to you and to your—to our—cause."

Popoca began to huff and protest, but Coyote silenced him again. Thaddius watched it intently, impressed by the command of this one, the respect given him by City Sovereign Popoca, and the abject fear shown to him by Abbot Dusibol.

He watched Coyote move to the cannon and place his hands onto the gold, caressing it, feeling the power of it. He stopped his strange massage at the ring near the back end of the long, cylindrical barrel, set with sunstones and rimmed with sapphires.

"Explain," Coyote demanded.

"It will throw balls of—" Brother Glorious began.

"I know what it will do!" an impatient Coyote snapped back at Glorious. "Explain to me the design."

Abbot Dusibol waved Glorious to silence and motioned to another nearby monk, a Behrenese man, Brother Adnis Ibn, who rushed over to Coyote's side, as did Popoca and Dusibol.

"Where did you get such gold?" Popoca demanded of the abbot.

"It is the bulk of our treasury."

"You were told to give me your excess."

"I thought you would prefer this." He motioned to the cannon, then nodded to Adnis Ibn to continue.

"Within this shield of gold are dozens, scores, of lodestones," Adnis Ibn explained. "Our magical Ring Stones, which can attract or deflect iron and many other metals. The magic of the gold keeps the energized magic of the lodestones contained within."

"Or most of the metal around it would be sent flying away," Glorious put in.

"Shut up," Coyote warned the fool, then motioned to the Behrenese monk to go on.

"Similarly, the gemstone ring at the base," Adnis Ibn explained, guiding the warrior to that place. "The sunstone seals the magic at this end, the sapphire keeps that anti-magic barrier limited and directional, so that the lodestones can be energized.

"The harness of the cannon, the armagrande, can be lifted onto wheels." He pointed out the axles. "And over there is the loading tray." He pointed to a trio of tripods supporting a semicircular slide.

"You charge the armagrande's lodestones, the loader rolls a ball into it, and it is flung out the other end with great force," Coyote said, nodding.

"Not I alone," Adnis Ibn admitted. "It takes a ritual of prayers from at least eight brothers, preferably a dozen brothers, skilled and strong with the sacred stones . . ."

He gasped when Coyote's hand came up, clutching his throat!

"The Abellican Ring Stones, he means," Abbot Dusibol quickly interjected. "Not sacred! It is habit alone that brought forth such blasphemous words."

To the side, Thaddius simmered with rage. The abbot was conceding everything here, every little bit. Throughout the production of this monstrous weapon, Dusibol kept selling it to the brothers as a joining of the two schools of magic. So, too, would this cannon bring closer the two peoples, Xoconai and Abellican. Thaddius had always known better. This was no act of diplomacy in play. This was a surrender, wholly so, to the Xoconai and their ways.

Coyote let the poor Adnis Ibn go. "When will it be ready to use?" he demanded of Dusibol.

"The finishing touches are being fabricated all around us. The blacksmiths are making gears that will be set to the harness, and side-carts where grenadiers can sit and work the levers for elevation and swivel."

Coyote waved that notion aside. "When will it throw the metal stones?"

"It can do that now."

"With what force?"

Dusibol nodded to Adnis Ibn.

At that moment, a Xoconai augur entered the room and rushed to Popoca. They whispered something Thaddius couldn't hear, then left quickly together.

Coyote watched them go, but turned back to the monk. "With what force?" he asked again.

"Great force, master," the monk answered.

"If you launched one of those metal balls at that wall, what would happen?" He pointed to the side wall, leading to the interior of the keep.

"That wall?" Adnis Ibn asked, pointing the same way. "It would go right through, splintering the wood, surely, depending upon how many monks, and how great their combined skill, were involved in the ritual."

"And the stone foundation wall of this structure? Would it crack those stones? Break bits away?"

The monk nodded to both.

"How many would it take to knock this foundation wall of these thick stones down?"

The monk looked at them for a moment and seemed to be considering the problem.

"Could a group of grenadiers launch enough balls and with enough force to do it?"

"Oh yes, I believe so," Adnis Ibn answered, his voice faltering as City Sovereign Popoca came rushing back in.

Popoca pulled Coyote aside, demanding his full attention, but not whispering, surely.

"She was seen, rushing into St. Rontlemore!"

"She?"

"The woman from Whispervale, we believe. Keridven the witch. The augurs—the same who were with you when you encountered her in that village—claim that they sensed her, then saw her fleeing for the monastery."

"She is dead," Coyote scoffed.

"You saw her body?"

"I saw the ashes . . ." The man stopped abruptly, took a deep and steadying breath, then added, "No, it cannot be her."

"You are certain?"

Coyote fumbled for a response, Thaddius noted, and noted too how agitated the man had become at the mere mention of this witch from Whispervale, wherever that might be.

"If it is truly her . . ." Popoca warned. "We have to be sure."

"Surround St. Rontlemore," Coyote told him. "Seal off every avenue of escape."

"We have many macana there now."

Coyote turned to Abbot Dusibol. "Get that armagrande up on its wheels, and a team to pull it, and a cadre of your brethren to serve as grenadiers," he ordered.

"Sir?" a flustered Dusibol returned. He looked to Popoca. "City Sovereign?"

"You heard him," Popoca replied. "We will get this woman, this witch, surrendered by the brothers of St. Rontlemore, or we will take her from them with all force."

"It is a fortress," Abbot Dusibol reminded them.

In response, Coyote pointed to Adnis Ibn. "He said your— what did you call it?—your cannon could knock down walls."

345

"It can, yes," Dusibol said, though he didn't seem very confident of that.

"Pray you hope that it will, for if not, know that I will cut off his head and tack it up on the inside door of your bedchamber."

"It will!" Dusibol said more firmly.

"Then to arms, good abbot," said Popoca. "You are finally getting your fondest wish, for this day will mark the end of St. Rontlemore's relevance, or it will mark the end of St. Rontlemore altogether."

That brought a cheer about the room, and Thaddius joined in, though only for appearance. He rushed from the room, fearing that Dusibol would assign him to serve on the grenadier crew or to perform some other function in support of the coming confrontation.

He hadn't the time.

He clutched his secret soul stone tightly as he rushed through the corridors toward his private chamber. He knew that Elysant needed him.

"She is not in port," Brother Edgar announced when he was called back into the abbess's room, much later that day.

"You have the logs?" Elysant asked.

The monk walked to the desk and dropped a large book onto the desk where Elysant sat with Keri. "The *Lauilli* sailed more than a month ago, destination unknown. She is not in port, nor expected."

"Eventually, she'll return," Elysant said to Keri, trying to comfort the obviously-distressed mother. "Patience will serve us well."

"No," Brother Edgar jumped in forcefully, startling both women. "Time is not our ally. Not with her here. They'll not suffer this magical creature to live. She is simply unacceptable to those painted-faced devils."

Keri grimaced at his description of the Xoconai. She understood why many here in Honce would feel so strongly about them—the Xoconai had certainly earned those insults and that hatred.

But she thought of Ataquixt.

She thought of Tuolonatl, who had forged a truce and then gone to Palmaris determined to make that truce mean something.

She thought of Kenzie. Was he to be considered a "painted-faced devil" by the monks of the Abellican Church, and by the people of the land resentful of the Xoconai?

She could never regret choosing to bring her dear, beloved Kenzie into the world, but doubts lashed at her with those harsh words from Brother Edgar.

"I caution ye not to be judging them all by the choices of the leaders here and now," she said. "The people of the west are of no singular mind, and at their extremes are no less diverse than the monks of the two abbeys that do battle here in Entel."

Edgar snorted.

"Enough, brother," Elysant insisted.

"You give them that generous mercy, lady," Edgar said to her.

"I wonder if you'll hold such feeling when they put you in the middle of their golden mirrors and roast you like a holiday bird."

"Brother," Elysant warned.

Keri was about to say more, but she knew from Elysant's look at her that such a course wouldn't be wise, not at this time. She knew, too, that Elysant understood her feelings in this, at least somewhat. The abbess didn't know about Kenzie's heritage, but Elysant, traveling beside Thaddius and Keri, had certainly seen many instances of the other side of the occupying Xoconai.

"Sadly, Brother Edgar speaks the truth about your presence here," the abbess said. "At least, the truth as we know it here in Entel, particularly since the arrival of this warrior, Coyote. We will have to be very careful and very clever. The Xoconai have been raiding the homes of the nobles and of the wealthy merchants—anyone suspected of having any gemstones or magical items fashioned of them. They have demanded that all the magic be surrendered, and have executed three who were caught with the contraband. They've even ordered us at St. Rontlemore to surrender our cache, but as of yet, they have not followed through on their threats to forcibly take them from us. I don't believe they'll risk an open battle. Not yet, at least. I hope I am right."

"You have to silence the magical song within you," Brother Edgar told Keri. "They will find you, and they do not share your generosity of spirit. They will burn you to ash and sweep up the remains of your magical dust."

"Brother, do be quiet," Elysant insisted. "Look at what this simple woman from another land has accomplished with these Ring Stones we hold so dear. Have you ever heard of such a thing as transforming the Ring Stones into a tattoo? It is miraculous."

"I have heard of something similar only once, Abbess Elysant. His name was Marcalo De'Unnero."

Elysant gasped at that.

"It was said that he absorbed the tiger's paw fully into his palm," Edgar went on. "That he lost himself within the ferocity of the magic."

Elysant held her hands out toward the man, begging him to shut up.

"She has to silence that magical song," the stubborn man finished.

"But how?" Elysant asked, shaking her head.

Keri knew that Elysant was not well-versed in the Abellican magic. As with most people, she had only a little affinity for the stones, if any at all.

Elysant moved to her desk and from a drawer produced a folded cloth, then opened it to reveal an orange gemstone streaked with milky white. "Do you know this Ring Stone?"

Keri shook her head, as she wasn't quite sure. "Sunstone?"

"Yes," said Elysant.

"Have you tried to use such a gem before?" Brother Edgar asked.

Keri shook her head.

"You need to," he sharply retorted. "That song of the sunstone to silence all other songs emanating from you is likely your only salvation."

Keri held the gem tentatively and sent her thoughts into it just a bit to hear its magical vibrations. "I do'no like it," she tried to explain, fumbling for the words. "Its song is not . . . beautiful. It clangs and strains."

"Those bitten by field vipers or hourglass spiders think it beautiful enough," Edgar dryly replied.

Keri stared at him curiously until she considered the other properties of the gem.

"Sunstone cures poison," Elysant explained. "And it silences magic. Brother Edgar is tactless, perhaps, but he is correct. You need to quiet the magic resonating within you." She nodded at the stone.

Keri took a deep breath and pressed it against her breast, falling into the flat notes and discordant vibrations of the gem's magic. She brought those magical vibrations forth and enveloped herself, much as she might have done with her serpentine to create a shield against fire.

She noted Brother Edgar, garnet and golden wand held up before him, nodding his approval.

So, it was working.

But it was also making Keri so very weak. Her stomach churned and she feared she would vomit. She took a deep breath and her ribs ached, particularly around the cloud leopard markings. Her hands burned as if she had left them too long in icy water, and her head throbbed.

She couldn't hold the sunstone's magic. She had to let it go. The discomfort wasn't like before, where the magic had pained her for her memories, no. This was quite a different feeling altogether. This pain was physical, as if the sunstone was assaulting her life energy, her very soul.

She gasped and dropped the sunstone to the floor. "I can'no," she said, sobbing.

Elysant was there at once, holding her close.

"It hurt," Keri whispered into the abbess's ear.

"This is not good at all, abbess. Not at all," she heard Brother Edgar say.

"We will figure it out," Elysant replied.

"Abbess, if they learn that she is in here . . ." His voice trailed off as Elysant stepped back from Keri, her eyes lifting toward the ceiling, a puzzled look on her face.

"Abbess?" asked Brother Edgar.

"I sense it, too," Keri said, similarly looking upward. She felt a presence there, like a ghost—her mind went back to a time in the caverns deep within the mountain where she had grown up, where the demon Fossa had trapped the souls of so many victims. "What is it?" she asked, near panic, and looked to Elysant.

The abbess had closed her eyes now and was nodding, confusing Keri and Brother Edgar even more.

Elysant's eyes popped open, a small gasp escaping her lips, followed by a deep and sudden inhale. "They are coming for us," she said with obvious alarm. "They are coming now, and they have a weapon that will take down our walls!"

"Abbess? Who?" Brother Edgar stammered.

"Now!" Elysant shouted back at him. "St. Bondabruce and the Xoconai. They are coming. They will take down our walls,

Brother Edgar. They have the means, a weapon." She shook her head, seeming unable to properly describe her claim. "The moment we have feared these long weeks is upon us. Gather the brothers and sisters. Send the common folk out of the abbey immediately. Put them to the streets. Gather the gemstones—all of them—and to the library, quickly. Go! Go!"

"A weapon?" Keri asked. A great fear welled within her, recalling another time she had seen a mighty Xoconai weapon in action.

"Yes. I don't know what it—"

"It, or who?" Keri asked.

Elysant looked at her curiously.

"I watched the Xoconai god Scathmizzane drop St. Gwendolyn abbey into the sea," she explained. "That is a weapon I would'no want to see reborn."

"No, no, and I remember your tale of St. Gwendolyn and I remember well the battle of St.-Mere-Abelle and the tales of Ursal's fall. No, my friend, this is a weapon, a physical creation. Some type of catapult or trebuchet or ballistae. Its name came into my mind as 'armagrande,' though I do not know that word."

Came into your mind? Keri thought, but didn't quite ask before Elysant began rushing about and pointing toward the door, begging her to leave.

"We must make all haste," Elysant was saying. She first rushed the other way, though, to a wall rack behind her desk to retrieve a marvelous quarterstaff of polished green wood laced with thin silvery lines. "We have tunnels to take us far away from this town square." Out into the hall she ran, waving for the guards, who were still watching Brother Edgar rush away, to come along. "All haste!" she kept yelling, and the guards took up the refrain. "St. Rontlemore is lost! All haste!"

The abbess didn't slow, sprinting to the lower levels, taking the stairs two or three at a time, and calling out the alarm with every stride. Keri kept up, but Elysant wasn't about to stop her panicked cries long enough to give her any answers. So too with any answers to the gasped questions and startled faces of the brothers and sisters she told to evacuate.

For there was no sound of battle, no calls from the outer halls of any force coming at them.

It was just Elysant, who somehow had found, or been given, or had guessed, that great trouble was imminent. Whatever had happened, it was clear that the abbess commanded great respect, for though those who heard her showed doubts or confusion at her call, none argued, and all, after the initial shock, leaped into action, heading for various rooms or toward the second circular stair, which led to the substructures of the stone keep.

Finally, all was in motion, with Keri standing beside Elysant in the main hall on the first floor. All the common folk who had been brought into St. Rontlemore were already swarming the door and rushing out onto the pavilion beyond. Elysant kept a count of every monk not escorting the common folk, all of them holding small bags and coffers, carrying weapons, and hustling for the stairs to the catacombs below.

"I see no enemy," Keri remarked.

"Soon," was all that Elysant replied.

"How can you know?"

The abbess turned to her, started to say something, but stopped, shook her head, and instead simply replied, "It does not matter. I know."

"Xoconai!" came a call from the opened monastery door.

Shouts of alarm, the townsfolk screaming and scrambling, came in through the open portals. Those few still inside hesitated, but monks were behind them, imploring them, assuring them that they were not the targets here and that their safety lay outside, away from St. Rontlemore.

They finally got the last of them out, as Keri followed Elysant up a tight staircase to a narrow ledge above the main doors, a platform set with small windows, other than the one large rectangular colored-glass affair directly above the entry doors.

"Go to the cellars," Elysant ordered the few remaining monks, who were looking up at her plaintively. "Collect all the books you can carry and be gone. You know the way. This is no surprise to us, my brothers and sisters. We have been preparing for this day for nearly a year. We knew they would come."

And there they were, Keri saw, and gasped. She stared out the window to see Xoconai macana ranks and mundunugu riders filtering out left and right to surround the abbey. They chased the peasants away, brandishing their tooth-lined paddles, even striking a few, though with the flats of their weapons.

She saw a group of Abellican monks coming next, behind some horse-pulled caissons and a single large cart upon which sat a cylindrical golden war machine.

"Elysant," she said breathlessly.

The abbess came up beside her, the two of them staring as the contingent of St. Bondabruce monks moved up to flank the war machine, placing their hands on handles set into the gold, six monks to a side.

"We have to go," Elysant said, pulling Keri's arm.

"I want to see."

Elysant, so very strong for a small woman, tugged her old friend from the window, spinning her about.

"We have to go now," she said.

"I'm no monk of St. Rontlemore, or anywhere else," Keri reminded.

"You, most of all, have to leave," Elysant insisted, tugging her toward the stairs.

Keri kept glancing back toward the door, but didn't resist Elysant's pull—and it proved very fortunate that she did not, for even as they entered the descending staircase, there came a succession of curious sounds from outside:

Whump!

"It will be far more precise when we have completed the targeting . . ." Abbot Dusibol started to explain.

"Just begin!" Coyote interrupted. "How accurate must your cannon be to hit a huge keep merely fifty strides away? It can reach that far, I presume."

The abbot nodded to his monks to take their positions holding the handles set into the golden barrel. The dozen began chanting immediately, calling to the magics set within the war machine, while a thirteenth monk stood back a few feet with a garnet, measuring the level of energy being created. A team of laborers worked fast to attach a feeder tray that would slide the shot into the back end of the cannon, past the sunstone and sapphire magical barriers.

Coyote winked at City Sovereign Popoca, who nodded his agreement. Coyote then moved to the nearest caisson and removed a heavy stone. He wanted to be the first to throw.

"On your command, abbot."

Dusibol looked to the cannoneer monitor, who nodded, which Dusibol, in turn, relayed to Coyote.

In went the heavy ball, rolling the last couple of feet down the feeding tray into the back, past the blocking magic, and into the charged lodestone barrel.

With a great rush of air, like the sudden gasp of a giant, the ball flew off, arcing only slightly before slamming into St. Rontlemore's stone wall, cracking the seemingly impregnable barrier and throwing splinters and shards of stone all about before a larger block fell to the street below.

A delighted Coyote jumped into the air, waving his arms at the laborers to be quick.

The monks chanted.

Coyote grabbed the rear of the cannon cart—he'd aim the thing manually, and with great pleasure.

The laborers fed the heavy balls onto the tray.

Whump! Whump! Whump!

Over and over again the armagrande let fly, a line of iron

balls flying out across the plaza, slamming into St. Rontlemore with stone-breaking force, shattering the great window above the door from the sheer power of the impact vibrations before Coyote could even aim for the easy mark!

Soon he had the cannon sighted in on the wall just above the massive wooden doors. With his great strength, the warrior lifted the back of the carriage slightly, lowering the angle, and he held it through several more shots, one skipping in low to crack against the stone stair leading up to the entryway, the iron ball ricocheting up high enough to fly right through the frame of that destroyed rectangular window.

Then came a line of missiles on target, splintering, and tearing apart, and finally knocking down St. Rontlemore's doors.

The heavy first missile struck the abbey with such force that the whole of the large keep shook—and then kept shaking as the lines of metal balls began battering the front wall. Only a couple of steps down the stairs, Keri and Elysant felt the shuddering of the barrage, heard the stone walls of their sanctuary breaking apart, heard the glass shattering all about the main hall, heard the massive wooden doors crack into kindling and explode inward.

Then came another, more frightening crash right behind, as a heavy missile soared through the opening just beyond the stairwell entrance, with the sheer force of its passing snapping the very air!

Down the two women ran, hearing the main hall of the

abbey being turned to rubble above them, dust and dirt and rat droppings falling all about them.

They came to the lower meditation chambers and sprinted to a second descending stair. Then down to the massive library, perhaps the second-best depository of knowlege in all Honce behind the great collection at St.-Mere-Abelle. A few monks were still gathering books.

"Go! Go!" Elysant yelled to them before she had even come off the stairs. "Away with you all."

Yet another set of stairs led to the catacombs, where many monks had been laid to rest through the centuries, and then still another stairwell, cleverly hidden under what appeared to be the capstone of a grave, which led down deeper, into tunnels far below the streets of Entel. Elysant was the last one in, and while other monks used their diamonds to bring up light, the strong abbess worked the lever to slide the heavy capstone back into place.

On they all went, through a maze, but one the monks had clearly traversed and practiced many times, for never did they hesitate at any T or fork in the tunnels. Sometimes they saw lights far up ahead from the brothers and sisters who had been first out, but the tunnels were so winding and turning that the handful of these last evacuees were mostly on their own, with only the light of their own making.

"Split," the monk in front said when they reached the next intersection, and three broke off to the right, the other two leading Elysant and Keri down to the left. Keri didn't have much sense of direction here, but she thought they were going primarily east. The tunnels were climbing, as well, and she could sometimes hear sounds of the street above her: wagons and hoofbeats, the chatter of merchants.

"You need to bring up a light," Elysant told her.

"Their glow is sufficient."

"No, bring up a light. Our group is splitting again very soon, and I cannot do it."

Keri fought within herself, reminding herself repeatedly that Elysant and the others had been there for her. She owed them this.

She unbuttoned the bottom few clasps of her shirt and slipped her hand under to touch the diamond on her belly ring. She heard the diamond's song and joined it in her thoughts, exciting the magic within, and soon enough filled the area about her with a light of her own.

Elysant called to the Abellican sister and brother up ahead, motioning them to the left with the next tunnel fork, while she led Keri to the right.

"Are you sure, abbess?" the sister replied as the group split.

"I'll not be away from you for long. You know where to go. You know the boat and where she is moored."

"We will not sail without you," declared the brother.

"Oh, but you will," Elysant replied. "The first of our order who reaches her deck—someone may already be there—will begin the hourglass. When it drains, anchors aweigh, do not doubt, and no pleading or arguing from you or any, or all, of the others will change that.

"But fear not, sister, for I intend to be there. Now, be quick. Our hourglass is turned!"

The other two exchanged a look, then rushed off along the side corridor.

"Here," Elysant said to Keri, reaching out her hand.

Keri took the offering, a pair of stones, one rich orange, the other a beautiful pale blue.

"Amber and aquamarine," Elysant explained, leading her along the main passage, then breaking off to the right only a few steps later. "Amber to walk across the water, and so you must, to be gone far from this place. And aquamarine to breathe underwater if that is your best place to hide."

"I can'no. I am here searching . . ."

"I know, your son. But it doesn't matter. You must be gone. If you cannot abide the sunstone's power to kill the vibrations of magic within you, you will be found and you will be killed. They knew you were within St. Rontlemore. Run, I say, run far from Entel. Run to Jacintha in the south, or across the water to Freeport, if you've the strength to get that far. This isn't an option, my friend. It is your only chance."

As she finished, they came around a bend in the corridor, which had become much more natural stone, limestone, and far down the end of a long straight run, saw the daylight. Elysant pulled Keri toward that distant opening, and soon they could smell the brine and hear the crashing waves.

Some twenty strides from the exit, Elysant stopped short. "Please be safe," she said.

"What about yerself and the monks?"

"We knew this was coming, though perhaps not quite like this, with whatever that war machine might be. But we knew by City Sovereign Popoca's recent actions and the edict placed on all magic that St. Bondabruce would eventually move against us, with the Xoconai supporting them. We prepared. We have a plan and a ship—that is the whole reason I was sent here to serve as abbess. I wish I could offer you passage, but—"

"You can'no," Keri cut in. "You would be putting that ship in great danger, and you've your duties to your church's order."

"I have responsibilities to my friends as well, and you are among them. So please, use the amber and run far from this place. I know you seek your sons and the *Lauilli*, but she's not in port and hasn't been for weeks. Truthfully, you're more likely to find her in Freeport than Entel."

"Take me there," she begged.

Elysant seemed truly torn, but she shook her head. "We're sailing north, though far to the east first. We cannot stay in the ocean lanes used by our enemies. If the Xoconai find us, or chase us, they will feel the full wrath of St. Rontlemore. We have many Ring Stones, and many who know how to use them well."

Keri sucked in her breath a bit at that.

"I promise you this: if we come upon the *Lauilli*, we will try to avoid a fight, and if it comes to that, I will try to save your sons, if they are aboard. That is all I can offer, my old friend."

Keri's head bobbed. She didn't like it, but she certainly understood it. "Freeport," she decided. "You believe that I can run all the way to Freeport?"

"Get to a ship—a Behrenese or Honce merchant—that has been loaded from the markets. Few sail south that do not moor in Freeport, or pass very near to the place, at least. Stow away. That is the best advice I can offer—well, that and get away from this place. Entel is not for you."

Keri nodded again and turned for the exit.

"My light," she said, glancing back.

"I know my way in the darkness from this point," Elysant assured her. "Worry about yourself, I beg."

Keri rushed back and gave Elysant a great hug, then turned and stalked for the exit, determined not to look back. A thousand questions swirled in her thoughts. What was this place, Freeport? How would she get there? What might she find? Would her enemies chase her there? How could she truly hope to find her boys? Why had she come?

And what was that monstrous Xoconai war machine? Had Scathmizzane returned?

She tried to fight the tumult out of her thoughts, moving determinedly, trying not to think too far ahead, trying not to be paralyzed by so much doubt, uncertainty, and fear, as she put one foot in front of the other.

She saw the beach just ahead, the waves breaking only a few dozen yards from the cave. From inside, it seemed quite deserted, so she went right out, noting at once that she was some distance north of the Entel harbor, the ships' masts visible around a rocky outcropping to the south.

She felt a punch in her side as she turned that way, or tried to, for it wasn't a fist that struck her, but a missile, a pair of weighted flying balls tethered by a leather strand.

A bola.

And as Keri tried to turn, the momentum of the weighted stones wrapped about her and slammed her hard, blasting her breath out of her lungs. She staggered and tried to turn for the water, tried to get her arms loose.

She saw them coming, mundunugu riders on their cuetz-pali lizards, scales brilliant green and golden-yellow in the sunlight.

A second bola flew in at her, lower, wrapping about her legs, cracking hard against her shins, and she was down in the sand, struggling. She rolled back and half turned as the soldiers bore down on her, two riders fanning out to flank her on either side, two macana warriors brandishing their toothy paddles, leaping down the bluff, and an augur behind them, up high in the windblown grasses, garnet sparkling, golden rod gleaming.

She understood and was afraid: the augur had caught her scent, her magical vibrations, and had tracked her through this last expanse of tunnels, which were too near the surface!

Keri fought to collect herself, to find a place of calm, a place of magic. She had to fall into the stones—what choice was left to her?

But too late, she realized, when the four closed, one coming right over her, macana paddle descending.

Stunned, hurt, and trapped, Keri tried to cover, tried to roll away, and felt the weight of the blow, a blinding, burning flash that threw her into a daze.

The macana warrior lifted his paddle for another strike, but then, so quickly, he wasn't there!

She couldn't straighten her thoughts out enough in that moment to understand. She just rolled and covered and waited for more blows to fall.

CHAPTER 22

THE ABBESS AND THE WITCH

Elysant came out of the tunnel in a full sprint, hips and legs churning to drive her along the sandy beach. She understood immediately the danger, both for herself and for her friend, and a flood of doubts nearly halted her, reminding her of her responsibilities to her church and those brothers and sisters under her care.

But this was her friend who had fought beside her, a great hero who had tried to save the world, and who was clearly about to die before her. In the face of that terrible reality, those voices of doubt gained little traction.

The soft sand slowed Elysant's charge, but at the same time it muffled her footsteps, and only the two flanking riders noted her at all, and that very late in the play. The two standing over Keri, the one lifting his toothed paddle to smite her, had no idea.

One of the riders cried out.

Elysant drove the front of her darkfern staff into the sand before her, ran past it, and leaped, using the strong pole as a brace to carry her higher into the air, where she laid out horizontally, legs coiled until the very last moment. She double-kicked her target's head and shoulder as she sped in, and the macana wielder never got the chance to deliver that blow upon Keri. He flew to the sand, facedown, and lay very still.

Elysant landed where he had been standing, quickly shifting to straddle her prone friend. She immediately pulled her staff back in close, then stabbed it out, spear-like, into the face of the second warrior, a woman not much taller than she. Her target's head snapped back, nose shattering, and she staggered, then slumped to her knees, hands reaching, trembling. She shook her head as if trying to throw off the blow.

But the warrior monk wasn't finished with her. Elysant brought her staff straight back in to her right side, trapped it with her arm, tip lowering toward the ground. As the butt of the weapon came up above her shoulder, she reached over to grab it again with her right hand, used her shoulder as a fulcrum, and rolled the weapon up and over, catching it with her left, too, then drove it down and forward to crack the skull of the kneeling Xoconai, who bounced weirdly, legs and head wobbling, before simply falling off to the side.

Elysant didn't see it, for out of the corner of her eye, she noted a flicker of movement. She spun right and brought the staff sweeping across to knock aside a javelin. Instinctively, she completed the turn back to the left, where a second missile flew in. Across came the staff, but too slow to fully deflect this second spear, and it drove against her left shoulder, knocking her back a step. She had her hand up to grab the javelin almost immediately, before it had fallen away, even before she realized that it hadn't penetrated her armor: the magnificent Robe of St. Belfour.

She kept the spear right there, turning so that neither of the mundunugu riders could see it clearly, dropped her staff to the ground, and spun down in a stagger, whimpering.

As the riders came in, left and right, Elysant pulled the spear back and yelped, as if she had torn it back from a deep wound. She scrambled awkwardly about it, finally lifting it up before her defensively, keeping her right shoulder tucked as if favoring it from some expected grievous wound.

The rider to her right lifted another missile, this time a set of bolas. Up they went, spinning about above the mundunugu's head, but only for a moment, for the faking Elysant exploded into action, leaping up with her right hand cupped on the butt of the spear. Her whole body worked as if one muscle, shoulders turning, hips turning, striding forward and half shoving, half throwing the spear at the approaching rider.

That attacker let her bolas fly too quickly as she reflexively tried to dodge, resulting in an errant throw that went harm- lessly wide of Elysant. That mundunugu needn't have dodged, for Elysant's throw came in low and caught her lizard right in its opened mouth.

Then came a third missile, this time in the form of a flying mundunugu as the thrashing cuetzpali bucked and rolled aside, trying to extract the painful spear.

As soon as she noted the errant trajectory of the Xoconai's throw, Elysant turned and rolled across the sand to gather her staff.

A second spear by the other closing mundunugu clipped

her on the back of her hooded head and skipped down along her spine, but it could not dig in through the magical robes.

Elysant came up with her staff in hand, the mundunugu charging past with a spear leveled as a lance.

Elysant presented her own weapon similarly, but as they crossed, she rolled the staff end down and out, then thrust it forward. Her strength, which was greatly enhanced by the magical Ring Stones of her bracer, clearly surprised the man, for the look on his face was one of abject shock as he was lifted and thrown from his mount, landing hard on his back as the lizard charged on.

The cuetzpali did not spin about for Elysant, but instead went to the fallen Keri, clamping its jaws on her leg.

Barely had it begun to dig in when Elysant's staff stabbed it through the eye. The monk grimaced at Keri's screams, though, the woman suddenly thrashing and kicking when the lizard went into convulsions, its sharp teeth tearing at Keri's pant leg and flesh.

Elysant couldn't help her friend then, though, for the first mundunugu she had taken from the saddle was coming in fast, spear stabbing.

The air filled with crackling energy, sparking and stinging, the force of it pushing Elysant to the ground and, she noted out of the corner of her eye, throwing the now one-eyed lizard through the air, trailing smoke in its flight.

Elysant feared that her position on the ground would cost her dearly, but no such worry, she realized, for the charging Xoconai warrior, facing Keri's powerful lightning shock, had suffered more of the power of it. The Xoconai woman staggered about, dropping to one knee, grabbing at her eyes. She finally shook it off and reached for her spear, but too late, as Elysant rushed past her and cracked her across the head with that darkfern staff.

The abbess spun about, surveying the four, seeing the other rider up, but limping away.

She looked to Keri and nodded, managing a strained smile, and started for the remaining Xoconai.

Keri didn't return Elysant's smile, horrified by the monk's last swing, which had sent blood and brains flying. And the pain was too keen in her shoulder, her shins, her torn leg. She looked at her lifeblood pouring out, and tried to focus enough to reach for her healing magic.

But the light changed then, so distinctly, as if everything were suddenly bathed in an orange haze.

And that haze intensified, and it began to sting, to burn.

Keri looked to her friend and followed Elysant's gaze back toward the tunnel. Up above it on the bluff stood the augur, golden wand extended and glowing, throwing its radiant cloud at the combatants.

Keri had not seen this magic, though it reminded her of the incineration executions she had witnessed within the walls of golden mirrors. Her eyes burned and watered. She felt as if she had been lying in the desert sun for far too long, and the heat was only growing.

She tried to call out to Elysant, but the abbess was already running back the way she had come, toward the augur, who seemed to realize the danger, reacting with a sudden start and a turn and then fleeing out of sight.

The light shifted back to normal, the heat diminishing.

Keri pulled herself up to her elbows, then grabbed at her torn leg. She looked at the woman before her, lying on her side near the smoking husk of the cuetzpali lizard, the sand bloody about her head, her hair matted red. The other way, one Xoconai limped away, struggling with every step. On the ground to the side lay another—the man who had been brandishing his weapon above her, she thought—facedown and not moving.

And over the other way, the woman whose face and head Elysant had just split wide open. Beyond her, her lizard mount, thrashing and struggling, clawed futilely at a spear jabbed deep into its mouth and throat.

Keri put it all out of her thoughts. She knew she had to reach into her wedstone, had to pull forth the healing magic, but it was all she could do to keep her eyes open as waves of pain and shock and sadness rolled through her.

She didn't know if the macana warrior behind her would wake up. She didn't know if the lizard would free itself of the spear and come raging at her, or if the escaping warrior would call for some friends.

Why had Elysant run off?

"Enough!" she said aloud, scolding herself. "Enough!" She

grabbed at her belly ring, cupped her hand over its base, and forced herself to listen to the magical song of the wedstone.

Elysant had charged in to save her.

What a miserable friend she'd be if she now just let herself die or didn't recover in time to help the friend who had so helped her.

She brought forth the healing waves, then sat up, gasping. As she started to pull herself to her feet, she saw Elysant sprinting back toward her.

The abbess came skidding up to Keri, grabbing her, supporting her.

"We have to be gone from this place right now," Elysant told her.

"You have to get to your boat."

Elysant shook her head. "Impossible. I would be leading the Xoconai to those I am sworn to protect. Our enemies are not far, and they are coming, I am sure. The augur . . ." She shook her head.

"You could'no catch him," Keri said.

"Can you walk? Can you run? We have to flee."

Keri nodded but kept leaning heavily on Elysant. She let the abbess lead, and to her surprise, Elysant headed straight for the water.

"You have the stones I gave to you?"

"I . . . I can'no . . ."

"You must."

Keri shrugged, not sure what it was that she must do here.

Elysant tugged her toward the water, then into the surf. The waves broke around them, bubbling white water rushing up to splash against them, its shocking chill and salty edge at first stinging Keri, but then soothing her injured leg.

Out they pushed, only to be thrown back by the next wave.

"Use the stone," Elysant begged. "They are coming!"

Keri heard the approaching enemies. She turned and saw them on the high bluff, pointing and shouting, lifting atlatls and golden wands.

The next wave came in, but it did not push the two women back, for now they were atop it, atop the water, running, limping, out from the shore. They pressed on and on, glancing back to see the beach swarming with macana warriors, many yelling back behind them to a group of mundunugu riders who were just then cresting the bluff.

The women kept running, holding each other for support as they fought to keep their balance while stumbling across the rolling water.

"The lizards can swim," Keri reminded her partner, and she released the magical song of the amber, dropping her and Elysant under the cold water.

Cold and quite deep already, and the two descended.

Keri brought forth the magic of the aquamarine, giving them breath even twenty feet below the surface.

Soon, the ocean floor was under their feet, and they stood facing each other, wide-eyed with amazement.

Keri tried to say something, to tell Elysant that she had never used this magic before, but all that came out were bubbles.

Elysant pointed—off to the south, Keri thought—then the abbess began pulling her along.

Together they loped with elongated strides across the ocean floor in the water-dimmed light. And they kept moving for a long while in the silence across the unfamiliar environment, until at last, Keri signaled to her friend that she could hold the magical song no longer.

She grabbed Elysant close and called upon the amber once more, and upon her malachite to lighten them even more as they ascended from the depths.

They came to the surface, their heads above the water, the beach and the pursuing Xoconai left far, far behind—indeed, they were nearer the harbor now, the moored ships in sight not so far to the south.

"They probably think us drowned," Keri quietly told Elysant. "For we should be."

But Elysant shook her head. "The Bondabruce monks know of the various gems, and know the two you used quite well, as we are so near to the sea. They use amber and aquamarine to catch the large-clawed shellfish that live in these waters."

Keri just held there in response, continuing the song of the malachite to keep them easily afloat. "Then what are we to do?"

"Exactly as I told you to do in the tunnel," Elysant replied. She pointed toward the harbor.

Keri nodded, her thoughts spinning, the dark wings of despair fluttering up throughout the passing minutes, then hours, as the sun descended toward the peaks of the Belt-and-Buckle.

They were still neck-deep in the water when Elysant picked

out their target, and there they waited until darkness fell, then eased their way together to the shadows beneath the prow of a merchant vessel, not far from a dinghy that was being unloaded.

When the last of the goods were out of that boat, the oarsmen climbed the net to the ship's deck. The two cold and shivering waterlogged women went back underwater, breathing with the song of the aquamarine, and eased their way to the dinghy, then came up, Elysant first, aided by Keri's malachite levitation, to silently and stealthily get over the dinghy's rail and slip under the tarp that had been placed atop her.

Keri came in next, barely settling beside the prostrated Elysant before they felt the shudder as the dinghy was hoisted up above the rail and settled into place on the deck of the merchant vessel.

They held their breath as the footsteps and words of the crew sounded all about them, and only breathed easier a long time later, when the deck had quieted and the ship began gliding out across the waves.

Exhaustion, mental and physical, took them both as they huddled together in the small boat, soaking wet and full of doubts.

CHAPTER 23

STOWAWAYS

"They went south," the augur decided, and told Coyote as much when the fierce man came down to the beach.

Coyote pointed to one of the macana warriors. "She thinks they drowned."

The augur shook his head. "We have been out on the rowboats. If she was out there, we would have sensed her. She cannot hide her magic from us. Nay, they fooled us and went south."

"There is a sand bar not far out," the macana interjected. "Beyond it drops straight off for perhaps hundreds of feet."

Coyote looked to the augur. "If they went down there, they would be beyond your senses. But so, too, they would likely be dead, or dying." As he finished, he turned the other way, to Abbot Dusibol. "How long?"

"To remain below the water? Minutes, perhaps a half hour for the most powerful of monks," Dusibol answered. "And even then, the aquamarine stone conveys no protection against the great pressures of the depths."

Coyote nodded and looked back to the augur. "So, they went to the harbor, you believe."

"I am certain."

"Why not north?"

"Falidean Bay," Abbot Dusibol answered. "Anyone who knows this area takes care to avoid the tides of Falidean Bay."

"We have augurs all about the docks," Coyote reminded the abbot.

"Perhaps they have already caught the scent."

The warrior considered that for a few moments, chewing his lip, weighing it all, and finally, shaking his head. "They knew we were coming, which means they knew, or she knew, that we could sense her magic and track her. Were you in that predicament, would you return to the docks? To Entel at all?"

"We believe that the monks of St. Rontlemore fled on a ship that was moored in the north. But that vessel put out to full sail before the two fighting here got off the beach, so they could not have caught up to their brethren. Perhaps they prearranged a rendezvous somewhere out at sea?"

Again, Coyote shook his head. "It was the woman, you are sure? The one from Whispervale?"

The augur nodded. To the side, the macana did as well.

"And the abbess," the augur confirmed. "Abbess Elysant, with her distinctive robe and that mighty battle staff. Unmistakably."

Coyote led them a bit down the beach, moving to get into better sight of Entel harbor. He paused, hands on hips, then lifted one to shield his eyes from the long glare of the low-riding sun, then pointed to sails, a merchant ship out on the horizon, sailing southeast. Then to a second ship which was only then going to full sail as it swept through the eastern rows of moored craft.

And a third and fourth vessel, readying to go.

"How many ships do we have in port, city sovereign?"

"Merchants?" Popoca asked.

"Warships. Tonoloya Armada warships."

"Two were expected this very day. Seven or eight are already moored, I believe."

"All seaworthy?"

When Popoca didn't immediately respond, Coyote turned on him. The man could only shrug. "Some needing repair and resupply, I expect."

"Give me five," Coyote said. "And bring the heaviest into the long wharf immediately. You," he added to the augur, "gather smaller boats, as many as you can fill with warriors, and get out there in the harbor. No more ships are to depart until they are fully searched."

The augur nodded, called for some of his charges, and ran off to the south.

"What do you know, Coyote?" Popoca asked, walking up beside him with Dusibol.

"I know where I would be. This witch of Whispervale is smart, so I know where she would be." He nodded his chin out toward the two vessels already at full sail and fast departing.

"Running to Freeport, beyond your reach," Abbot Dusibol said.

Coyote snorted a laugh. "There is nowhere in the world out of my reach. Not for her."

"Freeport's rules—" City Sovereign Popoca began, but Coyote cut him short.

"Are about to change." He turned to look to Dusibol. "Scurry back to your brethren. Gather your cannoneers, your armagrande, and your shot, and go with all haste to meet the heavy ship on the long wharf."

Dusibol stuttered as he tried to reply. "You cannot put the armagrande on a boat," he protested. "Its value . . ." His voice withered under Coyote's glare.

"Drag it to the best warship at the docks," Coyote insisted. "Put it up front. Take a carpenter and nail it there securely while you and your brothers prepare to power it. Chain, balls of iron, large and small."

"Grape," Dusibol said before he thought better of it.

The glare intensified.

"The small balls," he stammered. "We call them grapeshot."

"Why are you still here?"

And then Dusibol wasn't, yelling to Brother Glorious as he ran, calling for his brethren.

"You have two hours!" Coyote yelled after him.

"Where are you going, Coyote?" Popoca asked, skidding to a stop and swinging about.

"Hunting. Witch hunting. And all the way to Freeport, if I must."

"You think this woman worth all the risk and trouble?

We have the city wholly now, with Rontlemore razed and her monks fleeing."

Coyote snorted again, for now he knew. Without doubt, he knew. This wasn't just any woman, or just any witch, for that matter.

It was her, the woman who had clawed the skin from the avatar of Scathmizzane as surely as she had torn his skin in that cottage in the foothills those weeks before.

And so, yes, she was worth the trouble, all the trouble, and so much more.

He didn't bother to answer, just stared at the city sovereign.

"I would caution discretion in the waters about Freeport and on the island itself," Popoca offered. "The Chezru Chieftain of Behren is highly invested in the place."

"Do you think their armagrande could take a dragon from the sky?" Coyote answered flippantly, and walked off.

Elysant was relieved indeed when the first rays of dawn slipped through the holes in the tarp. She heard Keri beside her, groaning and twitching, and at first thought she had awakened her.

But no, Keri was in the midst of a bad dream, and was growing dangerously loud.

Elysant hugged her tight and whispered in her ear, and finally clamped a hand over her mouth and held her with all her strength as she came fast awake and ready to fight.

"Shh, I beg," Elysant whispered to her, and when Keri calmed, she removed her hand.

"Dawn?" Keri mouthed.

Elysant nodded. They had survived the night, and were now almost surely far, far from Entel.

But with whom, and where they were going, neither knew.

For a moment.

For then the tarp was pulled back, roughly and quickly, and the two women looked up into the blinding daylight to see the gleaming blades of curved sabers pointed down at them.

"'Ere now, who paid for these two?" one scruffy old dog barked.

"Get up out o' there!" another demanded. "And slow ye go or ye'll feel me steel!"

Elysant rolled to her back, holding her hands up unthreateningly. She could feel her darkfern quarterstaff under her right shoulder, but didn't dare make any moves for it.

Calls for the captain resounded across the deck. More sailors rushed over.

Elysant slowly sat up. "I am an Abellican sister," she said, quietly and calmly.

"Ye're a long way from a monastery," the scruffy man replied, and jabbed his saber threateningly, stopping it just a finger's breadth from her nose.

"St. Rontlemore, not to doubt," said another, a woman out of sight of the two in the dinghy. "Ah, but them monks there got sacked good. St. Bondabruce and the damned goldfish knocked down Rontlemore's walls to rubble."

Elysant glanced at Keri and shrugged, clearly unsure of how to play this.

"Damned goldfish," Keri mouthed to her, and then louder, as a more impressive man with a wide beard and a tricorne hat came up, pushing the saber wielders aside. "Aye, St. Rontlemore, but she's from St.-Mere-Abelle, as am I."

"You don't look much like an Abellican sister in that garb," noted the newcomer, whose fine clothing and fancy hat made her think him the captain.

"Looks can be misleading—sometimes purposely so."

"My friend here was out on a scouting mission from the mother abbey," Elysant said. "We were both in St. Rontlemore quite by chance when the goldfish attacked."

"She's lying," said the scruffy old man.

"What do you know?" the captain asked him.

"I know her." He pointed his saber at Elysant. "Not by chance at Rontlemore, unless she's meaning that she's the abbess by chance."

"Aye, Abbess Elysant," another sailor chimed in.

"And I know her," said another, coming up to peer over the side opposite the captain. He poked his finger repeatedly at Keri. "I seen her."

"You said that," said the captain. "Where?"

The man kept poking his finger, stuttering and mumbling as if trying to jog his thoughts. A woman came up beside him, her long hair braided over her left shoulder and tied with a huge red ribbon.

Keri recognized her.

"Connie," the woman said.

"Aye! Aye! Connie the tavern maid at One Last 'fore the Sea!" shouted the man.

"Well then, do you dispute this?" asked the captain. "Either of you?"

With a huff of breath, Elysant hopped to her feet, lifting her mighty quarterstaff beside her. She reached back to take Keri's hand, helping the woman to gingerly stand on a leg that was still clearly wounded.

"Are they wrong?" the captain demanded.

Elysant looked to Keri, then shook her head.

"So, now that we know who you are, why are you on my ship?"

"Sure that they be running from goldfish, and from Abbot Dusibol," reasoned the woman with the braided hair.

"That true?" the captain asked.

"We had nowhere to go, so we found your dinghy," Elysant admitted. "We will be no trouble, and will help where we may, and as you desire."

"No trouble? You're trouble just in being here. I want no tangling with the goldfish, nor with St. Bondabruce."

"Put 'em over the side," said the scruffy man who had recognized Keri. That started some grumbling all about, with more than a few of the crew clearly agreeing with the sailor.

"Well?" asked the captain.

"Well, what?" Elysant returned.

"Should we put you over the side?"

"You would lose half your crew in trying," Elysant promised, and when the scruffy sailor snorted, the monk's foot came up with the speed of a striking snake, catching him on the side of the head and launching him backward and to the deck.

"And I promise you, good captain, that I am not the dangerous one here," Elysant stated evenly. "We are from St.-Mere-Abelle, as I told you. I was sent to St. Rontlemore to secure the library and the sacred Ring Stones, and so I have."

"Where?" the captain asked, a bit of nervousness creeping into his voice as his eyes rolled about, inspecting the dinghy.

"Not here. Long gone, to the north. The goldfish and Abbot Dusibol sacked St. Rontlemore, but they'll find no bones and no treasures in the rubble they made."

"And what of her, then, the barmaid?"

"Connie, and no, that is not her real name, is a Sister Justice, sent as my eyes and ears within the city. Surely you have heard of the Brothers Justice, captain. Well, meet the first sister of that band."

She paused when she heard the word "assassins" being whispered among the crew. Elysant tried not to smile, but was thrilled that her gambit in naming Keri as a member of that order of those most deadly Abellican killers had seemingly paid off.

Even the captain's posture shifted then, one leg going back a bit as if he wanted to be ready to spin and flee.

But they were on a boat. How far could he go?

"You are bound for Freeport?" Elysant asked.

The captain nodded.

"Then that is where we will part ways," Elysant declared.

"Stowaways," the captain muttered.

"How much for the ride, then?" asked Keri, surprising him, and Elysant.

"What?"

"I'm not much for asking anything twice," Keri replied.

"Two to Freeport? Five silver, if they're working. A gold if—"

Keri sent a gol' bear spinning his way before he finished the answer.

"Now, get you gone," she growled. "You need not hear another word from me, nor am I wanting to hear one from yourself."

Elysant saw the man begin to puff up with pride, but only briefly.

Keri had played it perfectly.

The captain dispersed his crew to their posts. Some left grumbling, but nothing that seemed threatening.

"We've been sailing through the night," Elysant whispered to Keri. "We'll likely see the hills of Freeport by midday and tie up in the harbor before the sun drops below the western ridges."

CHAPTER 24

CONVERGENCE

K eri and Elysant stood as tall as they could manage, trying to see past the rigging and the yard and the high quarterdeck. For something was going on back there, they could tell from the reactions of the crew of the merchant ship.

The captain rushed past their position, lifting a spyglass as he went. He took the aft stairs two at a time to the quarterdeck and peered through his scope.

Elysant looked to Keri and shook her head, then broke the rules the captain had set for them and climbed out of the dinghy, leading the way to the captain. They heard a few protests from onlooking crewmen but ignored them. When they arrived, the captain lowered his glass and gave them a stern look, but nothing more than that.

He had other things to fret about, the two women realized, for the sea behind the ship was dotted with the sails of six ships.

The large, square-rigged sails of Xoconai warships, mostly.

"What do you know of this?" the captain asked Elysant.

"How would I know anything of it?"

"You were fleeing the goldfish—that is what brought you to stow away, of course, and now we see the Mirianic behind us teeming with goldfish. Pursuing us, perhaps?"

Elysant shook her head. "Is this so unusual?" she asked sincerely. "Xoconai ships put out all the time."

"Not like this," the captain told her. "Not so many all together on a course to, and so near to, Freeport." He handed her the spyglass.

Keri noted the instrument and recognized that it was much more than a simple tube with a pair of shaped lenses. It had gemstones, almost certainly magical Abellican Ring Stones, set into it.

She had seen a device like this before.

"Their decks are thick with soldiers," Elysant breathed, lowering the glass.

"They are not out on simple patrol," the captain agreed. "Nor on any long voyage, for they haven't the room to supply those numbers. No, they are in pursuit."

"Of us, you believe," Elysant stated. She handed the spyglass to Keri.

"The one ahead and farthest right is not Xoconai," she told both the captain and her friend. "Perhaps they are after her."

Even without raising the spyglass, Keri could see the logic there, for a warship was certainly closing on the vessel that was not Xoconai, another merchant ship, a barque, that had put out from Entel soon after this one.

Almost afraid to do so, Keri lifted the glass. Yes, she could see that the decks of the Xoconai ships were indeed crowded.

She took a steadying breath and called deeper to the magical item, enacting the chrysoberyl, the gem of far-sight.

She was glad she had taken that breath, for it took a long while for her to find her breath again when the image on those warships clarified. Xoconai macana warriors stood shoulder to shoulder across all five, at least a hundred warriors visible on each ship!

And there were more sails behind, too far for the naked eye to see, or even with just the normal magnifying properties of the spyglass.

"Eight warships, not five," she said.

The captain took back the spyglass and put it to his eye. Then, after a few moments swinging the instrument about, he lowered it, looking confused and shaking his head. "I count five, and the merchant one is about to be boarded."

"You do'no even know the magic of your own tool, then?" Keri asked him.

Even Elysant seemed surprised by that.

Keri pointed to the gems. "Far-sight," she explained.

"That is a Ring Stone?" Elysant asked.

"Ah," the captain said, and he, too, seemed very surprised.

"There are at least three more warships trailing, all at full sail, all laden to the maximum with soldiers," Keri explained.

"Hunting the two of you?" the captain asked.

"We do not know that," said Elysant. "Whatever this might be, it is surely bigger than the two of us!"

"This near to Freeport?" the captain said with a shake of his head. "A flappin' Xoconai army? It makes no sense."

"They caught the barque," the lookout called. The captain

lifted his glass again, but even without it, the women could see the Xoconai warship pulling up beside the distant merchant, who had struck her sails in compliance.

"They'll catch us before we make Freeport harbor," the captain said. "We'll strike and welcome them aboard."

Elysant glanced to Keri, then glared at the man. "Aye, you do that," she said. "As soon as we tell you to do it, not far out of Freeport's harbor."

"As soon as you . . ." The captain snorted. "And what, abbess? You will be gone, fleeing to shore? What? With my dinghy, you think?"

"No. We will be gone, but need nothing from you or your boat. Nothing except your silence. We were never here."

Keri looked about, doubting that demand would hold true if the Xoconai began asking the crew. Or even the captain, for that matter, for what did they have to gain in lying to soldiers about women they didn't even know?

"You ask that of me? Tell me why I shouldn't put you in chains and give you over willingly," the captain remarked, and the eavesdropping nearby crew all seemed more than ready to do just that.

"Because the spyglass has magic to it," Keri answered.

"'Twas given me by a nobleman after I saved him from shark-filled waters."

"The goldfish will take it from you, and might well kill you for having it. You did'no hear the edict echoing in the streets of Entel?"

"We're not in Entel now, are we? Not in Honce. Freeport is . . ."

"Sanctuary?" Keri asked, and pointed back at the fleet. "Are you so sure of that?"

The captain shifted nervously. "Well then, I give them you two and tell them the glass was yours," he warned. "Tell me why I shouldn't put you in chains."

"Are we really back to that?" Elysant asked.

"Because I know how to use yer spyglass," Keri answered. "And I have upon me more than a dozen gems more powerful by far. Try if you will, and I'll leave you dead, half your crew dead with you, and your damned tub burning and sinking."

The captain snorted.

"I would tell you to speak with those who have doubted my friend here before, but alas, they are all dead," Elysant told him. "We want no trouble, but if you start it now, the trouble will be more yours than our own."

He looked from one woman to the other, then to his nearby crew, then back to the women, who were both glowing white—a shield that most in this region knew well! At that point, the poor man seemed truly lost. And truly afraid, as Keri rubbed her thumb against the band of her ring, one that held both serpentine and ruby, the combination to create a fireball and protect the one who did it.

"How long before they catch us and demand a strike?" Elysant asked.

The captain looked at the distant fleet. Two ships had remained with the barque, but the other three were coming on fast. "Soon after midday?" he asked as much as answered.

"How close to Freeport?"

389

He shook his head. "It'd still be a sail of a couple of hours. Too far for you to row, surely."

"We aren't rowing." Elysant looked to Keri.

"Just keep her at full sail, fast as she'll go," Keri told him. "We beg you. You do'no like the goldfish any more than we do, or you'd have brought us right back to Entel." She looked around at the crew. "None of you do!" she reminded them.

"But we want to put you in no danger," she told the captain, told them all. "Keep sailing, fast as you can, and we'll be gone before any goldfish come too near in sight."

The captain stared at her long and hard, and Keri could well imagine the debate happening behind his eyes.

"You are supposed to be in the dinghy," he reminded the two.

"But we aren't," Keri replied, not giving an inch.

"Get belowdecks," he ordered them. "They might have eyes like this one." He held out the spyglass. "And I'll not be lying to them if they've spotted you."

The women exchanged skeptical looks, but it made sense, and with a nod, they went their way to the hold.

Keri noted that the captain never took his gaze from her, never blinked, as she walked to the ladder and down to the main deck. As she and Elysant made their way to the bulkhead, she heard the captain barking orders to his crew to keep the vessel straight and fast, but when she glanced back his way, she noticed that he was still staring at her and her companion.

"You think it's Coyote," Elysant said as soon as she and Keri found a quiet corner to be alone in the hold.

Keri nodded. "Has to be. On one of the three ships far

behind, I expect, for the other five were likely out as soon as the word of our escape reached the harbor. If Coyote was on one of those, I doubt the other three would have loaded so heavily and set right out."

"He knows that it was you back at St. Rontlemore, and he's going to chase us right onto Freeport, the possible troubles with Behren be damned."

Keri didn't disagree.

"If we even manage to get near to the place," Elysant added. "We can't run across leagues of sea."

In response, Keri turned back toward the ladder, lifted her shirt above her belly, and dropped a hand onto her belly ring. She stood there, wincing, chewing her lip, trying to consider all her options.

"You have an idea?" she heard Elysant saying, but distantly, for Keri's thoughts were on the black wings of doubt already rising within her. Unless she played this perfectly, and had more than a good bit of luck on her side, she was soon to be in a fight, no doubt, and a great battle with a fearsome, brutish warrior.

If she hesitated, Coyote or his warriors would surely kill her, and Elysant as well.

What then for her boys?

She thought to go to the deck and use her moonstone to fill the sails, but she shook her head, undecided. The pursuing warships might see the sudden change in speed on the ship they pursued, or might sense such a powerful use of magic. If they could get near enough the harbor to run off with the two gems

Elysant had given her, perhaps the Xoconai would rethink the route the fleeing abbess and witch might have taken, buying them lots of time to plan their next moves.

Unless, of course, the captain betrayed them when the Xoconai caught his ship.

Keri used the moonstone to send more healing over her and over Elysant, to mend any remaining bruises or cuts from the battle on the beach.

"We have a couple of hours if the captain's estimate is accurate," Elysant told her. "You rest, nap if you can, and I'll keep watch."

Keri thought to argue, but to what end? Elysant was right. She moved to the nearest hammock and pulled herself onto it, closing her eyes and trying to shut out the noise of the tumultuous world.

"If there is anything you can do with your magic, now is the time."

Keri heard the words distantly, the meaning slowly registering and taking her from her slumber. She blinked open her eyes to see Elysant standing over her.

"They're much closer," the abbess explained. "I fear we won't get near the island's northern harbor."

Keri rolled out of the hammock and followed Elysant far aft in the hold, through a door and up a short ladder to a room just above water level below the ship's quarterdeck. She didn't need a spyglass when she looked through the window there—the three pursuing warships were clear to see.

She looked to her companion, who shrugged, then led the way to the stairs to the main deck.

"Your sons are out there," Elysant reminded Keri when they came out into the midday sun. And more insistently, "If you have anything . . ."

Keri nodded. They were indeed. Carwyn and Kenzie. Somewhere. And they needed her. She could not, must not, forget that.

Keri's head rolled back as her eyes rolled back. She heard the song of the moonstone, her favorite gem, and she strengthened those vibrations and brought the magic forth.

The sails before her tightened and the ship lurched, gaining speed immediately.

"Get us to Freeport," she heard Elysant say, and when she looked to her friend, she saw beyond Elysant to the deck, where the captain and crew were nodding and working the rigging, thinking themselves fortunate to have found more favorable winds.

Keri knew that she couldn't keep this up for long before magical exhaustion would overcome her, and knew too that she needed to keep some energy in reserve if she and Elysant were to flee to the island. But she had to try to buy them some time, at least.

The sails stayed taut, the clumsy and too-thick merchant ship rushing along the calm seas.

But the warships were still behind her. Coyote was behind

her, too close and closing, though not nearly as quickly as before.

"I told you two to get down to the hold and stay there," the merchant captain said to Elysant, who was sitting against the quarterdeck wall, not far from Keri.

"You think the wind fortunate?" Elysant replied.

The captain stared at her with a puzzled look.

"Simple good fortune that we caught a channel of wind ahead of the pursuing warships?" the abbess went on.

"If you have something to say, then just say it. I have no time for—"

"She is filling your sails, you idiot," Elysant snapped at him, nodding her chin to the dark-haired witch. Keri didn't reply, didn't turn, didn't even open her eyes. She just stood there calmly, one hand on her stomach, covering her belly ring and the moonstone that she was using to create the magical wind.

The captain looked to the witch, his expression caught somewhere between surprise and consternation.

"Who are you?" he breathed.

"I already told you," Elysant replied.

He nodded to the stairs and motioned Elysant to follow him up to the quarterdeck. At the taffrail, he put up the spyglass. "They're still gaining on us," he said, and handed the spyglass to the abbess.

The three warships were very clear to see with the naked eye, but when she lifted it to her eye, even without using the instrument's magic, she noted the other Xoconai vessels, the two that had stopped the barque and the three that had been far behind, the ones likely under the command of Coyote.

Closing fast.

"We won't get near to Freeport," the captain said. "Then what? Did you two condemn me and my crew to the hangman?"

Elysant wanted to argue, but she couldn't. The thick merchant ship was moving well, but even with Keri's magic, the Xoconai ships were indeed gaining.

But up ahead now, Elysant could see the outline of a small mountain, and she knew it to be Freeport. She glanced back, gauging the pursuit, then ahead, trying to guess the distance to the sanctuary. She hustled back down the stairs to Keri's side.

"If you've more to give, then give it," she whispered.

Keri gave a little shake of her head. Elysant patted her on the shoulder and moved to the starboard rail.

"How did you know?" Keri asked, stopping her short.

"Know what?"

"How did you know that they were coming for me, for us, at St. Rontlemore?"

Elysant paused.

Keri opened her eyes and turned to regard the abbess.

"It is a story for another time," Elysant said.

"A tale I'd like to hear."

"For another place, then," Elysant quietly replied, subtly indicating crew members who might overhear, including the captain, who was coming down from the quarterdeck to join her.

"Have you more wind to give us?" the abbess added when Keri indicated that she understood.

The dark-haired woman looked back and shielded her eyes, then forward to note Freeport.

"I do'no," Keri said. "My song grows quiet now."

Elysant nodded and smiled, but knew that much more was going on here with Keri than the woman was letting on. She had seen this one in a full magic bloom, like a symphony of pure power and beautiful, momentous magic. The Keri she had known could outduel even the most powerful Abellican monks with the magical stones. The Keri she had known would have sailed them on a gale to Freeport already!

But she recognized that the woman wasn't lying to her, and that this relative impotence was deeply troubling her friend. Simply put, Keri was not all right. Something—her spirit, her inner harmony, her affinity for the vibrations of magic?—had broken. She was still creating a magical wind here and filling the sails, which was more than Elysant could ever have managed, and more, indeed, than most monks, even those with strong affinity to the sacred Ring Stones, could do.

For Keri, though, it seemed a pitiful exhibition.

But it would be enough, the abbess decided. It would have to be enough. She sat quiet at the rail, watching over her friend, eyeing closely any who came too near, and eyeing, too, the sails behind them, growing as the morning passed.

And the mountainous outline before them, growing, too, as the minutes passed.

By the time the sun had crossed its midpoint high above,

Elysant could see the mast poles of the few small ships in Freeport's shallow northern harbor. The captain hadn't been meaning to put in there, she believed from what she had learned of the usual Freeport run. Their course in leaving Entel had been to turn east and circle the island halfway around to the wide southern bay.

But that would take them past the eastern harbor, one that was always thick with Xoconai warships.

She went to Keri to tell her that, but the woman surprised her by turning on her first.

The sails began to luff a bit, and Elysant sensed that the magic was no more.

"We should be goin' now," Keri said.

"Can we make it? We've half a league to shore."

"We've no choice," Keri replied, taking Elysant's hand and pulling her toward the ladder. "We'll jump ship here."

They found the captain just ahead on the main deck near the base of the forecastle.

"That's not your intended harbor before us?" Elysant asked.

"Too shallow. We've too deep a keel."

"When would you begin your turn?" Keri asked.

The captain shifted uncomfortably as he considered her. "Closer in, but soon."

"We'll be gone from you," Keri explained. "You let us get a bit ahead and make your turn to the east—the wind'll be more favorable."

"And you will use us as cover," the captain reasoned.

Keri nodded.

"In my dinghy," the captain added sourly.

"We told you we were not taking it, or anything else from you," said Elysant.

"Except the spyglass," Keri added. "And that, for your own sake. Find us in Freeport and we'll give it back."

The captain considered that for a moment, then nodded. He led them to the starboard rail and looked ahead to Freeport Island. "Long swim," he said with a laugh, turning to regard the two women. "And in water known for sharks. There's no way . . ."

He lost his words and his breath when Keri and Elysant rose from the ground and flew out before him, Keri with her arms outstretched, Elysant securing her darkfern staff diagonally behind her shoulders, then climbing on Keri's back. They soared out past the forecastle and the bowsprit, angling down to the dark waters of the Mirianic, then touched down lightly atop the water, Elysant dropping from Keri's back, but, like the dark-haired woman, not going under the water at all.

Hand in hand, they ran across the water, up over the swells as easily as they might traverse a small sand dune on a beach.

"Captain!" came a cry from the lookout high above. He glanced up to see her jumping up and down in her nest, pointing her finger forward.

"Shut up and watch the sails behind!" he called back at her, then to the helmsman, he ordered, "Take us to port!"

He gave a long look back at the approaching Xoconai fleet,

then turned back and snorted with amusement to see that the two women were already almost out of sight.

It had been a strange journey indeed, and promised to grow stranger and quite tense soon enough.

Barely had that notion passed when he heard a call from a bullhorn behind, ordering him to strike his sails.

"Do as they say," he told his crew. "And not a word about our previous guests."

CHAPTER 25

NO SANCTUARY

B ounding across the water with the magic of the amber, leaping in long strides with the help of the malachite and the moonstone, Keri and Elysant soon came to the rocky north shore of Freeport Island, just to the west of the small fishing village in the protected bay. They crossed through a currently deserted market area to the cobblestoned trail south of that village in short order, and climbed the path to the top of the foothill ridge, where they could look back and down upon the village and to the waters beyond—indeed, where they could see most of the island, except that part blocked by the one mountain to the east of their position.

Over that ridge, the city of Freeport was clearly visible, and looking back, so was the Xoconai pursuit. The merchant vessel they had left was dead in the water, a warship up alongside her, soldiers on her deck. More alarming, though, were the rowboats coming in fast toward the fishing village, and the other Xoconai warships breaking east and west to go about the island. Keri and Elysant could see the ships signaling to each other, great flags waving.

Like a posse closing in on fleeing outlaws.

Keri lifted the spyglass and called upon its powers to look farther out to sea, to the trailing warships she had seen earlier in the day.

She gasped when she lowered the instrument.

"What?" Elysant asked.

"Coyote," Keri confirmed. She called more insistently upon the magic of the item and peered closer, then gasped yet again. "It is him, and monks, and they brought their new weapon."

"This is no coincidence," Elysant offered. "They seek us."

"They seek me," Keri corrected.

The two women rushed down over the ridge on the long trail to the city of Freeport, and paused at every high point to scour whatever coast they might see. The warships couldn't get around the island as fast as they could cross it in a straight line on foot, of course, but the signal flag message could, and there were plenty of Xoconai vessels already in the eastern port, and plenty of Xoconai warriors and augurs already on the island.

And soon, if not already, Keri realized, they would all be hunting for her.

She and Elysant had to get into the city and hide among the crowds there, she knew. And, eventually if not immediately, she was going to have to run away from Elysant.

"You have the sunstone?" Keri asked.

"I took no gems other than those affixed to my bracers and robe and the two I already gave to you."

Keri closed her eyes. She couldn't hide from those golden wands and the garnets.

To her horror and to her great hope, Keri could not *not* use the magic of her crystals, or of the tattoo she had created.

The two women crouched just back from the edge of the roof, a group of macana below them, being ordered about by an augur with a golden rod and garnet.

Keri and Elysant had leaped up here from the alley, aided by the malachite, obviously leaving their pursuers in a state of confusion below.

"In the building!" they heard the augur yell, and a trio of soldiers disappeared through the door below the two women.

Keri looked across the street then and noted the shadow of this building climbing the face of the one opposite as the sun lowered behind them. She pulled Elysant down beside her, realizing that they too would be outlined there if they stood upright.

"We have to be gone," Elysant whispered. "Across to another roof and beyond?"

"They are in there!" the augur yelled from below in the Xoconai language, which both women understood well enough. "Second floor! Go up!"

"He'll be on us every step, every jump, every building," Keri answered. She peeked over the edge.

The augur was there in the street with only two soldiers near him, the others either now in this building or moving along to and quickly through nearby doors.

"We have to be fast," Keri whispered. She grabbed Elysant's hand. "We must take them down and be gone from here."

"Take them down?" Elysant mouthed, and she felt magic flowing into her, felt lighter. Keri pulled her forward and up to her feet, rushing to the ledge, and she understood.

Down they leaped, down they flew, landing easily, as the malachite magic made them nearly weightless the moment before they hit the cobblestone street, landing right beside the three Xoconai.

Elysant fell straight to a crouch, spinning and sweeping out her leg to upend the nearest macana warrior. She came up stabbing her staff like a spear, driving back the second.

Keri focused on the augur, grabbing his extended arm and that golden pole. He turned and tried to swing at her, but she punched first, with a fist of stone that slammed him in the face, shattering his nose and cheek, snapping back his head.

He was stumbling, then falling, clearly unaware of the ground rushing up to swallow him, unaware that Keri now held the golden rod, unaware that his garnet was rolling on the cobblestones, soon to be snatched up by the witch.

A second stab, then a wide swing of the darkfern staff had the second macana warrior stumbling farther backward, clutching at his face. Ignoring him then, Elysant completed the swinging motion by cracking the other on the side of her head as she tried to stand, laying her low.

The two women ran off across the street and down an alley, followed by shouts of the still-standing warrior.

But they had the rod and gem, and this group, at least, couldn't so easily track them.

Would it matter, though? For the streets of Freeport were thick with Xoconai mobs, all led by augurs, pointing golden wands and holding garnets that sparkled in the late-day sunshine.

They turned a dozen corners and rushed through a dozen alleyways, scrambling and ducking every time they noted a roaming Xoconai gang. Shouts chased them, augurs likely sensing Keri's magic and calling out directions.

"We have to move to the docks and find a ship that's putting out," Elysant told her.

But Keri just held up her hands helplessly. They were in a maze of two- and three-story buildings, the tall structures huddled on narrow and winding cobblestone streets, full of ruffians and drunken sailors, merchants and vagabonds.

"Keep the lowering sun to our right," Elysant said. "The harbor is south."

"Get yerself there, then," Keri decided. "I can'no hide from them, but Elysant can."

In response, the abbess grabbed Keri and tugged her along, for she wasn't about to abandon her friend.

They came out onto a street, nearly crashing into a group of Xoconai who were running past the alleyway's exit.

The two women reversed immediately, heard one of the soldiers cry out, then, instead of continuing along the alley, went to a wall and up the wall, Keri calling upon the malachite once more to greatly lessen their weight, Elysant using the bloodstones of her magical robe to give her great strength. They made the roof just before the soldiers came running into the alley.

And thankfully, running right past them, heading for the far end.

Down went the women, and back the way they had started, out of the alley, across the street, and down another narrow channel.

Full speed they ran, turning wherever it seemed plausible, finding shadows and finally coming to a stop near the end of one dark alleyway, a bustling street just beyond.

"It can'no be much farther," Keri whispered. "You should go to a boat, and I'll get under the waves and there hide."

"We stay together," Elysant said, her tone leaving no room for argument.

The abbess edged up to the end of the alley, looked back to the left, then bent low and peeked around to the right.

She came right back in, though, motioning for Keri to stay very still and very quiet, and silently mouthing, "Xoconai right there" as she pointed down the street to the right.

Keri moved up beside her and crouched, listening, looking for clues.

"Keep the bucket," they heard a man say, followed by his laughter and that of a couple of others. "Farewell, my friend. Fair winds and following seas to you."

Keri looked at Elysant curiously.

That voice . . .

"Always," replied another man with a deep and resonant voice and an accent Keri did not recognize. "And you keep well, my young friend, Dabego."

Elysant tried to pull Keri back, but the witch shrugged the abbess off and peeked around the corner.

A tall, straight-backed, and well-muscled black man walked out from the shadows of the store beside the alley to join an enormous tan-skinned, bald-headed man who was covered in tattoos crown to ankle, and a Xoconai woman who had lost her right arm about halfway between elbow and hand. The stub was capped now in a fitted leather covering, with a curious metal implement on the end.

"Young Dabego is quite skilled," came that familiar voice once more, from the shadows under the awning. "And he has those long and delicate fingers—perfect for tight work."

"It is not me you had to convince, cobbler," the tall black man replied. "It was his mother."

"Cobbler?" came the response, full of insult and imperious huffing. "I am an artist, deckhand Massayo."

"Deckhand," the giant tattooed man echoed with a snicker.

"That is Captain Massayo, if you please . . . my artist friend," said the black man.

"Convince Dabego's mother?" the Xoconai woman asked.

"Our friend here would like to take on Dabego as an apprentice," Captain Massayo explained.

"The boy was born for this craft!" the artist in the shadows insisted.

Even as he spoke, the person in question, a boy, perhaps a

teenager, with shining black skin and a brilliant smile, came stumbling out under the weight of a pack that was far too large and heavy, apparently. He moved to the Xoconai woman, who reached for it until the huge tattooed man relieved them of the weight, hoisting it so easily with just one hand.

"We have to go," Elysant whispered, tugging Keri again.

But that voice. It came again. "The wide disk shield, a sword blade, a hook, a metal hand, and finally a long gaff. You can use the shield with any of them. Or with none. All will fasten to the interior groove of your end cap, except the shield, which will screw in quite securely to the outer ring."

Keri looked to Elysant, who was wearing as confused an expression as she. "An artist indeed," Elysant whispered.

"So, with one arm, you will wield shield and blade!" they heard Captain Massayo proclaim.

"The bolt has soul stone and sunstone in it to prevent gangrene and any infestation," came the familiar voice, and now, so suddenly, with a message equally enticing. "The magic will come to you whenever you feel discomfort. The cap will be a part of you, not an item of clothing."

"I know not how to use the gemstones."

"It matters not at all," the artist assured her. "Do you feel any pain now? Go ahead and try to feel the warmth."

"But she is Xoconai," Elysant whispered. "Why would she use such an item now?" Instead of pulling Keri, the monk moved up beside her.

The Xoconai woman stood with her eyes closed, then said, "It cannot be."

"But it is," said the unseen artist. "Like magic, because it is magic, don't you see? As I said, I am no ordinary cobbler. But enough of this. Begone now, and get Captain Wilkie and the others of your ilk sailing south with you."

"What do you think of so many goldfish swimming about Freeport's streets?" Captain Massayo asked the Xoconai woman. "The final fallout for the attack on the *Uey*? Popoca really wanted that gold, eh?"

"It was the largest haul ever brought up from the south," the Xoconai woman answered.

"A great haul," Captain Massayo agreed, grinning. "And you lost it."

The Xoconai woman's eyes widened in surprise, and she looked to the shadows with obvious alarm.

"Master Talmadge knows who you are and how you came to be with me," Captain Massayo stated, and now it was Keri whose face turned to an expression of utter shock. That voice! Talmadge? How could it be Talmadge, a man she had known so long ago in a far distant part of the world?

"Benny's boys really started something big and bad, we're guessing," said Captain Massayo, and there was no smile accompanying the claim.

"Then we should be long gone," said the Xoconai.

Keri and Elysant watched as the boy, Dabego, hugged Massayo, then the huge tattooed man, and then the Xoconai woman so very warmly.

"Whenever I put in to Freeport, you will rush to my ship and greet your mother," Captain Massayo told him, and Dabego nodded repeatedly, his bright smile so wide that it almost took in his ears.

Out from the shadows came the artist, indeed a man Keri had not seen in fifteen years, but one she would never forget.

Elysant pulled her back and she didn't resist this time, falling against the alleyway wall and finding it very hard to breathe.

"It's Talmadge. It's him," she whispered.

Elysant seemed confused.

"From the Wilderlands," Keri reminded the abbess. "From the docks of St.-Mere-Abelle—you remember. Talmadge, who warned us of the divine throwers approaching the great monastery."

Elysant's eyes went very wide. "How?" She shook her head. "It's the same Talmadge? You are sure?"

Keri peeked out again, then, seeing the area in front of the shop clear, Massayo and the other two moving down the street, She rushed out, pulling Elysant behind her. With a glance both ways, no Xoconai in the immediate area, the women went into the artist's shop, beneath the sign naming it as OOT O BOUNDS.

The man and the boy, who were standing over to the side, turned with a start when the door banged open, the man beginning a sharp protest at the sudden and rude intrusion.

Beginning, only beginning.

For then his jaw hung open, he blinked a hundred times, and he shook his head, obviously trying to make sense of what, of who, stood before him.

"It cannot be," he said breathlessly.

Keri rushed across the room and crashed into him, wrapping him in a great hug.

"Aoleyn," he whispered, and kissed her on the cheek a dozen times. "By all the gods, I knew I would see you again, and yet here I am . . ." He pushed her back to arm's length. "I cannot believe . . ."

"They're chasing us," Keri replied. "The Xoconai. I—we—must be gone from this place."

"Freeport? The goldfish are chasing you in Freeport? No, they cannot . . ."

Shouting from out on the street interrupted Talmadge, and he pushed Keri aside, ran to the front door, and peered out.

When he turned back around, having closed and locked the door behind him, his weathered face was ashen.

"They've no power here," he insisted, shaking his head.

"They sense the magic of Keri," Elysant explained. "They care not for propriety or rules in their desperation to catch her."

"Keri?"

"Me," Keri said. "I am Keri. Only Keri, forever Keri. The woman you knew is dead."

Talmadge stared at her incredulously.

"We haven't time," Elysant reminded.

The shouting voices outside came closer.

Talmadge started for the back of the room, pulling Keri behind him and waving Elysant along as well. He led them to a bookcase, then removed one old tome and reached in for a hidden lever.

The bookcase swung out like a door, revealing a small

chamber. He stepped aside and told Keri and Elysant to go in and hide.

"They sense me," Keri warned.

"Not in there," Talmadge told her. He seemed about to explain, but instead just shoved her in and pulled Elysant in behind her, closing the bookcase door just in time as the shop's street door banged with a heavy knock.

Keri and Elysant huddled against the back slab of that bookcase, ears pressed against it.

They didn't have to worry about any muffled sounds, for the voices beyond were hardly soft.

"Who have you in here?" demanded a man with a thick Xoconai accent.

"Myself and my assistant, Dabego, can't you see?" Talmadge answered.

"Where are they?" demanded another Xoconai, a woman this time.

"Where are what? Or who?"

"Augur!" the woman yelled, and Keri grimaced.

She understood what she would have to do if they were discovered. She told herself to be brave here. She wouldn't let Elysant and Talmadge die for her.

More arguing rang out in the shop, more voices, and in such a jumble that it was hard for her to make out most of it for several moments.

"Of course I have magical items!" she heard Talmadge protest as the others went quiet. "I am a trader throughout the lands, even with your own people."

"The edict . . ." a man loudly countered, his voice sounding older and so very thick with the western accent. The augur, Keri surmised.

"Tell me not of your foolish demands!" Talmadge shouted back. "This is Freeport, not Honce. You have no power here."

The room went quiet.

"What is this?" a woman said from the side of the main room wall to Keri's right.

"Leave it!" an obviously angry Talmadge shouted at her.

"A gown?" the woman said.

"But one thick with magical stones," said the older Xoconai augur.

Keri swallowed hard, her fists clenching. A dress filled with magical stones? She had made such a gown long ago as a gift to Khotai of To-gai, the wife of Talmadge. Could it be?

"Take it," ordered the augur.

"If you take it, you fight me," Talmadge warned. "And if you fight me, you fight the whole of this boulevard, do not doubt."

Keri braced herself against the bookcase, ready to burst out and lay low the Xoconai. Elysant crouched beside her, staff ready in hand.

"You are hiding more," the augur said after a long pause.

"I hide nothing. I am Talmadge the trader, Talmadge the craftsman, Talmadge the artist, who serves all who come to my shop, including the sailors of your armada. If you wish to buy something . . ."

He paused. "What are you doing? What is that?"

Keri knew.

"Back there," the augur said. "What is among those books?"

"What are you talking about?" Talmadge demanded.

Keri and Elysant straightened, hearing noise and feeling the thumps as someone, or more than one person, began shuffling about the books on the other side of the thin wooden backing.

"You lie!" the augur yelled. "Find them! Take him!"

Keri fell back, but Elysant went forward, bursting through the bookcase's door, knocking aside the macana warrior who was standing before it. Two steps and the abbess dove and rolled and came up to her feet swinging, taking out the legs of the Xoconai woman, then pressing ahead to stab her staff into the cheek of the old augur as he tried to turn and flee, knocking him to his back.

The man who had been shoved by the swinging door went after Elysant, and Keri started for him, but by the time she stepped out of the small room, Elysant had planted her staff on the floor, leaped up, and kicked her feet out, suddenly and brutally halting that charge. She landed on her feet, snapped her staff back around to knock the warrior's toothed paddle out wide, then reversed the staff in a single motion and threw it like a spear at the rising woman, who caught it more with her mouth than her slapping hand. She went back down again, writhing and groaning.

Inside the reach of the warrior's paddle, Elysant's hands worked like striking serpents, eluding every block, her stiffened fingers thrusting into the Xoconai's throat, a sweeping sidelong cut raking across his eyes.

Up came her knee into the man's groin. She fell back a step

as he lurched in pain, her foot barely touching down again before she sent it up high to slam him in the face. She pursued as he fell over, viciously punching him and kicking him, then leaping out to the side, pivoting and driving her foot hard into the head of the woman warrior as she again tried to rise.

Standing in the door, Keri didn't know what to do. She should call her magic, but which, and why?

She heard a yelp, then a groan, and looked across the way to see Talmadge driving a sword into the chest of the augur.

And not just any sword, oh no, but one she had known well in the war.

The sword of Aydrian, and of his father, the legendary Elbryan, before him. Tempest by name, a most marvelous weapon filled with craftsmanship, fashioned of the finest silverel by the Touel'alfar. The sword of a ranger, the sword of a king.

Back the other way, she saw the apprentice, a mere boy, smash the head of the fallen male warrior with a metal box.

Keri's knees went weak.

All of it, all the shadows, all the pain, all the guilt, swept back over her and she thought she would surely fall away, and almost hoped that she would.

Fall and die.

"Now what?" she heard Talmadge say, but she couldn't see him, couldn't see anything past the dark veil that had swallowed her, the opaque wall of her own eyelids, for she couldn't bear to see any more of this.

"I didn't ask for your help," Elysant answered.

Keri felt hands upon her, pushing her aside. Now she did

look, to find Talmadge hoisting the augur, the dead augur, into the secret room behind her.

The boy dragged the other man, Talmadge helping him to similarly stash the body, and as they moved aside, the Xoconai woman came flying in, hurled by a red-faced, angry Elysant.

"Tell them we did it, that we overwhelmed you all," Elysant offered, but Talmadge was shaking his head through every word.

"Now we run," he decided, and he shut the bookcase door, reached in, and locked it, then carefully replaced the books. "All of us."

He rushed to the side of the room, to an opened box. Keri could see the gown sticking up from its side, and she surely recognized it. Talmadge stuffed it back in and tossed Tempest in atop it, then darted all about the room, grabbing odds and ends—magical items, Keri figured—and threw them in as well.

"The toolbox," he said to Elysant, pointing to a small metal box.

He motioned to Dabego to take up the other end of the chest, and they all started for the door.

"I'll get you on a departing ship," he promised his old friend, the witch from the west. "Just keep sailing and don't ever look back."

"Get all of us on a ship, you mean," Elysant said. "You cannot stay here."

Talmadge didn't answer, and led the way, across the street, down an alleyway, then, surprisingly, down through a grate at the base of a building, into the sewers of Freeport. The foursome rushed on through ankle-deep muck, the meager daylight filtering in through similar grates along the way.

The man clearly knew where he was going, though, and soon they emerged into the water of a high tide, then ran splashing along the beach to the docks of Freeport's southern harbor.

And there, they found the two men and the Xoconai woman who had been with Talmadge right before Keri and Elysant had entered Oot o Bounds.

"Captain Massayo!" Talmadge called even as the tall dark man was about to get into a dinghy.

The man seemed quite surprised, to say the least, and Keri slowed and exchanged concerned looks with Elysant as the one-armed Xoconai woman came off the dinghy and back onto the dock.

Talmadge and Dabego set the box down on the dock, Talmadge bending over, hands on his knees as he tried to catch his breath.

"Good fortune that we caught you," he managed to say, then stood straight once more. "Take the boy back. He cannot stay."

"There is fighting right out there," Massayo answered, pointing to the sea, where indeed, there seemed a scramble of sails not far out of the harbor. "You think that safe?"

"There are three dead, or near dead, Xoconai in my shop," Talmadge replied. "Including a priest. Dabego must be gone from here, and I beg you, take these two women as well."

Massayo looked to Keri and Elysant, his expression sour.

"Mine is not a refugee ship," he answered, but did motion for Dabego to get into the dinghy.

"They will be of great value," Talmadge insisted. "You must. The Xoconai hunt them."

"Then I must not."

"I will pay," Talmadge insisted. "I beg of you, my friend." He rushed to the chest and popped open its lid, then removed the fabulous sword of King Aydrian. "Here, a fitting weapon for a great captain," he said, handing it over. "You must take them. For me, please. Take them south and leave them south."

"You too," Elysant said, moving to Talmadge. "We're not leaving you." She looked to Massayo. "Good captain, please. If you leave him here, they will find him and they will kill him."

"Get in the boat," Massayo told her, and she rushed over and took Keri's hand, pulling her to the dinghy.

"Go," Talmadge told them all. "I will find my way. I've places to hide . . ."

"No!" Keri said, pulling away from Elysant and moving back to Talmadge. "You promised me. On the docks of St.-Mere-Abelle, you promised me."

Talmadge wore a confused look.

"You said that one day we'd sail together to Jacintha," Keri told him. "Now, I hold you to that promise."

"Aoleyn . . ."

"Keri," she cut him short.

The two shared a long stare.

"Please," she begged. "I need you. You've no idea of how much I need you right now."

"The woman I promised was named Aoleyn," Talmadge teased, but Keri didn't crack a smile.

"Please?"

Talmadge motioned to the chest, set his toolbox atop it, then hoisted one end, Keri taking the other.

"Now, at long last, you work for me," Massayo grumbled at Talmadge as he shuffled past.

A very nervous and unhappy-looking Captain Massayo was the last aboard the small dinghy, with the giant tattooed man shoving off the dock, then dropping to the middle bench and heaving the oars with great strength and cadence, propelling them out quickly among the moored ships.

CHAPTER 26

PINQUICKLE'S FOLLY

"Stay out of the way," Captain Massayo told Elysant and Keri, not even bothering to turn around and look at them as he spoke. He stood at the prow of the dinghy, shielding his eyes and shaking his head.

"You have just taken your two best weapons from the field of battle with that order, captain," Talmadge told him.

Massayo didn't seem to be listening. He stared ahead, mumbling to himself.

"They're readying to sail," the Xoconai woman remarked, shifting to look past the captain on the crowded little boat.

"Put your back into it, Toomsuba," she then said, tapping the huge man on the shoulder. "Something is happening at the boat."

"That yours?" Talmadge asked Massayo.

"*Pinquickle's Folly*," he answered.

"Interesting name."

"Interesting story."

"What have we gotten ourselves into?" Keri whispered to Elysant.

"Better than what we had an hour ago, I hope," the monk replied.

They each leaned out of their respective sides in the dinghy, peering ahead at the sloop—they could see the name now. The crew worked the lines furiously to get the sails readied. Up above, a small figure was dangling at the end of a rope from the crow's nest, their foot in a stirrup of some sort. The person went out far to the side, suddenly, as if thrown by a gale, then swung back in toward the mast, but somehow avoided it and went out the other way.

"Chimeg of To-gai," the Xoconai told them, noting their interest. "She is the finest archer on the Mirianic. And I am Qua . . . Quixi, first mate of *Pinquickle's Folly.*"

Talmadge laughed at that, shaking his head. "Quauh," he corrected, and to the surprised Xoconai woman, he offered a shrug, a smile, and said, "These are allies, and among the best you'll ever know."

"They're readying the sails—Columbine's doing, do you think?" Massayo called back form the prow, turning to look at his first mate. "Has our bosun decided to take my sloop as his own?"

"He's a good powrie," insisted the behemoth rowing, and that made Elysant and Keri arch their eyebrows more than a little.

"Let us hope," Massayo replied, turning back. "If they get underway, we'll be sitting out in the middle of the harbor in a rowboat."

Talmadge turned fast to the right and the two women in

the back of the dinghy followed suit, to see a larger ship coming on at half sail, moving toward *Pinquickle's Folly*.

"That's Wilkie, aye?" Talmadge asked.

"*Port Mandu*," Massayo confirmed. "And there's Columbine," he added, pointing to a powrie at the rail of *Pinquickle's Folly*, waving his arms as if to urge the dinghy on.

"Faster!" Massayo ordered. "Someone help him!"

Elysant started for the rowing giant at the call, but Keri grabbed her arm to hold her back and motioned behind them. Over aft went the two women, both standing atop the water now, lessening the dinghy's load, and both grabbing on and pushing with all their strength, running behind the small craft.

"What?" Massayo gasped at the sight.

"You'll see, captain," Talmadge promised. "You'll see."

In short order, they came up alongside *Pinquickle's Folly*, with Captain Wilkie's *Port Mandu* just on the other side of her now.

"Get her moving!" Captain Wilkie called to Massayo. "There's a fight out there, and we'll be damned to the watery floor if we let the goldfish chase us off Freeport!"

"Do we leave them or do we stay?" Elysant asked Keri upon hearing that call.

"They're heading for a fight," Keri answered. She looked to Talmadge, standing over them in the boat, hand extended to help them back aboard the dinghy, then up to the sloop.

"They'll go where the goldfish cannot find us," Talmadge said.

"If they survive the fight," Keri returned, and her old friend shrugged.

"I need to return to St.-Mere-Abelle," Elysant insisted.

"There is always the spring," Talmadge told her.

She looked to Keri, then took Talmadge's hand and went into and across the dinghy, then climbed the netting to the deck of the sloop, with Keri and Talmadge close behind.

As soon as they were all aboard, the two women noted that other ships—other pirates and privateers, they figured—were putting out, or readying to do so.

"Where's my battle song?" Captain Massayo yelled, and Keri and Elysant gawked as a group of musicians ran to instruments set in a small corral on the deck and began a rousing tune.

"Behrenese," Elysant noted. "And powries all about. This Captain Massayo has quite the eclectic crew."

Port Mandu sailed past, *Pinquickle's Folly* falling in quickly, close behind and starboard flank.

"We counted eight giving chase from Entel," Keri said to Elysant.

"The ones out beyond the harbor were already in at port, or near port," Elysant said, shaking her head. "They cannot be the ones chasing us. They'd not have had the time to go all the way around the island."

"But was it just bad luck, or was the whole attack preplanned, and maybe as an attack on Freeport and the pirates and not just for us? How would they get word here fast enough to get those warships out the eastern port and up here fighting?"

"Monks," Elysant answered. "Abellicans strong in the sacred magic can do that. It's how I knew they were coming for St. Rontlemore." She turned a careful look over at Keri, who was relaxed now, sitting on the deck and leaning on the rail. "We are surely heading for a fight, a fierce one, no doubt. Are you up for playing a part in it?"

"No," Keri answered, and she wasn't surprised by the sharpness in her tone. "I want no part of it. This fight's not mine anymore."

"Can you be so sure?"

"I am so sure. Every night I pray to whatever god or fate might be listening in hopes that I'll not ever again kill another person."

"We've had fights aplenty since we joined together once more."

"I did what I had to do, and can only hope that none were killed."

"Some were killed," Elysant said grimly.

"By me, I mean. I do'no want to kill another."

"Even Coyote?"

The question hurt. It sent Keri's thoughts spinning to poor Dafydd, to her grief, to her responsibilities, to her past battles. And it hurt all the more because she honestly didn't know how she would react if she found the opportunity to destroy the ferocious man. On the beach outside the Entel tunnels, she had been attacked viciously, and as they were leaving, she certainly could have killed those attackers who had not already been sent to the afterlife by Elysant.

But the thought had gotten no traction in her heart, and quite the opposite: it repelled her.

"This is not my fight," she replied quietly through teeth gritted with determination.

"Aoleyn is needed," Elysant said, surprising her, and her response came swift and sharp.

"Aoleyn is dead."

Brother Thaddius could hardly believe the size and speed of this warship, with three tall masts, full-rigged, and a deck large enough to have three dozen archers firing on one rail alone. They had lain back for most of the chase, but after the initial engagement, had gone to full sail and rapidly caught and outpaced the lead Tonoloya warships even with the added weight of the armagrande and the tons of metal ammunition.

The captain of the ship had said little, other than to echo the commands of the fierce Coyote, who had taken control. Only once had the captain even looked back at the fierce warrior with doubt, when Coyote ordered them to run west around Freeport Island instead of east.

"If the queen of the desert kingdom arrives on her dragon, my cannoneers will promptly blow the beast out of the sky," Coyote told the captain. "The western course is shorter, and so the western course is ours. Our enemies have one escape from Freeport, and soon will have no escape from Freeport."

The captain merely nodded and settled back in his place.

Signals from polished mirrors flickered from the shore, and that was the last thing Brother Thaddius noted as he fell more deeply into the soul stone, using its spiritual ties to pull himself from his body, as Abbot Dusibol had commanded. He flew across the waves to the northernmost flashing mirror, to the signaling augur who awaited him.

Thaddius raced back a short while later, dismissed by the augur after hearing some startling news indeed. He thought to linger, to fly about the island to learn more, to better locate his friend, perhaps even to offer a warning to Elysant. But he realized that such a course might prove disastrous. Back in his physical form, he felt someone grabbing him by the shoulder and roughly shaking him. It took him a moment to realize that something heavy had been set upon his head, resting snugly above his ears.

Thaddius swallowed hard and was glad that he hadn't lingered about Freeport, hadn't learned more that would now no doubt be pulled from him.

"What do they report?" Coyote shouted in his face.

The monk hesitated and looked to Abbot Dusibol.

"Tell him, Master Thaddius," Dusibol instructed.

Before he could respond, a second spirit-walking monk called out, "They were tracked to Freeport City!"

Coyote spun about to regard the speaker.

"They are not along the northern coast, but two warships have blockaded the harbor in case they return and try to put out there."

Coyote snapped his glare back on Thaddius.

"It is true," Thaddius said, grimacing. In looking at the

other three spirit-walking monks, he confirmed the weight on his head to be a golden headband, one of those most clever and vile instruments that had been demonstrated to all the brethren at St. Rontlemore weeks before by the Xoconai augurs. A poor thief had been brought to the monastery's courtyard, and there questioned directly by City Sovereign Popoca. The man, understanding the price of conviction, had tried to evade the pointed questions, repeatedly, and each lie had caused the band to tighten wickedly.

The thief had only stopped lying when he was curled on the ground, gyrating in violent seizures, grunting in agony as he was dragged away for execution.

"There was a fight at some shop in the town," Thaddius elaborated.

"And?" Coyote prompted. He had no patience here, clearly, his facial colors flushing bright, spittle evident about his lips.

"An augur and two macana are dead," Thaddius reported, leaning back and wincing as he spoke, fearing that the ferocious and impatient man would strike him. "Their killers have fled, but to where is not known. Many are searching, but the city is thick with buildings and with so many people."

Coyote kept glaring, silently asking for more, and Thaddius saw no way out, for anything more he might provide, any answers to direct questions about the escapees, would certainly cause great trouble for his fleeing friends.

He felt the press of the golden band. Would he find the strength to lie and accept the pain as his skull was cracked and powdered?

"What more of—" Coyote started to ask.

"They've fled to a ship!" another monk who had been spirit-walking called out before Thaddius could speak. Coyote rushed from Thaddius to speak with the other monk.

"A ship in the southern harbor!" the monk reported.

"I saw them!" the fourth of the spirit-walkers called out, coming back into his body and stumbling out of his chair. He had been assigned to the southern docks, Thaddius knew. "The two women. I believe that one was Abbess Elysant herself! They went out from the docks in a rowboat. I saw them!"

"To where?" Coyote yelled at him.

"To a boat."

"What boat?"

The monk stammered. "Small . . . but bigger than the rowboat."

The impatient Coyote snorted, and Thaddius could see him fighting an urge to rush over and throttle the fool, who clearly knew nothing about ships.

"Did this boat perchance have a name?" the warrior said with all the sweetness of a headsman telling the condemned to move her hair out of the way.

"It . . ." The monk seemed as if he was about to cry.

"Were they still moored in the harbor?" Coyote yelled at him.

"No, they began floating away, behind another boat. A bigger boat."

"With no name."

The monk turned away.

"Get us around the island with all speed," Coyote ordered

the captain. "Point us toward any ships trying to sail out." He grabbed the last spirit-walker by the shoulder and hauled him out of his seat with one hand, then sent him stumbling toward the frigate's captain.

"Bring him with you to the prow," Coyote ordered. "Leave the band in place upon him!" he shouted at the augur who moved for the monk. "Have him point out the ship, or both, in question, and get me to them!"

"Pray don't harm him," Abbot Dusibol told Coyote. "He is needed on the armagrande . . ."

"The only one who will harm him will be him—if he lies," Coyote retorted. "I will have them, abbot. If I have to sink every ship in and about Freeport that is not sailing under the colors of the Tonoloya Armada, I will have them."

He gave a little laugh. "More importantly, I will have her."

"The abbess has damned herself," Abbot Dusibol replied.

Coyote didn't answer, but Thaddius understood the truth here. When Coyote referred to "her" specifically, he wasn't talking about the abbess.

Keri and Elysant stood tall on the quarterdeck of *Pinquickle's Folly*, peering ahead to port as the ship went to full sail and rushed out of Freeport harbor. They ducked and moved about, trying to see past *Port Mandu* as the crew of *Pinquickle's Folly* tried to pace her and not outrace her.

In the distance beyond, a wild battle was in full volley, with a handful of privateers running circles around a pair of Xoconai warships. Beyond the fight, a sixth small ship flying the red and black was burning and sinking fast.

The pirates clearly held the upper hand now, though, raining fire-tipped arrows all about the two larger vessels. One seemed abandoned, and Keri wondered if her crew had all been killed or chased from the deck. A dozen small fires burned on her and seemed to be growing uncontrollably as her sails luffed and flapped in the wind, and the only thing steering her seemed to be the rolling swells.

The five pursuing pirate ships apparently thought the same, for when the other warship, a large carrack, turned hard to starboard to flee, all five moved to give chase.

"Keep her steady, Benny," the two women heard Captain Massayo call out. "And be ready to cut through Wilkie's wake."

No sooner had he given the order when Captain Wilkie shouted out from his bullhorn to his escort ship. "That sling of yours got enough to make 'em miserable, Massayo?"

"Of course!" Massayo shouted back.

"Good, 'cause they're coming straight for us!"

A few heartbeats later, *Port Mandu* surged ahead and Benny cut hard to port, *Pinquickle's Folly* rolling over the wake of Wilkie's ship. Keri nearly fell to the deck but caught a handhold on a rope line, then turned her attention to the deck, where the giant Toomsuba was hauling back the thick, stretching band of a strange weapon, while others finished filling the pocket with pitch and embers.

Soon the sloop was running straight for the warship to join

in with her five pirate allies. Three trailed the fleeing warship, the other two sailing wide to flank her, and all five raining fiery arrows at their prey. Now trailing the speedy *Pinquickle's Folly*, Wilkie, too, turned to port, angling to stop the warship from getting out into deeper waters.

But the warship made no move that way, or any way, just running straight as fast as she could, either oblivious to the closing *Pinquickle's Folly* or simply having no choice but to try to crash past the newcomer.

"She's readying her forward catapult!" the lookout called, and Keri looked up to regard the woman named Chimeg. Keri blinked a few times, trying to makes sense out of the lookout's swinging movements, with direction changes that seemed truly impossible.

"Their catapult can't throw five hundred," Massayo yelled back to the lookout, and to the others. "First Mate Quauh, let the bullhead fling at six hundred feet."

"What is that thing?" Keri asked Elysant.

The abbess shook her head. "I have no idea. Bullhead?"

The ships closed.

"Six-fifty!" came the cry from lookout Chimeg.

"Clear!" Quauh shouted as she stood by a lever to the right of the war machine, counting out a few more heartbeats. Toom-suba and the others scrambled away from the stretched band, all lifting water buckets—in case of spillage from the pocket, Keri figured.

She was still studying the weapon, trying to make sense of it, when Quauh pulled the lever and let fly, the band contracting so fast that the witch gave a yelp of surprise. It took her a moment to even realize that the sling had thrown the payload, and she looked up and ahead just in time to see the spreading embers of the burning contents arc down over the prow of the warship, raking the deck, lighting a thousand fires on the deck and the sails and the ropes.

Keri winced and blocked her ears as screams erupted from the Xoconai vessel. The large warship's momentum halted immediately, and she banked hard to port. Keri wasn't very familiar with sailing ships, but from the angle of the shot and the way that payload had crashed across the deck, it was easy for her to envision a wheel like the one just below her, and a helmsman there—Xoconai, not powrie—catching the weight of it and now likely dead, or burning to death, probably falling to the side and taking the wheel with him.

Up ahead, Wilkie was turning hard again, but back the other way, to the west.

Massayo saw him, and *Pinquickle's Folly*, too, began another hard turn to port. Looking back over the taffrail, Keri understood, for another warship was in view.

"You two should get belowdecks," said Talmadge, coming up the stairs to the quarterdeck. "We might be first in on this next fight."

"I can fight," Elysant said.

"Oh, I don't doubt that," Talmadge replied. "And if we board or get boarded, you'll be sorely needed. But the first volleys, and as you can see, sometimes the entire battle, are all arrows and catapults and bullheads and ballistae, and the fewer unnecessary hands on deck, the fewer injured we'll need to tend with the fight on hand."

Elysant agreed and reached for Keri, but the witch didn't move, watching, mesmerized, as the five pirate ships raked the wounded carrack with arrows and catapults. The warship's sails flapped wildly as rigging lines burned and snapped, and the whole of the main deck and the forecastle burned and smoked.

She was fully broadside to *Pinquickle's Folly* now, and Keri could not avert her eyes as burning men hurled themselves from the deck to the sea.

Pinquickle's Folly continued her turn, and Keri turned opposite, unable to tear her gaze form the horrible scene.

Mesmerized by the horror on the carrack flying the flag of the Tonoloya Armada.

The horror on the warship named *Lauilli*, she learned, when the stern came into view.

CHAPTER 27

FIRE AND WATER

Elysant heard the gasp before she spun about to consider her friend. Even then, it took her a moment to look past Keri to find the source of the witch's distress.

The abbess's jaw dropped at the same time Keri dropped off the stern of *Pinquickle's Folly*. Elysant called after her, but Keri was already some distance away and speeding across the ocean, running with the power of amber, leaping into short flights with the power of the moonstone, but staying low to the water all the way.

Talmadge ran up beside the monk. "What is she doing?" he cried, bending over the rail, having obviously seen Keri's drop from the boat. "Where is she?" he cried frantically, looking down as if expecting to see the witch struggling in the wake.

Elysant pointed out to the east. "Her sons are on that ship,"

"Sons?" Talmadge slapped the taffrail, then gasped when he spotted the distant figure bounding across the waves. "Aoleyn," he lamented, shaking his head.

Elysant turned to regard him. "She's always chasing trouble."

"Trouble is always chasing her," the craftsman corrected, and Elysant could not disagree.

"More Xoconai warships," Talmadge said then, and Elysant followed his gaze, then his pointing finger back to the northeast, to a pair of schooners coming around the eastern end of the island's southern harbor. Before them, four of the five pirate vessels began a starboard turn to meet the new threat, while the fifth had turned back to get to the wreckage and hopefully the survivors of the sixth pirate ship, which lay dead far beyond the listing *Lauilli*.

"At least the pirates won't mistakenly shoot Keri dead," Elysant muttered.

"Come," Talmadge said, putting a hand on her shoulder to turn her about with him. "Trust in Aoleyn . . ."

"Keridven."

"Keridven, then," Talmadge agreed. "She's beyond our help, and we've our own fight brewing."

"A big schooner," Elysant said, looking forward to a third enemy, a lone warship coming around the western side of the island, throwing a tremendous spray.

Port Mandu and *Pinquickle's Folly* were aimed right for her.

"A frigate, not a schooner," Talmadge corrected her, and he blew a sigh at the sheer size of the vessel. "And likely with more archers on her deck than we've got crew on both our ships combined."

"That sounds promising."

"Massayo is too smart to go deep into this fight," Talmadge assured her. "And Wilkie's as fine a captain as is sailing the coast.

They'll get close enough to make her turn and present a target for that bullhead." He nodded to the giant sling. "We have that one advantage. We can hit her before her catapults can reach us. If we're lucky, we'll then cripple her mainsail. Then Massayo and Wilkie will turn hard and put fast back to the open sea and the southern waters. I don't think you'll be needed for any fighting, but your strength on the lines when they call for that turn might help."

"What about Keri?" She turned back as she asked the question. If they weren't fighting this frigate fully, they certainly weren't going to slow on their retreat.

"Trust her. You've no choice."

The flames tickling the sails were dying, and that seemed a fitting symbol to Keri as she leaped and ran and flew across the ocean. For the *Lauilli* was surely dying, and all aboard her were likely dead or dying.

Images of Carwyn and Kenzie flashed in her thoughts. She remembered the day Carwyn and Dafydd had joined the family, still boys, but headstrong and impressive even then. She remembered the first time she had cradled Kenzie in her arms—a day of hope and optimism, the promise of a brighter future for all. And a day, a moment, of love such as she had never before or since realized.

She leaped past debris in the water, past bodies floating facedown, and with one great explosion of magical energy, she flew to the deck of the ruined carrack.

Arrows were sticking everywhere. Dozens of bodies of Xoconai sailors lay strewn about, pincushioned with arrows. The helmsman and another sailor stood pasted to the wall of the quarterdeck, held fast by the pitch that bound them to the wall. *Pinquickle's* bullhead throw had hit the mark indeed. Tattered sails flapped, angry beams creaked, flames whispered and hissed, but still, the ship seemed quiet to her.

Deathly quiet.

She stood there for many heartbeats, frozen in fear, locked in the horror of a reality she simply could not emotionally process at that time. Back the other way, she saw more flotsam, more bodies. Far, far back, she saw someone thrashing in the water, and her first instinct nearly sent her over the rail to rescue the poor soul.

But her boys . . . where were her boys?

She was grieving them, as surely as she had Dafydd. She felt herself almost sinking in despair, her knees weakening.

A wave caught the *Lauilli* at a bad angle and sent the ship in a short spin, and the jolt knocked Keri sprawling but also broke her from her downward emotional spiral.

"You do'no know," she reminded herself, and almost as soon as she had whispered the words, she heard a sound below. She rushed to the forward hatch and down the stairs to the hold, then stopped and gasped, barely catching herself as she slipped in a pool—nay, a pond!—of fresh-spilled blood.

A single figure moved about across the way, a Xoconai sailor, holding a macana dripping small streams of blood. Before Keri could even call out, the sailor lifted the weapon and caved in the skull of a man shackled to the beam of the hold. The sailor stumbled back and spat, her face and mouth struck by the backsplash of blood and brains, and, as if angered by that, she pushed forward and whacked her victim again.

Keri just stood there, taking in the garish scene of this chamber of slaughter. She thought of the lair of the demon dactyl, for this seemed equally horrid to her, a chamber of absolute murder. All about the hold were battered and bloody men and women, most shackled upright with their arms up high to the beam, but with some strapped to hammocks, and a couple of others, including one small girl just to the side of Keri, crumpled on the floor in death. The wounds to all were obvious and plentiful and surely mortal. None were Xoconai. They were enslaved, Keri understood, impressed into service, all bound and all, it seemed, brutally murdered.

"Bloody dog buccaneers," Keri heard the Xoconai sailor say, and she looked up to see the woman striding across the hold toward her, rolling her macana with every step. "You think you will get me, do you?"

She lifted the weapon, screamed, and charged, closing the gap in short order, lifting the macana to strike Keri down.

And then flying away at the end of a lightning bolt as Keri stamped her foot.

The sailor landed halfway across the hold, falling back to the floor and bouncing another ten feet, where she lay groaning and struggling to rise.

Keri paid her no heed, instead rushing about the hold desperately.

To a man whose skull had been hit so hard that one eyeball had popped out and was hanging over his cheek.

To a woman whose blood stopped squirting from her chest just a heartbeat before Keri got to her.

To a young man, barely more than a boy, curled against the wall. She fell to her knees before that one, turning him, crying, knowing he was dead, and fearing it was Kenzie.

It wasn't, but still the tears flowed.

She knelt. She clawed at her face. She screamed in denial and anger at the sheer wrongness of this scene.

She rocked back and chanced a glance to the side, to see the Xoconai woman struggling to kneel.

Keri wanted to kill that woman.

For all the pain, for all the guilt, for all her desires to make the world a better place, Keri wanted to kill that woman.

She turned as she rose to her feet, even took a step toward the sailor, when out of the corner of her eye, she spotted something, someone, she could not ignore.

Carwyn, hanging from the beam, covered in blood.

"No! No, no, no!" she cried, rushing to him. Magic wrought of fury, of fear, of denial, flowed through her. Her muscles tightened with the power of bloodstone. She hit the beam about the shackles with a jolt of lightning without even realizing it. Her hands became stone and she leaped up, crashing against Carwyn, grabbing the chains, and pulling her legs up to plant her feet on the beam on either side of the shackle base.

Hissing and growling, scrambling and scrabbling, more red rage than thought, more animal than human, the witch brought forth the bloodstone strength to surge through her as never before, and with a great tug, she straightened her legs and tore free the shackles, she and Carwyn falling hard to the floor, splashing in the lake of blood.

Still she scrambled, out from under her son to hold him, to cradle his head, to call to him. Her hands became flesh again as she stroked his bloody cheeks, and one depressed beneath her gentle touch, for the bone shaping it had been shattered.

Shattered by the Xoconai sailor, she knew.

Snarling, Keri snapped her head around to see the woman, who had regained her footing and now stood shakily. Beyond and behind her, a door burst open and an eyeblink later, a crossbow bolt flew out.

Keri got her hand up to block it, but her hand was flesh now, not stone, and the bolt went right through her palm and scratched and stabbed into her cheek. She slapped it away reflexively, hardly registering the pain.

"Kill her!" she heard the female sailor cry. "Abellican!"

A dozen thoughts spiraled into tangents in Keri's mind in that single instant. She didn't know if Kenzie was in here.

She had to search!

And what others might she save, poor victims who did not deserve their fate? But how?

Her thoughts could not keep up with her hopes.

Through the door came Xoconai sailors, intent on murder, rushing to kill her.

"Ma?" came a soft whisper. Carwyn was still alive.

Keri stood fast, her muddled thoughts clearing under the singular instinct to save her child. Her body surged with magical physical strength, and she ignored the pain in her hand and her cheek and with the bloodstone magic effortlessly hoisted Carwyn up into her arms, cradling him as if he was but a small child.

The approaching attackers slowed, even stopped and gawked at the strange sight of the diminutive woman so easily lifting and holding a large and muscular young man clearly twice her weight.

"Just shoot her dead," someone said, and Keri heard a crossbow crank and lock.

Keri understood the language, every word, and she was glad of that when she heard the confused murderous sailor ask, "Why are they glowing white?"

"If ye be stayin' on the deck, get yerself to work!" bosun Columbine shouted at Elysant and Talmadge. "If ye be runnin' to hide, then get off the damned deck!"

The two moved to the stairs of the quarterdeck and noted the commotion, where the giant Toomsuba was tugging back the thick sling to the locking pole, while a pair of powries waited beside a smoking pot. They were wearing gloves and holding long tongs. To the side, a trio of people with skin as dark as Massayo's handled more conventional payloads, sorting chains and stones of various sizes.

Talmadge stepped onto the stairs to the raised afterdeck and glanced back.

"We fight," Elysant told him.

Talmadge kept climbing, but paused and looked back to

signal his agreement with the sentiment. He turned back, coming over the lip of the higher deck, and looked at the listing Xoconai carrack. He shuddered and gasped in surprise, reactions that were echoed all about a moment later when the sound of a great explosion and a warm shock wave from the fiery blast washed over *Pinquickle's Folly* and every other nearby ship.

Even the music stopped.

Elysant scrambled up the ladder enough to look over the taffrail just in time to see a burst of flames lifting from the dying carrack, curling mushroom-like into a rising ball, flaming planks and decking flying from it every which way.

The mainmast of *Lauilli* remained, but with only the upper yardarm still attached, looking like a great burning cross, and one that wouldn't stand for long as the entire hull of the ship began to splinter and pop open, becoming a giant burning wooden rib cage.

"Aoleyn," Elysant whispered.

"Get to work or I'll put ye to the sharks!" Columbine howled at the two, and at all the startled crew. "If we're not makin' that shot and makin' it right, we're all for the bloody sea!"

Elysant almost tripped and fell when Talmadge stumbled past her on the tight stair, her gaze locked far behind to the smoke and carnage, certain that she had just lost a dear friend.

With both Carwyn and herself protected from the flames by her serpentine shield, Keri used her moonstone, malachite, and amber yet again, leaping, soaring, through a huge gap in the blasted and burning hull. She barely touched down in the water before springing away again, a great jump that sent her near-weightless form long and far from the disintegrating *Lauilli*.

Still, she barely got away from the carnage of her explosive fireball, and felt the splash and swell as the huge and heavy mainmast crashed into the sea just behind her.

And her luck barely held again and again as burning planks fluttered and spun down all about her.

She hadn't meant to let loose such a blast—not like that! She had hoped to sting and drive off the Xoconai attackers, but her rage and fear had taken over, had brought her fully into the same feral power that she had wielded against Tay Aillig and Scathmizzane and other enemies those years ago.

She tried not to think about that, cursed herself every step to drive it out of her mind. She was juggling many gemstones here—too many!

Another long stride and she dropped the serpentine fire shield, and brought up instead the magical song of her wedstone, calling to it, bringing forth its power to send into Carwyn as he held on to life by the tiniest of threads.

Pinquickle's Folly was far away now and sailing strong, though into headwinds. She couldn't slow. For her sake and for Carwyn's, she had to catch that ship.

With stubbornness and unbreaking resolve, she ignored the exhaustion and balanced the amber and the malachite to keep her atop the sea, the bloodstone so that she could have the strength to keep her son secure in her small arms, and the moonstone and the wedstone to alternate short and swift flights and bursts of healing magic.

She gained steadily. She saw the other ship running with *Pinquickle's Folly* make a wide turn to port, heading out to deeper waters.

Anticipating that Captain Massayo's ship would do the same, she began angling slightly to the left.

But then the world changed again.

Elysant went to work with furor, telling herself that she had to uphold Aoleyn's legacy, to do justice to the witch's sacrifice. She used all the strength her bracer could give her to hoist a large metal ball and carry it back toward the pocket of the now-locked giant sling.

She glanced to her right, over the prow of *Pinquickle's Folly*, to see *Port Mandu* beginning its swing out to the left, out toward the open Mirianic. Now the Tonoloya frigate was clearly in view, just a few hundred yards away.

A gleam of gold caught her eye, and the sound of monks chanting drifted to her ears.

Elysant dropped the iron ball, which hit the deck with a great thud.

"Secure that!" Columbine yelled above the renewed battle music, but Elysant ran forward instead, leaving the heavy ball for Talmadge and the powries.

"No, no," she shouted to Captain Massayo and his Xoconai

first mate, who stood together at the starboard prow rail, near the sling's release lever.

Both turned to regard her curiously.

"No! Turn! Flee!" Elysant shouted to them, for she knew. She just knew. "It is Coyote! The armagrande!"

"We close and cripple her!" Massayo shouted back, but his sentence was punctuated with a sudden tumult, a rush of noise, puffing and whooshing like the noise of a child spitting watermelon seeds in rapid succession—or more accurately, she thought, like a giant spitting coconuts!

Port Mandu had turned to lure the frigate to starboard, or at least to get the attention of the crew and give Massayo's ship time to close and let fly the bullhead's payload. Instead, though, that turn had merely put her broadside to the approaching warship, which should have still been far out of range.

Broadside, and what a wonderful target, indeed.

A line of projectiles reached out from the frigate's prow, a rain of metal that was continually adjusted as it flew and so was soon locked in on Wilkie's ship, cannonball after chain after cluster of sharpened blades and small balls smashing in, tearing in, spinning in, to crash and splinter planks and masts, to spin through sails and cut rigging, to create a hailstorm of deadly design.

Port Mandu shuddered repeatedly and continuously, moving as much sideways as forward under the relentless, awful barrage. Everything shook and splintered, the crew on the forecastle cried out and fell silent and began a dance of shudders and jolts as the grapeshot ripped them apart. The sweep of destruction and death moved all the way to *Port Mandu*'s stern as the metallic storm swept the length of the ship.

Time seemed to stop for the gawking onlookers on *Pinquickle's Folly* in those terrible moments as they watched their friends and their sister ship so suddenly and violently die, both flesh and bone and wood quite literally shredding and splintering before them.

In mere heartbeats, *Port Mandu* wasn't crippled, wasn't listing, Elysant thought, for those terms didn't do the image before her justice. No, there was no ship. It was gone, just gone, reduced to flotsam and driftwood.

Massayo stood with both his hands upon his head, tearing at his hair, staring helplessly.

Still the deadly rain continued.

First Mate Quauh yelled out to Benny, "Hard to the wheel now!" and *Pinquickle's Folly* began her bend to the left and the open waters.

"The other way! The other way! Keep to the enemy's port rail!" Elysant pleaded, for the cannon was starboard of the bowsprit, and she suspected that the Xoconai crew could not easily maneuver that massive armagrande on a rolling deck. Even if they managed it, the monks would likely have to begin their chanting to empower the lodestones all over again, buying *Pinquickle's Folly* some time.

"All the way about! Turn and run!" Massayo yelled.

"We cannot outrun her," Quauh insisted.

"No choice but to try," the captain replied. "Hard turn, Benny!"

"No!" came a booming shout from the quarterdeck, a call so commanding, so obviously enhanced with some magic, that all on deck spun about. Even Benny stopped his work and the ship broke the turn. Up onto *Pinquickle's Folly* flew Keri, midship, bearing her burden. She laid the broken form down beside the mainmast and stalked forward.

"It's him, Coyote," Elysant said as Keri ran past.

"I know."

"The armagrande—the cannon—is starboard of her bowsprit," Elysant pleaded with Massayo. "Keep us to her port rail. Use her bowsprit and jib as a shield!"

"We cannot outrun her," Quauh said again.

"I'll speed us to close and shoot, then you run straight past her port rail and then out across her stern," Keri told the captain.

"What madness," Massayo replied.

"Cap'n?" Benny called.

"They're turning!" Chimeg called from above.

"Port helm forty, Benny!" Quauh ordered. She looked to the witch. "You claimed that you could speed us. I would suggest you get to it."

Keri didn't run to the quarterdeck; she jumped and flew, landing and spinning and bringing forth her moonstone wind to pull tight the sails.

On the deck before her, the captain and bosun helped the sling crew in adjusting the angle of the bullhead to shoot over the forward port rail.

The witch ignored them. She had to keep the sloop moving ahead of that turning frigate or all would be lost.

446

"Steady and straight, Benny!" Quauh yelled out, and Keri nodded. It was all about speed now. If she could keep those sails full, that frigate would not be able to align and get the armagrande its shot.

"Five hundred yards!" Massayo called to Quauh, and to the musicians, he prodded, "Play! Play with all your hearts! First Mate, mark the distance and let fly as you will!"

When he turned back to view Keri, though, his smile vanished, revealing his great doubts to the witch who stood on the small quarterdeck.

But the first part was working, Keri knew. They were going to get their shot, but the frigate likely wouldn't—unless they had some way to easily turn that golden cannon.

Moments later, the sloop shuddered under the shock of the firing bullhead. The throw was true, but low, most of it smashing against the port prow, with only a bit flying over to tear at sailors and sails—enough to ignite the jib and cause some scurrying about on the frigate's forecastle, but nothing, it seemed, that might cripple the larger craft.

Just below Keri's position, Massayo cursed. "How long?" he asked Keri. "Now we have to run."

"We go right past her port rail," Keri growled back.

"Her archers will sweep clear our decks!"

"Do as I told you," the witch demanded. "You've no other course before you."

She locked stares with the captain, and answered his doubting expression by showing him his full and straining sails—even though the wind was not behind them.

447

Massayo threw up his hands and ran forward to Quauh, who began barking orders to Benny.

The sloop charged ahead, then bent back slightly to port, running a course parallel to the frigate, whose forecastle and port rail were now lined with crossbowmen and Xoconai warriors lifting javelin-loaded atlatls.

More than one voice on *Pinquickle's Folly* yelled out to beg Massayo to turn aside, and more than once did Massayo glance nervously back to Keri. The musicians stopped playing, looking to each other with obvious alarm.

But Keri was sure that she was right in this desperate attempt, and knew that Massayo understood that as well. They could evade the frigate for a short while, but they couldn't possibly outrun her long enough to get to waters too shallow for pursuit.

They needed to hurt her more.

But first, they had to survive the close encounter, and when the frigate's archers lifted their bows, the sloop slowed, bereft of the magical breeze. For Keri had dropped the magical wind and rushed down to the main deck and port rail, readying, waiting, her focus going to the water before the closing frigate. She called to the magical zircon she had set in her anklet.

With the battling ships still thirty yards apart, bow to bow, and thirty aside, port to port, up came the bows.

And up came a berg of ice, bursting from the ocean depths so suddenly just before the speeding frigate, colliding with the prow, just left of the bowsprit, throwing sailors from their feet, and more than a few over the rail.

These Xoconai were veteran sailors and seasoned warriors,

though, and those who could recovered quickly and lifted their weapons to return a volley.

And up came the wind from Keri, a great wall of air reaching forth, slamming those bolts and arrows and javelins even as they came free of their throwers, whipping them up and about and every which way except for the one their launchers had desired.

The frigate's sails luffed flat and even reversed, the huge ship shuddering as if in a sudden gale—as indeed, it was!

Xoconai sailors grabbed the rails, the masts—anything!— and held on for their very lives, as did the team of monk cannoneers, Keri saw as the ships began their pass.

As did Coyote! He stood against the mainmast, staring hatefully at her.

Keri lifted right off the ground, her arms spreading wide, one hand grasping a guide rope to keep *Pinquickle's Folly* from sailing out right under her as she fell deeper into the magic. She was truly exhausted, truly pained, those black wings of doubt and guilt chasing her yet again.

But Carwyn lay on the deck behind her, dying, perhaps already dead, and surely dead if they did not get away from the fierce monster staring at her.

And Kenzie . . .

She didn't look back to the smoldering mess that she thought his grave.

She looked back in time instead, to the distant mountain of her youth and to the definitive statement she had made to the Coven of Usgar witches those years ago, when she had used her magic to throw them down and show them their evil ways.

And so, she made that statement again, using the very same magical combination.

She called upon the ruby in her ring, sending wisps of flame spinning out with the wind. Now the enemies ducked and covered their eyes, the wind showing small lines of fire, stinging and burning. Little fires erupted about the deck of the frigate, most blown out immediately by the howling gale of the witch's wrath.

So ferocious came the storm that the floundering frigate leaned to starboard under the blow. More than one sailor tumbled over that far rail to the icy Mirianic.

Coyote never moved, never stopped glaring at the witch. Never stopped wickedly smiling. For all the chaos on his large warship at that moment, for all the little stings and likely a few lost hands, Coyote was staring at her and smiling. He knew her, who she really was.

And so did she.

She took great pleasure when an arrow stabbed down from on high, taking the man in the shoulder.

Still, he didn't flinch, didn't move, other than to reach up and tear out the missile, throwing it aside, his wound healing almost as soon as the blood began spurting. And he never took his eyes from the witch as he did!

"Hard to port, Benny!" Quauh yelled, and *Pinquickle's Folly* dove into a steep port turn, rushing behind the frigate. "Catch the wind full!"

The witch dropped her breeze and reached her thoughts to her anklet once more, this time to catch the song of the graphite bar.

How she wanted to strike at Coyote directly! How she wanted to melt him where he stood!

But she could not, for the angle had changed and now he was blocked by the high quarterdeck, and she could not anyway, for this little sloop had no chance of survival if they could not hinder the frigate's pursuit.

Her blast of lightning reached up high to the top yardarm of the mizzenmast. It wasn't her strongest bolt, surely, for the continual release of such powerful magic had taken a heavy toll on her energies, but it packed enough of a jolt to break free one side of that aft sail, which flopped, causing even more confusion and distress on the floundering enemy vessel.

Keri moved back to the quarterdeck, resisting the urge to go to Carwyn—Elysant was over him then, protecting him with the flap of her nearly invulnerable robe.

"Get us away!" the abbess begged.

CHAPTER 28

THE SECRET SAVIOR

Brother Thaddius collected himself and patted out a few wisps of flame on his robes. He looked about the deck to see the battered Xoconai crew, many rushing to somehow reset the mizzen, while others ran about with buckets and heavy blankets to put out the little fires caused by the splash of the burning pitch and the hot winds, and still others throwing lines to crewmen who had been blown overboard by the witch's powerful display.

The monk tried to keep a grin from his face. It was so good to see his old friend putting the monstrous Coyote in his place.

It was easier to hide that look of satisfaction when he glanced over at Coyote, though, for the man hardly seemed humbled. A wide smile splayed across the cochcal's face, his eyes locked on the run of the sloop as she passed behind the frigate and broke for the south.

"Water! We are taking water!" came a yell from belowdecks.

The captain ran over to Coyote.

"The iceberg split a seam, forward starboard," another

sailor yelled from the hold. "Iceberg!" he yelled again in obvious disbelief.

"Have your brothers any magic that can help in repairing a cracked hull?" Coyote called to Abbot Dusibol.

The monk considered it for a moment, then held up his hands.

"Zircon," another monk suggested. "Freeze the area of the leak."

"That might work," Dusibol told Coyote.

"Send one of your monks to get it done."

Abbot Dusibol grabbed a nearby brother, fished about for the appropriate gem, and sent him rushing to the ladder.

"All extra hands to the hold to bail," Coyote told the captain. "And get this ship aligned and in chase to strike at that sloop. If they escape, your head will escape your shoulders, as well."

"I've crew in the water," the captain replied.

Coyote flashed him a stare that frightened Thaddius for the poor captain! The monk leaned on the cannon and looked out to his right, to the fleeing sloop. He knew the range of the weapon, and a few heartbeats later, as the frigate came around, he knew that the sloop was about to take a profound and likely fatal beating.

"Take down her sails, Abbot Dusibol," Coyote instructed. "I want to see the witch's face as we send her to the bottom."

The abbot nodded and moved over to take the place of the monk he had sent to freeze the ship's wound.

"Let us chant, brothers," Dusibol ordered.

Brother Thaddius briefly slipped one hand into a pocket

in his robe before reaching forth and grasping his two handles on the armagrande. He began his chanting with the others, as he had with the barrage that had destroyed the larger pirate vessel—an attack that had pained him greatly.

That last time, Thaddius's heart and his magical energy weren't really into the magical song. He had secretly contributed little magical energy to the armagrande assault.

This time, though, his heart was indeed behind his task, and he brought forth every bit of the magical power he could manage.

But not in the way Abbot Dusibol might be imagining.

"Come on," Massayo implored Keri. "Back to the quarterdeck. We need wind!"

"Your sails are already full," Elysant countered, stepping between the man and Keri, who knelt on the deck, magically tending her broken son.

"We need more."

"Give her time!" Elysant scolded. "This is her son!"

"Look behind us!" Massayo shouted back. "We don't have time! If she wants to save her son . . ." He let the thought just hang there.

Elysant did look back.

The frigate wasn't pacing them, but was indeed turning in line for the armagrande. She couldn't deny Massayo's warnings.

"Keri?" she said. "Your son has to wait or we are all doomed.

Please . . ." She halted and gasped audibly when her friend looked up, as hateful an expression as she had ever seen stamped upon the dark-haired witch's face.

"Do not call me that," she said.

Elysant was truly confused, her expression clearly revealing that.

"Keridven of Whispervale is no more," the witch said, rising. "Our enemies know who I am, and now, again, so do I. I am Aoleyn of Fireach Speuer."

She walked past the abbess and the captain to the sloop's taffrail, and there brought forth as much wind as she could manage, though it was nowhere near as powerful as before. Even with her determination brimming, Aoleyn simply did not have enough magical energy remaining to strengthen the run beyond this small wind. Still, *Pinquickle's Folly* leaped away, her mast straining.

Only for a moment, though, for a line of missiles spewed from the pursuing frigate, and Aoleyn spun about and called upon every last bit of energy she could muster, throwing that wind wall behind them in an attempt to deflect and defeat the power of the volley.

It wasn't nearly enough.

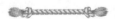

Thaddius tried to hold his concentration. He grimaced as he felt the initial spew of the cannon, but he knew that he had to time his own action perfectly to be most effective.

They were throwing chains mostly, high for the rigging, but now they loaded the feeding tray with the second wave: heavy balls and deadly grapeshot to clear the deck.

Thaddius clutched the cannon handle, and within that grasp, secretly clutched a very powerful sunstone. His magical energy was fully tied to the cannon then through the handles and the ritual, and so he brought forth the sunstone's full magic and threw all his might to inject it into the weapon, weakening the lodestone magic, countering the efforts of the other monks.

The stream of metal vomit continued forth, but now began to splash short of the fleeing sloop.

Thaddius heard Coyote yelling at Abbot Dusibol.

Thaddius redoubled his efforts with the sunstone, covering his growls to make it seem as if he was increasing his efforts with the cannon instead of against it.

Now the stream was falling far short—for Coyote's protests had distracted Dusibol, and Coyote's threats had upset the other monk cannoneers, weakening their concentration.

Finally, Dusibol called for a halt in the firing.

Thaddius let go of the handles and stood straight, as did the others, all looking at a fuming, questioning Dusibol.

"What happened? How is this possible?" he demanded. "We held the shot far longer—longer than this one and the one that destroyed the other ship combined!—when we leveled St. Rontlemore!"

"Something is amiss, abbot," one of the others insisted. "I feel interference."

Thaddius started to slip the sunstone back into his pocket,

but in noting Coyote striding toward the cannon, the dangerous man's face a mask of rage, he instead just subtly flicked the sunstone behind him, sending it over the rail. He could only hope that he wouldn't need it again to aid the ship carrying his friends.

He breathed a bit of relief when word came up from belowdecks that the ice seal wasn't holding and the frigate was again taking water.

"Catch them!" Coyote screamed at the captain, but his call was simply an expression of rage-filled denial.

Even without the magical winds of the witch filling her sails, the sloop was pulling away.

"Abbot!" Coyote yelled at Dusibol. "Again! Again!"

Dusibol looked to the now-distant pirate sloop and held up his hands helplessly. "We cannot reach that target."

Coyote flew into a rage and decked the abbot with a heavy fist. He stormed about, screaming at the other monks, screaming at Dusibol as the man tried to stand, screaming at the frigate's captain, who was, in turn, yelling at his crew to sort their rigging.

But it was over. Even Coyote knew it.

Soon after, the frigate turned and limped back for Freeport.

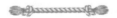

Aoleyn felt the sting as a chain clipped her shoulder.

She heard the sails tearing behind her, heard Chimeg cry out from above, then fall silent, heard the commotion on the deck as Massayo and his crew scrambled for cover.

The wind wall she had created had turned some of the

volley, and had diminished the speed and power of those missiles flying through, but they wouldn't outlast the rain of death, Aoleyn knew.

And then, for a moment, all that she knew was a heavy punch in the chest and the hard rail of the quarterdeck against her back and neck.

She looked down to see a metal ball rolling off her lap and across the planks.

More missiles flew in, but now above her, coming in high without the force of her wind to impede them. She managed to half turn and look up, to see poor Chimeg hanging upside down from the mast, her foot looped in the harness she used to execute her deadly dance. The skilled archer's bow fell from her hand, spinning down to the deck, and Aoleyn, only half-aware of the sights before her, watched its descent, mesmerized.

Aoleyn spent a long while staring at the weapon lying there on the deck before she even realized that the sails weren't being hit anymore, that the sloop wasn't being hit anymore and was still gliding swiftly to the south.

Then Elysant was there beside her, grabbing her, hugging her.

"You did it!" she said repeatedly, but Aoleyn knew that she had not. "Please come back to us!"

"I'm here," Aoleyn assured the abbess, her senses fully returning. She felt a tremendous pain about her chest and ribs, but thought she'd be all right. "Help me up."

"Come, we'll get you tended," Elysant said, but Aoleyn brushed her away.

The witch limped to the taffrail and saw the line of missiles dying away, splashing nearer to the firing frigate than to *Pinquickle's Folly*.

Aoleyn spun about once more. "Go to my son," she ordered Elysant, and then, before the abbess could answer, the witch leaped away, flew away, up to the hanging Chimeg, falling into her wedstone to bring forth the healing magic even as she got there.

"Get someone up here to help her get down!" she shouted down to the deck. "And gather all the wounded."

Only a few minutes later, having used the very last of her magical powers, exhausted as fully as she had ever been, Aoleyn collapsed on the deck beside Carwyn, surrounded by several others, all seriously wounded, Chimeg included.

The last thing she heard as she slipped in and out of consciousness was a call that the frigate had turned, then a great cheer from *Pinquickle's* crew.

Despite the apparent escape, the rest of the crew ignored their own exhaustion and, for many, their wounds, and worked hard to keep the sloop running south, then veering to starboard, setting a course to the southwest and the shallow, reef-filled waters along the Behrenese coast, where a frigate could not possibly follow.

EPILOGUE

It was dark when Aoleyn again opened her eyes, the sky above her thick with stars. She basked in that beautiful sight only for a moment, though, remembering the dire predicament all about her.

She rolled to her side, then sat up beside Carwyn and immediately fell over him.

How much easier she breathed when she discovered that her son was still very much alive!

She dropped her hand to her belly ring and fell into the song of the wedstone, then filled the young man with the warmth of magical healing once more. After only a couple of moments, he awakened, opened his eyes, and took in a great gulp of air.

"Ma?"

"I'm here."

"Where's here?"

"On a boat, sailing south."

"The *Lauilli?*"

"The *Lauilli*'s dead, Carwyn. Your brother is dead."

461

"Dafydd? Aye . . ."

"Kenzie," Aoleyn clarified.

Carwyn sat up, showing surprising strength for one who had been so grievously wounded. "Kenzie? Where? How?"

"The *Lauilli* is dead," Aoleyn repeated. "Blown apart. None survived."

The young man nodded. "But where is Kenzie?"

Aoleyn started to repeat her previous response, but stopped as she realized that Carwyn had heard her. "Where is Kenzie?" she hesitantly asked.

"North, and maybe far west, last I knew," said Carwyn.

Aoleyn could hardly breathe. "Kenzie wasn't on the *Lauilli*?" she asked slowly and deliberately, enunciating every word so that there could be no misunderstanding here.

Carwyn shook his head.

Aoleyn fell over him, sobbing with joy and hope, her mind spinning at the roads that might soon lie before her.

After a while, she felt a hand on her shoulder and looked up to see Elysant. She put her hand on that of the abbess, nodding and smiling and crying.

"Are your powers regenerated?" Elysant asked quietly.

Aoleyn sniffled and nodded. "I'll give you more," she told Carwyn.

But Carwyn, staring at Elysant, shook his head. "Others, Ma. I think she means that you're needed elsewhere."

"Chimeg is in a bad way," Elysant affirmed. "And Perridoo the powrie's wound is infested, I fear."

Aoleyn nodded, spent just a moment kissing Carwyn once

more and hugging him close, then followed Elysant about, first to Chimeg, then to the powrie named Perridoo, and when both were resting comfortably, to several others.

Aoleyn was exhausted enough to go back to sleep when she had finished, and intended to do just that, when Talmadge joined her and Elysant, motioning for them to come forward.

"I keep my promises," he said to Aoleyn at the prow, looking out to the southwest and the multicolored, fabulous lights of a sprawling city. "Jacintha, Keridven . . ."

"Aoleyn," both Aoleyn and Elysant said together.

Talmadge looked from one to the other, then gave a little helpless laugh. "Jacintha," he repeated. "That is the seat of Queen Brynn's power, the greatest known city south of the Belt-and-Buckle, and by my reckoning, north of the mountains, as well! Tomorrow, you and I will walk the streets of Jacintha together, as we once vowed, long ago."

"Not so long," Aoleyn answered. "And will you tell me of Khotai?"

She didn't miss the shadow of pain that crossed Talmadge's face, but the man nodded. He put an arm about her shoulders and pulled her in close to his side.

They tied *Pinquickle's Folly* to a mooring buoy as dawn began to break two days after the battle.

Aoleyn and Elysant got out of the way but remained near the prow, taking in the magnificent sight as the brilliant colors, shining domes, spires, and minarets of magnificent Jacintha came into clear view.

They were still staring and shaking their heads in amazement when Talmadge returned to them, the captain and first mate at his side.

"Let me now formally introduce you two wonderful ladies to Captain Massayo Mantili," he said to them. "A dear friend who financed me with favorable terms when I set up Oot o Bounds in Freeport. You can trust him as surely as you can trust me."

"Talmadge has told me all about you," the captain said with a wide smile and an extended hand to Aoleyn. "We are honored to have you aboard, and grateful. We'd not have escaped that row without you. I give you my first mate, Quauh . . ."

He paused, his gaze leading the others to look at Elysant, who was staring hard at the Xoconai woman with obvious suspicion, even contempt.

"I do not blame you," Quauh said to Elysant. "We live in difficult and often confusing times."

"Quauh is no enemy—far from it!" Massayo said. "The Xoconai would hunt her as eagerly as they hunt you two."

"I was once your enemy," Quauh admitted. "And now I owe my life to Captain Massayo. More than my life, for I have learned better than those views I took with me to Entel."

"And now you're staying here? First mate?" Elysant asked.

"Aye, and gladly."

"Until she becomes captain of my second ship," Massayo said. "She was a captain, you see, in the Tonoloya Armada."

"You betray your own people?" Elysant said.

"Sometimes it is necessary," Aoleyn answered before Quauh could.

"What are your plans?" Massayo asked the two guests.

"Back to Honce," Aoleyn answered. "I must."

"And I," Elysant agreed. "Sail me to St.-Mere-Abelle, I beg of you, and I will make sure you are fabulously rewarded."

"Alas, I cannot," Massayo replied. "Winter fast approaches, and should I try such a journey, at best I would be trapped in the cold north for many months—not that we'd have a chance of getting there, in any case. *Pinquickle's Folly* is a not a ship suitable for the swells and deep winter waters north of the Mantis Arm and into the Gulf of Corona, and we'd never slip along the coast unnoticed."

"The reward—"

"Perhaps next year," Massayo cut Elysant short. "Our course now is south, far south, to islands of beauty and freedom and safety."

"Come with us," Talmadge interjected.

"Us?" Aoleyn asked.

"Aye. I've nothing left in Freeport after the . . . incident. Captain Massayo has great plans."

"And I could use a craftsman of Talmadge's skill on my crew," Massayo put in. "And I could use you, both of you."

"Undoubtedly," Elysant said dryly.

"And perhaps you will find your gain greater than ours in such an arrangement," Quauh said. "To see the world is no small thing. For you, sister . . . ?"

"Elysant," she answered. "Sister Elysant, Abbess of St. Rontlemore."

"The information you will learn along the southern trade routes will help your church's cause greatly in their dealings with my people . . . with the Xoconai. You cannot fully appreciate their desires for your homeland until you fully appreciate the treasures they seek along these routes.

"And for you," she said to Aoleyn, "there is rest, and perhaps clarity for your clouded mind. Safety for your son to recuperate fully, and to better learn his craft at the hands of Talmadge."

"On this small boat?" Aoleyn replied doubtfully.

"Forget this boat, good lady," Massayo told her, and that smile returned, one of promise and intrigue. "At my side, you will find ways to pay back the Xoconai invaders, I promise. And the next time you see a frigate like the one we battled, we will put it to the bottom."

"Because of her power," Elysant said, indicating Aoleyn.

"With or without her," Massayo replied. "Sail with me this season. I ask for no commitments beyond that, so I offer none. But come, rest, and I expect that you will better understand the road before you."

They left it there, with Massayo and Quauh going off to organize the crew.

"Carwyn will stay," Talmadge told Aoleyn. "He has a long recovery ahead of him."

"I've another son out there, somewhere in the north," Aoleyn explained.

"But they can find you," Elysant reminded. "You cannot hide from them—not unless you learn how to mask your magic."

Aoleyn looked at her curiously for a few heartbeats. "You're joining Massayo's crew," she accused.

Elysant chewed her lip for just a few moments before nodding. "Unless I can find an audience with the Chezru Chieftain of this desert kingdom and convince her of the need for her assistance in the north, then yes, that will be my course. I will sail with Captain Massayo."

"How will you report to your brethren?" Aoleyn asked. "Surely, they would wish to know what happened to the Abess of St. Rontlemore."

"The same way I knew about the cannon rolling for St. Rontlemore before we spotted it," she answered. She turned to directly face Aoleyn's confused stare and elaborated, "Brother Thaddius will find me. Spiritually, through use of his soul stone." She moved to the port rail and looked to the south.

"I want to know more of this trade," the abess explained. "And I want to learn more of the first mate who once captained a Xoconai ship."

Aoleyn stood there, truly torn. Kenzie was out in the north, somewhere. Would Coyote remember him among the many young men and women he had taken from Whispervale and the other towns? Would he make the connection between Kenzie and her and go and find him? Could she find him first? Where would she even begin to look?

Or would her efforts simply lead the fierce warrior to Kenzie?

"You are full of trepidation and despair," Talmadge said to her, breaking her from her thoughts. "I've spoken with Elysant and with your boy, Carwyn. You are full of grief and guilt. Sail with us to the Pirate Isles, to Port Seur."

"You've been there?" Elysant asked.

"No," Talmadge replied. "But I've heard of it a thousand times from my patrons. Warm water, warm winds, and no one to tell you what to do. Hurt no one and no one will hurt you. A place of perfect respite. Sail with us, Aoleyn. It might be just the adventure you need to find your way."

"My way is to my son."

"Your way back, I mean," Talmadge clarified. "Find who you once were. Find Aoleyn of the Usgar, the hero of the war. Once you have, you will be better prepared for the search of your lost son."

Aoleyn looked to Elysant, who just smiled and shrugged and said, "I spent most of my life on the coast of the Mantis Arm. I am no stranger to the sea or the sailing ships that challenge her. I do not doubt what Talmadge believes for you."

"Then I suppose I'm a sailor," Aoleyn said, surrendering.

"No, good lady," Captain Massayo called from across the deck. "You are better than that. You are a buccaneer!"